The Secret Kings

Brian Niemeier

Other Books by Brian Niemeier

The Soul Cycle
Nethereal
Souldancer

Principal Characters

ELENA BRAUN: Originally a chimera generated from Nakvin, the Project Exodus heads, and the fragments of nine souls. Mother of Tefler. Though a reincarnation of Thera, she became goddess of the White Well during the Cataclysm. Currently resides with her mother and her son in Avalon.

CELWEN: Pilot of the Night Gen flagship *Sinamarg*. Daughter of Zan, the souldancer of air.

TEG CROSS: Mercenary. Kethan by birth. Spent his youth in a succession of criminal gangs. Deserted from the Mithgar Navy's Special Operation Forces. The Cataclysm's aftermath set him on a long odyssey in search of home.

KELGRUN: Leader of the Shadow Caste, the occult group behind the Arcana Divines, the souldancers, and ultimately the Cataclysm itself. Formerly resided on Tharis in the guise of a disgraced Guild Master. Continues his catastrophic schemes from a more advantageous location.

NAKVIN: Former pirate and current queen of Avalon. Mother of Elena. Inherited the Light Gen throne from her father, the demoness Zebel. Strives to protect her kingdom from Shaiel.

SHAIEL: Regnal name taken by Void souldancer Vaun Mordechai after attaining godhood from the Words of Creation. Imprisoned in the White Well by Elena, he was freed to oppose Zadok's judgment. Now leads a military and metaphysical campaign to dominate all of creation.

ASTLIN SYKES: Childhood friend of Teg Cross. Abducted by Kelgrun, who transformed her into the souldancer of fire when he took part of her soul. Escaped after the Cataclysm to terrorize Mithgar. Befriended and married Xander. Murdered by Zan, the souldancer of air, but passed through the Nexus and returned from the light beyond. Has vowed to free all souls from Zadok.

XANDER SYKES: Husband of Astlin. Son of a Nesshin chieftain and a human agent of the Night Gen. His clan were slaughtered by Hazeroth, Shaiel's first Blade. Journeyed across Mithgar for revenge against the gods and demons responsible for his people's murder. Received the light beyond from Astlin and deterred Zadok's judgment.

Prologue: Port Concordia

The *Theophilus* touched down on Crote just in time to prevent Teg from painting the cramped tub's walls with his brains. He'd never taken to confinement, voluntary or otherwise.

As Teg debarked into the damp chill air, he thought of the weary survivors huddling in the habitat pod—which, like the ship's two other sections, was basically a big steel drum—and contemplated the improbable; one might say *miraculous*, chain of events that had brought them together.

His memory of the golden city was as faint as a childhood dream, but Teg knew that the *Exodus'* voyage had come to ruin at Tzimtzum. The deaths of Jaren and Deim, Elena's transformation, and Nakvin's heartbreak over having to leave her, felt like tragedies witnessed by someone else.

They were, in a way. Teg had worn Sulaiman's body back then. His rugged good looks had since been restored by the same demonic regeneration that had ensured his survival over these wretched years.

Too many years, thought Teg. *I should've let the Cataclysm take me.*

1

Instead he'd escaped through a door that, to his surprise, had left him in a cave system beneath the mountains of Tharis. Teg had thought the desert planet couldn't get any uglier. Then he saw what the fire had done to it. The grey dust plains lay under a sheet of black slag. Noxious fumes filled the once dry air, and soot clouds hid the suns.

Even more surprising, Teg wasn't the only one to survive. A reclusive Nesshin cult had lived and worshiped in those caves for generations. The years had thinned their ranks, and the fire killed off half the remnant. Disease, starvation, and suicide had reduced them to a number that the *Theophilus* could accommodate—barely.

Fifteen years toiling on a world of toxic asphalt to cobble a ship together. Five years more confined to the cluster of damp reeking barrels they'd shot into space in the hope of finding somewhere decent to live; where Teg could start over and leave all the horror behind.

Hoping that such a place even existed seemed vainer with each barren rock and charred moon they found. If they'd known beforehand about the ether—that only a patchy, mostly unnavigable residue remained—they'd probably have stayed put and died.

Instead, they'd salvaged what they could from Melanoros, crammed themselves into an ether-runner with little to run in, and lived.

Hopeful signs appeared just when all seemed lost. For instance, last month the ether had gradually begun thickening. The leading theory was that the universal medium was spreading out from the fire's origin point at Mithgar, and would replenish itself in time.

In any case, the survivors had made more progress in the last four weeks than in the previous four years. They'd found a world whose brown and grey atmosphere looked like the clouds of heaven compared to the blasted skies of Tharis. Now they'd landed, and Teg praised the only god he knew.

Thanks, Elena.

"You look like you have seen a ghost."

Teg turned from the daunting view—a double ridge of dark, ice-flecked rock girding a lake that filled the narrow trough between peaks—and faced the man who'd spoken.

Black gravel crunched as Yato Freeman approached along the shore, barefoot. Why not? It wasn't as if his feet, or the brown habit that befit his priestly station, could get much dirtier.

"This is the right place to find them." Teg pointed toward the lake, where the bones of drowned buildings languished beneath the reflection of a murky sky.

Yato's grimace tugged his gaunt face down toward his scruffy goatee. Teg unconsciously ran a hand across his own beard, which had grown rather unkempt itself.

"That used to be a valley under an ice dome," said Teg. "Local traders ran a port down there. Doesn't look like anyone survived when the fire fell."

Yato's dark eyes stared into the cold, silent depths. "May Zadok judge them worthy."

An icy wind blew down from the ridge, reminding Teg that Crote's glaciers may have retreated, but its northern latitudes were hardly paradise.

"Did you see any signs of life from the Wheel?"

Yato shook his bald head. "The equatorial settlements felt the

3

full brunt of the fire before the seas covered them. If the ice failed to save this port, then none were spared."

Five crewmen loitered about the landing site. None had strayed far from the ship, and all stared at the broad mountain vista with wary fascination.

Teg waved to them. "Spread out and search. If it's useful and portable; grab it. We meet back here in an hour."

Teg's foray along a glacier-carved gully turned up nothing besides scattered ice formations like fragile abstract sculptures; not that he'd hoped to find anything but an hour's solitude. The light was fading when he sat down on a boulder to remove pieces of the pervasive black gravel from his boot and rub some warmth back into his toes.

Is this all there is to look forward to—flying from one dead sphere to the next; scrounging to survive?

It might've been asking too much, but Teg wanted something more than brute survival. He was ready to go home.

The scream echoed from the mountainside, followed by the sounds of something that Teg knew well—violence. He sprang to his feet and made it several yards before realizing that one of his feet was bare. After a hobbling sprint back to the rock and a moment of fumbling with his boot, he raced back down the gully.

The *Theophilus* came into sight below. Along with the ground, the two spars connecting the ether-runner's three pods formed an equilateral triangle. But it wasn't the ship's rusty grey hull that stopped Teg in his tracks at the edge of the landing site.

A figure was lurching about the otherwise deserted landing

4

site. No, there were two—a Nesshin scout who'd come back early or never left, and something hairy that clung ferociously to his back.

Teg watched the pair's thrashing with grim fascination. He took the aggressor tearing at his shipmate's back for a wild animal—until the victim fell motionless onto the gravel, and his attacker set upon him with something that gave off a metallic glint.

Deeply ingrained reflex put Teg's gun in his hand. The revolver's greater weight and poorer balance compared to his lost zephyrs offended his sensibilities, but accuracy wasn't a factor here. He'd have balked at shooting into a brawl, even if he hadn't been years out of practice. Luckily, power and accuracy now took a back seat to noise.

Teg scanned the hillside above the landing site, judged it to be clear, and pointed the gun's muzzle upslope away from the ship. The recoil jolted his wrist and the report made his ears ring when he pressed the trigger.

The aggressor reared back, stopping its attack short. Other men charged onto the scene, but Teg's eyes were riveted on the creature that sat astride his shipmate.

It wasn't an animal, but a man with ragged pelts covering his scrawny frame. His left hand clutched a length of crudely sharpened metal. His right forearm ended in a cauterized stump. A matted red mane and beard framed cloudy eyes that had once been emerald green. Teg knew those eyes, just as he knew that they could no longer see him.

The crude blade stabbed downward as its wielder gave a bestial cry.

Teg's boggled mind would only let him yell, "Stop!"

There was a dull crack like someone hitting a leather sofa with a broom handle. The would-be killer slumped forward and rolled onto the coarse ground beside his intended victim.

Yato stood over them, a wooden club in his hand. His rapid breath sent up clouds of mist.

Teg holstered his gun and ran toward the priest. Reaching the unmoving pair, he knelt to check their vitals.

Yato nodded at the unconscious Nesshin. "Is Ehen badly hurt?"

"He'll be fine. Probably just blacked out." Teg brushed aside the copious beard of Ehen's attacker and felt relief wash over him when he found a pulse. "Frankly, I'm more concerned about this one."

Confusion colored Yato's voice. "I doubt I gave him worse than a concussion. What is this savage to you?"

"He was my boss," said Teg, unable to take his eyes off Jaren Peregrine's ravaged face. "The worst I ever had."

1

Cook stared down at the targeting screen of a *Serapis* gunnery station, his crooked teeth set on edge, and glowered at the pursuing corvettes. The four ether-runners were painted a darker grey than the giant ship they hunted, which would have made them hard to spot in the black of space if they hadn't flown in perfect formation all the way from Keth.

Two keel-lengths off our stern—far enough to avoid the Working suppression field with room to spare.

A burst of light flashed on each corvette's bow, and four impacts on the *Serapis'* stern sent tremors running through the deck under Cook's bare feet.

While keeping us within point blank range of their weapons.

Not that enemy fire was a serious concern. The suppression field negated energy weapons altogether and stripped projectiles of their Workings, making the corvettes' torpedoes little more than irritants. But to be fair, they were irritating enough that Cook thanked Zadok he wasn't on the Wheel.

The people on this ship have been through so much, he prayed. *Just let me get them to safety.*

Right now, safety was a pipe dream. Even if the four corvettes weren't a concern, the scores of other ships at Shaiel's command were another story.

Cook glanced over his muscled shoulder at Gid, the most senior living member of the *Serapis'* original crew. The white-haired shipwright stood upon the backup Wheel, and though its glowing surface illuminated Gid's lean form, it failed to shed much light on the dim confines of the auxiliary bridge.

"Those Lawbringers don't know when to quit," said Cook.

Gid didn't turn to face his gunner, probably because his senses were focused through the Wheel on the four corvettes.

"Cadrisians never did, whether they served Shaiel or the Guild."

Cook winced. "Just our luck, running into them as we were leaving Keth. Any thoughts on how to lose them?"

"I'm rated on the Wheel for moving ships in and out of drydock," Gid snapped. "I couldn't outrun them on the *primary* Wheel, which is just as well since it's in a total vacuum."

A flood of recent memories brought pangs of grief that displaced Cook's anxiety. The series of tragedies that had played out on the bridge seemed to have happened mere minutes ago; not days.

Zan's death was still a raw wound on Cook's heart. He'd mourned Astlin, too—until he heard Tefler's wild tales of what he'd witnessed in Kairos. Cook might have doubted his own memory if not for the white sword that Tefler had given him before vanishing as suddenly as he'd returned.

Four more shots slammed into the stern, raising distant alarms and rattling Cook's bones as if he stood on a drumhead.

He'd have asked for a damage report, but the *Serapis'* skeleton crew of shipwrights was so busy fixing damage that none remained on the bridge to report it.

Luckily, Gid had firsthand knowledge of the ship's wounds. "They've compromised the hangar doors." His voice held audible strain. "Emergency fields closed the breach, but Workings or no, another hit to the same spot could do real damage."

Cook felt sweat beading on his lumpy brow. "What if we made a break for the ether?"

"We'd need to drop the suppression field so *Serapis* could make the transition," said Gid. "She's a tough ship, but even momentarily exposing her to full-power enemy fire is too big a risk, especially in our condition."

"But with the field down, we could shoot back."

Gid finally turned, adjusted his gold-rimmed glasses, and said, "At fast-moving targets one-tenth our size? You could probably shoot down one of them. I might get another if I delay the transition and get really lucky. That leaves two fully armed corvettes with an even bigger opening to pummel us."

The shockwaves that coursed through the ship caught Cook off guard—not just for their intensity, but because unlike all the others, they came from the bow. Only a painful collision with the gunnery station kept him from falling to the deck.

Cook shouted over the ringing in his ears. "I thought dropping the field was too risky!"

Gid was on one knee, clutching the Wheel railing in a white-knuckle grip. "It is. Those shots came *through* it!"

Horror darkened the pilot's face. Cook rounded to check his station's forward screen. His brow furrowed when he saw nothing—at first. The next moment revealed swift angular shadows flitting over the stars.

Nexus-runners!

Green-white light lanced from the sharp bow of an onrushing black trident. The *Serapis* trembled, and her steersman cried out.

The suppression field won't stop them. We need to drop it and return fire. Cook almost voiced these urgent thoughts, but the din of disarmed warheads striking the stern resumed.

Before he could form another plan, Cook's screen alerted him to a whole new kind of trouble. A small shadow, perhaps one quarter the size of the others, broke formation and hurled itself toward the *Serapis*. Cook watched in morbid awe as the inbound object resolved into an elongated black diamond, its sharp point aimed straight at the *Serapis'* tapered oval hull.

It's going to ram us.

Cook braced himself for an impact that, somehow, never came. He turned back to Gid, who'd regained his feet but still looked shaken.

"Where did it go?"

The sleeve that Gid wiped across his forehead came away wet. "Don't know. Should've torn through us like a bullet through a can. It's just gone."

Cook double checked the tracking system's readings. As usual, Gid was right. The dwarf nexus-runner should have crashed right through the main bridge canopy.

If there'd still been a canopy to crash through.

"Hold the fort," Cook shouted as he bolted out the door in a race between bridges and against time.

Cook knew he was too late when he saw someone lying motionless against a bulkhead, his face obscured by the relative gloom of emergency lights. The two foot thick ceramic steel barricade had stood in place since the main bridge's total decompression, and Cook tried not to think about the cause of the breach as he knelt to check the still figure.

The man's grey uniform marked him as one of the few original *Serapis* crewmen—at least he had been. His dry skin was still warm, but no pulse beat beneath it. Cook recognized the dead man's salt and pepper hair and lined forehead.

Petty Officer Grahm.

Cook and Grahm had escaped divine wrath, cataclysm, and shipwreck with their lives. Now, somewhere in the emptiness between worlds, something had cost Grahm his.

Without shedding a drop of his blood.

An ugly bruise at the base of Grahm's skull hinted at the cause of death. Cook had seen similar injuries in victims of crashes and falls. A full autopsy might prove him wrong, but he surmised that Grahm's spinal cord had been detached from his brain—internal decapitation.

Cold dread tempered Cook's urgency. Grahm was a thirty year navy veteran, with most of those years spent in security. Yet he'd died with his weapon holstered and without any defensive wounds. He'd been struck from behind by crushing force delivered with pinpoint accuracy. In all likelihood, he never knew what hit him.

Grahm had been stationed at the intersection of three corridors leading to the bridge. He'd mainly been there to keep the foolish and curious—especially children—away from the compromised area. Since he'd almost certainly stood facing the main corridor, the fatal blow probably came from the direction of the bridge.

Cook stood and inspected the bulkhead. Its matte grey surface was pristine, except for the warnings emblazoned across it in red, yellow, and black.

Nothing could have passed through that door without blowing it open, or at least exposing the whole section to vacuum. Yet the dead crewman testified that the *Serapis* had been boarded by enemies unknown.

But how?

Cook had figured that the ramming ship would try a boarding action, but he'd expected chaos and destruction; not a single casualty.

And eerie silence.

The enemy's stopped firing. They definitely had people on board, then. The only question was—

The boarding ship is a nexus-runner. That's how.

Saving Tefler from the Fire Stratum had given Cook a crash course in Night Gen translators, which had the ability to turn people and objects into prana, beam them through the ether, and rematerialize them elsewhere. Translation normally required line of sight, but placing the departure point *inside* the general target area would make a blind jump much less risky.

They could be anywhere!

Cook slowed his racing pulse with a series of deep breaths. If his hunch was correct, the enemy had translated into the hallway and were proceeding on foot. That limited where they could be.

The auxiliary bridge wasn't their target, since they'd have

passed Cook on the way. He'd assumed that the Lawbringers wanted the *Serapis* itself, but their Night Gen allies were clearly after something else.

Cook's mind raced to think of other targets of value on board. The silence was so oppressive that he almost wished for the distant thunder of dud torpedoes hitting the stern.

Like the one that blew the hangar open.

A seemingly random hull breach. The sudden ceasefire when another ship had entered from the bridge. Unknown killers stalking the halls.

As Cook turned these jumbled pieces over in his mind, a terrifying picture started to emerge.

He dashed back the way the way he'd come. Sparing a final glance at Grahm's still form, Cook made a silent vow—not to avenge his shipmate, exactly, but to honor the man's death in the line of duty by taking up his charge.

Cook knew where Grahm's killers were going. He would meet them there. But he'd stop by his quarters on the way to pick up a little welcoming gift.

2

They definitely came this way.

Cook fought to calm the rage that burned his blood when he saw the second and third corpses—both men he knew; both clearly stabbed to death. He fought down his gag reflex when he rounded a corner and saw most of a fourth.

The pitiful heap—too small to have been a grown man—lay upon red-stained steel deck plates in a corridor leading to the hangar. The pieces were sliced so cleanly that their raw ends looked like polished crimson marble. The hallway smelled of blood and approaching storms.

Reason spoke over Cook's wrath. Whatever had butchered the fourth victim was unlikely to have run the third and second through, let alone to have bloodlessly dispatched the first outside the bridge. The differences in style, subtlety, and skill were conclusive.

There's at least three of them.

Cook stalked along, the ever-present engine hum masking his footfalls. The metal deck felt cool under his bare feet, in contrast to the warm metal tucked into his belt that pressed against the small of his back.

Voices emanated from the next hallway, beyond which stood a main hangar entrance. Cook froze in place at the corner. Though hushed, the voices were clear enough for him to make out words, and although the words were in Gen, he'd read enough of Captain Malachi's books to get the gist of the conversation.

There were indeed three men—Night Gen, judging by their strange dialect. They were trying to open the door that had sealed shut during the hangar breach. Someone or something called Izlaril, most likely a fourth member of their team, had already entered by some way denied to the rest.

Cook knew that some nexists had the power of personal translation. Was this fourth intruder one of them? However he'd gotten in, his allies seemed to resent being left behind.

Quiet words faded to incoherence under the click and clatter of tools, until Cook heard a phrase that turned the fire in his blood to ice.

Shaiel's Blade

Who were these Night Gen talking about? They couldn't mean Hazeroth, since Astlin had left nothing of Shaiel's last Blade but a charred skeleton. Irallel had coveted the title, but she was hardly in any shape to fill the vacancy since, thanks to Xander, she was now a living flood buried under an ancient seabed.

But according to the Night Gen, Shaiel's Blade was on the *Serapis* with them.

"Damn the Smith," said one of the Gen. *"If not for his tinkering, I'd cut this door like paper."*

Another of the Gen chuckled. *"Surely that was the point of his tinkering."*

15

The sounds of work stopped. *"Quiet yourselves,"* hissed the third Night Gen. *"Or keep distracting me, let Izlaril take the prize, and trust our lives to the greycloak steersmen's restraint."*

A knot formed in Cook's gut. He didn't know what the greycloaks sought, but the Gen's threat implied that Shaiel's people were only toying with the *Serapis*. Cook knew his enemy. The games would stop the moment they got what they wanted.

Cook scanned the broad, sparsely lit corridors. Not a friendly soul in sight. No use sending for backup, either. The enemy could be gone; the *Serapis* an expanding cloud of hot vapor behind them, by the time help arrived. And the outmatched security officers would probably end up like the bodies in the hall.

The prospect of taking on three armed, murderous Night Gen—and who knew what else—didn't thrill Cook. But a resounding metallic thud and gloating laughter from the direction of the door made up his mind for him.

Cook glanced around the corner and immediately wished he hadn't. Two Night Gen in dark green uniforms stood at the far door with their backs to him. The final member of their team kept watch on the hallway. The lookout's yellow eyes narrowed as they caught sight of Cook, and his ashen brow creased in anger.

Surprised, Cook froze as the lookout charged him. The Gen's hair trailed him like a black silk streamer tied to the base of his skull. He already held a short sword, its matte steel blade poised to eliminate one more threat.

The thought of his shipmates lying cold in their own blood roused Cook from his stupor. He pivoted back around the corner and pressed up against the wall. Keeping time by his enemy's rapid footfalls, he ducked when the moment was right and kicked out into the hall.

A sense of timing honed by years in the galley served Cook well. An onrushing shin collided with his outstretched calf. The Night Gen tumbled past him but gracefully turned the fall into a roll that brought him up in a crouch facing Cook.

The Gen's angry leer became a disgusted frown. "The clay tribe are as soft as their name," he said in heavily accented Trade. "We smother cripples at birth."

"I'm not crippled." Cook swept his leg in a blurring arc that connected with the flat of the short sword, sending it clattering down the hall. He stood and looked down at his foe. "Just ugly."

The Night Gen rose into a fighter's stance, but his eyes suddenly widened. Cook saw the alarm on his foe's face and heard footsteps approaching from behind, the direction of the hangar door. He and the Night Gen lunged in different directions at the same time.

Rising to one knee in the adjacent hallway, Cook turned his eyes toward a deep rending sound like a chunk of ice falling free of a glacier. An area encompassing the intersection of two walls, and extending for three vacant feet on all sides of the corner, buckled in ways that made Cook nauseous. The warped space slammed back into position, but the affected section of wall crashed down in a jumble of irregular sharp-edged pieces.

"*Watch your aim, Pelm!*" Cook's first opponent cried down the hangar corridor. "*Unless you want me to end like that boy.*"

Cook recalled the pile of cleanly sliced meat. *Pelm. I'll remember that name.*

17

Most likely shaken by his close brush with messy death, the first Gen wasn't ready when Cook sprang. Surprise was just one advantage of attacking head-on. More importantly, closing with his opponent would buy him some protection from Pelm's space-warping.

Cook ended his leap with his leading foot stomping on the deck and his rising palm planted under his foe's chin. The Gen's head snapped backward, sending him reeling. Cook slid behind the dazed Gen, secured his enemy's arms in a tight hold, and forced him down the hallway toward the hangar doors.

Another Night Gen stood halfway down the hall on the right, his hands empty of weapons and shock etched on his grey face.

You must be Pelm.

Cook doubled his pace, pushing the groaning Night Gen before him like a battering ram. Except it wasn't a door, but a murdering Gen, obstructing his path. Cook threw his semiconscious burden forward. Pelm reflexively reached out to stop his comrade from falling, and Cook used the opening to land a flying kick to Pelm's face. Both Gen toppled to the deck.

Just one Night Gen remained—a weaselly fellow with shoulder-length hair who turned away from the exposed guts of the hangar door and drew a short sword as Cook rushed him.

The Gen slashed at chest level. Cook ducked under the whistling blade, and a breeze fanned his bald scalp. Maintaining his forward momentum, he jammed his elbow into the Gen's solar plexus. Another gout of air—warm and moist this time—told Cook that he'd driven the wind from his opponent's lungs. The Gen duly dropped his sword, doubled over, and fell gasping onto his side.

The door caught Cook's trained eye. He straightened to his full height and looked over the intricate locking mechanism exposed by the removal of a foot-square panel.

These folks know their stuff. They already bypassed the Worked failsafe and most of the mechanical backups.

A weird yet familiar tearing sound sent a chill down Cook's spine as a terrible force tried pry it out of his back. The agony wrenched a cry from his throat and drove him up against the door.

A mental image of disjointed meat and metal incited fear that temporarily suppressed Cook's pain. He spun to face the hallway and locked eyes with Pelm, who stood a stone's throw away, blood streaming from his nose and mouth; his hands thrust forward.

Cook had wondered what kind of weapon could instantly dissect anything from human flesh to steel sheets to space itself. Now he knew that Pelm didn't wield such a weapon. He *was* the weapon—a particularly vicious breed of nexist.

And Cook's inattention had left him defenseless at point-blank range.

Pelm's face contorted in a vengeful scowl. The air in front of him wavered, but the spatial distortion stopped within a foot of Cook's face.

The first Night Gen staggered to his feet behind Pelm and gestured toward the hangar. *"He's inside the anti-nexic field!"*

The Night Gen's earlier conversation made sense, now. Besides being a souldancer, Mirai Smith was a nexist capable of otherworldly engineering feats. He must have rigged a way to suppress nexism like the *Serapis* disrupted Workings. The anti-

19

nexic field had protected the door from Pelm. Now it protected Cook, who offered a silent prayer of thanks.

The implications weren't lost on Pelm, who fumbled to draw the short sword at his belt.

The third Gen's sword lay within reach of Cook's foot. He kicked the weapon straight up, caught the hilt, and threw it. The sword's graceful journey ended with the blade buried in Pelm's throat.

While the nexist lay choking on his own blood, the first Gen retrieved his sword and lurched toward his cornered, unarmed foe.

Despite his misgivings, Cook reached back and slid the warm, smooth sword from his belt. The uncanny lightness of Cook's blade almost threw off his parry, but its white curve met stark grey steel and checked the Gen's blow with a clear ringing like silver temple bells. The opening was all Cook needed to lay his last opponent out with a knee to the chin.

Not the last, Cook reminded himself as he turned to the hangar door. His back still stung. Luckily the white scimitar's blade made an adequate mirror. The wound reflected in lavender hues was much less serious than he'd feared—just a small gash below his right shoulder. The bleeding wasn't bad enough to risk a trip to the infirmary; not if Shaiel's Blade was on board.

Besides, he could get it stitched up later.

Cook tucked the scimitar back into his belt, reached into the guts of the door, and finished the Night Gen's work for them.

The heavy doors parted in the center with a hiss. Cook's heart lodged in his throat when he imagined being blown through an inch-wide opening into a vacuum left by a failed emergency containment field. His muscular chest rose and fell with a sigh of relief when the doors slammed open, revealing a fully pressurized hangar.

The cavernous space was no less of a shambles, though. The once grey floor had been scorched black and buckled in several places. The few remaining cargo containers that held the last of the ship's supplies were strewn at odd angles like the building blocks of a child colossus.

Scratch that, Cook thought as he looked past the onyx trident of the *Kerioth* to the hangar's main door. *It's even worse.*

The massive shutter lay in a single twisted piece on the deck—blown off its hinges by pinpoint torpedo fire. The opening yawned like a giant mouth full of broken teeth, and Cook felt the deck turn to quicksand when he saw the oblong hulls of four corvettes brooding in the dark beyond.

They're matching our speed but holding their fire—which is good, considering how accurate their gunners are.

Since he couldn't do much about the tailing ships at the moment, Cook dragged the two incapacitated Gen from the hall, locked them in a cargo container, and resealed the inner door. He felt isolated, but not alone.

Cook climbed the stairs to a second story catwalk. The metal grates underfoot rattled despite his best efforts at discretion. The prevailing charred smell was even stronger up here, with an acrid undercurrent. The faint stench heightened his unease.

You're down there somewhere, Cook thought as he surveyed the mess below. Yet there was no sign of the enemy.

Had he misheard the Night Gen? After all, Cook could see that the other shipside hangar doors were all sealed. Even if someone could open another without leaving traces of tampering, reaching the next closest door would require a long detour to port or starboard.

Cook searched his encyclopedic memory of the *Serapis'* layout. Besides a few hatches that were even less accessible than the doors, the only other ways into the hangar were a system of pipe and cable-strewn ducts that a small, exceptionally limber child might be able to crawl through; and from outside, which at the moment was a hard vacuum.

What about nexism? Unlikely, since Mirai Smith's field had kept out the Night Gen.

Normally, Cook would take a situation like this as proof of his own fallibility. But the situation was hardly normal. These weren't pirates out for loot; they were servants of a self-styled Void god. Who knew what they wanted—or what they'd do to get it?

Cook shuddered. More than one book in the late captain's collection told of beings with stranger powers than nexism. If anyone could dredge up servants like those, it was Shaiel.

"Gid," Cook sent through the stud on his ear, "I'm in the hangar. The damage is just like you said. A boarding party entered from the main bridge. Three Night Gen. Possibly a fourth man—or something else. They killed four of ours. I returned the favor to one of them; locked up two more. What's the situation down there?"

The silence that answered Cook's sending chilled him more than the cold metal grill under his feet. The feeling of motion assured him that Gid was still on the Wheel. Which meant the ship's comm was damaged—or jammed.

"If you're sending, Gid, I'm not receiving. Keep the channel open. I'm going rat hunting."

Cook descended the stairs to the main deck where an impossible sight made his heart miss a beat.

I know this was the one I locked!

Yet there it was. The cargo container; its doors wide open. A quick check confirmed the suspicion that twisted Cook's gut. Quiet, bloodless death had claimed both Night Gen in the time it had taken him to walk downstairs.

Shock washed over Cook's body, leaving gooseflesh in its wake. His chest tightened as he cast about the huge space in vain. But his will, trained as rigorously as his body, asserted control.

Breathe. You're in the main hangar on the Serapis. *There are ten shipping containers, a parked nexus-runner, and a killer on the loose. That's just one thing that wasn't there before. Just one problem to solve.*

As Cook's panic subsided, his senses sharpened. He felt the hard deck underfoot and vibrations from the engines far below. He heard the constant bass note of their hum and the regular beat of his own pulse.

Cook strode toward the *Kerioth*. Nothing else moved in the black mirrors of its three-bladed hull. A section of cracked grey paint stretched between him and the ship, as if the deck had seen a hundred summers and winters. The area was clear with nowhere to hide. He hesitated only a moment before proceeding.

Paint chips crunched with each step, and Cook felt like he'd pulled a fire alarm in a library.

He took one more step and froze. There were no other footsteps, but there was something else.

Cook advanced two more paces. There it was, almost undetectable over the engine vibrations—light impacts on the deck behind him, synchronized exactly with his stride.

Cook rounded on his pursuer and saw no one. He focused on his surroundings—the cargo containers, catwalk support struts, and the steel-paneled walls—letting his senses inform his mind without judgment.

Someone less acquainted with weirdness might have dismissed it as a trick of the low light, but something was there. A distortion in space; not like one of Pelm's, stood between him and the nearest container. It was about the size and shape of a man, and Cook's detached calm shattered when two dark, human-seeming eyes opened in the warped space corresponding to the thing's head.

Cook failed to keep his voice from trembling. "Izlaril? Shaiel's Blade?"

"Yes."

It might have been the direct answer, delivered in a deep airy voice, that stunned Cook to silence. That, or seeing an invisible man fade into view as if his bare flesh were a screen that had just been switched on.

Izlaril filled the silence. "The souldancer of fire killed the last Blade. Is it true that you fought him man-to-man?"

The memory of claws digging into his lungs shocked Cook awake. He studied the new Blade. Though more robust, Izlaril didn't project anything like Hazeroth's menace. A lank mane of black hair framed his face, which challenged Cook's for the Middle Stratum's ugliest.

Cook gave a curt nod. "It wasn't much of a fight. I'm lucky to still be here."

"Yet you are here. Few of Hazeroth's prey can say the same. That makes you a threat."

Cook tried to read Izlaril's face. The angular features, marred by strange welts that looked like gridiron burns, betrayed neither thought nor emotion.

Knowing what he wants might help save the ship. I need to get him talking.

"You're a good choice to fill Hazeroth's shoes," said Cook, "killing your own men like that."

"You killed their pilot. With no way to escape, they faced capture and shame."

Cook frowned. "You killed your men to spare them from dishonor?"

"No. To set them free."

Reflexively, Cook backed toward the *Kerioth*.

Izlaril didn't budge. "There is no death; only reunion with the Nexus. So you also believe."

"How did you know?" Cook blurted out.

"You made Atavist signs over the bodies."

Panic stabbed up Cook's spine. "How long were you following me?"

"Since you came into the hangar."

Terror urged Cook to keep backpedaling, but he took hold of himself again. The one thing he knew for sure was that running from Izlaril would be impossible.

Izlaril took a cautious step forward. He didn't appear to be armed.

Cook stood his ground and raised his guard. The Blade seemed just as wary of him, so it was time to get answers while he could.

"Nice vanishing act," said Cook. "I don't know of any Workings that could make you invisible. Is it some kind of nexism?"

Izlaril inched closer as he shook his head. "They tried to give us nexism but only made us invisible to it."

The allusion to creating nexists stirred memories of shadowy historic events—none of them pleasant.

"There are more like you?" Cook asked, if only to stall his foe.

Izlaril now stood less than twenty feet away. "Not for a long time now."

"Shaiel must be really fond of the *Serapis* if he sent his Blade to taker her back."

"Shaiel's Left Hand wields the Blade," Izlaril corrected Cook, "and his Will directs it. They would sooner see this ship destroyed than retaken."

"Then what do you want?"

Izlaril pointed over Cook's shoulder to the *Kerioth*. "To retrieve Shaiel's kin and property."

He's after Smith!

The souldancer must have known it, too. Why else hole up aboard the *Kerioth* behind an anti-nexic field? But Hazeroth had hunted the souldancers because one of them was a gate to Shaiel's prison. What use did Shaiel have for them now that he was free?

Cook didn't get the chance to ask, because Izlaril made his move. He closed the distance between them with sure, rapid steps that spoke less of preternatural speed than inevitability.

The first blow came—a jab at Cook's left side that he twisted to evade. Cook threw his momentum into a cross to his opponent's face. Izlaril blocked, but just barely.

Something didn't sit right with Cook. Izlaril was good. His form, which called to mind pictures of Guild mercenaries from the Purges, was textbook perfect, and Cook hadn't laid a hand on him yet. But he didn't fight like you'd expect of Shaiel's chief cutthroat.

I need to end this now.

Cook threw a feint at Izlaril's eyes. The Blade lifted a hand to block, and Cook drove his knee into the area exposed by his opponent's raised elbow.

The oddest sensation followed. Cook knew the crunch of broken ribs, but Izlaril's bones didn't break. They *moved;* bending to distribute the force of impact before popping back into place like a dented plastic bin. The blow didn't knock the wind out of Izlaril's lungs. He didn't so much as grunt.

What is *he?* Cook wondered. He tried to back away, but for some reason he couldn't distance himself from his foe, as if Izlaril knew all of Cook's escape routes before he tried them.

Cook renewed his attack with greater speed. Izlaril turned every blow, never seeming to fully exert himself. Cook tried another feint. Izlaril ignored the ruse. His scarred face retained its neutral expression as his fist hammered Cook's left biceps, momentarily numbing the whole arm.

Izlaril threw a seemingly halfhearted kick that Cook nevertheless barely dodged. Cook's muscles ached and his lungs burned while Shaiel's Blade wasn't even short of breath.

Fighting him is like trying to tear down a brick wall by shouting at it!

Cook didn't see the blow that sent him rolling across the deck, his head pounding in agony. He willed himself to get up, and while still on his hands and knees, he saw Izlaril striding inexorably toward him.

In that moment, Cook knew how he'd been played. Izlaril's creators had failed to produce a nexist, but they'd made something worse—a monument to brutal efficiency that existed only to free the living from the prison called life.

Cook spared a moment to reflect on Izlaril's beliefs, which were really just the ultimate logical conclusion of his own. But his shipmates' faces flashed before his eyes.

Sorry, Cook told Zadok, rising to his feet as his right hand reached behind his back. *Now's not a good time.*

Izlaril's gait never seemed to change, yet he closed with his victim faster than his pace should have allowed. Cook was ready though. He swung with all his strength, and the Blade of Shaiel walked into the white scimitar's flashing arc.

What happened then removed any possibility that Shaiel's Blade was human. Izlaril contorted in ways that would have snapped a normal man's spine. His trunk moved just beyond the white sword's tip, but something—possibly a stray air current— nudged the blade just enough to sink into his flesh.

Not even the best fighters could remove every foreshadowing of their attacks. The mind signaled the limbs, and several other muscle groups supported their motions.

Yet Izlaril's leg moved on its own, sinking the ball of his foot into Cook's hip, which separated from its socket with an audible pop and a red flash of pain. Cook fell to one knee but kept his grip on the sword stuck in his foe like a climber clinging to the rope holding him over the abyss.

Izlaril looked down at the mirrored blade protruding from his stomach. Blood streamed from the scalpel-straight wound, and Cook caught a whiff of seared meat. The burning smell intensified when Izlaril grabbed the crossguard. The skin of his hand shifted through myriad colors as it sizzled, and for the first time, his expression changed to a grimace.

Cook fought to keep his hold on the hilt, but he was reduced to one hand; the other being needed to keep him up. Despite the pain it must have caused him, Izlaril clasped his other hand on the sword and wrenched it from Cook's grasp. The blade struck the deck with a chiming note.

Izlaril stood over his disarmed foe. His wound had compressed itself into a thin line shedding only a thin trickle of blood, though the palms of his hands were still discolored and raw.

He gave Cook a solemn nod.

A blur of motion was Cook's only warning before absolute darkness claimed him.

3

Crote was a dirty slushball. Tharis was a blasted hellscape of fused volcanic ash and toxic gas. Teg was sure that nowhere else could possibly be worse.

Keth proved him wrong.

"I am setting course for Mithgar," Yato said from the pilot's seat of the *Theophilus*. Framed against the view of Keth through the Wheel pod's grubby window, the Nesshin steersman's bald head looked like a beige planet orbiting a red-orange star—a star that had been Teg's home sphere.

"No," Teg told the back of Yato's wrinkled head, "you're not. When I left Keth, it wasn't on fire. Now it is. I'd like to know why."

Yato turned his seat—a shabby affair salvaged from a wrecked drifter and bolted to the Wheel.

"The rest of us need safe harbor more than you want answers," Yato said. Did his face have new lines? "You cannot believe that anything survived down there."

Teg studied the globe of roiling flame that turned silently in space. "I can only stop believing what I know isn't true."

Yato swiveled back to face the front window with a frustrated snort. "Sentimental folly! Our supplies are low enough without dawdling here."

"Too low to make Mithgar; especially with an extra mouth to feed."

Once again, Teg pondered whether he should have just left their new passenger on Crote. It would be one thing if Jaren could lend the *Theophilus* crew a hand. But the former pirate captain no longer had one to spare. His decrepit physical state and near total amnesia didn't recommend him either, even though Yato had healed his eyes.

Yato's right. I am getting sentimental.

"Thera bed me," Yato cursed under his breath.

"Am I that irritating?" asked Teg.

"Yes, but that was not meant for you." Yato gestured to a point in high orbit. "This concerns me more."

Teg leaned over the pilot's chair for a better look.

How did I miss that?

Turning quietly in high orbit, the vortex yawned wide enough to swallow the *Theophilus*. Its ragged disc resembled a hurricane seen from above, but with no atmosphere to sustain it.

"Any clue what it is?" asked Teg.

Yato's bony fingers danced across the makeshift control panel wedged between his chair and the window.

"There's a rip in the ether. Huge volumes of elemental air are flowing out."

"I'm no expert," said Teg, "but I feel pretty safe calling it an Air Stratum gate."

Yato nodded. "We agree for once."

"Remind me to buy a sweepstakes ticket. What caused the rip? The Cataclysm?"

"Not if air flow through the gate has been constant. Judging by these concentrations, the vortex has been here for less than a week."

Teg sidled up beside the pilot's seat. The chair's occupant reeked like a month's worth of soiled laundry. Worse, Teg knew that he himself didn't exactly smell like a rose.

"All I wanted when I joined you Nesshin on this flying scrap heap was to get home; to settle down someplace without demons and dead men. I'm not giving up just because the front door's locked—and in flames."

Yato sighed. "Why should you? Knowing when to quit is a mark of good sense. Yet curiosity compels me to ask. How will you get past the flames?"

No matter how many years he'd lived with it, the constant rattle from some elusive cranny of the ship's ductwork still distracted Teg. Ignoring the irritant by force of will, he thought back to his youth, the last years of which were misspent smuggling contraband to and from the sphere below.

A lot's changed, he thought with a laugh both wistful and bitter. He'd barely reached his teens before his father's death and his mother's arrest drove him to finish his upbringing in the cutthroat Kethan underworld.

Back in those desperate exhilarating days, he'd believed in nothing but the money in his fist; hoped for nothing but the next job.

To be honest with himself—and aboard the leaky tub that would probably be his tomb, there was no use for anything but brutal honesty—Teg had maintained that outlook practically unchanged for twenty years.

Not that he was ashamed. His was a sturdy philosophy, practiced throughout history by renowned and accomplished men. In all likelihood he'd have kept to his ways till they put him in the ground.

But then he'd seen the Circles, and died. And the girl with rose-colored eyes had pulled him back from the Void with a black miracle.

After that, Teg didn't believe anything. He *knew*. And he envied those with only faith.

The faint clatter reasserted its hold on Teg's thoughts, making him mindful of the air coursing through the ducts. He hunched down next to the pilot's ear.

"Let's go through the vortex."

Yato's face, when his head spun toward Teg, looked as if the steersman had swallowed a hot brass casing.

"The Air Stratum is an endless hostile waste! You would strand us there?"

Teg pointed at the swirling storm. "No, look. It's basic cosmology. Diagrams show the Strata stacked on top of each other, but that's a dumbed down version of the truth."

"Well, yes," said Yato. "The Strata relate to one another much like the dimensions of mundane space."

Teg gave his voice a conspiratorial tone. "So all of the Strata are actually *here*. That gate marks a spot where the Air and Middle Strata intersect, and the ether touches all of them. That gives us a fixed point for navigating all three."

Yato ran his fingers through his scraggly beard. "You suggest that we fly straight into the Air Stratum, transition to the ether, and emerge back onto the Middle Stratum under the fire barrier, guiding our course by the gate."

"Brilliance like that is why we haven't butchered you for stew meat," said Teg, slapping the threadbare headrest.

"In that case," Yato said, let me shed more light upon your scheme. There is no guarantee that the gate is stable, or that the ship would survive a trip through even if it were. Supposing we do make the passage without mishap, the Air Stratum is notoriously unnavigable. Lastly, if by God's grace we manage to stay on course through a perpetual hurricane, we don't know if the fire reaches down to Keth's surface. We do know that the flames extend into the ether, so making the transition anywhere within the atmosphere may kill us."

Teg paused for a moment. "Is that all?"

Yato sighed. "You should tell the others if you insist on gambling with their lives."

"Sounds fair. But don't fret. I'll be right back to give you moral support."

"Zadok help us," Yato groaned.

Teg sat on the patchwork deck plates and swung his legs down into the tube that bridged the Wheel and habitat pods. "If not him, I'm sure *someone* will."

We're not going to crash.

Realizing that they *couldn't* crash without something to hit intensified Teg's nausea. *Theophilus* careened through the Air Stratum's endless sky, tossed like a kite by shifting gales. Yato's grimacing, sweat-streaked face told of his battle to control the ship, and the violently pitching deck showed that he was losing.

The pilot's chair was the only seat in the Wheel pod, so Teg had to brace himself by threading an arm and a leg through the exposed pipes that traversed the walls. His joints burned, and he expected the next jolt to pop his aching shoulder out of the socket.

Looking beyond Yato's mortal struggle with the Wheel, Teg saw a world of cloud in constant flux. The window's webbed circle frosted and cleared with a suddenness that betrayed wildly shifting temperatures. Light from the Fire Stratum filtered in through the ether, continually switching between a smoldering sunset, high noon, and everything in between.

At least the view's nice, thought Teg. But a grim yearning seemed to haunt the frenzied dance of wind, water, and light.

A grunt from Yato pulled Teg back into the moment. The ship took a sudden dive, almost fulfilling Teg's prophecy of a dislocated shoulder. Far below—or ahead, there was really no difference here—loomed a thunderhead that made his jaw drop. Blue forks of lightning arced across its charcoal face and set its inner depths ablaze. The shockwaves of its thunder shook the *Theophilus* like an infant's rattle.

"Turn!" Teg shouted over the din of God's own kettle drums.

Yato's voice emerged through clenched teeth. "No center of gravity. Drifters useless. Something's pulling us in!"

Teg watched the monster cloud fill the whole window. The storm might've been large enough to swallow a planet.

Come to think of it, unless the wild ride had totally muddled Teg's sense of direction, the storm corresponded to Keth's position on the Middle Stratum.

"Let it pull us in," Teg called to Yato.

"What?"

"That storm is Keth. Ride it down, and when we get to a depth that equates to the lower atmosphere, take us into the ether."

Yato turned from the blacked out window to scream at Teg. "The cloud is constantly changing! Chances are we'll transition into the fire or the sphere's crust."

Teg only took a moment to make up his mind. "This way, we explode or live. The other way, we starve to death. Your choice."

Resignation hardened Yato's face. He looked back to the window.

Teg couldn't suppress a grin as the dark, lightning-torn sky faded to a rosy haze.

His smile likewise faded as the rose mist flared into an inferno.

"Keth's ether is burning all the way from low orbit to the core," Yato cried above the wail of alarms.

Teg heard screams echoing from the habitat pod below. He squinted against the growing brightness, searching the ethereal blaze for some way—any way—to cheat death just one more time.

"Our elemental ward can't repel the heat," Yato said. "The hull is close to melting!"

Teg didn't focus on the steersman's words, because something even more important commanded his attention. Far below—or above; it was all relative at this point—he saw an anomaly. It was like a sunspot, but instead of darkening the flames, it warped them into whorls and eddies that defied the burning current.

"See that countercurrent?" Teg shouted over the alarms and howling flames as he lurched forward to point out the window.

"More than one," Yato corrected him. "I'm seeing scores of interdimensional gates."

"Get as close as you can to those gates and bring us out of the ether."

"Staying here is a much easier way to commit suicide."

Teg laid a hand on Yato's shoulder. "Relax. Only a Guild house has that many gates. If it's still standing, we've got a chance. Bring us out a mile or so above it just to be safe."

Though he didn't speak Nesshin, Teg inferred from the grave tone and martial cadence of Yato's words that the steersman was praying. The desperate litany reminded Teg of another pilot, much younger than Yato when he died, who'd petitioned mysterious powers.

The last of the rose mist vanished. Outside the window there was only fire.

4

It was, of course, a complete waste of time.

Or it would have been if Elena's perceptions were limited to one temporal frame of reference.

Reclusive by disposition, her apotheosis hadn't made Elena any more comfortable with large numbers of people—even though she herself now *was* a large number of people. But her mother insisted that they hold court together each day.

To her rose-colored eyes, the great hall of Seele was a gossamer screen; the crowds mere shadows projected onto it. The light of the Well shining down like an empyrean noonday sun was always present to her, as were the three essential forms that cast every shadow.

The Nexus, soul of Zadok, flanked by two lesser nexuses belonging to Thera and Shaiel. In all the world, they alone were real. They alone existed in and of themselves, relying on nothing else.

Although that's not quite true. Vaun Mordechai had been host to part of Thera's soul. Elena had contained, and still possessed, all of it. Both had been walking inter-Strata gates—souldancers—divinized by infusions of primordial forces.

The previous petitioner staggered back into the throng gathered between the double row of slender pillars as the next stationed himself at the foot of the dais where Elena and her mother sat enthroned.

Everyone else would see a proud son of Gen nobility standing to make his plea. Elena saw only a mirage.

The slender ray from the White Well that sustained the supplicant shone through Thera's Nexus. They shared that in common. Yet the slight pale girl he would see upon the throne, her long waves of ginger-brown hair untamed by a white circlet, wasn't a mere speck of Thera's image but the goddess' whole and perfect shadow.

The shadow-speck wore a forest green suit of clothes that matched the eyes framed by his golden hair. He bowed deeply to Elena and her mother.

"Lady Souldancer. Your Majesty. I am Roen Mentem, heir to my august house, which long held in fief from your Majesty's predecessor of happy memory…"

White silk robes and night black hair rustled as Nakvin discretely fidgeted. Seated at Elena's left, the queen of Avalon radiated dignity and vigilance, though her silver eyes betrayed signs of roving thoughts.

Elena continued entertaining Roen's petition, though the act approximated talking to herself, while simultaneously hearing the prayers offered at that moment by the million shards and half-shards of her Nexus.

Twenty years of experimentation had taught Elena to use extreme caution when answering prayers. She wasn't omniscient, being limited to what her shadow and shards perceived.

Composites of hers and other nexuses were unreliable, since all three gods could block or modify the perceptions of shared fragments. Worse, the full consequences of her interventions were largely obscured by the restrictions that Zadok's shadow Szodrin placed on Kairos.

"...gave his life liberating Avalon from the baals before confiding the papers' location." Roen's eyes, which had been fixed on Nakvin, darted briefly to Elena before he continued.

"Were the situation less dire, I would not trouble you with the concerns of my house. Nonetheless, this court has earned renown as a place where mortal wisdom is put to shame, and a worthy appeal may overturn even death."

A susurrus passed through the crowd of nobles, craftsmen, laborers, and sages.

"Lord Roen," Nakvin's musical voice rang out above the chorus of whispers, "what exactly are you asking for?"

The hall fell silent till Roen answered. "I ask that your royal and divine daughter graciously obtain the location of my late uncle's letters patent. She needn't raise him from the dead. Merely inquiring of his spirit should suffice."

Nakvin turned to her daughter. *Is that even possible?* she asked without words.

Elena recreated a young girl's cat, dead six days in a Medvia house fire, and revoked the life cord of a Dawn Tribe acolyte condemned for profaning a Mystery. At the same time she thought to her mother, *His uncle was a shard of Zadok. Roen will have to ask Szodrin.*

One pearly fang emerged to bite the corner of Nakvin's full lip. *Good luck with that!*

As her mother gave Roen the verdict, Elena studied the three divine souls whose shadows covered the world. Zadok looked to her originally mortal eyes as a vast obsidian pyramid. Her higher order intellect discerned the myriad layers of pure knowledge, fundamental laws, and universal decrees that comprised the first Nexus—just as she knew the composition of her own black diamond.

The black cube, though; there was a puzzle.

Shaiel shared nothing with her. His Nexus, his mortal shards, the Strata and spheres he ruled—the Lord of the Void guarded all as jealously as Roen's uncle had guarded his wealth.

Elena had never quite mastered human emotions. As she contemplated the silent monolith from which cords of gold descended alongside those of silver, she felt an unpleasant hollowness in her heart.

Was this envy? The concept of wanting something enough to hate those who had it intrigued her.

A new voice entered Elena's thoughts; not from her mother, but from the cube, cold and viscous as chilled oil.

I feel your gentle eyes upon me, sister. Is the sight they show you not fair?

Nakvin touched Elena's silk-clad arm. *Are you alright, sweetheart? You're shivering.*

Elena ignored both questions and directed one of her own at Shaiel. *What do you want?*

I do not forget your betrayal, he said. *But I may yet forgive, and restore your rightful seat in the Void.*

All for the bargain price of betraying my mother's kingdom.

It is no treason, Shaiel said. *What claim have even kings against gods? However, I require neither regicide nor matricide. Simply withdraw your protection from the realm and regain my favor.*

A merchant prayed for a safe journey, and Elena blinded the highwayman who lay in wait for him.

The end result is the same. You butcher my mother. And my son.

Shaiel's words lost all congeniality and became absolute cold given voice. *You speak more rightly than you know! My servants in the Strata march from triumph to triumph while I wear down your defenses by a thousand subtle ways. Already I stand at Avalon's gate. Grant me passage and gain leniency. Defy me…*

A Nesshin girl, huddled in a sour-smelling place, finally despaired of Zadok's grace and begged Thera to bring her and her friends painless deaths before they burned alive. Elena would have ignored her, but for the familiar voice carried down through a duct from somewhere above.

Elena continued her verbal joust with Shaiel while searching the doomed girl's soul. Soon she found the right memory—a man with a lean body like chiseled wood; his scars gone, his sandy head and beard showing signs of grey, but with the same hard dark eyes.

Teg.

The girl was Thera's shard, and her memories were now Elena's own. The ship was a jumble of scrap welded into three tapering cylinders connected by two shafts. Desperate survivors crowded aboard the makeshift lifeboat in a last attempt to escape a dead sphere.

Keth was even deader, but Teg Cross hadn't known that when he'd led the Tharis refugees there. He'd hoped to find a habitable region below the burning stratosphere by flying through the ether but had only sent himself and his shipmates into the fire.

Elena honey, what's wrong?

My Left Hand will pull down her walls and rip the marrow from her bones.

Elena delegated lesser aspects of herself to deal with her mother's worry and her brother's threats while she focused on Teg's dilemma. He was a shard of Zadok, so she couldn't reach him directly. The same went for most of his shipmates, though one belonged to her, and another to Shaiel.

That opened up possibilities. Expending enough power to put out the firestorm or even move the ship to safety might weaken Elena's defense of Avalon. But Shaiel wasn't so constrained.

She interrupted his blustering. *One of your aspects is about to burn up in Keth's atmosphere. Didn't you notice, or don't you care?*

I notice much, sister. For instance, I am aware of Teg Cross' presence aboard that ship. I recall killing him once before. You, on the other hand, risked waking Elathan to raise him.

Elena supposed that helping Teg before had been quite a risk. Intervening now would entail an even bigger one. Her deliberation took hardly long enough for a light wave to traverse the hall, but Shaiel would notice the pause.

And another second could mean Teg's life. She decided.

Save him.

Shaiel's laugh held all the humor of orphans dead from exposure. *Why not save him yourself?*

And spend myself elsewhere so you can force your way in here? I don't think so.

My view is better out here, Shaiel said. *That ramshackle ship's hull will fail any moment now; though the occupants may broil to death first.*

Bring the ship in safely, said Elena, *and I'll give you Temil.*

It was Shaiel's turn to pause. Elena gripped her throne's armrests while her brother thought and her friend died.

What is one sphere? Shaiel said at last. *I can take it as I please.*

Elena knew she had him. *You haven't been able to yet.*

Wrath froze Shaiel's grim mirth. *And how will you depose the Shadow Caste in all their might when you cannot save a paltry ship?*

How did I stop Szodrin's judgment?

As I recall, the victory you claim belongs to a pair of mortals.

They were under my direction, Elena said, *and they're not mortals anymore.*

Shaiel scoffed. *I cannot imagine such a boast containing the least mote of truth.*

Unsurprising. Your intellect wasn't always divine.

Elena's jab had its desired effect when Shaiel answered. *You think yourself greater than me? You, who huddle in the cellar with the rats you call kin? Hear me, my arrogant sister—I could not only forsake your swordarm friend, but prolong his dying agony by decades, and you'd be powerless to thwart my will. Yet unlike you, I retain some respect for our ties of kinship.*

You'll save the ship, then? Elena asked.

A sullen silence followed, which Shaiel broke an instant before the ship would have exploded.

I will grant it safe passage to the surface, though I offer the passengers no protection against what awaits them there.

Thank you, Elena said.

Do not thank me. Your pet cutthroat certainly won't. But remember your pledge. I will hold you to it.

"The court of Seele is adjourned." The authority in Nakvin's voice almost hid her concern. "Any petitions we didn't hear today will go to the top of tomorrow's docket. Thank you all for attending."

Elena returned her full attention to the throne room. Lord Roen was stalking away amid a gaggle of richly dressed hangers-on. The other nobles and yeomen crowded into the galleries stared at Elena until the court officers ushered them out.

Even when the outer halls finally swallowed the shuffle of retreating footsteps and the hum of hushed conversation, a company of courtiers, soldiers, and servants remained. Elena and her mother were never truly alone—not here.

Nakvin turned to her daughter, her regal façade broken by the worried frown on her lips.

We need to talk. My chambers. Now.

A squad of royal bodyguards in green and gold uniforms under silver breastplates escorted Elena and her mother along the labyrinth of opulent corridors that wended through the palace of Seele to the royal apartments. Every wine-red silk carpet, every birchwood panel engraved with hunting scenes; every graceful alabaster fixture boasted of a culture at its zenith.

Perhaps this tribe deserved the name of *Light Gen*. Yet boasting often concealed fear, and even the brightest day inevitably succumbed to night.

The perfumed corridors finally gave on a covered footbridge with arcaded walls of elegantly carved white limestone that offered a sweeping view of forested slopes on both sides.

Having spent her version of childhood confined to sterile labs and ships' engine rooms, Elena still found live greenery somewhat confusing. It was a pleasant confusion though, fascinating as a difficult equation or the workings of a complex person's soul.

Elena had met only a handful of truly interesting people. She thought of one such individual and hoped that Shaiel would honor his word.

The ring of the soldiers' spurs and the clatter of their spear shafts didn't fully conceal the whisper of the women's skirts sweeping the white marble tiles or the distant rumble of a waterfall inexorably deepening the tree-lined gorge at its base.

Elena glanced from the guards to her mother. *Why are they following us?*

They're here for our protection, answered the queen.

What threat can they stop that you or I couldn't?

Nakvin sighed. *It's tradition. Protocol annoys me too, but it's more for the people's sake than ours.*

Tradition doesn't annoy me. Thoughtless adherence to it might endanger others. Considering the threats we face, couldn't an elite military squad be put to better use?

Nakvin gave her daughter a bemused look. *There's more to consider than logistics.*

Elena spent the rest of the short stroll puzzling over the queen's words. She had yet to reach a conclusion when they turned at the bridge's intersection with a wide hallway and stopped at set of double doors clad in golden filigreed ivory.

A man uniformed in the royal household's archaic livery reached for the near door's scrimshawed handle. But before the servant could perform his function, the door swung outward to reveal a mousy slip of a girl exiting with a bundle of white linen tucked under one arm.

"Hi, Ydahl," said Nakvin.

Besides fulfilling Elena's original purpose of saving her mother from the Cataclysm, Nakvin's return to hell had ignited a rebellion that saw her ascend the vacant throne of Seele and culminated in Seele's conquest of the Circles—or rather the first eight.

Misfits, malcontents, and outcasts of all kinds had flocked to Nakvin's banner. Perhaps the least of these was Ydahl, who now served as the queen's chambermaid. The dead girl, whose homicidal mania had damned her, froze on the threshold and lowered her plain face rather than look at Elena.

"I put on fresh sheets, mum." Ydahl barely managed more than a whisper.

Nakvin smiled. "Good job. Go ahead and run the old ones down to the laundry."

The dead girl managed to nod without lifting her eyes from the floor. She slipped past the doorman and the guards and dashed down the hall. Even in the shafts of daylight streaming through the tall arched windows, the pale green velvet of her gown looked as dim as if she stood under a perpetual raincloud.

With the queen's path made clear, the doorman resumed his duties and opened the door wide for Nakvin and Elena's entry to the royal apartments. The guards were dismissed, except for two who remained to stand guard outside.

Mother and daughter passed into a corridor of polished cherry wood smelling of cloves and lit by golden lamps. The door closed, shutting out the day and leaving only a soft, warm glow.

"Sorry about Ydahl." Nakvin made a small sound halfway between a laugh and a sigh. "I think the tension's getting to her."

"She's afraid of me. That's normal."

Nakvin laughed. "Who knows what dead people think?"

Elena gave her mother a sidelong glance. "I do."

"Wait a minute." Nakvin planted herself in front of her daughter. "The dead don't have life cords. How can you read their minds?"

"Only shards of the Nexus need silver cords to mediate telepathy with other shards," Elena said. "My nexus can make direct contact."

The two of them continued past comparatively simple doors to their left and right on their way to a second set of double doors lavishly carved with stylized floral patterns. The queen herself took hold of the brass handles cast in the shape of falcons' heads and pushed the doors wide.

"Deim used to say that wisdom meant fearing the gods," Nakvin said as she stepped onto the intricately woven Thysian rug that carpeted her sitting room. "I just think Ydahl's being a bit paranoid. It's not like you're going to smite her or something."

Elena entered the queen's apartments and shut the door behind them. No lights burned in the windowless chamber, though none of its more frequent visitors were hindered by darkness. The ghost of a sweet, spicy scent lingered.

"You said it yourself. She has no silver cord, and I'm the embodiment of a nexus."

Nakvin fell back onto one of two sofas flanking a low table of mahogany polished to mirror smoothness. Her silk robe splayed out across the satin cushions.

"Ydahl's not the only one you're making nervous. You were out to lunch at the end of the audience."

Elena pondered how much to tell her mother. Shaiel's designs on her kingdom gave Nakvin troubles enough. Learning that her daughter had made a pact with him to save one of her old friends would only compound her worries.

"And why not?" Elena replied, stationing herself near one end of the couch. "I've explained how tedious it is hearing your subjects' petitions."

Nakvin's head, which she'd craned back onto the couch's backrest, lolled to face her daughter. "It's no more fun for me, but it comes with the job."

Good. The conversation was already veering onto a side issue. Elena had a response prepared to ensure that the discussion stayed lost in the weeds.

"Your job; not mine. I didn't intend to take up residence here."

"I'm glad you did, though." Nakvin's smile turned up a corner of her mouth, exposing the point of one fang. "More importantly, so are my people. They'd have fallen apart by now if we had to face Shaiel alone."

Now to sever the thread, Thought Elena. "You realize that's not my concern."

Nakvin shrugged. "I'm sure a goddess has bigger things on her mind. Speaking of which, what *were* you daydreaming about earlier?"

The queen must have inherited a double share of her grandfather's cunning. It was the only explanation.

Elena weighed her options. She could try more misdirection, but another attempt was less likely to succeed than the first. She could simply lie, and she had no moral qualms against doing so, but Shaiel—and Teg, if he survived—could eventually expose what she sought to hide. Then again, baring her thoughts to her mother now would cause equally irritating complications in their relationship.

It occurred to Elena that she could make the queen forget the whole line of inquiry, but such a mental violation *did* elicit pangs of discomfort.

The sound of someone shuffling down the hallway toward the chamber relieved Elena's burden. The latch clicked, and one door gently creaked open, admitting a cone of soft golden light that spilled across the floor with the shadow of a slim figure at its heart.

"Are there any sweet rolls left?" asked a groggy masculine voice.

Nakvin's silver eyes gleamed as they looked to the door. "Hi, Tefler. Breakfast was six hours ago."

Elena turned. Her son leaned in the doorway, clad in a short-sleeved shirt of white cotton with a crimson device merging serpent, bird, and fish that she still found unnerving. He rubbed his head with one hand, further mussing his light brown hair, and ambled into the room.

"So...no, then?" Tefler said as he puttered about the table. The silver tea service chimed as he lifted the empty kettle's lid. His varicolored eyes had no difficulty in the dim light.

"You slept through today's audience," Nakvin said flatly.

Tefler's voice brightened. "That almost makes up for missing breakfast."

"The doorman said you left early yesterday and came in late. Where were you?"

"Anris took me to see some local points of interest," Tefler said. "If I'd known about the spooky stone rings down here, I'd have come sooner. Did you know there's one on this hill? The townsfolk turned it into a pavilion. I'm glad you kept that stuff around."

Nakvin exchanged a wary look with Elena. The queen hadn't merely invaded the other Circles. She'd expanded her domain into those she'd conquered. Now hell was almost entirely Avalon, but even the queen of Seele and heir of Zebel couldn't remake every infernal acre to her liking. Tefler's ruins, predating the reign of any baal, resisted her influence—as did the lowest Circle, and what lay beneath it.

"I need to have a talk with Anris," Nakvin said.

Tefler spread his hands. "For not letting me go alone? He's a malakh. Guarding's not what he does. It's what he *is*."

"And you're not a member of the Khemet pantheon or Almeth Elocine. He's *my* army's captain; not your personal bodyguard."

"So? If your army ever has to fight Shaiel, the grape warrior won't do you much good. Trust me on that one."

Nakvin gave Elena another knowing look. "We'll just have to count on your mother."

"Yeah," said Tefler. "Thank God for...I mean..."

Grateful for the distraction, Elena sent forth the smallest exertion of her power.

"There are more rolls in your chamber," she said.

Tefler turned to her, beaming, for just a moment before he

51

sprinted from the room. "Thanks, Mom," He called back from the hallway.

"You really spoil him," Nakvin said. "You know that?"

"Compensation for letting the greycloaks raise him. Besides, he's a grown man. His personality and dispositions are set by now."

Nakvin's face fell. "It's hard to express how much I hope you're wrong.

5

There was fire above and fire below.

But Teg already knew that.

He walked the half mile from the *Theophilus'* landing site at the center of the Guild house's roof to the southern edge. A hundred yards to his right, a massive fissure belched gouts of flame into the sweltering—but miraculously not ignited—air between the surface and the burning stratosphere. The fiery chasm traversed a quarter of the black plateau's diameter and continued down the south wall as far as Teg could see.

Who knew? The breach might span the whole mile to the ground.

Teg's eyes wandered over the panorama below. Rolling prairie stretched away under the burning sky, the dead grass tinted red-gold by lofty flames. Farther south a web of rivers broke the plains into flat-topped hills.

Teg turned slightly eastward, to where the sea shimmered like molten gold in Midras' forge. He could make out the delta where the Rove, of which every lesser river below was a tributary, reached its end.

Fifty miles or so inland, filling a wide river valley between two high bluffs, lay Salorien, the greatest city of the Second Sphere.

Teg squinted. The city's tallest buildings stood in the river basin and didn't rise above the surrounding hills. On a clear day the dreary housing blocks of Northridge would be visible, but a haze that smelled of distant forest fires hid the top of the bluffs. No lights shone through the murk, and neither ship nor drifter glinted in the once busy sky lanes between the city and the cube.

"Yato." The pervasive traces of smoke coarsened Teg's voice as he spoke into his ear stud. He stood at the edge of the ship's meager range, but incredibly, the broken and burning Guild house was still boosting the signal.

"Do not fear," the steersman replied. "I haven't decided to strand you in this smoking ruin—yet."

He'd long since grown used to Yato's grim humor, but the harsh—and accurate—description of Keth stung Teg more deeply than expected. After all he'd suffered and sacrificed to get home, what if there was no home to go to?

"Did you see any signs of life in the city on our way down?"

"All I remember seeing was fire," Yato said, "and lots of it."

"We came here hoping to find some remnant of civilization, and you didn't even look?"

"I was fighting to hold the ship together. There is evidence that the Guild erected a global field to protect Keth from the Cataclysm. Instead of repelling the fire, the ward absorbed it, and the feedback destroyed the Guild house. I doubt anyone on the sphere survived."

Teg rubbed his irritated, watering eyes. Even if Yato was right, the Guild wasn't responsible for Keth's demise. Deim had lit the fire, but Vaun had given him the match. "Like they say on Temil, don't bet against Kethans. Are we good to fly?"

"Surprisingly, yes. Our survival alone qualifies as a miracle. It must have pleased Zadok to bless us with a functional ship in the bargain."

"Then I owe him a drink," said Teg. "Warm up the drifters. We're heading into town."

Yato clicked his tongue. "We need not have wasted a trip had your people been more sensible. Why build Salorien's Guild hall so far from the city?"

Teg smiled to himself. "The Steersmen had a stretch of riverfront all picked out, but the city fathers doubled the land tax. Building way out past the safety of the valley sent a message—the Guild stood above local politics and history. They got the second part wrong."

Teg crept through a shabby park that was the sole clear landing site in Northridge. The yellow light cast down from the burning sky froze the world in an eternal morning before a storm. Every step within the square block of greenery bounded by run-down buildings brought back long lost memories.

There was the drinking fountain that served as the neighborhood social hub and trading post. The graffiti scrawled across its square brick pedestal had grown thicker since Teg had seen it last, but he still recalled the day of his tenth summer when an older, fatter boy had thrown him against one of the fountain's hard edges during a fight.

An even more vivid memory followed, helped by the sweet scent of dead leaves. Teg's father had returned from another long absence to find his son curled up on the attic floor, bloody and crying. Teg's fear of another beating succumbed to even worse shame when his father had just stood over him silently before turning and descending the stairs.

Teg had risen early the next morning and waited at the door to the basement workshop—the door that he and his mother both knew better than to open—for his father to emerge. Though weary from a long night's work, the elder Cross had taken his son out and begun his instruction in certain skills that Teg still found useful from time to time.

The daily lessons continued until summer departed along with his father. Yet the knowledge remained. Teg had spent the first week of fall planning and executing a pair of petty burglaries. Then he'd hidden in the bushes beside the walk leading to the fountain.

When the bully who'd beaten him approached, Teg had cut his arm with the fat boy's favorite pocket knife—stolen from the edge of the park's wading pool while its owner swam—before tossing the knife down at its bewildered owner's feet.

The dead cat whose throat had been slit with the same blade came next. Its limp carcass slapped wetly against the older boy's round belly before tumbling to the ground. Teg followed it, throwing himself to the concrete hard enough to skin his elbows. He never raised a hand against his foe but just lay there, screaming.

After all this time, he still smiled to remember how the inevitable crowd of witnesses—including an even larger, notoriously short-tempered boy who'd been the cat's owner— had given Teg his revenge.

"Some weather we're having!"

The greeting pulled Teg out of the past and back to the present-day park, where an old woman was ambling along the shrub-lined path toward him.

Teg looked up at the raging vault of fire. "Yeah. Let's hope it clears up in time for the fireworks show. Any idea what happened?"

"It's not the cold." The old woman's voice was surprisingly close. "It's the damp."

Several things occurred to Teg, not the least of which being that it was warm as high summer and so dry that his mouth seemed to be lined with cotton.

Teg stifled a curse. His longing to speak with someone he hadn't been stuffed inside a rickety tub with for five years had made him sloppy. Only now did it dawn on him that she wore a purple winter coat.

A bony hand grasped Teg's shoulder from behind. His gun was in his hand before he'd fully rounded on his assailant. When he did, he found himself pointing the bulky revolver at Yato's lean, wide-eyed face.

"Why did you leave the ship!?" demanded Teg.

Indignation replaced Yato's shock. "I've been trapped aboard that ship as long as you have. Am I not allowed to stretch my legs?"

Teg lowered the gun but didn't holster it. "This hasn't come up before, so I'll let it slide. But for your own sake, never sneak up on me in a potentially hostile situation—which pretty much means from now on."

Yato looked as if someone had told a ribald joke about his

mother. "I was concerned for you. Something was odd about that woman, and you didn't seem to notice."

Nearly shooting the man who may have been the last living steersman had distracted Teg from the woman in winter clothes. Now he spun back around and saw to his dismay, but not to his surprise, that she was gone.

"Please tell me you saw where she went."

"I did not." Yato sounded as flustered as Teg felt. "Perhaps she wandered behind the hedge."

Teg doubted that even he could vanish behind a row of dead bushes in a coat like that, yet no sign of garish purple showed through the withered leaves. Grubby toys poked out of the brown grass here and there, eerie monuments to owners who'd never returned from their supper or their beds.

Teg raised his gun again. "Get back to the ship. Seal the hatch, raise the aura, and don't let anyone on board unless I say so."

"What is it?' Yato asked. "What's happening?"

"I don't know," said Teg. "But when somebody pops up and disappears like that, it's never good."

The fiery firmament seemed to press down closer. Not a leaf stirred.

"No," Yato said in his best tone of defiance. "We go back together."

The offer was tempting, but Teg's burning need to know what had wrecked his world overcame his good sense.

"This isn't my first time around the block. That's not a metaphor. I used to live here. There are some places nearby where I think I can scrounge up supplies."

"Very well," said Yato. "We press on together."

Teg faced his steersman again. "No good. If I cash in, it's one less mouth to feed. If we lose you, we lose our only way off this rock."

Yato's smile softened the resignation in his voice. He clapped a hand on Teg's arm.

"Friend, you belittle your worth. Only I can fly our poor ship, but I cannot fly her through the flames again. Even if I could, and even with one less hungry mouth, there is nothing left to feed us.

"It has been a grand voyage, but this is the last stop. Our survival now depends on yours, and I shall do all in my power to ensure it."

Without another word, both men strode through the park gates and into the silent city.

There was no sign of the old woman—or anyone else—in the street, but the wide tract of pavement was far from empty. Drifters sat on their skids by the roadside, caked in years' worth of dust. To all appearances, their owners had simply parked and walked away for good.

Teg continued forward, stepping carefully around piles of desiccated trash that the wind had gathered here and there. The crunch of pebbles under his boots shattered the stillness like gunshots.

"Look there," Yato said, stabbing a finger up the street.

Of course, Teg had already seen what the steersman was pointing at. A line of cars cordoning off the intersection was hard to miss, but he preferred to tackle puzzles in their turn.

Drifter drives explained how the cars had been stacked, three high in places. The prominent presence of police vehicles—and even one drifter bearing Guild Enforcer markings—explained who'd erected the barricade. What Teg remained gallingly ignorant of was *why*.

The same question clearly galled Yato. "Perhaps there was civil unrest. The Guild's hand in the Cataclysm spurred the townsfolk to riot."

"Possible, if they found out what hit them."

Teg cleared his mind of presumptions and scanned the nearby buildings. Most were concrete boxes four or five stories tall abutted by older brick structures. The firestorm overhead gave everything a nicotine stain tint, and Teg felt like he'd walked into an antique photograph.

Broken windows and traces of fire damage did suggest some kind of disturbance. Teg was starting to side with Yato when he noticed that most of the damage was confined to the low rent housing on the upper floors; not the small businesses at ground level.

Even less consistent with a riot, the prevalence of broken glass on the sidewalk ruled out hooligans throwing bricks from the street. Dust-stained sheets still hung limply from more than one shattered window.

They were broken out from the inside.

What really decided Teg against the riot theory, and chilled him despite the stifling heat, was the total absence of dead bodies.

A second look confirmed his initial shocking observation. There were no dust-covered lumps balled up in the gutters, no mummified forms slumped over the wheels of inert drifters; no human ragdolls hanging halfway out of dark windows.

Teg asked the obvious. "Where are all the dead people?"

Yato, looking as if he'd startled a scorpion in his shoe, darted glances in every direction. "The authorities must have removed them."

"Okay," said Teg. "Why did they leave the rest of this mess?"

"Perhaps they can answer," Yato said, tugging on Teg's sleeve.

Teg looked in the direction his steersman was facing. A small knot of people stood in the middle of the road between him and the barricade. Their posture and expressions were neutral.

"Hey," Teg greeted them. "Where are all the dead people?"

The small band didn't answer. Instead they moved toward the newcomers as if out for a casual stroll.

More unnerved than the situation should've warranted, Teg pointed his gun at the unarmed civilians.

"That's close enough. We're not here to make trouble, but we will if we have to."

The approaching townsfolk, whose ranks of both sexes and all ages seemed larger than at first glance, continued forward as if Teg's gun were no more threat than a balloon.

Only then did Teg realize what had set his nerves on edge. Most of the oncoming band—scratch that; *crowd*, wore winter clothes despite the oppressive heat.

"It's not the cold," said a familiar voice on Teg's left. "It's the damp."

Yato gave an indignant grunt that became a scream.

Nothing could have prepared Teg for the sight of the old woman from the park digging plastic fingernails the same purple as her coat into the side of Yato's neck. It may have been a trick of the light, but Teg thought he saw the woman's hand brighten and her impassive face grow ruddy as Yato paled.

Teg put a bullet through her eye. The shot left Teg's ears ringing as she and Yato fell to the dusty street. Only the steersman got up, pressing a hand to his left ear instead of his bleeding neck.

Teg's senses kept telling him things he'd rather not know. The woman in the purple coat lay dead, but her wound had bled far less than it should have. Also, the shot had failed to scatter the advancing mob.

I hope they're just deaf.

Teg grabbed Yato's arm and strode briskly away from the following mob, which now filled the street from the barricade to the park. They all wore winter clothing.

It was winter in Salorien when the Cataclysm hit, Teg remembered.

He breathed deeply to slow his racing heart and focused on guiding Yato down the trash-strewn road. The steersman staggered along, weaker than the slight bleeding from his shallow cuts could explain.

We need to get off the street. Teg searched his surroundings and his memory for shelter. The park had minimal cover and might hold more hostiles. The buildings across the street were all fronted with floor-to-ceiling windows that wouldn't even slow down determined pursuit. The mob certainly qualified, though Teg had no clue what they wanted and he wasn't about to stop and ask.

Teg glanced over his shoulder and gaped when he saw that the ambling mob had somehow halved his lead. He broke into a run, all but dragging Yato with him. The ashen steersman was panting when they turned left at the corner of Nailand and Scrimm and ran right into a small army of blank-faced citizens in winter clothes.

The old lady in the purple coat stepped from the crowd. Both of her fully intact, lightless eyes stared at Teg. Her wrinkled mouth moved, and though the clatter of a hundred slow footsteps drowned out her words, he knew she was warning him about the relative discomfort of the cold and the damp.

Yato pushed his guide away with unexpected strength. "They are dead, not men. Hide your eyes!"

The irony of the curse Teg muttered as he covered his face with his arm no more escaped him than his eyes escaped the white light that shone from Yato.

The prana burst lasted only an instant but left Teg dazzled. He heard Yato wheezing beside him as if struggling to breathe through a crushed straw. The din of approaching footsteps had stopped.

Teg's vision cleared. He saw Yato kneeling on the pavement, shaking as he tried to stand.

The dead of Northridge stood before him, their faces flushed; their eyes bright as those of wolves who've run down a wounded stag.

Teg lost count of how many times he fired. Each shot dropped one of the ruddy mob, but the others pressed forward unfazed. Though they swarmed the priest like flies drawn to roadkill, the hand of one dead Kethan brushed Teg's. A sudden chill sapped the strength from his arm, and only with a desperate effort did he hold onto the gun.

Listing his sins would have taken Teg a month, not counting

meal breaks. Now, as his longtime companion—and his only escape from the restless graveyard that had been Keth—vanished under a press of grasping corpses, his cries dwindling to groans, Teg added another shameful deed to the list.

He turned and ran for a narrow alley on his right.

The hungry dead were easy enough for Teg to shoulder past, though he suffered more than one flesh-numbing touch. He staggered into the alley and crouched between two dumpsters behind what had been a Shianese restaurant. The expected stench of rancid grease and rotten vegetables was long gone.

The dead men—if that was the right word; these were nothing like the ones in the Nine Circles—hardly let Teg catch his breath before filing into the alley.

I wonder if I'd go back to hell. Teg entertained the temptation to quit running only long enough to draw a deep breath and bolt for the alley's far end.

6

Teg emerged from between two brick buildings onto a steeply sloping street. The dead were already stalking the road in twos and threes as dozens more funneled into the alley behind him.

Scanning the street in growing desperation, Teg spotted one place that looked completely free of hostiles. A tower of burnt umber brick stood uphill on his left where the road turned a corner.

Teg knew 1616 Foothill—a ten story block of cheap flats that had housed working class families before fire ate the sky. With multiple easily defended entrances and a rooftop overlooking the whole ward, he couldn't ask for a better fallback position.

Teg's hackles rose, warning him of dead hands seeking his neck. He dashed across the street, weaving between stalled cars and heaps of trash, and bounded up a short flight of concrete steps to reach the double steel doors at the building's entrance.

Finding the door unlocked, Teg's pounding heart leapt. Rushing in blind vexed him, but there was no time to subject the entrance to the Formula—or even a lesser, cursory search. He pressed his shoulder to the olive drab steel and pushed his way in.

No sooner had Teg gained entry than he whirled back toward the door and threw the lock. He breathed a sigh of relief when the deadbolt clicked home.

Teg surveyed the lobby. Orange-gold light seeped through narrow wired glass windows. A security desk cloistered behind a transparent metal sheet stood across from the doors. No trace remained of its last occupant.

Moving into the small reception area on the right, Teg noticed that the still air felt uncomfortably thick. The smell of plaster dust and rotted particle board stung his nose. A collection of metal frame chairs and a low plastic table, all covered in dust, took shape as Teg's eyes adjusted to the gloom. The silence was total.

He was alone.

Probably not for long, thought Teg. There were other ways in. It was only a matter of time before his pursuers found them.

The shock of losing Yato clutched at Teg's mind. He shifted his focus to survival. Berating himself was a luxury that would have to wait. Getting better informed of his situation was priority number one, and that meant heading up to the roof.

There was no power to the elevator. Teg found the stairs and made his way upward in the sparse light of windows placed at every other turn. He proceeded carefully, checking each landing and the inevitably vacant hallway stretching beyond it before climbing to the next floor.

The possibility of getting trapped on the roof occurred to him during the ascent. Recalling the building's two fire escapes, both of which rose to the top floor, allayed Teg's fears. From his unobstructed vantage point atop the tower, he would plot the best route back to the ship.

And after that?

The next part was still fuzzy. Maybe Jaren would come to and hatch a brilliant escape plan.

Teg shook his head. That would be just like old times, but Keth had proved that the past was dead.

He'd just set foot on the fifth floor landing when Teg's eyes alerted him to the first anomaly he'd encountered since entering the building.

The hallway was empty, but in the dim light Teg saw that the last door on the left stood open.

The sight gave Teg pause. He tightened and slackened his grip on the gun as he weighed the possibilities.

Was it an ambush? No one had passed him on the stairs, which were the only set, meaning that anyone lying in wait for him must have already been up here. Judging by its location, none of that apartment's windows faced Foothill Street, so its occupants couldn't have seen Teg coming.

What about the fire escape? Teg doubted his single-minded foes were creative enough to climb up and lure him into a trap with an open door.

Another possibility lightened Teg's heavy heart. Could there be survivors?

The signals were mixed. The dead seemed too stupid to leave doors open on purpose, but anyone who left doors open by mistake was too stupid to survive.

The apartment's resident might have been killed years ago while stepping out for the mail, leaving his front door ajar. A pair of footprints in the dust, facing the door, ruled out that scenario. It had been opened from the outside, and recently.

Teg crept into the hall to satisfy his morbid curiosity. What he found froze him where he stood. Besides the two small, fresh footprints facing the open door, the only other tracks along the entire length of the hallway were his own.

Teg strained his ears for any sound and heard only his own rapid heartbeat. At length he inched forward until he could read the number on the open door—503.

1616 Foothill Street, Apartment 503. The address was familiar, though Teg couldn't quite remember why.

Applying the Formula on the door might've calmed Teg's frayed nerves. But the high likelihood of deadly foes hot on his trail forced him to give the living room beyond a quick once-over before stepping inside.

Shafts of hazy light slanted down from four windows on the right, leaving four gold-orange squares on the floor. Depressions in the worn carpet showed where furniture had stood—for a long time, judging by their depth.

A family lived here once, observed Teg. Uncharacteristic nostalgia came over him when he thought of all of the birthdays and holidays that must have been celebrated within these walls.

It was no use pining for an imaginary past. Here and now where he had to live, his world was dead and the apartment was empty.

Or was it? Teg thought he heard a floorboard creak somewhere down the hallway off the living room. He listened but the sound didn't come again.

Teg flexed his fingers. The numbness caused by the dead men's touch was gone. He tightened his hold on his gun and slipped into the dim hallway.

The smell of dust prevailed everywhere, but a rosy fragrance impressed itself on Teg's mind; not a scent, more like the ghost of one. It was probably just his senses rebelling against the barren sphere, but he didn't dismiss the occurrence outright.

Five doors lined the hallway. The third on Teg's left stood ajar. The opening looked like a narrow brass pillar gleaming in the dark.

That room has a window.

Had the dead come in through it? There was only one way to find out.

Teg burst through the door and into a bedroom, hoping to surprise anyone inside. He succeeded. A dark shape huddling just beyond the lone window's light rose from its knees with a startled gasp. The figure's slight build informed Teg that it was a woman—or had been.

Not that it mattered. He'd seen women in the flower of youth, wrinkled grandmothers, and freckle-faced girls descend on Yato like ants swarming a beetle. Whatever these people— Teg's people—hand been, the Cataclysm's aftermath had warped them into something loathsome. He had no compunctions about putting any of them in the ground where they belonged.

The thing that might have been a woman stared at Teg with red-rimmed blue eyes that widened when they saw him. The hood of her dark brown jacket obscured the rest of her fair-skinned face.

Teg pointed the barrel at her forehead, pressed the trigger, and heard an empty click.

"Sulaiman?" She asked with confusion; not fear. Her light

Kethan accent made the name a poem—a sad one.

"You know Sulaiman?" Teg asked, keeping the empty gun trained on her.

The woman's black skirt rustled as she stepped forward. "You aren't him?"

"Why would you think I was?"

"You look just like him."

"No I don't!" Teg said an instant before he recalled that his denial had exceptions. After all, he'd walked out of Tzimtzum with golden hair and sapphire eyes. Both hair and eyes had slowly darkened, a process that Yato had credited to Teg's infernal regeneration following the form of his soul.

None of which explained why the last survivor of Keth had mistaken Teg for Sulaiman Iason.

Until Teg remembered how the abomination that nearly killed Elena had looked when it lay dead in the *Exodus'* engine room.

The woman now stood in the shaft of amber light shining through the window. She pulled back her hood with delicate hands, freeing blood-red hair that spilled almost to her shoulders.

The sight of her held Teg riveted as he holstered the gun. Now he understood why this address was so familiar.

"Astlin?"

Astlin's face brightened. "Teg Cross. It's really you."

Teg approached warily as if expecting her to vanish like a dream. Of all his old friends, Astlin was the one he'd least expected to see again. Not only had most of the Middle Stratum's population died in the Cataclysm, Astlin had vanished twenty years before the doomed expedition that had lit the fuse.

"I hope so," said Teg.

Wariness became suspicion. Not only was Astlin the sole survivor in Northridge, she hadn't changed since he'd last seen her, aged seventeen.

No, thought Teg, *that's not right.* It wasn't even that Astlin hadn't aged in forty years—though that did seem to be the case. Something *was* different about her; something hard to put into words. She seemed more present, more *real,* than anyone he'd ever met.

A smile turned up the corner of Astlin's mouth. "You look great." She cocked her head slightly. "A little rough around the edges, but..."

Teg gently took Astlin by the shoulders and guided her away from the window.

Astlin's brow furrowed. "What are—"

Teg pressed a finger to his lips. She got the message and fell silent.

"I know how you feel," he whispered, "The last time I had this many unanswered questions, I'd studied for the wrong exam."

Astlin gave him a skeptical look.

"Okay, to be fair I never studied, but that doesn't matter." He hooked his thumb toward the window. "What does matter is the city full of atypically spry corpses on the hunt for their next meal. Since all the local dining spots are closed, we're on the menu."

"The whole city?" Astlin's voice wavered. "We're the only ones left?"

Teg gave her firm arms a squeeze that he hoped felt reassuring. "Questions later. Right now we need to get off the sphere."

He took a gamble and prayed it would pay off. "Your ship's on the roof?"

Astlin shook her head.

Teg's hope dimmed. "Okay, where is it?"

"I don't have one."

Wrath and despair strove for dominance in Teg's soul, but simple shock triumphed. "You've been here this whole time? Everyone thought you were missing."

Astlin slid from his grasp with a backward step. Her face hardened, and her eyes focused on something only they could see.

"Everyone was right. I've been back for less than an hour."

"How the hell did you get here?"

"Not hell," Astlin corrected him. "Kairos."

It was Teg's turn to furrow his brow. "Where?"

Astlin spread her hands in exasperation. "You said 'Questions later'."

Footfalls echoed from the landing. Teg's muscles tensed. He turned away from Astlin, drew his gun, and ejected the spent shells. Brass casings chimed as they hit the bare wood floor.

"There's a dead army between us and my ship," Teg said as he dug through his jacket and pants pockets. "They already ate my steersman, so here's the deal—I blow your brains out; then mine. Let's hope I've got two more bullets."

Astlin's delicate hand clutched his shoulder. "You can shoot me later. Where's your ship?"

Teg found one fresh cartridge and kept digging. "In the park. Might as well be on the moon."

"Wait here," said Astlin. "I'll be right back."

"You'll never make it."

Footsteps approached from the hallway outside the bedroom. Teg gave up searching and loaded the lone bullet.

"Close your eyes and hold still."

Teg turned to level the gun at Astlin's head.

She was gone.

A visual search ruled out any exits besides the closed window, which to judge by the dust hadn't been opened; and the door, which Teg had been facing.

Had he simply imagined meeting Astlin?

Yeah, let's go with that.

Teg faced the door again and held the gun to his temple.

"...not the cold," a whiny, tremulous voice announced from down the hall.

"Oh, fuck that!" said Teg.

The old woman shuffled into the doorway, her purple coat immaculate; her head intact. "It's—"

The enclosed, wood and plaster-clad space magnified the gun's report. Teg wouldn't have heard the end of the old hag's sentence even if his last bullet hadn't shattered her jaw and decorated the far wall with her skull's contents.

Its surprisingly meager contents...

Another dead person—this one dressed as a postman—stepped over the hag's body on his way into the room. Others could be heard filing along behind him.

Teg stowed the gun and threw the window open. He stuck his head out and saw an emergency ladder bolted to the outer wall beside it. A sea of the dead surrounded the building's base, so Teg pulled himself onto the weather-stained rungs and climbed.

The ladder ended in a set of arced railings bolted to a waist-high ledge enclosing the rooftop. The surface was coated with adhesive sheets of a pebbly material that was originally white but had suffered discoloration from dust, cooling system runoff, and sun damage.

The sun's no problem anymore, Teg thought as he looked up at the all-encompassing fire. A moment ago he'd almost killed himself out of despair for losing Keth. Now he hoped to live long enough to kill Vaun for cursing it.

Teg strode across the roof, wending between plumbing vents and corroded boxes housing Worked air pumps that heated or cooled entire flats. Northridge spread out around him—a mass grave disguised as a rundown neighborhood. He could see over the hill of the same name to the barren northern plains. Beyond them loomed the Guild house, only half-hidden by the horizon.

Did you smug bastards do this? If so, your master plan backfired, and I'd go back to hell just to rub your noses in it!

Teg rounded the corner of a large air pump. A young man stood not ten yards away, his face red; his flesh slightly swollen like a corpse just beginning to bloat. He wore only a sleeveless cotton shirt, shorts, and socks.

At least he's dressed for the weather, Teg mused as he drew an old pocket knife—not an ideal weapon, but it was his last.

Teg backed off a few paces. The man who'd died in his skivvies didn't move, so Teg turned back.

And came face-to-face with a silent mob.

They shouldn't be here.

No way did they all climb the ladder, and the door to the stairs was across the roof on Teg's right. Getting from the stairway side to the ladder side would've meant passing him.

The world seemed to spin around Teg, and he wheeled to take in the whole rooftop. They were everywhere now, fencing him in. Most were dressed in winter clothes. Some muttered a particular phrase, nonsensical in this context, with clockwork repetition. All had vacant, greedy eyes.

The first one came forward. There was no signal given and no sign of a rational plan.

The dead man, wearing a blond beard, a long tan coat, and fingerless gloves, walked up to Teg like a bum asking for change. Teg's knife cut two fingers from the bum's outstretched hand, but the wound didn't slow his advance. Another slash opened the dead man's throat, spilling remarkably little blood. That did slow him, and burying the blade in his eye put him down.

Dull nails tore Teg's jaw. Blood soaked into his beard as creeping cold numbed the wound.

"It's not the cold, it's the damp."

With a growl, Teg turned his head and saw the old woman leering over his shoulder. Her body was whole, but his blood reddened her purple nails. She stood on her tiptoes and brought her crooked teeth toward his neck.

Something long confined broke free. Teg rounded on the dead hag and stabbed her until she died again. He doubted it would take this time, but technicalities didn't concern him.

Cold hands groped for him—first one pair, then three; then ten. It didn't matter how many. Teg unleashed ruthless butchery on all of them; dealing mortal wounds like a light-fingered gambler passing cards around a table.

The darting blade stopped. Teg realized a second later that

he'd cleared a circle big enough to dance in. His right arm was numb; whether from the touch of dead hands or the strain of his grisly work, he didn't know.

Slaughtered corpses ringed his feet. Shuffling, sometimes mumbling corpses filled every other free inch of the rooftop.

Teg's scratches had already healed, but the cold was slower to leave his numbed flesh. Though he didn't regret firing his last bullet, he wondered if slitting his throat would do the job before the dead could do it for him.

He was raising the blade to find out when the whine of drifters drew his eye toward the park, above which three bullet-shaped pods connected by a pair of angled spars hovered.

Teg couldn't help but smile. *She actually got that scrap pile in the air.*

The *Theophilus* arced over the intervening buildings and came down heavily atop 1616 Foothill.

The old housing block wasn't built to take the weight of an ether-runner. Then again, neither were the teeming dead, several of which were crushed between the ship's two lower pods and the sagging roof.

Teg's joy fled when he saw the morbid crowd still massed between him and the ship.

At least he had a reason to fight, however hopeless the odds. Teg readied the knife and stepped forward.

Astlin stood beside him, though she hadn't traversed the corpse swarm. One second the space at Teg's right was empty. Now it contained her. He had no other way to describe it.

Sometimes indescribable things were good. So far, this one qualified.

"Close your eyes," Astlin said, facing the horde's renewed advance.

Teg grabbed the plush sleeve of her jacket. "Are you about to channel prana? Because if you are, my priest already tried that. It's like pouring chum in a shark tank."

Astlin's eyes stayed fixed on the front row of dead men, who were almost within arm's reach.

"I can't channel prana," she said. "No silver cord. I do have some authority, though."

"What?" asked Teg. "You'll tell them to disburse or—"

Three glowing points like gems carved from blue light shone above Astlin's brow. Heedless of her warning, Teg was still staring at them when their inner brilliance blazed forth. Unlike a prana burst, the blue light wasn't blinding. It was unspeakably beautiful, and looking into it filled Teg with awe unlike anything a mortal could inspire, along with all the peace and comfort he'd failed to find on Keth.

An elbow jabbing his ribs failed to fully rouse Teg from his ecstasy. He did hear Astlin say, "Come on. I don't know if I can move you onto the ship, and now's a bad time to experiment."

Teg once again became aware of the dead men gathered around him. They weren't frenzied; nor did they appear to be harmed. All of the dead on the rooftop merely stood and stared at the light.

"What happened to them?"

"They died in the Cataclysm," said Astlin, "but the surge of prana reanimated their bodies. They don't have real minds anymore; just echoes. But it's enough for this to work."

"What is this?" asked Teg. "It's really nice."

"I'll try to explain. Let's get on the ship first."

Teg nodded. Even as he and Astlin walked through the dead mob that parted before them, he couldn't take his eyes off the light.

The sagging roof creaked under Teg's feet, and he leaned on Astlin the rest of the way to the drive pod hatch. She paused as if deep in thought. A moment passed under the empty collective gaze of the dead before the stained pitted hatch slid open with a hiss.

Astlin swept onto the ship in a rustle of dark skirts. "Come on!"

Teg wondered absently who'd opened the locked hatch, but he didn't need her urging to follow her aboard.

Only when the hatch thudded closed, sealing them within the ship's dank stuffy interior, did Astlin douse her lights.

Teg's mental sovereignty returned, shattering his peace like a fallen chandelier.

"The high wasn't worth the crash," he groaned.

"I warned you," she reminded him.

He pointed Astlin toward another door set into the sheet metal wall. "This way."

Astlin gave him a questioning look before opening the door and passing through. An industrial concert of mechanical noise filled the engine room beyond. The hot air smelled of oil and lightning.

The deck pitched as they moved through the room, and Teg caught Astlin's arm before she fell against the rail encircling the engine. He ushered her into the short hallway beyond and closed the door, shutting out the racket.

"Thanks," she said, smiling sheepishly.

"Thanks, yourself. This was a pretty lousy day till you turned it around. That reminds me—how'd you do it?"

Astlin's face retained a half-smile as she studied her feet. "A lot's happened since I saw you last."

Teg suppressed flashbacks of a chase through dark woods, scaling treacherous peaks, and staring into a mirror at a face not his own.

"No kidding."

A vibration ran through the deck, and Teg felt a sudden weight pressing down on him as the ship rose on its drifters.

He flashed a surprised look at Astlin. "I thought you were flying. Who's on the Wheel?"

She met his eyes, and her smile grew till it lit her whole face. "I'll introduce you."

They climbed the tube connecting the drive pod to the Wheel pod. Teg emerged onto the patchwork deck plates and saw an unfamiliar steersman in the pilot's seat.

Not entirely unfamiliar—the smooth scalp rising above the threadbare headrest reminded Teg of Yato's, though the newcomer's head was clearly shaved; not naturally bald. This new steersman also seemed more youthful and robust than the gaunt, wizened priest.

A flurry of activity through the cockpit window caught Teg's eye. The ship had already risen some distance from its improvised landing pad, and its nose was angled toward the rooftop below. Teg watched as the roof caved in, taking dozens of Salorien's restless dead with it.

Astlin made small hitching sounds beside him, her body

trembling slightly. It took an effort for Teg to repress the same sense of loss that she must have felt.

I can't go home, he thought. *But somehow, I'll get even.*

The ship turned away from the grisly scene and climbed to a safe distance high above the ground but below the fiery ceiling.

The pilot left the Wheel and strode aft. Teg saw him to be a very young man—perhaps only a year or two older than Astlin's apparent age—stocky yet strong, wearing a short brown robe with cloth strips wrapping his calves and forearms. Ignoring Teg, he wrapped Astlin in a tender embrace.

"I am sorry," the young man told her. "We're too late."

"Don't I get a hug?" asked Teg.

The young man gave Teg a disapproving look. Astlin gently pulled herself away from him, dried her eyes on her sleeve, and motioned toward her fellow Kethan.

"This is Teg Cross. We grew up together."

Teg favored the young man with a toothy grin. "Hi. Nice flying."

Astlin positioned herself beside the young man, draping her arm around his shoulders. "This is my husband, Xander." Just speaking his name seemed to lift her spirits.

Xander's grey eyes narrowed. "Have we met before, Mr. Cross?"

"I was stranded at the ass end of space before you were born, by the look of you," said Teg, "But looks can deceive."

"Yes." Xander gave a slight nod. "They can. Forgive my poor manners. As guests on your ship, my bride and I are grateful for your hospitality."

Teg pointed at Xander. "Technically, you're a pirate. So now we all have something in common, whether it's heritage or profession."

Astlin's sweet laughter suddenly turned to a startled gasp, and she stared wide-eyed at something over Teg's shoulder.

Before Teg could react, three silver lights shone from Xander's brow. Facing them was like standing before a lightning bolt that had been frozen to constantly shed its glory. Teg froze in awe as Xander produced an ebony spear from nowhere and hurled it with a sure hand toward the drive tube opening.

There was a sound like a butcher cleaving a hog carcass, and the awful lights went out. Teg turned and saw the same bum he'd stabbed to death on the roof pawing at a hole in his chest. After a moment the vagrant fell to the deck and stopped moving.

Teg crept toward the corpse. The man was dead again. The spear that had killed him was gone.

He pressed the intercom switch on the wall. "Boys, this is Teg. We might have stowaways on board—the cannibal kind. Search the drive and habitat pods, and exterminate anyone you don't recognize with extreme prejudice."

"A verdilak," Xander spat. "My father told tales of the dead who feed on life. The sphere is overrun with them?"

"Yes," Astlin said darkly. "We need to get away from Keth."

"That's a pretty tall order," said Teg, "since the upper atmosphere's on fire."

Xander resumed his seat at the Wheel. "I think I can guide us past the flames."

"We got lucky our first time through the fire." said Teg. "Surviving a second trip will take a miracle."

"Miracles are in greater supply these days," Xander said.

"Astlin and I can move anywhere in sight, or that we know from memory, with a thought. The Wheel makes me one with the ship. I should be able to move it, as well."

Teg fixed an expectant look on Astlin. "Since there's a good chance your husband is about to get us all killed, now's a good time for that explanation."

Astlin bit her lower lip. She looked back and forth as if searching for an escape route. At length she let out a sharp breath.

"I guess it started when me and Xander died."

"You two are like them?" Teg jabbed an accusing finger at the corpse on the deck.

"No!" Astlin held up her hands, palms outward. "Those things are fragments of fragments; not even full Nexus shards."

Teg folded his arms. "You said you don't have a silver cord. So you're not part of the Nexus, either."

"You're basically right," Astlin said with a sigh. "But that's like saying a lake is a raindrop because neither one is a river."

"Yato tried to explain all that Nexus stuff with metaphors," said Teg. "Save us both a lot of time and give it to me straight."

"Look," Astlin snapped. "I'm not a philosopher!"

"Why not show him telepathically?" suggested Xander.

Still facing Astlin, Teg replied, "Why don't you focus on steering us through the fire?"

"I have already brought us safely through," Xander said.

Teg spun toward the front window. The roiling flames were gone, replaced with a starry black curtain.

"You two are handy to have around," Teg whispered to himself.

Astlin approached to stand beside him. "When I died, I

found a way through the Nexus to…somewhere else."

Teg turned his eyes from the window and saw that Astlin was still staring through it.

"Somewhere else?" he repeated. "Like heaven or hell?"

Astlin slowly shook her head. "There's a world beyond this one—a place where no one has a silver cord. Where everyone is *real*."

"I'm not real?"

Astlin faced Teg. Her eyes were like sapphire lenses granting him a view of unfathomably distant light.

"No," she said softly. "Everyone here is a part of a nexus." Iron resolve hardened her expression. "That's why I came back. You're all puppets on silver strings, but I'll cut you free."

Teg broke the ensuing silence. "That's really thoughtful. The people of the universe will love your plan. In fact, you can tell them about it right now since the Nesshin I've been hauling from Tharis are probably the only other folks left."

Xander laughed. "That would be poetic justice, since my people were nearly wiped out. But I know of another ship carrying survivors of the Cataclysm."

"That's right," Astlin said. "The *Serapis*!"

Teg's eyes widened. "Big, grey ship with curvy things sticking out the back? That *Serapis*?"

Astlin nodded.

"I thought a god ate it," said Teg.

"Yes," Xander said, "but our friends fixed it."

Teg stepped up to the pilot's chair and leaned on the headrest. "This I've got to see. Do you know where she is?"

"Here, until a little while ago," said Astlin. "You must've just missed them."

"They will head for Temil next," Xander said.

"This scrap heap has one thing going for it," said Teg. "It's light and fast. We can catch the *Serapis* before she makes Temil."

Xander turned to the navigation panel. "I will set a course."

"Good. If they've got provisions to share, we might not starve." Teg clapped Astlin's shoulder. "I'll introduce you to the others—if dead people haven't eaten them."

7

The more Astlin saw of the *Theophilus*, the more amazed she became that twelve people had lived in its cramped confines for five years.

"She started as three dreadnaught turrets that were too hot for my old crew to fence," Teg told her as she stepped from the tube's last rung to the habitat pod. The humidity and mix of smells reminded Astlin of a kitchen or a laundry, stirring up memories of her old life, along with unexpected nostalgia.

Teg turned left through one of two doors in the narrow hallway. Astlin followed him into an oblong room filled with the surprising scents of soil and water.

A complex lattice of metal rods and plastic pipes hung under lighting panels that covered the center of the ceiling. Green leafy vines twined around the lattice, while what looked like squash and potatoes grew in knee high square bins below.

"Welcome to the garden," Teg said when he saw her admiring the plants. "We hung sun lamps and opened a pinhole Water Stratum gate for irrigation. It's never been enough to feed everyone. We were planning to stock up on Keth, but you saw how that went."

BRIAN NIEMEIER

Astlin ran her hand through greenery struggling to thrive in the cold and dark of space. Fine mist falling from the pipes clung to leaves and pods like dew.

"Speaking of that burning mausoleum," said Teg, "what brought you back from the dead?"

"At first I came back for Xander," Astlin said pensively, "but I realized that everyone needs saving." The glories of the light that had welcomed the monster she'd been, healed her, and made her real came flooding back. She felt a deep longing for the joy she'd abandoned, like a young soldier leaving home to fight a distant war.

"No argument here," said Teg. "How do you plan to save them?"

Astlin gave a start. "I don't know, yet. But if I can escape, so can others. I'll free everyone I can from Szodrin, Thera, and Shaiel."

"Shaiel?" repeated Teg.

"One of three gods who rose up after the Cataclysm," Astlin said. "Shaiel wants to rule the Middle Stratum from the Void. He already conquered Cadrys; probably Mithgar, by now."

Teg rubbed his bearded chin. "Have you met this Shaiel character?"

The divine tribunal in Kairos came back to Astlin like a nightmare of falling through ice into black waters. "Yes."

"Does he dress in grey and talk like a bad actor in an old opera?"

Astlin's memory lost its dread, and she failed to hide her smile. "That's him."

At length Teg gave a curt laugh. "I did a job with that creep.

86

Him taking over the universe is the worst thing I can imagine."

Before Astlin could ask any of the questions raised by Teg's comment, he moved to the end of the room and opened the only other door. Hushed voices on the other side rose to urgent chatter as he stepped through.

Astlin hurried after him and found herself in a chamber shaped like a tin can. Triple rows of recessed bunks lined the curving walls on her left and right. A narrow passage ran up the middle, floored with metal grates.

A long steel table flanked by parallel benches, all welded in place, stood at the room's center. Four men and one woman sat around the table while four children ranging from toddlers to adolescents watched their elders' heated debate.

Standing at the table's foot, Teg took the brunt of his shipmates' agitation.

"Everybody relax," he said.

"Relax?" said a middle-aged man with wispy hair and a lined mouth that gave him a permanently downcast look. "You trade Yato for a man-eating stowaway and tell us to relax?"

"Fine," said Teg. "Next time I won't tell you anything."

"Saba'd rather be right than alive," said the lean, rosy-faced woman with her hair gathered in a knot. "He's still vexed we made it past the first month."

Saba rose and jabbed his finger at the woman. "You won't be joking when a verdilak's sucking on your neck, Marse." Suddenly he jumped back from the table and yelled, "There's one of them now!"

With a collective gasp, everyone else stared at Astlin. Their accusing glares struck her speechless.

Teg planted himself beside Astlin and laid his hand on her shoulder. "You only wish someone this pretty would suck on your neck, Saba."

"Hi, I'm Astlin." She gave Teg a sidelong glance. "My husband is upstairs."

A small girl perched on the edge of a top bunk giggled. "Her hair is like the one-hand man's!"

The comment stoked Astlin's curiosity. Red hair was practically unknown beyond Keth, and even there it was rare enough to get her teased at school. Was this tiny ship harboring another Kethan?

Astlin turned to Teg, who'd gone strangely quiet. "Who's she talking about?"

Teg headed toward the back of the room. Those seated on the right side of the table rose to let him by.

"He keeps to himself, mostly," said Teg. "Come and say hello."

Astlin made her way past a roomful of wondering eyes to the last column of bunks where Teg crouched. There, propped up against the back wall on a worn mattress, lay a figure that Astlin found eerily familiar yet marvelously strange.

"I think his hair is a shade lighter than yours," Teg said of the scrawny man whose mane and beard were vivid red and whose right forearm ended just above the wrist.

"Who is he?" Astlin nearly jumped when the maimed man's piercing green eyes fixed themselves on her.

His face reminds me of Damus, she realized. *And his eyes are like Szodrin's. Could he be a Gen?*

"Meet Captain Jaren Peregrine," said Teg. "He's not the

captain of this ship. Or any ship, since his last two exploded."

Astlin peered into Jaren's eyes. They shone with a fierce, though haunted, light.

"What did you see?" she wondered aloud.

"Jaren doesn't talk much these days," said Teg. "At least not in actual words. We picked him up on Crote. The last place I saw him before that…would take a while to explain."

Driven by a force she couldn't name, Astlin stooped down and reached toward Jaren.

"It's alright," she said. "I can talk directly to his mind."

Jaren's left hand darted out and grabbed Astlin's wrist.

"Gleamed like gold," he rasped. "The Fire."

Astlin wrenched her hand free with a start. Jaren leaned back against the wall as if nothing had happened.

"That's the most coherent thing he's said since we found him," marveled Teg.

Astlin barely heard him. Memories of terror, madness, and pain seared her soul.

The hall door swung open. Astlin stood to face the dour-looking young man who stepped into the room.

Marse spoke first. "What did you find, Ehen?"

Ehen's long dark hair shook with his head. "I searched from bow to stern. Those of us in this room—and the new steersman on the Wheel—are the only ones aboard."

"Excepting poor Yato," said a wrinkled man with a long grey beard seated at the table, "we've come out none the worse for wear."

Teg nodded. "Let's keep it that way till we catch up with the *Serapis*."

8

Only the faint light of the Middle Stratum's farthest star betrayed the presence of the *Sinamarg*. A dim glint like tarnished silver outlined the Night Gen flagship's sharp angles while its onyx planes remained immersed in the utter darkness beyond the last star's sight.

The *Sinamarg's* hull, looking from below like a great pentagonal gem, its two leading edges elongated to a dagger point, likewise overshadowed the fleet of lesser nexus-runners that hung below it—frozen raindrops under a storm cloud.

Yet to Celwen, the great ship was as close as her own body— and just as subject to her will. She suppressed her impatience with the orders constraining that will as the *Sinamarg* and its fleet waited at the edge of space; turned not toward the living spheres ripe for conquest, but the utter darkness that had hidden her people for an age. The fleet's disposition struck her as frustratingly backward.

Damn Lykaon! A redundant curse. The demon prince's hunger to regain his throne compelled him to serve as Shaiel's Left Hand. Having already sacrificed his pride, he would not hesitate to offer up the Night Gen fleet for his ambitions.

Celwen stifled a bitter laugh. Lykaon knew better, but the Lawbringers he commanded thought her people the worst terror of the dark. Nothing else could explain the foolish summons they'd sent into it. Actually meeting what they'd summoned would teach the greycloaks otherwise.

As if answering her thought, the ship alerted Celwen to a disturbance just off the starboard bow. She turned her magnified vision in that direction and saw, not an object approaching through space, but a distortion in space itself.

Celwen watched enrapt as the empty blackness warped and bubbled like molten plastic. The frothing surface formed blisters that swelled and somehow took on substance. The extruded sacs clustered together in a doughy mass that resembled a cancerous jellyfish whose tumors held a metallic luster.

The fleet's comm channels erupted in a telepathic cacophony. Celwen phased out the crosstalk with an effort and concentrated on the creature apparently birthed from the darkness itself.

Scans showed that the being or object—no means at her disposal could tell precisely which—dwarfed every vessel present but the *Sinamarg*, approaching twenty percent of the flagship's mass. Its density, internal structure, and overall shape were in constant flux. No individual life signs could be distinguished with any consistency.

A shiver ran down Celwen's spine. *It's them. The Anomians.*

Every child of the Night Tribe knew the tales. There were places within the non-place of infinite darkness where no nexus-runner dared trespass. These utmost reaches of the Middle Stratum, where nature's laws were better thought of as suggestions, were the haunt of the Anomians.

Which race they'd belonged to, none could say. But it was whispered that these ancient Factors had perverted transessence to escape the limitations of their nature. The most disturbing accounts held that they'd succeeded—and lost their souls.

The fleet stopped chattering with itself and started bombarding the weird visitor with transmissions in every available medium.

At length, communication attempts ceased. A silent moment passed.

Perhaps they will lose interest and leave, Celwen hoped.

A coiled tendril burst from the hideous clump of blisters and shot toward the fleet. Celwen raised the flagship's defenses, but a consensus of her telepathic overseers belayed her impulse to open fire.

The tendril darted under the *Sinamarg* and its powerful shields. A bulb on the pseudopod's end released a cloud of smaller spore-like projectiles that showered a group of *Aqrab*-class ships. Most of the nexus-runners repelled the attack with flashes of blazing light.

One crew reacted too slowly. The living projectiles latched onto their ship's trefoil hull like barnacles on a seagoing vessel's keel. Webs of rot spread out from the impact sites, turning black crystal to running sores.

Celwen again sought permission to fire—this time on the tainted ship—and was again denied. Her resentment became panic when a pair of nexic waves revealed that something had translated from the infected nexus-runner to her own ship. Internal sensors could make no identification.

How is this possible!? Nexic translation rendered a living creature and its personal effects into pure prana that traveled along that being's silver cord. One could translate through almost anything—except a nexus-runner's shield.

The only explanation chilled Celwen's blood. *Unless whatever just came aboard is alive enough to translate but enough like inert matter to confuse the shield.*

Celwen cringed. She could feel the invading presence spreading along the ship's corridors like parasites burrowing through her veins.

Why isn't anyone stopping it?

The question became moot when the invasion did stop—right outside the bridge doors.

Celwen's awareness snapped back to the bridge. The suddenness of her emergence from the sympathetic interface left her briefly disoriented. She cast about the large room until her gaze fixed itself on her own reflection—tall and slender in her pilot's jumpsuit, dark hair spilling to her waist; all shaded black in the polished obsidian floor.

I am myself. The corruption is not in me.

Yet the words were difficult to believe.

The shouting of a security team alerted Celwen to a commotion at a set of double doors in one of the room's six matte grey metal walls. The three men, wearing dark blue jackets over black shirts; sweat slicking their black hair and beading on their ashen skin, stood ten paces from the door and argued over who should dare to move closer.

Hideous rasping and slapping emanated from the other side. Rather than sounding aggressive, whatever lurked beyond the door gave the impression of something cautiously probing for nearby danger, like a blind man feeling his way along a clifftop.

It breezed through sixteen security checkpoints to get this far, Celwen thought with growing fear. *Why let a simple door keep it from taking control of the ship?*

From her position near the room's apex where the tapering left and right walls met the front view screen, Celwen turned to the command crew gathered near the wall opposite the shunned door.

Her worthy superior Captain Velix always saw possibilities in even the most difficult situations. Now Celwen saw only frustration in the tight set of his jaw. Even Admiral Raig, imposing in his wholly black uniform, hesitated to issue orders.

A differnt fear, much like standing on the edge of a precipice, washed over Celwen an instant before the doors behind Raig and his officers slid open. Her vague dread intensified to near-panic, like a dream of falling she couldn't wake up from, when a grim band of soldiers loped onto the bridge, bowed beneath armor that rang like crossed blades with each step.

The squad processed to the center of the room. Though unfamiliar with the tools of Middle Stratum warfare, Celwen perceived their armor as not only arcane, but combining pieces from many different cultures. Yet eclectic taste was the newcomers' least odd quality. In the shadows behind their slitted masks, Celwen caught flashes of yellow eyes and long teeth. Their speech was the snarling of muzzled dogs.

They were not Flesh Thieves—not *Isnashi*. These beasts had never been of Celwen's kind. They hailed not from the darkness beyond all worlds, but from the pits beneath, and nothing could ease her revulsion at having to bear them on her ship.

A dread figure loomed over the pack, solitary despite his feral honor guard. His bronze helm, crowned with the jagged antlers of no natural beast, hid his face. A pelt too large for any normal wolf covered his broad shoulders. Perhaps the skin belonged to the monstrous lupine head carried aloft by the standard-bearer at his side.

The towering figure pointed at the door that held back the invading abomination. His voice was a guttural peal of thunder. "Open."

The security team turned to him and stared wide-eyed. Even the horrible thudding at the door ceased.

"Prince Lykaon." Admiral Raig ran his fingers through his white hair and cleared his throat. "This intruder poses an unquantified threat. It would be prudent to wait for additional security personnel before exposing ourselves to further risk."

At the merest gesture of Lykaon's hand, one of his honor guard marched toward the security team. He seized one of the hapless security officers, ignoring the rest as if their short swords were made of foam rubber.

"Again," Lykaon said. "Open."

Raig nodded to Celwen. Against her personal judgment, but in keeping with her duty, she released the command lock barring the intruder's way.

The door opened on a riot of alloyed flesh, as if a colony of primitive sea creatures had fused with the wreck they fed on and grown to absurd size, filling the hall with shuddering, cilia-wreathed stalks.

His head wedged in the crook of the man-beast's bulging arm, the security officer shrieked when his captor tossed him into the open maw of chaos.

Celwen screamed as the mass enveloped the struggling man with a chorus of sucking sounds. His own muffled screams continued for far too long after his body disappeared in a knot of tendrils and cysts.

"Easy, Lieutenant," Velix said to Celwen. His steady voice brought her immediate calm.

Lykaon's men laughed like jackals. He himself watched in silence.

"We pledged Shaiel our support in return for his," shouted Raig. "If you bring my officers to harm, our alliance is at an end!"

A pseudopod burst forth from the mass bearing a bulbous growth larger than a man. The flesh-colored bulb turned brown and peeled back, releasing a stench like burning metal and spoiled milk along with a roughly manlike figure.

The creature from the bulb tottered forward, the pod that had birthed it shriveling to nothing as it advanced. A final sheath of veined plastic-like material sloughed off, revealing a crooked bipedal form draped in ribbed membranes that grew from its hunched shoulders.

Celwen watched in morbid fascination as furry scales like those on moths' wings bloomed upon the membranes, making the whole look like varicolored robes. But the head perched atop the stubby neck belied all kinship with Gen, human, or any clean race.

Thick fibers like grey twine wound around a misshapen gourd served as the monstrosity's face. Whorls opening at irregular intervals held what Celwen took to be eyes, while a variety of mouth parts resembling those of leeches, lampreys, and spiders nested inside others. She guessed that the few empty openings functioned as ears.

The abomination stood before Lykaon's guards, multiple organs on its face blinking, sucking, and smacking.

"Name yourself and your purpose," Lykaon said.

A tendril lanced in from the hall and coiled around Lykaon's throat. His retainers shouted curses and howled as they hacked at the ropy outgrowth to no avail.

A sickly golden nimbus surrounded Lykaon. He grabbed the constricting tentacle with one hand, his gauntleted fingers sinking into its rubbery surface. Grey-brown fluid seeped from its metallic veins.

The tendril uncoiled and tried to withdraw, but the demon prince held it fast. Golden light poured from his hand into the tendril and coursed through it into the hall. The tendril and the mass attached to it melted down to a tarry residue that clung to every surface of the corridor as far as Celwen's natural eyes could see.

An even more startling revelation came when she cast her own nexic sight over the ship.

He froze out the invasion. It is all gone!

All, except for the many-eyed, many-mouthed aberration cringing before the prince.

"The outer darkness must dull the wits of all that dwell in it," Lykaon said. "Shaiel's Left Hand compels you. For the last time, name yourself."

A confluence of gurgles, clicks, and chirps from the creature's mouths produced syllables approximating words. "Liquid Sign."

Lykaon grunted. "You sought to take this ship."

"Wanting Song was to incorporate properties of Those That Do Not Exist and their ship," said Liquid Sign. "All processes of Wanting Song now permanently inert."

"Because it presumed to conquer what is mine by conquest."

Raig charged forward, but was halted by the ring of snarling guards.

"Conquest?" he cried. "This was meant to be diplomacy; not piracy!"

At some covert signal, Lykaon's guard parted. Raig drew back, but the demon prince strode past him toward the bridge officers, who stood dumbstruck in his path.

Celwen couldn't blame them. Even from her position on the control dais she felt the mindless terror of a rabbit cornered by wolves.

Lykaon overshadowed the bridge officers like an iron pillar. Velix alone faced the demon unflinching.

With the time-distorting speed of sudden violence, Lykaon locked Velix in a chokehold. The square-faced captain's grey skin darkened and his green eyes bulged as Lykaon squeezed. A sound like dry wood cracking broke another officer's trance, because she screamed when Velix's limp body slid from Lykaon's arms to the deck.

"He cannot move, yet he still feels pain." Lykaon didn't bother to face Raig, but there was no mistaking who was being addressed. "He dies slowly. Hours or days. He stays here. Anyone raising hand or voice against me dies with him."

Anger chased away Celwen's fear. But prudence tempered her wrath. She wordlessly contacted the nearest translator station and ordered Velix evacuated to the infirmary. His broken body vanished in a green-white flash.

Silence swallowed the chaos that had gripped the bridge. Celwen expected Lykaon to bluster and rage; to issue ultimatums for the one who'd defied him.

Instead his masked face stared straight at her.

"She dies," he told his men.

"Wait," shouted Admiral Raig. "Lieutenant Celwen is joined to the ship. Her death could endanger us all."

"And needlessly at that," said Celwen, relieved by Raig's intervention. "I have done nothing against you."

Lykaon approached the dais. The deck seemed to shudder beneath his footfalls.

"You lie," he said. "You burned with rage when I broke your captain."

An overlooked possibility dawned on Celwen. Her blood froze. "You are a telepath?"

Deep grating laughter emanated from beneath Lykaon's helm. "I hear your heart's beating and smell its desires. You care for the captain."

Celwen swallowed a sudden lump in her throat. "He is like a father to me."

"What of your real father?"

Guilt and sorrow besieged Celwen. She fought to muster her courage even as it bled away, but the wounds of her own making cut too deep.

The gloating in Lykaon's voice almost made her wish for the death he'd threatened. "You betrayed him. To his death…or worse?"

Celwen willed herself to offer a defense, but her lips moved soundlessly.

"Very well," Lykaon said, "Your shame is enough."

Raig shot Celwen a stern questioning look. She averted her eyes.

Lykaon turned back to Liquid Sign. "These escapades try my patience, Anomian. I'd not be made to suffer them had Shaiel's Right Hand kept faith. Answer quickly. Will you serve my lord against his foes?"

Liquid Sign twitched in myriad unnatural places and ways. The colored scales of his enveloping membranes rippled as if in a stiff breeze.

"Soon after we attained liberation, They Who Exist Beyond scoured us from the spheres and drove us into the outer darkness," Liquid Sign explained. "Many iterations later we sought to return and incorporate new properties, but Those That Do Not Exist forced us back as they fled the Guild."

Lykaon barked a cruel laugh. "Conquest lures us both. I defied the master of the known world, expanded his empire beyond the conquests of Great Zolgadr, and thenceforth ruled one third of hell. Now I serve a just god and command your ancient foes. Join us and none will stand against you. Refuse and we shall finish the work the old gods began on you."

"You do not know the plague that will be loosed upon the spheres," Celwen warned.

"Not just the spheres," Lykaon corrected her. He turned back to the Anomian. "Answer me. Will you serve Shaiel?"

Liquid Sign's many eyes rolled. His myriad mouthparts drooled.

"We will serve."

9

Astlin studied the squares etched into the piece of sheet metal on the table and moved one of the steel washers that, along with an equal number of hex nuts, served as game pieces.

Rosemy, the youngest Nesshin girl, sat on the tabletop across the board from her and giggled as her nut took Astlin's washer.

"You're pretty good." Astlin praised her with a smile. "Who taught you?"

Rosemy beamed. "My daddy. He made the game for me."

Seated in the stuffy confines of the habitat pod, Astlin pictured a life spent entirely aboard the *Theophilus*; a father struggling to give his daughter something remotely like a childhood. Her smile faded.

"Your daddy must love you a lot."

Rosemy looked down at the board and stirred the pieces with the rasp of steel on steel. "He died."

Memories of two lifetimes flooded Astlin's mind like a radio dial stuck between stations. Whatever that meant. Fragments of the world beyond seldom made more sense than the remnants of dreams.

Astlin slid another washer into the girl's reach. "I lost my dad, too."

Rosemy took the piece and turned it over in her small hands. "How did he die?"

"I don't know." Her father's unknown fate was an aching wound that even Astlin's rebirth hadn't healed.

"My dad got burned when the engine caught fire. Mom said he saved us." Rosemy took Astlin's hand and slid the washer onto her little finger like a ring.

Astlin's grief and affection compromised in a half-smile. She tried to remove the makeshift ring, but Rosemy grabbed both of her hands.

"No," the girl insisted. You keep it."

"But your game will be missing a piece."

Rosemy's dark braids whipped from side to side as she shook her head. "No one else plays with me now. Zay says he's outgrown it."

She glanced at the nearby bunks where her exhausted shipmates—including a bristly haired boy probably a year older than her—napped.

"Teg says we're going someplace with other kids and real games," said Rosemy. "But if you keep your piece, you'll come back for a rematch."

Astlin leaned forward and kissed Rosemy's forehead. Holding up her finger with its steel ring she said, "I promise I will."

Xander's voice booming over the intercom shattered the temporary peace.

"We are in sight of the *Serapis*," he said, and Astlin divined the great ship's peril from the urgency in his words. "They're under attack!"

Standing beside Xander's seat on the Wheel, Astlin stared through the cockpit window in dread and growing anger. A rattle from deep in the ship's ductwork further strained her nerves.

The huge oval wedge of the *Serapis* with its backswept aft pylons clearly stood out against the stars. Four smaller oblong shapes trailed it like roving shadows while a number of obsidian-edged craft—she counted three—flitted in and out of the dark.

The creaking of old boots on the deck betrayed Teg's approach, but just barely. Astlin turned to see him dressed in the same grimy shirt and frayed pants as before, but now his gun was in his hand.

"Four corvettes." Teg fed six bullets from his pocket into the revolver, closed the cylinder, and slid the freshly loaded gun into a shoulder holster worn under his patched olive coat. "It's nice to see a familiar sight. I don't recognize the three gnats, though."

Astlin faced the window and crossed her arms protectively. "They're nexus-runners—Night Gen ships."

"That didn't help," said Teg. "But come to think of it, they look like tiny backwards versions of the *Exodus*."

"You can reminisce later," Xander said. "Right now your shipmates—my people—need safe haven, and seven ships stand against us."

Teg sidled up to Xander's seat and leaned on the armrest across from Astlin.

"It might look that way," said Teg. "But those ships aren't here for us. They want something aboard the *Serapis*. They have a boarding party tossing her, and they don't expect outside intervention."

Astlin cocked an eyebrow. "You can tell all that from here?"

Teg pointed at the trailing ships. "Those corvettes are covering the stern." His finger tracked the weaving nexus-runners. "While the Gen run interference. They're not shooting, so they have people on the *Serapis*. The hangar's their extraction point. That's where we need to be."

"I will bring us in for a landing," Xander said with more than a hint of sarcasm.

"Nice initiative," said Teg. "Bad idea. Judging by how those corvettes are keeping their distance, I'd say the *Serapis* has her suppression field on. It doesn't seem to affect nexus-runners, which we should all keep in mind, but hitting that field will turn us into a flying brick."

Astlin cast anxious looks between Teg and Xander. "What can we do?"

"Whatever it is," said Teg, "we should do it fast. Once they have what they need, those nexus-runners can take the *Serapis* apart."

"A skeleton crew of engineers and refugees cannot hold off trained soldiers for long," Xander said. "We must destroy the nexus-runners."

Teg shook his head. "Those corvettes need to go first. Then the *Serapis* can lower the field and let us land. Plus the boarding party loses its ride and keeps the Gen from getting trigger happy."

"You are skilled in war, my friend," Xander said. "We'll take the corvettes first."

"Chalk it up to experience," said Teg. "But even Almeth Elocine would have his work cut out going four against one."

Though no longer one with the Fire, Astlin's former bond

with the all-consuming force gave her sudden inspiration.

"Bring us in close," she told Xander. "I'll even the odds."

"Can you make it onto their ships?" asked Teg.

"If this works," said Astlin, "I won't have to."

It was a big *if*. Astlin had once wielded nexism to rule cities and tame souldancers, but she'd been cut off from the Nexus. Then again, she was basically her own nexus now.

The corvettes flew in a staggered line. The nearest ship's blocky hull grew larger in the cockpit window as Xander steered the *Theophilus* closer.

An alarm chirped from somewhere on the instrument panel.

"I think they see us," said Teg.

White-orange tracers streaked into the night as a chain cannon on the corvette opened fire. Xander pivoted the *Theophilus* to the left. The drive pod stayed fixed in space while the connecting spar—and the rest of the ship—rotated around it. The habitat and Wheel pods ended up opposite their starting points, and the bullets cut through empty space.

"They didn't expect that," said Astlin. "Why aren't we upside-down?"

"The pods are gyroscopically oriented," said Teg. "You can spin the ship around any of them."

"Yes," Xander said with a grin. "This is a ship of many secrets."

Astlin kept her focus on the corvettes as the *Theophilus* canted and spun clear of incoming fire. When the nearest ship's tapered rectangular hull filled the window, she closed her eyes and reached out with her thoughts.

Many people, some in grey cloaks; most in dark blue uniforms, milled about each corvette's bridge. Most wanted to win glory for sphere and family. All feared and served Shaiel.

Exerting her will over the command crews of four ships taxed even Astlin's strength. She knew she had little time to act before their shipmates stopped them. In her haste, the fourth corvette slipped from her overextended grasp.

Your allies are about to turn on you, she made the three remaining crews' own thoughts tell them. She hastily added, *Escape the Nexus. Find the world beyond.*

Near exhaustion, Astlin broke telepathic contact. She gripped Xander's arm and said, "Get us out of here."

"Why?" asked Teg. "What's—"

The three nearest corvettes fired, though not at the *Theophilus.* Bullets chewed all four ships' armor, while torpedoes punched through their hulls.

Xander was already banking away from the enemy line when the leftmost corvette veered across the others' path. Astlin didn't see how many ships collided, but the resulting blast rattled every loose bolt on the *Theophilus* and forced her to lean on Xander's backrest for support.

Teg grabbed Astlin's shoulders and spun her toward him.

"You can blow up ships with your mind!?"

It took Astlin a moment to gather her wits under a flood of fatigue and guilt. "No. I made their crews blow each other up."

She hoped they'd followed her last advice.

"Not all of them," Xander said. "The farthest corvette escaped destruction."

"No big deal. The gyroscopes aren't all that's left from the turrets." Teg slapped Astlin on the back. "One-on-one. I like those odds."

106

Warmth flooded Astlin's face, and she hoped she wasn't blushing. Before she could speak, a heavy impact rocked the Wheel pod.

Xander's voice was grim. "The nexus-runners are firing on us."

Astlin barely saw the three jet black, trefoil shapes speeding toward them before Xander wheeled the *Theophilus* about and ran. Green-white rays flashed past the window.

"Do the mind explosion thing again!" yelled Teg.

Astlin struggled to stay on her feet as the deck lurched. She cast about for the Gen pilots' minds, but her soul dashed itself against barriers like solid iron walls.

"They're shielded from nexism," she shouted back. "I can't break through."

Teg sprinted for the drive pod tube. "Okay. We fight them old school. Xander, warm up the Wheel pod gun. I'll jump on the drive pod turret. Astlin, can you take the gun on the habitat pod?"

"I think I can do better." Astlin disengaged from the Night Gen ships and cast her will across the battlefield to the last corvette. She didn't have the strength to take on the whole bridge crew, so she focused on the steersman.

With a final push Astlin entered the corvette pilot's mind. He was Paredh, a newly ordained Bhakta in Shaiel's priesthood. His brothers' betrayal had left him confused and afraid. The damage they'd done to his ship burned like raw wounds.

But he had his orders—watch the heathen ship's hangar and keep the stolen nexus-runner from escaping until Shaiel's property was secure.

Astlin wondered what property Paredh meant. Was it the *Kerioth* itself? Unable to find the answer in the young steersman's mind, she looked through his Wheel-magnified senses.

And saw someone dear to her sprawled upon the hangar floor.

"Cook!" she cried aloud.

"We'll eat *after* the dogfight," said Teg.

Astlin barely heard him. She pictured the *Serapis'* hangar in her mind's eye and was there.

10

The scene that greeted Astlin was like looking at time with double vision. Shipping containers still lay scattered on the blackened deck from her fight with Fallon a lifetime ago.

But here, it's only been a few days.

A burst of light from behind her broke Astlin's contemplation. She turned toward the mangled hangar door and saw what looked like a fireworks display on a starry night.

Looking closer, she saw the *Theophilus* leading the Night Gen ships on a wild chase. Emerald light streaked from the nexus-runners' black spear tip bows, but at Xander's command the small ether-runner pitched and rolled clear of their fire.

Astlin's spirits rose as blazing red bolts lanced out from the *Theophilus*. The drive and habitat pods swiveled at the ends of their spars, returning fire on the pursuing Night Gen. The chase spiraled past the lone remaining corvette, stubborn as a hunting hound, that still blocked the approach to the hangar.

Astlin considered invading the last steersman's mind, but she didn't know if her weakened will could bridge the distance.

It's alright. Xander and Teg will find a way.

And right now, Cook needed her more.

Astlin followed the fleeting image of Cook lying splayed on the deck. Her distant secondhand vision left her unsure if he was hurt.

Or dead.

She pushed the last thought away. Cook had lasted longer than her in their first fight with Hazeroth, and he wasn't even made of brass like she'd been. No way a bunch of Night Gen had done what Shaiel's Blade couldn't.

She would find Cook, get him patched up, and—when the *Serapis* was out of danger—have a long overdue celebration with all of her friends.

It's only fair, she reminded herself. *They missed the wedding.*

Astlin entered the *Kerioth's* shadow. Red and green flashes from the battle outside pushed back the darkness in short bursts. The fitful light revealed a body lying on the deck.

Many thought Cook's lumpish form ugly. To Astlin, who saw his true beauty, every hurt done to him was a dagger in her heart.

Astlin knelt down beside Cook. There was no blood, but dark bruises ringed his neck. His breath was a shallow whisper. A familiar white sword lay at his feet.

"Cook?" she said softly. "It's Astlin."

His thick lips moved, but his eyes stayed closed as he whispered, "You came back."

She fought the urge to take him in her arms. "I'm right here."

Cook's voice fell to a low hiss. "Glad we could talk one last time."

A wave of panic nearly swept Astlin away. She reflexively looked into the ether and saw Cook's silver cord dimming to a hair-thin line.

He needed a medic. Though she could reach the infirmary with a thought, Astlin wasn't sure if she could bring Cook along. He would die without help, but trying to move him might be no less fatal. Her fatigued will couldn't decide.

Casting about in desperation, Astlin saw the stud on Cook's ear. She gingerly pressed the blue stone between her thumb and forefinger, being careful not to jostle him.

"Medical emergency in the hangar," she sent on all channels. "Cook's hurt—*bad*. Please hurry!"

Cook's soul blazed like the last gleam of a fading light. "No! Send them back. It's not safe!"

"The Night Gen," said Astlin. "They're still here."

"They're dead." Cook's frail voice held fear as solid and sharp as a blade. "He killed them. Killed me."

Anger melted Astlin's dread. "Who did this?"

"Shaiel's Blade."

A different kind of dual vision sent Astlin's thoughts spinning as she flashed back to her last battle with Hazeroth. The demon prince had almost left her worse than dead. He would have, if not for Xander's sacrifice.

Astlin sent her thoughts into the hangar's every nook and cranny. She sensed no one spying on her from behind the jumbled containers, or leering down from the catwalks. All six of her senses testified that she was alone with Cook.

What if Cook was wrong? How could she detect a soul on the verge of death but not his attacker? According to Cook, that attacker was Shaiel's Blade. But Hazeroth was dead. Astlin knew that better than anyone.

It was far more likely that a team of Night Gen had ambushed

Cook and left him for dead. His warnings of Shaiel's Blade and his urgings to call off the medics were just delirium.

But Cook was the wisest, most sober person Astlin had ever known. True, she could remove all doubt by prying the memories from his fragile soul. Instead she took him at his word.

"Cancel that emergency call," she sent again. "There's a serious threat in the hangar. Stand by while I deal with it."

There was no reply. The sending was either broken or jammed.

If help was coming, it was rushing into a trap. If not, Cook would die.

It's up to me, Astlin realized. No more lives would be lost today—except for Shaiel's Blade.

"And if it's Hazeroth," she thought aloud, "I'll kill him again."

"Run," urged Cook. "He's dangerous."

Astlin gave a joyless laugh. "Me too—even more than before. And I'm always learning."

The corner or Cook's pale mouth turned upward, though his eyes didn't open. "Gonna go now. Don't you follow me yet."

Astlin's heart raced. Her stomach tied itself in knots as she faced the brutal fact of Cook's death.

"Break free of the Nexus, Cook!" she pleaded. "Hold on to yourself. I know you can do it!"

Cook's uneven brown eyes did open then. He looked at Astlin, and his smile grew.

"Don't think so," he rasped. "Always said trying to stay us causes pain. Wouldn't wanna be a hypocrite."

Cook's eyes fixed themselves on Astlin. His chest fell with his last words and didn't rise again. In the ether, silver light flashed from his body like a lightning bolt striking the heart of the Nexus. The looming black pyramid swallowed the light, leaving the small corner of creation that had belonged to Cook in darkness.

His eyes, Astlin thought as tears filled hers. *His eyes are still bright...*

She spared a moment for her grief. Then she stood and set her sights on revenge.

Where are you? Astlin wondered, redoubling her visual and mental search of the hangar.

Hers was the only conscious mind. There were no nexic ripples in the ether, not even from the *Kerioth.*

Which should've been impossible. Even though it was idling on low power, the nexus-runner should have stirred the rosy mist and lit it up like a beacon.

Astlin had piloted the *Kerioth* before, but the Night Gen ship largely remained a mystery. All nexus-runners might have fields that blocked nexism like the *Serapis* blocked Workings. Or Mirai Smith could have built one.

Smith. Besides having a gift for invention, he was the souldancer of Kairos. Shaiel had been obsessed with capturing him, just as he'd hunted Astlin when she'd been the souldancer of fire.

Shaiel used his Blades to get what he wanted. He still wanted the souldancers, and one was hiding on the *Kerioth* behind an anti-nexic field.

Astlin hurried to the ship's front port side. The boarding ramp was retracted; the main hatch locked. There were no signs of forced entry. She circled the hull and found every other entrance in the same condition.

The only openings were the landing gear skid wells. Checking the already tight spaces, Astlin saw that they were entirely sealed off from the ship's interior, except for a small defrosting vent that not even a young child could fit inside.

Driven by an equal need for answers and vengeance, Astlin thought of the crew quarters where she and Xander had been confined. She willed herself from the hard hangar deck to the smooth, gel-like floor of the *Kerioth's* cabin.

The room was pitch black. She noticed the nexus-runner's usual synthetic smell and caught traces of a metallic yet floral scent.

Suppressing a shiver, Astlin heard a low hum.

I was right. The ship is ready to launch. Smith just needs the last corvette out of his way.

Astlin tried sensing nexism and was relieved to feel energy coursing through the ship. There was another strong power source moving on the deck below and…something else that slipped through her weary grasp like oil. She projected herself into the stronger power's path.

The corridor was long and narrow, lit only by glowing green cables and indicators scattered upon the walls. The air was stuffy; the steady hum slightly louder.

Astlin soon oriented herself. The engine room lay up ahead at the hall's aft end. Weapon and navigation systems were housed behind her in the ship's bow.

A soft rustling sound coming from the engine room startled Astlin to full alertness. She strained her eyes, but the gloom hid the source of the noise.

I don't miss being a souldancer, but thermal vision would come in handy right now!

There was no other sound, but Astlin noticed rhythmic tremors moving through the deck in time with the engine's pulse. Her anxiety grew as the invisible wave rushed toward her.

Astlin revealed her crown, driving back the darkness. In the azure light she saw, not someone moving across the deck, but a section of the deck *moving*.

There was a rasping wail. A mound of small dark gears rose out of the floor, and a sallow death's head emerged.

"Quench that hideous light!"

Astlin obliged with a sharp exhale. "Smith. What are you doing down here?"

"Evading Shaiel's grasp! Would have wrecked the engine if not for me."

She raised an eyebrow. "Shaiel tried to sabotage the engine?"

"No, his Blade!" Smith's mass of gears coiled past Astlin, positioning his face behind her. "Listen—he's coming!"

Alarmed, Astlin peered down the dim hallway and once again saw nothing. If there were any other souls besides her and Smith, the nexic waves coming off him and the ship concealed them.

"I don't see any—"

Smith's shriek cut her off. Astlin turned and saw nothing at first. Then she glimpsed fleeting movement high on the left wall.

Something like see-through putty squeezed itself out of a small ventilation duct. At first she thought it was a man—his horribly contorted flesh mimicking the wall-mounted pipes behind him. But it had to be a trick of the dark.

Tentacles made of countless tiny gears lashed out from

Smith's shapeless mass. The transparent thing from the vent twisted to avoid the gear whips and dropped to the deck. With a series of awful popping sounds it stood, almost invisible in the half-light, but definitely shaped like a man.

Astlin stifled her shock and reached out for the barely visible creature's mind. Her strength hadn't returned yet, and the slick surface of his thoughts repelled her.

At least I know he's the slippery one from before.

"Do something!" Smith cried as he uselessly flailed at his evasive foe.

Astlin let her sapphire light fill the hall. Smith screeched and turned his corpselike face away.

As if stepping through a warped mirror, Smith's enemy made himself seen. He was stripped bare; his muscular yet nimble frame marred by a long diagonal wound on his side. A mop of long black hair hid most of his ugly face.

Unfazed by Astlin's crown, he ripped a sturdy pipe from the wall and pointed its broken end at Smith. White steam poured out. Astlin backed away from what she thought would be scalding heat, but as the torrent washed over Smith, she felt unearthly cold.

The strange man broke off a section of pipe and crimped the end, stopping the flow of liquid air. Though he lacked any protection from the cold, only his hands were harmed; though to Astlin the blackening looked more like severe burns than frostbite.

She was also unhurt, but the same couldn't be said for Smith.

The souldancer of Kairos filled most of the space between his attacker and Astlin. Smith's body looked like a dead tree made of dark oiled metal. Frost coated his many twisted limbs and his grimacing skull-like face.

"Stop!" Astlin warned the pipe-wielding man. "If you kill Smith, we'll be sucked through his gate."

Ignoring her, he swung the pipe and knocked a chunk out of Smith's midsection. Frozen gears scattered with the sound of a car roof in a hailstorm.

Astlin got ready to project herself away, but Smith's Worked body held. His enemy dropped the pipe, which clattered down among the souldancer's gears. His hands free, he reached into the hole he'd made in Smith's trunk and pulled out something pale that shone with hungry crimson light.

Astlin recognized the object and recoiled. The expressionless mask had last covered her sister's stolen face. The gem on its brow wasn't a ruby, but a cursed relic that had eaten many souls—including hers.

Revulsion became defiance. "I can't let you have that," Astlin said.

The man spoke in a deep soft voice without taking his eyes from the mask in his hands.

"Shaiel's property isn't yours to withhold."

The man held the cursed mask out before him. The ruby blazed in mockery of Astlin's light, and doused it.

Through her horror, Astlin saw Smith's body shudder. With a ringing crack, the frozen layer sloughed off, revealing live writhing gears beneath. A thin tendril whipped out from the thawed mass and latched onto the gem in the mask's forehead.

Shaiel's agent drew back, his knuckles white as he held on to the mask. Discordant chimes rang out as the gem broke free. Smith took the ruby into himself, hiding the terrible light, and swarmed down the corridor past his foe like a nest of metal bees.

Still holding the mask, the man let his hand fall to his side. He turned to follow Smith.

"Shaiel's Blade?" Astlin called out to him, making the title a challenge.

"Yes." the Blade of Shaiel turned back to face her. "You are the souldancer of fire?"

Astlin fought back unwelcome memories. "I was."

"You killed Hazeroth?"

"Damn right I did," Astlin said.

"You've won great honor," said Shaiel's Blade. "More than the one who fell before you."

The jab at Cook's memory ignited Astlin's rage, and her grief fed the blaze.

"That man—the man you killed—was the noblest, gentlest soul in this broken world." Astlin clenched her fists. "He saw what I was; what I'd done. And he forgave me."

"He loved you." Shaiel's Blade, ugly inside and out, never changed his blank expression. "You could see it in his eyes, before the Nexus took him."

Unlike Cook, Astlin had escaped the Nexus. She'd found the way to the world beyond, the true world where Zadok had lived before making his cheap imitation. There, all her crimes were washed away and she was crowned with unearned glory.

Yet she'd chosen to return; to retrace Zadok's path in the hope of saving those he held in silver chains. She came with authority from beyond; less than the gods of this world, but enough that the prisoners she came to free might be tempted to worship her if she wasn't careful.

Hiding her crown took effort, like keeping a spiritual muscle flexed.

After the Blade spoke, Astlin let go. A constellation of three blue stars hovered before her brow. Their brilliance grew as her scream rose in volume. Sapphire light melted every shadow before her.

Shaiel's Blade squinted like a man staring at the sun. He didn't retreat or look away as she rushed him.

Astlin was no longer made of elemental fire, but her speed rivaled its swiftness.

She collided with Shaiel's Blade, knocking him off his feet. He grunted from the impact, but the muscles under his bare skin squirmed, bending him in impossible ways.

Astlin suddenly found herself locked in a python-like hold. Though her opponent lacked her raw strength, his unnatural contortions evaded her fists and elbows. She tried to pry herself free, but his flesh twisted out of her hands.

"You are fierce," Shaiel's Blade spoke into her ear, "but unskilled. Hazeroth must have been weaker than his legend claims."

The already dark hallway grew dimmer as the Blade's hold cut off blood flow to Astlin's head. In desperation, she racked her clouding mind for a way out—and found only one.

I wanted to know if this would work...

Astlin pictured the hangar. She was there as herself, but for one mind-bending moment she was also Shaiel's Blade in the nexus-runner's darkened corridor. Finally she stood on the *Serapis'* singed deck; then folded to her knees, her head swimming.

Need to focus.

Astlin's will restored her mind and body to balance, and she rose again to her feet.

A deep groan made Astlin turn to see Shaiel's Blade on his hands and knees, shaking as he slowly stood. Cook's body lay between them.

With Cook's killer now in arm's reach, Astlin saw the white sword resting on the deck nearby. With a thought its light hilt was in her hand. The curved, mirrored blade sang as it cut through the air.

Having just regained his feet, Shaiel's Blade gaped in shock. His torso bent absurdly far backwards, and Astlin's slash severed only a few strands of his greasy hair.

But her foe's other defenses slipped. Mustering all of her will, Astlin battered down the gates of his soul.

She saw his mind laid as bare as his skin. Bred and trained to remove all sense of self, Izlaril Nizari was the last Son of Haath—a living weapon wielded by...

Something else. Something much, much worse.

Behind Izlaril's reeling form, Astlin saw the monstrous shadow of a wolf outlined in sickly golden light.

The shadow wolf's growling formed words in her mind. *Shaiel's Left Hand wields the Blade, my pretty one. I won't suffer you to wrest it from me!*

Astlin's light blazed again without her command. Sapphire strove against gold, and finally the wolf image vanished like smoke in the wind. But the effort cost Astlin a moment's concentration.

Izlaril leapt into the opening, striking Astlin's wrist and

sending the white sword flying from her hand. It chimed like a bell as it struck the deck and slid under the *Kerioth's* landing gear.

Izlaril's blow had been more surprising than painful, but the distraction left Astlin open to another attack. His leg pistoned out, driving the ball of his foot into her stomach. The stars crowning her head went out and new ones flashed behind her eyes.

"*That* hurt," she admitted, "but if that's your best shot, you're in trouble."

By all appearances, Astlin's body in this world was identical to those of Zadok's shards. It was even made of prana-based matter. But unknown to Izlaril, it was made much *better*.

A look of awe came over Izlaril's marred face. "Will you bring reunion with the Nexus?"

"Sure, I'll kill you," Astlin said. "But you don't have to rejoin the Nexus. You can be free."

"Selfhood is torment."

Astlin heaved a frustrated sigh. "Why does everyone say that?"

Izlaril punched her in the face. The impact left her ears ringing.

One thought penetrated Astlin's pain and fatigue. *He* can *hit harder!*

A burst of light flooded the hangar before a violent tremor shook the deck.

It was Izlaril's turn to be caught off guard. Astlin willed herself into the air above him. The glare and noise of the blast confused him until the instant before her fall-assisted kick hammered into his head. Astlin teetered when she landed but regained her balance. Izlaril fell flat on his back and lay still; not even breathing.

Astlin turned. Through the hangar door she saw a fireball that had been the last corvette. Amber tracers continued pelting the wreckage for a moment after the explosion subsided.

Those shots came from the Serapis. *That means the field's down.*

As soon as the thought came to Astlin, the upside down "V" of the *Theophilus* surged into the hangar. The drive and habitat pods sent up sparks and left dark streaks on the deck as the etherrunner skidded to a stop thirty feet away. She saw Xander seated on the Wheel and gave him a weary smile.

Arms like iron made flesh locked themselves around Astlin's throat. She struggled, but her enemy's muscles writhed like snakes, tightening their hold. She heard and felt something pop in her neck.

"There is a way to kill you," Izlaril breathed into her ear. "We shall find it together."

Xander disappeared from the Cockpit window. In the same instant he stood beside the grappled pair. Silver stars blazed upon his clean-shaven head.

"You have laid hands on my beloved," Xander said like a judge passing sentence. A black spear tipped with a diamond blade appeared in his hand. "I'll strike the head from your shoulders." He raised the weapon for a fatal thrust.

"Can you strike before I snap her neck?" asked Shaiel's Blade, sounding honestly interested in the answer.

"I can," said a familiar voice.

Teg stood beside the *Theophilus*, his right foot still on the threshold of the drive pod hatch. He must have been aiming his gun at Izlaril, but to Astlin it looked like the barrel was pointing at her.

Izlaril laughed.

"Do not—" was all Xander had time to say before the muzzle of Teg's gun flashed. There was a loud crack. A far harder and more painful blow than anything Izlaril could deliver slammed into Astlin's chest, and she fell back into nothingness.

11

"Serieigna!" Teg heard Xander cry. The Nesshin fell to his knees beside Astlin, who lay on top of two extremely ugly men—one of whom had been about to break her neck until Teg shot her.

"Sorry!" Teg called out as he dashed to Xander's side. "Guess I'm rustier than I thought."

Xander glared at him, shaking with rage. "You are sorry!? She saved your life, and you shot her!"

"Honestly," said Teg, "this isn't the first time that's happened."

Teg raised his gun again as Xander sprang to his feet, but Astlin's irate husband wasn't interested in venting his anger on Teg. Instead Xander stretched out his free hand toward the naked man who'd been lying under his wife and who had now risen to a crouch.

Thunder roared, ringing Teg's bell worse than the gunshot. The naked man flew across the hangar and smashed into a cargo container, leaving a dent in the orange-painted steel.

"Nice," said Teg. But Xander was already standing over his wife's attacker, who lay on the deck clutching something white in his hand.

Teg had caught a glimpse of the strange object before he'd shot at its bearer. The man had held it while he'd strangled Astlin, and more impressively, had managed to hold on to it when Xander blasted him into a metal box.

Now that he'd taken a longer look, Teg recognized the pale mask. Its emotionless face seemed to stare at him, and the distance didn't soften its malice.

"The mask," Teg called to Xander. "Get rid of it!"

Either Xander couldn't hear, or he didn't listen. He raised his spear and stabbed it down to skewer the man at his feet like a pig.

In all his years, whether on the countless spheres of the Middle Stratum or in the nine pits of hell, Teg had never seen anyone or anything move like Xander's intended victim did then. He flowed to his feet in a series of motions that hurt Teg's eyes and pressed Vaun's mask onto Xander's face.

Xander clawed helplessly at the false porcelain face. It was his voice but Vaun's words that boomed from the mask's unmoving lips.

"You mocked me in Kairos, young Zadokim. I do not forgive your blasphemy, and there are none now to shield you from justice."

Xander collapsed.

"Nobody listens to me," Teg thought aloud.

A rising hum made Teg glance to his right. The *Kerioth's* black spearhead of a bow swung toward him. A sudden sense of freefall threw Teg off balance, and he fell prone as the nexus-runner's nose passed overhead. The concurrent feelings of weightlessness and massive downward force turned his stomach.

Both sensations passed and Teg raised his head, coming face-to-face with the second ugly man. Correction—an ugly corpse.

Lying next to a dead man didn't disturb Teg; nor did the man's ugliness. The fact that he'd clearly had considerable strength and speed, yet someone had killed him bare-handed, was another story.

Too bad, thought Teg. *Here's hoping Zadok makes you prettier if you come around again.*

Astlin lay opposite the corpse, curled up on her side. A dark blotch stained the front of her jacket.

A shockwave crashed over Teg. He rose and turned to see the *Kerioth* blasting out of the hangar. It sliced through the cloud of corvette debris like a black trident and vanished between the stars beyond.

"Cross!"

The sound of his name reflexively drew Teg's eyes toward the *Theophilus.* Ehen stood beside the habitat pod, where he'd manned the turret in lieu of Astlin. The gunner was stabbing a finger at something behind Teg as more debarking Nesshin gathered in the *Serapis'* hangar.

Teg spun and found himself facing another ugly man—the living, naked one—who limped forward dragging Xander's motionless body.

"Hi," said Teg. "Where do you think you're going?"

The ugly naked man brushed past him. "Not your concern."

"It must be somewhere important," said Teg. "And clothing optional."

"Make way," the rude, ugly, naked man said to the Nesshin congregating around the *Theophilus.* "Your ship now belongs to Shaiel."

Teg fell in behind him. "No. Shaiel didn't build this rust bucket. It would probably look much nicer if he did. But we built her, so she's ours."

The would-be thief ignored him, hobbling toward the *Theophilus* and her crew while dragging Xander behind him.

Teg leveled his gun a hand's breadth from the back of the naked man's grungy head.

If I miss at this range, I'll take up drinking again.

The target didn't turn his head, but his free hand shot out and twisted the gun from Teg's grip with a deft motion that snapped his trigger finger like a twig.

Ehen lunged forward, but Saba held him back.

Teg clutched his wounded hand as his gun clattered on the deck. "Damn that hurts! I'd apologize to Deim if your boss hadn't killed him."

The ugly man stopped. "Your associate died at Shaiel's hand?"

That got his attention! "Yeah," said Teg. "Saw it myself."

The naked man turned, showing his ugly face. "You have seen Shaiel?"

"Way too much of him," Teg said. "He killed me, too. But he did a piss-poor job."

The man's blank expression never changed, which showed discipline. But when his arm struck out with no visible warning, Teg knew he'd picked a fight with something perverse.

Teg managed to twist away from the blow so it snapped his collarbone instead of crushing his throat. He tried to ignore the sharp explosion of pain, but his foe landed a kick that shattered Teg's kneecap and sent him crashing face-first to the burnt deck.

It was hard for Teg to decide which hurt worse—his injuries or the infernal gift that drastically sped up his healing. The one certainty was that his enemy didn't expect his unnaturally fast recovery, or he would have struck again sooner.

Teg rolled sideways, favoring his injured shoulder and leg as bones and ligaments knitted themselves back together. The momentum helped propel him to his feet—one foot, actually. His right knee still couldn't support his weight.

His enemy stood right there facing him as if neither of them had moved. Teg did take some satisfaction from noting that his foe had dropped Xander. The masked Nesshin lay unmoving several paces away.

Without warning, vicious blows crushed Teg's jaw and ribs. He used all his willpower to stay focused on Xander, draw his knife, and fling it underhand at the porcelain mask.

Shaiel's toady sprang into the knife's path with inhuman speed. The blade imbedded itself in his forearm.

Teg reached into his pocket, pressed a handful of loose bullets between his knuckles, and hammered his enemy's floating ribs. Or what would have been ribs if some strange reflex hadn't moved the bones away. Nevertheless, the bullet tips left bloody wounds that punctuated the recent cut in his foe's side.

A blindingly fast elbow to his already broken jaw sent Teg reeling. But Saba had given in or been pushed aside, because Ehen bull rushed their common enemy. The edge of the ugly man's hand slammed into Ehen's neck, toppling him in mid-charge.

Teg saw an opening and leapt in, locking arms around his foe. The ugly man wriggled like a sack of eels, but Teg held on despite bursts of agony from his mending bones.

"Get the gun!" Teg grunted. Ehen didn't respond. His limbs jerked feebly.

"If he dies," said Teg, "I'll get real grouchy."

With a nauseating series of pops, the ugly man's wrists, elbows, and shoulders bent in ways that no god intended. A startling burst of strength reversed Teg's hold and caught him in his opponent's loathsome grasp. Ropy arms and burned fingers constricted Teg's neck while his own knife slit his throat.

I recognize that sword, Teg thought when his foe twisted his head to the left. The white scimitar was the last sight he saw before a sound like green wood snapping filled his skull, bringing oblivion.

12

"...still breathing," a feminine voice said in a familiar lilting accent.

Teg's sight returned, showing him blue eyes staring from a fair-skinned face framed by blood red hair.

"There was five, six of 'em," he mumbled. "Jumped me in the park."

"Keth is gone, Teg," Astlin said softly. 'We're on the *Serapis*. Can you remember?"

The distant lights partly eclipsed by skeletal catwalks and the smell of char and ether jogged Teg's memory.

"I shot you."

Astlin's eyes narrowed. Her lips formed a crooked frown. "Yeah. You did."

The dull aches that attended Teg's efforts to rise told him that enough time had passed for his wounds to mostly heal.

"Sorry," he said through gritted teeth.

Astlin helped him sit upright on the deck. "You were trying to help. At least now we know I can take a bullet."

Teg's clearing vision alerted him to the absence of Astlin's jacket and the pristine skin beneath the bullet hole in her dress.

"What happened to your chest wound?"

"It's like knowing you're in a dream," Astlin said at length. "I can influence things, including my body."

"You can't die?"

Astlin wore the expression of someone watching the horizon for storms. "If I'm hurt bad enough, I'll wake up. Short of that, I can conform my body to my soul."

Teg laughed. "Kind of like how Sulaiman's body turned back into mine."

Confusion clouded Astlin's face. "What happened between you two?"

Teg's aching knee protested as he stood. "After you disappeared, I went to hell."

"I never knew I meant that much to you," joked Astlin.

Teg fixed his eyes on hers. "No. I went to the *actual* Nine Circles. You could ask Jaren if he weren't a vegetable.

"We killed one Circle's lord. Doing that sprung three even worse demons, each of whom gave me a curse. I pledged myself to another demon for a cure. He switched me and Sulaiman's souls; Worked my new body—or something—so it heals ungodly fast. Over time it did like you said; made my flesh conform to my soul."

As he spoke, Teg rubbed his midsection and felt box-woven cotton. A downward glance confirmed that he wore only his long underwear.

"Where are my clothes?"

Astlin shrugged. "They were gone when I came to."

"That murdering snake took them," said Marse. She and the

rest of the Nesshin stood nearby—except for one of their number who lay under an oily drop cloth. "And that's not all he took."

"Xander!" Astlin said with a quick indrawn breath. She cast frantic glances around the hangar. "There's just…*nothing* where his mind should be. Where did Izlaril take him?"

"Wherever they went," Teg said as he glowered at the empty space where the *Theophilus* used to be, "they took my ship."

He rounded on the Nesshin. "And you people just stood there?"

"Easy, Teg," a masculine voice, scratchy from disuse, said from across the hangar. "We already lost one man. No sense losing more."

Teg spun to face the voice's source. Jaren stood, disheveled but alert, in the *Kerioth's* former landing site. His green eyes were fixed on the white sword at his feet.

"Besides," Jaren added, "that old death trap already got us where we need to be."

Teg's jaw dropped. "You're awake? What the hell is going on?"

Jaren gave him a sidelong glance. "I was hoping you'd tell me. The young lady must have jarred something loose, but the dam only broke a minute ago. Besides that, the last thing I recall is pulling the trigger."

"You mean firing your front-loaded rodcaster at Mephistophilis?"

"No." Jaren frowned. "Firing my zephyr at Zebel."

Teg exhaled sharply. "That leaves a lot of ground to cover." A thought occurred to him. "Astlin here could probably transfer my memories to your head."

Jaren held up his remaining hand. "No, thanks. I've had my fill of telepathy. And in case you forget that, the telepath who raised me taught me how to block it. Just tell me what I missed—the old-fashioned way."

"Fine," said Astlin. She visibly fought to keep her composure, but her voice broke. "Everything burned. Teg and his crew spent years flying from one dead sphere to the next. He landed on Keth to find the sky burning and everyone dead; not that they stayed in the ground.

"A few days ago, I died and came back to free my husband and everyone else from the Nexus. We helped the *Theophilus* escape and fought our way onto the *Serapis*. But a necromancer god's minion killed my friend and Teg's friend and kidnapped Xander!"

"And he stole all my stuff," said Teg. "She forgot that part."

Astlin wheeled on Teg. "Are you always this selfish?"

"Mostly," Jaren said. "But it looks like Vaun's cutthroat—I assume he's the necromancer you meant—left the sweetest plum behind."

Jaren tapped the white sword's hilt with his bare foot and winced.

Teg approached the scimitar, bent down to pick it up, and dropped it with a yelp as pain shot through his hand. The mirrored blade rang against the deck like a chime.

"The bastard's hot! Must've been cooked when the nexus-runner took off."

Astlin glided over and took up the sword. "I don't think that's the problem."

"That's the same blade Sulaiman used on Elena," Teg told

Jaren. "He came out of nowhere; nearly killed her. You remember seeing the sword again after that?"

Jaren rubbed his shaggy chin. "Honestly, no."

"Me either," Teg went on. "Somehow it vanished from the *Exodus* and ended up here."

"Xander took it." Astlin stared at the blade. Unlike everything else cast in its white surface, her reflection was normal; not purple-hued. "He went through Kairos and stole Elohim from Vaun's room."

Teg's brow furrowed. "Who's Elohim?"

"It's one of God's names," Saba called out from where he sat beside a shipping container.

"That's what Xander called the sword," Astlin said. "Sulaiman talked about a weapon that could kill gods. I think this is it."

"It should come in handy then," said Jaren.

"This is your interim captain, speaking," an older man's voice boomed over the intercom. "Now that security's back online, I'm looking at a dozen or more stowaways having a tea party in my hangar. Care to explain before I blow you into space?"

"And then he took my stuff," Teg told Gid.

Gid sat at the head of the small gathering, set in relief against the star field framed in the window behind him. The elbows of his grey jacket rested on the table's darker matte surface. His hands in turn supported his chin. He eyed Teg over round glasses whose gold rims threatened to slip off his hawkish nose.

"Let me make sure I understand the situation." Gid's eyes passed to Astlin, Jaren, and the aging security officer at the back of the conference room before he pointed at Teg.

"You rode out the Cataclysm on Tharis, cobbled a ship together from spare parts with a band of Nesshin, and went searching for a new home. You found your old boss on Crote and brought him aboard."

Gid's finger moved to Jaren. "Even though he was a feral amnesiac."

The arc of his gesture ended at Astlin. "Then you made it to Keth, where she and her husband saved you from a horde of dead cannibals."

Gid laced his fingers. "Your jury-rigged ship somehow fought off the small fleet pursuing mine, and you boarded us for a showdown with a homicidal maniac who serves a self-styled god. He wiped the floor with you—including a couple of demigods—before making off with one of them."

Teg raised his hand. "And all my—"

"Your stuff, yes," repeated Gid.

Teg pulled at the sleeves of the dark green, ill-fitting jacket he'd stripped from a dead Night Gen and tried to ignore the itchiness of the matching pants.

"You got it," said Teg.

"If that wasn't enough," Gid continued, "somebody hijacked the *Kerioth*."

"It was Smith," said Astlin. "Izlaril was after him, too."

Gid's chair hissed softly on the carpet as he slid back from the table. He stood and paced the room, rubbing his shock of white hair.

"And now, you want asylum—along with your whole ragtag crew."

"You're undermanned," said Jaren. "We'd be useful."

Gid stopped beside Jaren and leaned down next to him. "Really? You weren't much use stopping the killer of four security officers and the cook!"

"Was he a good cook?" asked Teg.

Gid straightened his back and pushed his glasses up. "Exquisite."

"Be serious," said Jaren. "Me and Teg are worth ten of him."

"*If* you are who you say," Gid shot back, "then two decades ago you sicced an unholy terror on this ship. Thanks to that little stunt we lost half our crew and spent twenty years stuck up a tree. I should shove you out an airlock!"

Jaren met Gid's gaze. "That would be a mistake. Vaun lost seven ships and scores of men today. He might have let you off if you'd given him what he wanted. Now you're on the wrong side of his warped honor code. He'll keep coming till he gets satisfaction."

"Don't forget who rattled the hornets' nest," said Gid.

"It doesn't matter," Jaren said.

Gid scowled. "Let's be clear. The only reason you're not spending the rest of this voyage in the brig is because I can't spare the security staff."

Astlin leaned forward, her eyes pleading. "You're right to be angry, Gid. Maybe Cook's death—every death today—is our fault. But there's still a chance to save Xander."

"I didn't mean to sound dismissive." Gid took off his glasses and pinched the bridge of his nose. "It's good having you back. But excuse my bluntness for pointing out that you're supposed to be dead. Did you just need a few days to get over it?"

Astlin's eyes wandered across the starry panorama behind him. "To you, I just died a few days ago. But it's been years for me."

"Xander pulled a reappearing act, too," said Gid. "Though you put a novel twist on it. Can we expect Cook to come strolling in next?"

"He rejoined the Nexus," Astlin said sadly.

"What about my security team?' asked Gid. "Rendon was fourteen, but the Night Gen slaughtered him like a calf. Doesn't he deserve another chance to live?"

Astlin sighed. "It's not about deserving. You've had dreams that you knew were dreams?"

"It's called lucid dreaming," said Jaren.

"Escaping the Nexus when you die is like making yourself have a lucid dream when you go to sleep," Astlin said.

"That's rare, I'll grant you," said Gid. "But there are people who say you can learn."

Astlin shook her head. "That's just getting out. Coming back is like picking up exactly where you left off in a dream you had years ago."

Teg whistled. "How can anybody do that?"

"I had someone to come back to," said Astlin. "I want to help everyone. But right now, nobody needs me more than Xander."

"I get it." Teg reached over and squeezed her hand.

Gid's face softened. "We'd never have left Mithgar if not for you and Xander," he told Astlin. "So believe me when I say that we're just not equipped to mount a rescue. Let's get to Temil and see if anyone there can help."

Astlin sat back in her chair and nodded somberly.

"Meanwhile," Gid continued, "Peregrine, Cross, and the Nesshin can stay." He jabbed a finger at Jaren and Teg. "You two are on notice. I'm the only steersman now that the devil-queen's gone. Step one inch out of line, and the ride's over. Got it?"

Teg cocked an eyebrow. "Zebel was here?"

"Her name's Nakvin," said Astlin. "She took over hell. It's called Avalon now."

Jaren gaped. "Nakvin's the queen of hell? That's even more insane than her being here!"

"She didn't stay long," said Gid. "From what I gather, Shaiel wants her throne."

"I was close," Teg interrupted. "Zebel's her mom."

"No," said Jaren. "Zebel is her dad." He answered Teg's blank stare with a word. "Shapeshifter."

Teg folded his arms. "Either way, she's got no love for Vaun and a kingdom at her command. Did she leave her contact info?"

"She's a demon," said Gid. "Try sacrificing a chicken and burning incense."

Teg shivered. "No chickens."

"You just reminded me how hungry I am," Jaren said.

"Same here," said Teg. "Where's the wardroom?"

Gid frowned. "Meal service is suspended till we hire a new cook."

Astlin rose from her chair. "I'll fix you something in the galley."

"You sure?" asked Teg.

She nodded. "Cook was giving me lessons. It'll take my mind off things."

Teg stood and eagerly fell in behind her. Jaren followed.

"Looks like it's back to the Wheel for me." Gid sighed. "I'll keep us on course for Temil. If there are leftovers, feel free to bring some down."

The three newest *Serapis* crewmen filed from the room and into the eerily empty hallway. Teg couldn't help comparing the giant Guild ship to the *Exodus*. Though it was the smaller of the two, the *Serapis* felt more spacious.

There was a subtler difference that took Teg a minute to pin down. Isolation wasn't a problem aboard the *Exodus*, where you always felt like you were being watched. But a sense of loneliness haunted the *Serapis*. And an air of tragedy, like a house where a lovesick poet killed himself.

These dreary thoughts led Teg back to a question he'd meant for Astlin. "What's it like—the other side?"

The three of them walked on for what felt like a long time, with only the rhythm of their footfalls on steel deck plates breaking the silence, before Astlin spoke.

"In some ways it's a lot like here," she said distantly. "You know how your dreams never make sense to anyone else?"

Mercifully vague memories of dreams aboard the *Exodus* came back to Teg, and he left his curiosity unsatisfied.

13

"Is the nexus-runner holding its course?" Izlaril asked from behind Xander.

Shaiel's Blade stood at a deferential distance from the Wheel, where something unholy steered the *Theophilus* with Xander's body. He felt the worn seat under him but couldn't so much as lift a finger.

"The Zadokim senses its presence." The voice, muffled by the mask on his face, was Xander's. But it wasn't he who spoke. "My wayward brother seeks asylum on Temil. He will find that not even the Shadow Caste can hide him from me."

"As you will, lord," Izlaril said.

Shaiel kept Xander's eyes fixed on the starry expanse ahead. He could in fact sense the *Kerioth's* nexic waves rippling through space like a death worm's wake in sand. The reckless speed of Mirai Smith's flight betrayed the souldancer's fear of what pursued him.

And fear he should. Shaiel's thoughts were icepicks plunged into Xander's mind. *I am well pleased with my new Blade. From him there is no escape.*

Answering took all of the meager willpower left to Xander. *You toy with the agent of a power beyond your understanding!*

Shaiel's laugh was like a steel blade sawing through ice. *Your concern for my welfare is touching, Master Sykes. But I know what truly concerns you. Rest assured, she will receive my attention in due time.*

Xander fought to quell his fear and wrath. *Release me before Zadok punishes your meddling.*

Zadok will not interfere. Is not our contest—your strength against mine—the very trial he wished to make?

You are evil given substance, Xander replied. *Astlin and I bear a light that reveals your strength as a passing shadow!*

Indeed, Shaiel mocked. *How fares your light now?*

It is not I who will defeat you.

Shaiel's answer was a storm of mirth and rage. *Who will vanquish me? Your darling bride? As the culmination of prophecy, a maudlin twit ruled by passions that alternately drive her to save and murder orphans is quite a disappointment, don't you think?*

A sudden calm quieted Xander's anger. *That passion served her well enough to best your greatest servants.*

None have truly faced my greatest servants, Shaiel boasted. *That is a mercy I shall soon revoke. Your trollop, the harpy of Avalon, and even my traitorous sister will cower and fall before them.*

A warbling chime from the control panel announced the *Theophilus'* entry into Temil space. Through the Wheel's enhanced vision, Xander saw the third Cardinal Sphere as a bright blue dot. A dark angular speck revealed the nexus-runner's presence.

Xander's voice once again spoke Shaiel's words. "We have him."

The *Theophilus* gained speed, closing with its quarry.

Shaiel turned Xander's head toward the Blade, who stood on the patchwork deck in Teg's shabby pants, shirt, and olive coat.

"Man a gun. Disable the nexus-runner when I bring us in range."

Izlaril melted into the Wheel pod's shadows. Though Xander heard nothing but the high whine of overtaxed engines, he imagined Shaiel's Blade creeping down the tube toward the drive or habitat pod turret.

Xander's eyes faced forward again. Temil's sea-blue orb, flecked with islands of green, filled most of his view. The black mote had resolved into the *Kerioth's* three-bladed hull.

You are violating sovereign space, Xander warned the god in his head. *This isn't just fraternal sentiment. What are your true plans for Smith?*

Is your banter meant to draw out my closely guarded designs? Shaiel scoffed. *No need to pry when my aims are no secret. Perfected souldancers are Strata incarnate, and Smith knows the making of souldancers.*

Xander's confusion vied with his shock. *Why create more souldancers? You are already free.*

Is your mind so limited that I must make every connection for you? The Void must triumph; not only in the Middle Stratum, but over all.

The horrible conclusion that dawned on Xander left him fighting to stave off panic. If Shaiel made his own souldancers, perfected them, and tainted them with Void, the Strata they embodied would become extensions of his own domain.

As I said, Shaiel gloated, *none can escape.*

The drive pod turret opened fire on the *Kerioth*. The nexus-runner rolled left to evade, but Xander's stomach clenched when two streaks of red light lanced into its stern. Dark plumes of vapor burst into space.

They must be stopped!

Again, who will stop us? Shaiel chided. *You, who cannot move your least finger without my leave?*

Another scarlet bolt struck the *Kerioth* amidships. The nexus-runner ceased evasive action and drifted toward the blue-green sphere ahead.

"She is adrift," Shaiel sent to his Blade. "I will bring us alongside. Make ready to board the nexus-runner and retrieve her pilot."

Xander desperately cast about for some way to keep Smith out of Shaiel's hands. His search delved into the ether, where another shock lay in wait—a huge metal structure like a fortress hanging in the rosy mist.

That is why we saw no defenses on approach, Xander thought. *Temil's fleet is hidden in the ether!*

Where they will continue to hide, Shaiel answered. *The Shadow Caste ever skulk about in secret. Nothing so mundane as a skirmish between two small ships will make them show their hand."*

The *Theophilus* slid up next to the *Kerioth's* sharp-edged flank.

Izlaril's deep voice came over the sending. "Ready."

Despite the dire situation, a transcendent sense of calm returned to Xander. Shaiel barred him from exerting his will, but sometimes there was more strength in letting go.

Xander let his light blaze forth. Silver radiance filled the

Wheel pod and shone through the cockpit window like a spear of white fire cutting through Temil's night and the ether behind the sky.

The Void grasped the shaft of light and broke it like a black iron fist. Shaiel's laughter clawed the inside of Xander's skull.

Such a minor nuisance will not drive me out, boy. Your soul, mind, and body are mine.

Take them, Xander replied. *My heart belongs to another.*

The space between Temil and the two smaller ships wavered like a heat haze. A massive shape emerged from the ether—its silver hull tinted light blue by the sphere it guarded.

Xander couldn't help admiring the elegant yet aggressive lines of the Temilian battleship's hull; even as its gun batteries trained themselves on the *Theophilus.*

I am sorry, Serieigna, but better we part for a time than allow Shaiel his triumph.

The battleship gave no warning before it opened fire.

Celwen found Raig in a secluded alcove of the *Sinamarg's* sunless agriculture system. She hadn't needed her nexic second sight. The artificial grotto lit by phosphorescent fungi served as his usual retreat from the stress of command.

The admiral sat cross-legged on a rock jutting into a black pool, his eyes closed in meditation. Urgency tempered by deference prompted her to speak at a volume slightly above the pervasive echo of trickling water.

"Admiral, I must have a word with you."

"If you must," Raig said in a voice as cool as the moist air.

Celwen had racked her brain for the right words to say during the long walk from her quarters. Now she simply spoke her mind without flattery or guile.

"Sir, you must remove Lykaon from this ship!"

Raig's blue-green eyes opened. The foxfire glow made them shine like gems in his lean face, and his cap of silver hair gleamed like a crown.

"I could order it," he said. "Can you state a compelling reason why I should?"

The question caught Celwen off guard. Her already strained composure broke, and she dropped all formality.

"Velix has been euthanized," she nearly shouted. "Even now, the wretched spawn of our mortal enemy takes his place!"

Celwen spoke truthfully. Through the nexic window in her mind she saw Liquid Sign pacing the bridge with hideous, unnatural movements.

"These are worse than insults. They are acts of war authored by Lykaon—the envoy of our supposed ally!"

Raig unfolded his legs and stood in one smooth motion. He lithely hopped down from the rock to stand before her.

"Shaiel is indeed our ally," he said. "Expelling his Left Hand would end that alliance. Should I make a foe of the Void god in the name of old enmities?"

Celwen couldn't believe what she was hearing. "What has Shaiel's friendship brought our people but humiliation and death?"

"Shaiel has given us Mithgar," said Raig. "Would any Night Gen prize life and limb above victory over the Guild?"

The veiled accusation fed Celwen's shame and stoked her anger. "The Fire defeated the Guild. Should we sacrifice good men to harvest fallen fruit?"

145

Raig cast a furtive glance around the grotto before drawing uncomfortably close, and Celwen realized a startling truth.

He is not just toeing the line. The admiral is afraid!

Afraid of what? Shaiel's wrath? That was the most obvious answer in light of how freely his Left Hand dealt out pain and death. Raig clearly wished to preserve the alliance with Shaiel, but Celwen suspected that his dread had a deeper source.

Raig now stood close enough to smell a trace of medicinal herbs on his breath. Despite the cool temperature, his ashen skin and black shirt were damp with sweat.

"I saw the Purges," he whispered. "I remember the day we fled the light of the stars for unending darkness—forever, many feared. You are young, with no memory of the light. So I do not hate you for conspiring with the men who drove us into the dark."

Celwen's blood froze. Her body went rigid. *I was so careful!*

"You wonder how I know," said Raig. "Rest assured, your benefactors' methods hid your treason from the telepaths."

Raig gripped Celwen's arm, wrenching a gasp from her throat.

"Your father fought beside me in the Resistance. Did he tell you? Perhaps not. Few veterans of the Purge wish to relive our disgrace. I of course launched inquiries when he disappeared. Imagine my dismay when they all came to dead ends."

Celwen's voice returned, though it trembled. "My father took his own life."

Raig shook his head. "So I believed for a time; reluctantly. Ilmin's mention of a Gen souldancer in his report from Mithgar revived my doubts. Your exchange with Lykaon confirmed them—and ancient suspicions that enemy spies followed us into exile."

Celwen tried to squirm out of the admiral's grip, but he held her fast.

"So you see," Raig continued, "Shaiel's servants have given me more than dead officers and an empty world. That is a fair price for closure."

Raig released Celwen. She rubbed her arm, though his firm yet gentle grip hadn't left a bruise.

"Shaiel's beast ordered my death," she said. "Did you deny his bloodthirst just to indulge yours?"

"On the contrary." Raig straightened the sleeves of his black jacket. "I intervened because you are a skilled officer, and executing the flagship's pilot will hardly bolster our fragile morale."

Dizzying relief soared above the morass of Celwen's emotions. "You will not strip me of my post?"

Raig drew himself up. Looking every inch the seasoned officer he said, "One must carefully manage treacherous allies. Henceforth I am placing you on alternate duty."

The order aroused Celwen's suspicions. The admiral wasn't one to mince words, but she still half-expected a permanent posting to the brig.

"A new assignment? Of what sort?"

"The *Sinamarg* has been rerouted to Temil," Raig announced. "This morning their defense force shot down a vessel carrying high-ranking agents of Shaiel. Lykaon identified the Third Sphere's rulers as the same cabal responsible for creating the souldancers."

Celwen's unease grew. *He would not tell me this without reason.*

"You are reassigned to fleet intelligence until further notice," said Raig. "Your first mission is to ascertain the Shadow Caste's capabilities and objectives."

"I accept," Celwen said. "But I make no admission of guilt."

"You are a spy now. The Shadow Caste will kill you as such—unless you are *their* spy. Either way, I am spared from executing the flagship's pilot." Raig moved past her, his boot heels clicking on the wet stone.

"Wait!" Celwen called after him. "My father—is he still on Mithgar?"

The cavern's echo carried Raig's parting words. "He died over Keth five days ago."

14

Teg sat back at a navigation console on the *Serapis'* backup bridge and loudly munched on bread and cheese that Astlin had grilled but no one else had eaten. Even Gid, who'd been at the Wheel all the way to Temil, had suddenly lost his appetite.

But his shipmates' loss was Teg's gain. Tough stringy cheese served between slices of burnt toast was a lavish delicacy after living on bland rations.

The interim cook herself stood against the wall to the right of the Wheel, frowning sheepishly.

"Sorry guys," she said. "I think I turned the grill up too high. I'll do better next time."

Teg gulped down another bitter, salty bite. "Don't beat yourself up. This is the best I've had in years."

"I don't want to know what you fed me while I was catatonic," said Jaren.

"Everybody shut up!" Gid snapped. "I'm getting an answer from Temil."

Astlin rushed across the darkened room to the Wheel. Its fluorescent glow gave her a ghostly look.

"Put them on," she said.

Gid shook his grey head, but a moment later a smooth masculine voice filled the room.

"Greetings, *Serapis*. You are speaking with the Temil Defense Service's special diplomatic branch. We have received your request, and after thorough review, have opted to deny you asylum."

"Thorough?" said Gid. "It's only been fifteen minutes!"

"This decision is binding and cannot be appealed until our security status is reduced from high alert," the diplomat said. "Approaching closer than lunar orbit will be considered a violation of our sovereign space, to be met with all necessary defensive measures up to and including lethal force. We apologize for any inconvenience."

"There's debris from my friend's ship in your sovereign space!" Astlin argued. "My husband was on board. At least tell me what you did to him."

Gid sighed. "They cut off the channel. We'll be twisting in the wind till they call back."

"Remind me to bill them for my ship when they do," Teg said around another mouthful of charred bread and cheese.

Jaren shot him a scathing look. "Shaiel's goons are already on our tail. How many more are coming now that Temil shot down his Blade? We need somewhere safe to hide."

"Temil is the closest thing to safe in the Middle Stratum," said Gid.

"I always wanted to invade a planet," said Teg. "What better time than now?"

Gid rounded on him. "There's at least one battleship out there, and probably more where that came from."

"And we have a Working suppression field," said Teg. "Let's see them stonewall us when we turn it on and blow right past their ships."

"There's more than just ships." Astlin seemed to be staring into the distance, as if she could see through the walls. "They have a field of their own around the whole sphere. It extends into the ether, and it blocks nexism."

Teg grunted. "Sounds like Keth tried the same thing, only Temil's worked."

Astlin turned on her heel and marched toward the door. "I'm going down there."

"Don't be stupid," said Jaren. "We can't get close enough for a good view of the surface. Have you ever been to Temil before?"

Astlin looked down at the deck. "No."

"I have," said Jaren. "It's mostly water with small, widely scattered islands. Odds are a blind jump will land you in the ocean miles from rescue."

Teg finished Gid's grilled cheese, dusted the crumbs off his black shirt, and stood. "There's a way around that problem."

With all eyes watching him, Teg spoke to Astlin. "Xander moved my ship off of Keth. Stands to reason you could get a ship onto Temil."

Astlin brushed a hand through her red hair. "It might work. But with a ship the size of the *Serapis*? I wouldn't want to endanger everyone."

"I saw something interesting while I was out there shooting down Night Gen." Teg circled around the nav station and stood facing Astlin. "They left a ship on our bridge."

Astlin stood on the stolen nexus-runner's control dais, guiding the Night Gen craft through Temil space like an obsidian dart. Smaller than the *Theophilus'* drive pod, the eight-sided black prism would be hard for the Defense Service to detect.

At least she hoped so; mainly for Teg's sake.

"Thanks for coming," she told the ex-pirate strapped into a seat in the cabin behind her, "but you'd be safer if I'd come for Xander alone."

Teg finished checking the Mithgar Navy revolver he'd chosen from the *Serapis'* armory and holstered it across from the short sword on his left hip. Both the grey blade and the dark green uniform he wore had belonged to an ally and victim of Izlaril.

"Xander saved my life," said Teg, "but I'm here for my ship; not him."

"What if they blew it up?" asked Astlin.

Teg leaned back and folded his hands in his lap. The dim green light made him look corpselike.

"Then they probably blew your husband up with it, and we're both wasting our time."

Astlin didn't hide the dread that Teg's words caused. Xander's trail ended on Temil, but she still couldn't sense him.

What if he's right? What if Xander is...

"Don't worry," Teg said with surprising gentleness. "I wouldn't be here if I thought Xander and the *Theophilus* were a vapor cloud."

Astlin couldn't hold back a bittersweet laugh. "Thanks, Teg."

"Don't mention it. You'll find Xander. I'll take back my ship and, God willing, everything else that freak show stole from me."

"Don't celebrate yet," Astlin said. "We haven't even made it to the surface."

"Just get close enough to make sure we don't end up in a mountain or underwater," said Teg. "Then do that vanishing and reappearing trick on the ship. It'll be easy."

Astlin scanned the space around Temil. Though the way looked clear, several massive forms waited in the ether. "Unless we're spotted first."

"Relax," said Teg. "Nobody's around for—"

A vast black shape like a stretched out five-sided arrowhead suddenly filled the upper third of Astlin's vision. She feared she was hallucinating, but if she was seeing things, so were the captains of the dozen silver-blue Temilian warships that emerged from the ether.

"What's wrong?" asked Teg. "You look tense."

"Something big just showed up in orbit."

The black arrow gave off a nexic wave that made Astlin feel like she was standing in a hurricane. Green-white bolts rained down from the giant nexus-runner onto the sphere and its defending fleet. The deadly storm pummeled the defending ships but beat harmlessly against the shield.

A stray bolt hit the field directly ahead. The shockwave nearly knocked Astlin off her feet.

"Talk to me," said Teg.

Astlin shook the fog from her head. "It's a nexus-runner. Bigger than any I've ever seen! It's routing the Temilian ships, but the shield's holding."

"We need to make our move while they're distracted. Wait too long and we might get mistaken for one of the big boy's friends."

Astlin searched Temil's surface. Even to the ship's magnified sight it still looked like a big blue ball speckled with green.

"I can't find a landing site."

"Worry about landing later," said Teg. "Just get us inside the shield."

"I'm not sure how deep it goes," Astlin said with rising fear.

"Give it your best shot!" Teg yelled over another blast.

Astlin tried to let nexism guide her, but interference from the massive ship and Temil's shield left her nexically blind.

I love you, Xander, she thought as, with clenched teeth, she willed her miniature nexus-runner into Temil's atmosphere.

In the next moment, she and the ship were soaring gently over deep blue waters. The sea and sky mirrored each other. A warm breeze gusted against the bow.

"We're not dead," said Teg. "Good job."

Astlin's word of thanks became a shout as an unknown object sped past on the right.

"Did I speak too soon?" asked Teg.

"Something almost hit us," Astlin said. "It moved so fast I couldn't tell what it was."

As she spoke, another mystery object darted by; then another. Countless more followed, giving Astlin the impression of a school of jellyfish in flight.

"There must be hundreds of them," she said. "They're all headed the same way, over the horizon."

"Where are they coming from?" asked Teg.

Astlin traced the objects' flight path back and upward into orbit. She gasped when she saw their source.

"It's like something you'd find washed up on the beach after an oil spill," she thought aloud. "Only bigger than the *Serapis!*"

"*What's* bigger than the *Serapis*?"

"The thing that's hiding under the giant nexus-runner. All the little blobs came from it."

"Is it a ship?" asked Teg.

Astlin focused her magnified senses on the fleshy metallic hulk hanging under the even larger nexus-runner, and the shapeless things still streaming from space. A wave of dizziness forced her to look away.

"They're...*everything*," she said. "And nothing."

"You'll have to clarify that for me," said Teg.

Astlin surfaced from the sympathetic link and faced him. "That's the problem. Whatever we're dealing with, they're not like anything else. I can't even tell if they're manmade or alive; solid or liquid. And they keep changing—so fast I can't keep track. That must be how they're passing through the shield."

"That can't be good," said Teg. "What're you gonna do?"

Astlin plunged back into the control interface. "Follow them."

Teg started to speak, but his back slapped into his chair as she accelerated, knocking the wind from his lungs.

What are you? Astlin wondered, staring at her odd shapeless quarry. *And where are you going?*

She didn't pretend to understand what was going on, but the blobs seemed to be working with the Night Gen, who were allied with Shaiel, who'd taken Xander. Besides, their attack on Temil right after Izlaril and her husband had disappeared in orbit couldn't be a coincidence.

A dark line appeared on the blue horizon up ahead. The blobs were converging on it.

"They're all heading for a big island up ahead," Astlin told Teg.

"Is there a little island with a tall white tower on it?" he asked.

Astlin scanned the distant shoreline. Sure enough, what looked like a giant ivory horn thrust skyward from the sea.

"We're coming up on it fast," she said.

"That's the Guild house," said Teg. "The city of Vigh is on top of the cliffs beyond."

"You think the blobs are some kind of weapon?"

"The Night Gen are giving them cover fire," said Teg. "I doubt they're balloons for the kids."

Picturing the Night Gen bombing children kindled Astlin's rage. "They shot first. Let's shoot back."

Astlin imagined herself striking out at the blob-weapons, and streaks of green-white light stabbed into the hideous flock from the nexus-runner's sharp bow. Several of the ugly sacs burst into clouds of oily smoke. Brown dust like mushroom spores rained into the sea.

"Did you get them?" asked Teg.

"A few," said Astlin, frowning at the slightly diminished ranks of flying jellyfish. She was searching for a way to destroy all of them before they made landfall when one blob turned from the flock and shot straight toward her. Its impact against the hull felt like a warm peeled grape hitting her skin.

"What now?" Teg shouted when he heard her cry out. "Don't keep me in the dark."

Astlin's pulse raced. Fighting down her disgust she said, "One of them latched onto us!"

The feeling that the ship's senses transmitted next—like a swarm of maggots eating her skin—nearly made her gag.

"It's doing something to the ship," Astlin said.

Teg threw off his safety harness, sprang from his seat, and rushed to her side. "Is it cutting through the hull?"

Astlin shook her head and fought the terror that came when she realized what the blob was doing.

"It's not cutting through," she said. "It's turning into the ship and turning the ship into *it*."

"Transessence?"

Astlin considered Teg's question as she tracked the hull's rapid transformation into a hybrid of ship and blob.

"I think so," she said, "but on a level I've never heard of before."

The scattered displays and panels providing the cabin's only light turned from green to red as alarms sounded.

"That can't be good," said Teg.

Checking the depth of the rot showed Astlin that he was right. "It's about to breach the hull!"

Teg drew his gun. "Where's it coming from?"

"Shooting it won't help," Astlin warned him.

"Shooting helps everything," said Teg.

Astlin glared at him. "You say that to everyone you've shot?"

A sight carried through the ship's vision took Astlin's mind off the argument. The city of Vigh had come into view, silver and crystal towers rising from a coastal plain above sheer cliffs.

The blobs were swarming over buildings. She watched in horror as glass and steel veins spiderwebbed out from flesh bags clustered on tower walls. She could just make out crowds pouring into the streets, their screams drowning out the breaking waves below.

Sympathetic pain like molten metal burning through skin and muscle drew Astlin's focus back to the infection consuming her ship.

"They're eating the city," Astlin said, "and us."

"Any ideas?" asked Teg.

"Just one." Astlin powered up the nexus-runner's translator and focused on the spreading corruption. Since the rot was partly made of the ship itself, it was hard to isolate from uninfected areas.

With only seconds left before doing so would puncture the hull, Astlin activated the translator. A bubble of green-white light surrounded the ship and momentarily blinded her.

Her sight returned. The rot was still there.

"We need to abandon ship." Astlin searched the shoreline and saw a vast expanse of soft, secluded marshland. Before Teg could object, she directed the translator to evacuate him. Pale green brilliance washed out the cabin's red half-light, leaving Astlin alone on what was now a plague ship.

She took some comfort in knowing that Teg was safe—safer than her, at least. The problem now was finding a place to crash the ship before making her own escape.

In the city below, the plague carriers had consumed what might have been a shopping center. The building's roof and walls sagged like wet clay of multiple brown, grey, and metallic hues. Thick black smoke poured from the windows and doors, but what emerged next chilled Astlin's blood.

Twisted shapes lurched out of the smoke. No two were alike, and none gave any hint of what they'd been before the transessence plague fell from the sky. Most seemed to be made of the same metallic clay as the building they shambled from.

The largest had a head like a giant rotten fruit with one large ragged opening. Boneless tendrils hung from its hunched shoulders where arms should have been as it slouched blindly into the frenzied crowd on legs like stunted tree stumps.

I need to get away from the city! Astlin thought. She was turning the tainted ship out to sea when the feeling of maggots gnawing on her skin gave way to the sensation of ants crawling over it. Her hackles rose, and the fine hairs on the backs of her hands stood on end.

It's some kind of field. Where's it coming from?

The answer revealed itself. White-capped waves churned by an unseen force radiated out to sea from the ivory tower's island. The invisible field passed over the city, melting plague blobs and everything they'd infected into pools of tar.

To Astlin's relief, the energy wave also burned the infection out of her ship. The alarms went silent and green twilight filled the cabin once more.

Those plague blobs live on transessence, she thought. *The Guild house must have a Working suppression field like the* Serapis, *only big enough to cover a city!*

Smoke rising from the streets marked where suddenly powerless drifters had crashed. Astlin's heart sank, but the oddly low number of wrecks both consoled and puzzled her.

High above, the mother jellyfish folded in on itself and vanished. But the gigantic nexus-runner remained, keeping up its bombardment of the planetary shield out of what Astlin could only imagine was pure spite.

Pins and needles stopped pricking Astlin's skin. The sea around the tower grew calm.

Whoever's in there didn't hesitate to use that weapon on their own people.

That fact raised more questions. The white tower was Vigh's Guild house. Had the Brotherhood survived the Cataclysm under Temil's shield?

And did they have Xander?

Astlin still couldn't feel her husband's presence, but Teg's calm mind stood out from the panicked masses below.

Every Guild house was just a shell for a warren of pocket dimensions. No way she could will herself inside. Luckily, no one was more qualified to help her break in than Teg.

Attention, Night Gen craft. The message imprinted on her mind through the ship's nexic comm gave Astlin a start.

Proceed directly to the indicated docking pad on Alabaster Island, the telepathic message continued, giving the impression of a coolly detached male voice. *You are granted landing clearance for the magisterial campus. Any deviation from the authorized approach vector will be answered with lethal force.*

An image came to her mind's eye—a square of dark, veined elemental stone amid well-ordered gardens in the shadow of what seemed less like a tower than a pearly spike nailing the land to heaven.

I'll come back for you, Teg, Astlin vowed silently, taking care to hide her thoughts. She turned toward the island and started her descent.

15

Celwen struggled up onto the beach. The sea had scoured most of the foul tar from her suit. But she lay shivering on the wet sand until the shock of entering Temil's atmosphere in an Anomian pod—like riding inside of a large animal's intestines— finally faded. The magnified sound of her own breathing drowned out the lapping waves.

I am nothing; the mission is everything, she thought.

Celwen often used that mantra to persevere through adversity, but this time the words rang hollow.

Raig knew of her treason. Accomplishing her mission to infiltrate the Shadow Caste and bring down the shield would give him enough proof to have her executed. He already thought her expendable, as his musing that the pod might penetrate the shield but leave her behind had shown.

But what choice do I have?

That was defeatist thinking verging on self-pity. Celwen forced such thoughts from her mind and considered her options.

She could make contact with the Shadow Caste—if they

really ruled here as Lykaon said—and seek asylum instead of betraying them.

Then what? Hope that Temil held out against the combined might of Shaiel, the Night Gen, and the Anomians? The chances of surviving such a siege, even if her former benefactors held influence here, were slim to none. The odds of them handing her over in a doomed appeal to Shaiel's mercy were much better.

When given two bad options, Celwen thought, *make a third.*

The overwhelming force that Lykaon had brought to bear on Temil hadn't escaped Celwen's notice. Her strategic training indicated the presence of something that Shaiel greatly valued—and feared.

Her only hope of survival depended on finding it first. Luckily, a nexic burst she'd felt to the southwest gave her a place to start looking.

Celwen stood. The surf rolled around her feet as she removed the breathing mask from her mouth and tasted warm salt air. She brushed fine sand and the last of the dead pod tissue from her suit. Water beaded on the slick black fabric and rolled off, leaving her dry as she strode up the shore.

The beach ended at a line of tall grass shaded by a stand of low trees. Celwen drew back her suit's tight-fitting cowl and shook her long dark hair free. The new smell of green growing things filled her nostrils like an exotic perfume as she stole into the woods.

Teg hid the body in a broken freezer in the basement of a defunct sport shop.

The moldy building's water had been shut off long ago, but

Teg stripped off his reeking clothes and did his best to clean the muck from his skin with an old drop cloth.

After donning the brown long-sleeved shirt, belting on the tan canvas pants, and slipping into the grey polymer jacket his victim didn't need anymore, Teg threw his mud-caked Night Gen uniform on top of the corpse.

"No hard feelings," Teg told the dead man who'd seen him trudge out of the swamp. If the fool's last act hadn't been screaming about invaders from the marsh, he'd be sleeping off a concussion instead of going room temperature in a deep freeze.

Teg checked the pockets of his new clothes and turned up the usual wallet and keys, plus a well-used folding knife with a horn handle, a pack of waterproof matches, an empty tube of insect repellant, a plastic comb, and a cheap pair of sunglasses.

Documents in the wallet identified the grizzled-looking deceased as "Amit Scrope" and declared him a "Protected Citizen".

Didn't protect him from a crushed trachea.

Combing the slime out of his hair, Teg consoled himself with the knowledge that Astlin could have picked far worse drop zones.

Wakerife Marsh was a rambling expanse of coastal swampland bordering Temil's capital of Vigh. Over hundreds of years the marsh had largely resisted the city's attempts at southward expansion, thanks largely to persistent legends about strange goings-on in the untold miles of stagnant lakes and waterlogged woods.

Teg had learned to use the local folklore to his advantage during a stint running guns to this very shop. Decades back the last owner had vanished amid fantastically wild rumors. The place's unsavory reputation was probably why Scrope's cries had gone unheard.

If Teg was lucky.

No sense waiting around to find out.

Teg reluctantly ditched his bulky holster and stowed his gun inside the jacket with Scrope's knife. He debated keeping the ID to get past checkpoints, but his sandy hair and lack of a tan would quickly betray the ruse. Instead he pocketed the dead man's cash and tossed the wallet into the freezer before shutting the lid.

Making sure that his new pants concealed the short sword strapped to his thigh, Teg climbed the stairs to the back door, put on the scuffed sunglasses, and stepped into an empty carpark lit by the tropical sun and green-white bursts of orbital fire.

Suspicion over why a local had been heading to the same old smugglers' den as him prompted Teg to retrace Scrope's path. The man's rather obvious trail led down the highway's muddy shoulder to a light green drifter. Though grimy and dented, it was relatively new.

Figures that the last sphere we find is the only one that didn't burn back to the stone age.

Anticipation lightened Teg's heart and fingers as he approached the derelict vehicle.

It's been too long.

After a slow start, the Formula quickly reconstructed the last minutes of Scrope's life. Based on the relative age of impressions left in the mud by the car and its pilot, Scrope had started walking down the road roughly half an hour ago; a few minutes after landing.

Before that he'd been drifting down the westbound lane. With blobs invading from the east, that made sense. What didn't make sense was finding the car safely parked; not crumpled into a meat-filled steel ball.

Teg knew what a Working disruption field felt like, and he'd felt a big one right after getting dumped in the swamp. One didn't normally flee an invasion at a leisurely pace, and if Scrope had suddenly lost power at speed, the first tree in his path would've saved Teg some trouble.

Had Scrope been forewarned to land ahead of the field? Possible, but unlikely. If he'd known when the field would be used, he wouldn't have been caught in the middle of nowhere.

Dismantling the dash with Scrope's knife hinted at the answer to one mystery and brought up several others. Though years more advanced than any Teg had seen, the drifter's parts were still identifiable—all except for a strange box hidden behind the control yoke.

The box just fit in Teg's palm. Its casing was some kind of ceramic-polymer hybrid totally bereft of markings—no model or serial numbers and no branding. The only breaks in its smooth grey surface were small ports for wires leading to every main control system.

Someone landed the drifter for him.

A beaten green case on the passenger side floor caught Teg's eye. It contained hooks, spools of heavy line, plastic floats, small steel weights, and colorful fake bugs. That and the shiny blue earpiece left on the driver's seat told the rest of the tale.

Teg felt a pang of sympathy for the man whose fishing trip had been cut short by a war he hadn't caused, whose escape had been cut short by parties unknown, and whose life had been cut short while he'd been looking for help.

Since fretting wouldn't bring Scrope back, Teg focused on the problem at hand. He was trespassing on foreign soil at best. At worst he was behind enemy lines. The locals' high technology—and their willingness to control people with it—would make staying unnoticed a pain in the ass.

To say nothing of recovering his ship and his friend's husband from whatever secret hole the sphere's rulers had stashed them in.

The Defense Service probably blew them both to hell, Thought Teg. That possibility would make things easier. Which was why he doubted it was true.

Teg picked up Scrope's discarded sending stud and almost checked to see if it was working again. Instead he cut the mystery box out of the dash, attached the stud and a handful of floaters to it with some waterproof tape from the fishing kit, and tossed the whole package into a murky stream running beside the road.

Further interruptions were unlikely, so Teg conducted a thorough check of the cockpit, trunk, and engine. When no other suspect devices turned up, a little more tape saw the controls fixed and Teg flying down the road behind them.

Astlin took in the landscape beyond the nexus-runner's open hatch. Neatly trimmed hedges enclosed lavish lawns. Calm pools mirrored a sky torn by green-white flashes, and the steamy air smelled of roses.

All of these matched the telepathic impressions she'd received. What struck her were the differences.

Rich carpets woven in complex patterns of red, purple, and gold covered the ground from the black and grey stone landing pad all the way down a broad gravel path as white as the tower at its end.

Soldiers standing at attention in sky blue uniforms lined either side of the path, the barrels of their rifles angled toward the ground. Their faces showed no emotion.

A shorter line of people waited at the edge of the landing pad. They wore expensive-looking suits and dresses, and sweat beaded on their foreheads. One of them—a tall man with a square fleshy face and receding blond hair—called up to her.

"On behalf of the Assembly and all our citizens, welcome to the Free Sphere of Temil."

This is weird, thought Astlin.

The speaker went on like a politician running for ward boss. "It's my privilege to extend you every honor and courtesy."

Astlin didn't have time for speeches. She rifled through the speaker's mind for any knowledge of Xander.

The politician—she'd gotten that one right—was Kroylan Renneker, a senex of Temil's Assembly. His gloating contempt for the people he supposedly served belied his claim that the sphere was free. Actually a cabal of government, military, and business leaders ruled Temil as absolutely as any monarch.

Which, oddly, Renneker thought Astlin was.

They turned away the Serapis, *but they're giving me a queen's welcome. Why?*

"…emerged from the crisis of the Guild's fall to forge a society according to the pattern of reason…" Renneker continued.

Astlin ignored his words and dug deeper into his thoughts. It didn't take her long to figure out that Renneker knew far less

167

than a real ruler should. He had no information on Xander, and his false impression of her as a visiting head of state came from a council of advisors called the Magisterium.

While Renneker droned on, Astlin expanded her mental search to the other five dignitaries. None of them knew any more than the senex. Their thoughts were a mix of amused fascination with her and anxiety over whether the council of Magists could hold off the invasion.

The Magists, Astlin noted, *not the Defense Service.*

She unconsciously played with the steel washer that encircled her finger. Seeing her ring of base metal reminded Renneker of a riddle the Magists' messenger had told him.

Gold is most queens' fortune; hers was brass.

The stray thought shook Astlin to her soul. She swept down the boarding ramp, onto the lush carpets, and past a stunned Senex Renneker, who halted in mid-speech as she marched by.

The welcoming committee burst into angry chatter. Renneker urged her to wait, but Astlin kept going until she stood amid the silent double row of soldiers.

The Magists knew about her shadowed past. There would be a spy here—if not one of the local figureheads, then someone who seemed to be guarding them.

The soldiers' minds gave up no answers. Either Astlin was wrong, and Temil really was governed by civil servants chosen by the people and advised by a council of elders, or the sphere's secret rulers taught their spies how to hide their thoughts.

With Xander's life on the line, Astlin took a gamble.

"Someone here works for the Magists," she said. "Take me to them."

A young soldier with a friendly face stepped from the line, gave her a slight bow, and said, "It would be a pleasure, My Lady."

The soldier started toward the white tower, and Astlin joined him. Abandoned beside the landing pad, Renneker and his friends fell silent.

16

Teg sped up the coastal highway in his stolen drifter. The sea was a glittering sheet of blue glass on his right. On the northern horizon, luxury resorts towered over Vigh's fabled Silver Strand.

Folks ascribed the *silver* moniker to rumors that you could get anything there—if you had enough of it. Multiple stretches on shore leave had confirmed the tales, but this time Teg's search would take him across the reach to what had been the Guild's private island.

The knife-edged Gen ship loomed over the capital like the white tower's heavenly shadow. The intervening atmosphere lightened the ship's black hull to a washed-out grey, but the pulsing flash of its assault on the shield was as bright as lightning.

Teg was so busy staring at the sky that he almost plowed into the woman standing in the middle of the road. Instead his peripheral vision gave his reflexes just enough warning to slam on the brakes.

His pulse pounding in his ears, old habit overcame Teg's shock enough to train his senses on the stranger he'd nearly flattened.

She looks like one of the stiffs in the hangar, he thought, comparing her black hair and grey skin to those of Izlaril's dead friends.

The female Night Gen—which Teg surmised she was— showed remarkably little fear for someone who'd been about to lose a fight with a two ton vehicle. She stood facing him, her chest level with the front bumper, so close he could make out the sharkskin sheen of her tight black suit. Her green eyes matched the drifter's paint.

Teg considered hitting the accelerator and running the Gen down anyway. After all, her side were the aggressors, here. But it occurred to him that she wasn't currently *with* her side. He'd rather not kill her till he found out why.

Sliding his right hand into the jacket pocket that held his gun, Teg beckoned the woman with his left.

She readily complied. Teg angled the still concealed gun toward her as he lowered the driver side window to frame her pretty head.

"What?" he grumbled.

"It is good that I found you," she said in a strange accent.

"Why?"

"We are both fugitives. You came here on a stolen nexus-runner."

Teg discreetly thumbed back the gun's hammer. "How did you know?"

"I can see what others cannot," she said, "like the gun in your jacket. Now put it down, let me in, and we can talk."

"Nope." Teg applied the accelerator, and the drifter pulled forward.

The Gen woman stood dumbstruck in the middle of the road for a second before she ran after him, shouting something he couldn't make out.

Teg slowed the drifter. After a moment, the woman caught up.

"Wait," she huffed, jogging beside the window. "We can help each other."

"You first," said Teg. "Tell me who you are and why you're here."

"I am Celwen." She paused before saying, "I deserted from the Night Gen fleet."

"Better go wait over there." Teg pointed to the muddy shoulder of the road. "The highway patrol will really want to talk to you."

Celwen's expression was determined, but her eyes betrayed fear. "I will be sure to tell them about you."

Teg stopped the car. "Okay. Get in."

Celwen hurried around to the passenger side while Teg raised his window. She threw the tackle box in the back seat, climbed, in and slammed the door behind her.

"Thank you," she said breathlessly. Her grey skin glowed with sweat. She smelled like she'd gone diving in runoff from a shoe factory.

"You're welcome." Teg had the gun drawn and aimed at her face before he finished the sentence. "Now tell me why I shouldn't kill you now and dump you back in the ocean."

Celwen glanced at the gun barrel for only a moment before her eyes met Teg's.

"I am running from both sides," she said, her calm audibly fraying at the edges, "just like you."

"I'm not running from anyone," said Teg.

Realization gleamed in Celwen's green eyes. "You are hunting, then. I can help find what you seek."

The Night Gen's claim piqued Teg's curiosity. "Can you find a ship?"

Celwen's focus seemed to wander far afield. "I can tell you that another vehicle is approaching us from behind."

Teg wasn't stupid enough to look away from his prisoner, but he did check the rear-view mirror out of the corner of his eye.

A light blue drifter rounded a bend about a mile behind them. The sun glinted off its mirror finish.

Teg stuffed the gun back into his pocket and eased the drifter up to speed, being careful to stay under the limit. He kept one eye on the curving road ahead and the other on his odd passenger while stealing glances at the trailing vehicle.

Trailing, but definitely gaining. Soon the silver-blue drifter had fallen in behind them, matching their speed roughly ten car lengths back.

Sweat loosened Teg's grip on the wheel. He maintained his course and speed, expecting sirens to blare and lights to flash from the other car at any moment.

I'm probably just being paranoid. The blue drifter didn't have police or military markings, whatever that was worth. The two figures dimly visible behind the tinted windscreen might be an ordinary couple out for a leisurely drive.

Along an exposed seaside highway during an alien invasion.

"Can you see who's in that car?" Teg asked.

After a brief pause Celwen said, "Two men in dark blue jackets and pants. Mirrored glasses hide their eyes."

Standard issue operators, thought Teg.

Then again, Celwen might be lying to him. He couldn't think of a reason why she would, but that didn't mean there wasn't one.

Teg fell back on a time-tested method for spotting a tail. He slowed down and sped up at random, climbed to the drifter's limited flight ceiling without warning, and swerved between lanes.

In short, he drove like a moron.

Civilian drivers would have passed him. Police would have hit their lights and pulled him over. Whoever was piloting the blue drifter matched Teg's every move.

"Yeah, they're following us," said Teg.

He mashed the accelerator into the floor. Celwen gave a curt squeal as she was pushed back into her seat.

Teg took a few sharp turns at speed and got back on a straight stretch before checking the mirror again.

The blue car rounded the last corner. Teg expected it to quickly close the distance, but for some reason the almost certainly faster vehicle hung back.

Celwen twisted around to look through the back window. "Have they given up?"

Teg hoped so, but he knew a more likely explanation. "They're probably trying to shut us down by remote. We need to lose them before they figure out they can't."

Vigh's infrastructure refused to cooperate with Teg's plan. The road ahead wended toward the still distant skyline in a series of cliff-hugging curves. He saw nothing to either side but uninterrupted woods on the left and a wire fence on the right above a sheer drop to the sea.

"Here they come again," Celwen said.

The mirror told Teg that he'd been right about the blue car's superior speed. Now that his pursuers had realized they couldn't stop their quarry remotely, they seemed hellbent on doing the job up close and personal.

Teg could handle a drifter better than an average slob off the street, but he wouldn't list it among his specialties.

His tail was clearly far more practiced. Despite Teg's best evasive driving, the blue car charged up alongside his, wrenching a cry from Celwen as it thudded into her door. Teg's mind raced and his muscles strained against the other driver's attempts to force him off the road and into the trees.

"Up ahead!" Celwen yelled.

Teg shifted his focus from the blue drifter beside his to the road, where a wickedly sharp curve lay just ahead.

"Duck!" said Teg.

Celwen got the message when he drew his gun and aimed at the passenger window. She bent down and covered her head an instant before Teg fired. The gunshots drowned out Celwen's screams as glass pebbles rained down on her. The blue car's dark window spiderwebbed but didn't break. Still, the other driver got the hint and fell back.

The road ahead looped hard left around a small inlet. There was no way to slow down in time, so Teg floored it. He thought of warning Celwen, but if her ears were ringing as bad as his, she wouldn't hear him anyway.

Teg wasn't an expert on how drifters worked. He did know they were based on the same Workings as protective auras and airlifts, and that the column of force needed a solid surface to push against—which was why they were useless in the Air Stratum.

Water alone couldn't support drifters either, which was why Teg whispered a prayer to Thera as he spurred the drifter to its top altitude, scraped over the roadside fence, and soared past the edge of a sea cliff.

The other side rushed closer, and Teg thought they just might pull it off. But time slowed, the opposite cliff seemed to pull back, and Teg's stomach lurched into his chest as the drifter fell.

The blue car flew over them, and Teg couldn't help smirking when he saw it come down, hard but intact, on the other side. Then the cliff face reared up and hid his view of the road.

Even at full power, the engines did little to slow their fall. The car pitched downward, and Teg saw one last chance. Sporadic mounds of rock broke the surface of the waves. He poured all of his effort into landing on a target no bigger than his vehicle. Even if he aligned the drifter perfectly, it might still slip off the irregular rocks.

A bone-rattling jolt coursed through the cockpit as the force column made contact with a patch of rock. Teg's relief was fleeting, because the car wobbled for a moment; then plunged toward the sea. Cast onto the waves, they'd be pulverized against the rocks.

The ringing in his ears had subsided enough to hear Celwen's scream as they hit the water. Sea spray fountained up past the roof and surged in through the broken window.

As his final, all too human act, Teg threw his arms around Celwen in a futile protective embrace and waited for impact.

It may have been several seconds before Teg realized that no impact came.

He and Celwen disentangled themselves and stared through the windscreen. The car floated just above the water. Waves lapped against the sides.

Teg lowered his window and looked into the clear water. A bed of submerged rock lay directly beneath them.

He turned back to Celwen, who sat beside him drenched and shivering.

"So you can find my ship?"

Celwen slowly nodded.

"Good," he said.

Teg's smuggling days had acquainted him with Vigh's shoreline. Scanning the area, he found a safe route onto the small beach at the inlet's base. From there, he could skim along the shallows to a hidden cave system connected to the sprawling network of drainage tunnels under the city.

Teg smiled. If the *Theophilus* was anywhere near Vigh, it was as good as his again.

17

Astlin followed the soldier into the white tower, which unlike other Guild houses was a tall open shaft; not a big empty box. But the trademark three-stepped gate platform bracketed by four reception desks stood right in the middle, and Astlin's military escort led her toward it across the oddly empty white floor. Their footsteps were lost in the distant heights.

"Where is everyone?" she asked, eyeing the metal pin on the soldier's blue jacket with the name *Capgrave* stamped on it.

"The lobby was cleared because of the orbital strike," Capgrave said. "It's standard security protocol, but we'll make an exception for you."

Astlin faced him. "Your leaders—your *real* leaders—have my husband. I need to see them."

Still smiling, Capgrave activated the gate and directed Astlin toward the large ball of light that hummed atop the platform. She suppressed the urge to look back, climbed the steps, and strode through the gate.

Astlin's formerly silent heels now clicked on polished stone. She passed down a short hallway, pushed aside a yellow banner covering the exit, and stepped onto a wide disc of gold marble. Windows spanned from the floor's edges to the ceiling, alternating with banners—each a different solid color—and broad columns of the same golden stone.

Where am I? She could still sense Teg at the edge of her nexic awareness, so she hadn't left Temil.

A cool breeze smelling of grass and the sea stirred Astlin's black skirt from behind. She turned and saw to her surprise that the gate was now a set of doors made of many wooden frames holding small panes of glass.

Should've brought my jacket.

The open doors gave onto a green terrace whose manicured lawn ran to a sandstone parapet. Long blue and white streamers flew from slender poles planted along the low wall. Past the wall the land fell away, and beyond that shining silver waves stretched toward the azure sky.

That sight and the sensations that came with it hinted at fond memories from one life or another, and Astlin embraced the faded echo of joy as she left the door and approached the table in the middle of the room.

Before she'd taken ten steps, the grass and salt scents gave way to the aromas of smoked meats and cheeses, stuffed olives, and dried fruits piled into brightly painted dishes on the scuffed tabletop. The feast could have served a family gathering—or, Astlin thought darkly, a council of robbers.

The lone man seated at table hadn't been there when she'd entered. Now he seemed to fill the whole room, though his height was average and the body under his robe of red-gold silk, which matched the banner behind him, was lean.

Astlin would never forget the man's face no matter how many lives she lived. The furrowed skin framed by a greying beard and wiry receding hair; the small square glasses perched upon the crooked nose and the eyes hard as weight stones behind their lenses—all had been burned into her mind at the burning of her flesh.

Moving as if in a trance, Astlin seated herself in a cross-framed chair facing the man who'd once plunged her into a living nightmare of madness and fire.

"Are you going to talk," he asked at length, "or are you just going to sit there staring daggers at me?"

Astlin fought to keep her voice even. Her eyes never left his. "I think I'll do both."

With a sigh, he plucked a walnut from a brass bowl and held it between his thumb and forefinger. "Why not have a bite instead? Try the cured ham."

Astlin's hand balled into a fist. "I don't want anything of yours, Kelgrun!"

"Don't you?" Kelgrun arched one bushy eyebrow. "What about knowledge—of Shaiel's new host, for instance?"

Despite herself, Astlin couldn't prevent a quickly indrawn breath.

Kelgrun smirked. "His ship got a taste of our new battle cruiser's guns. We'd have shown him better hospitality, but he barged in unannounced."

Anger fed Astlin's resolve. "Where is he? Give me a straight answer, or I'll rip it from your mind."

"Will you? I saw firsthand what you could do before..." Kelgrun waved his hand over her. "So go ahead; try to read my mind. Any page. Rip it out. Frankly I doubt you've still got the nerve. Whatever's beyond the Nexus, it tends to make you people soft."

Astlin must have failed to hide her surprise, because Kelgrun spoke again.

"I've been around a while. Do you really think you're the first of your kind I've seen? It's a small world, and nothing new in it!"

In her shock, a portion of Astlin's power slipped its leash. Her anger lashed out at Kelgrun, hungry to avenge the pain he'd caused. His will turned the blow with a subtlety she hadn't expected, but even his skill couldn't fend off her greater strength for long.

Astlin closed her eyes and leaned forward, planting her hands on the table. She tore through Kelgrun's defenses. Sweat rolled down his face, and his left eye twitched as he struggled hopelessly to keep her out of his mind.

You disfigured me, she reminded him. *It's only fair if I return the favor. Cut your eyes out.*

Kelgrun's left hand twitched as it removed his glasses. His right hand jerked toward a silver carving knife.

Another will intervened. Though weaker than Kelgrun, its wielder caught Astlin off guard and broke her mental hold on him. A third nexist; a fourth, then a fifth, joined Kelgrun's defense. Their combined power forced Astlin to break off her assault and drove her back into her chair.

Her head pounding, Astlin opened her eyes to see that she now faced six men instead of one. No two came from the same tribe or race. All wore luxuriant silk robes similar to Steersmen's, but instead of black each man's robe matched the vivid color of the banner behind his seat.

She wondered where the five had come from, and if the banners hid secret gates.

Kelgrun's right hand had kept its grip on the nut throughout the nexic duel. Now he cracked it with a loud snap.

"Poor form, child," he said, donning his glasses again. "You'd best control that temper. Or better yet, give it free rein. You made such a lovely monster, and your career as a savior was doomed before it began. Now, thanks to that love-struck boy you'll always fall somewhere in-between. No matter how many shards you steal, Zadok will just cleave off more."

Astlin spoke with a conviction she didn't feel. "If Szodrin keeps bringing souls into this world forever, I'll keep doing everything I can to free them—*forever*."

"Have you told your darling husband this plan?" Kelgrun asked. "Perhaps my brother Magists and I should hold on to him for you."

Dread quenched the last spark of Astlin's anger. "Xander is here?" She couldn't keep her question from sounding like a plea. "He's alive?"

Kelgrun exchanged a look with the blue-robed, dark-haired man at his left before saying, "Somewhere between life and death, actually. Don't blame us. We'd be enjoying his company now if we could get that pestilential mask off. Sadly, unexpected forces of the most dangerous sort are inhabiting his body, so we'd best not wake him."

Astlin swallowed the lump in her throat. "Give...give him back to me."

Kelgrun leaned back from the table, a wounded expression on his face. "And give up my only insurance against being brutally murdered at your hands?" He shook his shaggy head. "No."

The other Magists chuckled.

"You're holding Xander hostage," Astlin accused.

Kelgrun shrugged. "Whatever terms are easiest for you to understand. Regardless, you should avoid prying into our minds or dazzling us with your crown, for poor Xander's sake."

Astlin spoke through gritted teeth. "What if I pick up this chair and bash your sick heads in?"

"That's right out," said Kelgrun.

Holding back her fear and rage, Astlin said, "We're only talking because you wanted to. Why am I here?"

Kelgrun popped the shelled nut into his mouth and crunched on it as he spoke. "You're here now because you passed our little test down at the landing pad." He grinned at a bald man in mustard-colored robes. "Belar didn't think you'd find our guide."

"I did."

Astlin's eyes followed the high, nervous-sounding voice to its source and saw a small man in pine-colored robes who sat hunched over the table, feeding thin strips of meat through a black web pulled tight against his face. Not quite a veil, it looked more like he'd pulled a fishnet stocking over his head. His unkempt goatee poked through the mesh, and dull brown hair peeked out from under his black velvet cap.

"Don't boast, Gien," Belar said in the thickest Temilian accent she'd ever heard. "You're offending our guest."

Gien suddenly stared at Astlin. His ice blue eyes held an animal hunger that deeply disturbed her. She noticed that he'd finished his meat and was gnawing his own fingertips. Blood trickled down his pale, trembling hand.

Astlin averted her eyes, letting them come to rest on Kelgrun and marveling that she found the sight of him a relief.

"What do you want with us," she asked, "me and Xander?"

Kelgrun steepled his hands. "A while back we set in motion a series of events that were to culminate in the Last Working, Thera's return, and the end of the cosmos. Sadly, we miscalculated certain variables. A great deal of time and effort went to waste."

"You want to rip out part of my soul again?"

"No need," Kelgrun said. "We've got the original piece—along with all the rest—thanks to your friend Smith."

"Smith." Astlin made the name a curse. "He's working with you?"

"His life's ambition is to build a god. What better partners than us?"

Astlin folded her arms. "He already made a god."

"Only a larval one," said Kelgrun. "Under our auspices he can succeed where all others have failed."

"So Thera can destroy everything? She'll probably start with you."

"Thus, our need for you and Xander," Kelgrun said. "Smith claims that you two thwarted Zadok's designs. If so, perhaps you can help us control Thera. The pseudo-incarnation inhabiting Xander's body may offer an extra advantage."

Astlin pointed at Gien. "If you think me, Xander, and Shaiel will help you control Thera, you're crazier than the guy who eats his own fingers."

Gien's smile showed pink, crooked teeth.

"Assuming you're right," Kelgrun said, "disappointing us would have unpleasant consequences—especially for your friends."

The floor seemed to give way under Astlin. "Friends?"

Kelgrun scowled. "Don't insult us. Our capabilities exceed the Guild's at its height. We've confirmed at least two other infiltrators. One translated from your ship to the swamp, where he murdered one of the plebes. Another killed an intelligence officer at a secure docking facility last night. He must have hidden aboard that ragtag ether-runner."

Astlin strove to hide her sudden dread. *The only one on the* Theophilus *with Xander was…*

"You've sent a pair of wolves among our sheep," Kelgrun lectured her. "Both are quite elusive, but no matter. Both have been drawn inexorably into our trap."

18

"One crab cake," Teg told the vendor. "No onion."

The mingled aromas of fish, vinegar, and old hot grease wafted from the sidewalk food stand. Glancing at Celwen standing on the wet pavement behind him, he added, "Make that two."

The local underground had changed since Teg's last visit, and a detour through a narrow side-tunnel had forced them to ditch the car. By the time they'd wound their way through the drainage tunnels and surfaced in the heart of Vigh, night had fallen, bringing rain with it. The clouds rolling in from the sea weren't thunderheads, though the continued Night Gen barrage against the shield above looked like green-white lightning.

Teg paid for his order with Scrope's money and turned to offer one piping hot, paper-wrapped cake to Celwen. Her green eyes studied the package skeptically from under the hood of Scrope's borrowed jacket.

"You spent all day running from your own people and the local spooks," he told her. "Eat."

"Quiet!" Celwen hissed. "Someone may be listening."

Teg looked up and down a commercial block with half its

gaudy signs unlit and a dozen screens counting down the fifteen minutes till curfew. Just before the next intersection to the west, yellow lights blinked on a police line cordoning off the front of a building where a drifter had crashed.

"I think we're the worst ones out tonight," he said.

After a moment's pause, Celwen took the crab cake. Her agile grey fingers undid the wrapping and pressed the steaming morsel to her lips. She chewed the first bite slowly; then finished the rest in two greedy mouthfuls.

Teg savored his own portion, along with the memories evoked by the taste and aroma. Finished, he wadded up the wrapping and pitched it in the gutter where the swift current carried it away.

"What now?" asked Celwen. "My people and the Shadow Caste are locked in a stalemate that I am expected to break."

"Now you tell me why you deserted from the side that's putting on the nonstop light show."

Celwen studied the sidewalk as she spoke. "My people want to wipe out yours. I would not answer the clay tribe's bloodshed in kind."

"You're the only Night Gen opposed to genocide?"

"No!" Celwen's head jerked up. "At least, I doubt it. Understand, my people embraced conformity to survive. Dissent is prohibited, and the telepaths are vigilant."

Teg mulled over the answer. "You're sure my ship's around here somewhere?"

"Yes and no," Celwen said. "It is hidden far from Temil; far from the Middle Stratum. But the entrance to its hiding place is nearby, somewhere below."

Teg looked eastward to where the side street ran into the Strand. A big empty lot occupied the corner. Amid the luxury hotels towering on both sides of the main thoroughfare, it stood out like a missing tooth.

Rain cascaded down signboards fixed to the wire fence that encircled the lot. The older signs looked to predate the Cataclysm, and Teg recognized one bearing the logo of a major Temilian construction company. The faded picture on the same ad showed a glittering new hotel that had yet to rise.

That's where Gray's used to be, he recalled. The upscale inn and gambling establishment had been a monument to Vigh's more refined past until an ether-runner crash two decades before the Cataclysm had leveled the place.

With all the new construction around here, it's odd that they never rebuilt…

A drifter sped into the western intersection, rounded the corner, and lurched to a halt near the police line. The car's shiny exterior reflected a constellation of lights, screens, and signs. All of its doors opened at once, and four men in dark clothes stepped into the street.

Celwen pressed up against Teg's back. He felt her slick diving suit through the soggy jacket.

"Agents of the Shadow Caste," she said. "How did they find us?"

Back in the direction of the empty lot, part of the fence running along an alley rattled. A sudden breeze might have shaken the wire, but Teg hadn't felt any.

Strange.

The rainless man-shaped space at the top of the fence was

much stranger. It disappeared so fast that Teg would have doubted his eyes if not for Astlin's account of something similar.

Teg slid his hand into the pants pocket where he'd stuck his gun. His fingers closed around the checkered grip.

"I was wrong," he said to Celwen. "Something way worse than us is sneaking around."

She turned toward a gift shop on the other side of the street and tugged on his arm. "We should run."

"You're right." Teg pulled free and started toward the alley fronting the fence. "But now I know where my ship is. Besides, my friend's counting on me. Come on."

Teg jogged up to the fence and was pleased when Celwen followed. Shouts and the sound of sensible shoes rapidly striking wet pavement told him that the local spooks were inbound.

"Give me the jacket," he told Celwen.

Removing the stolen garment exposed Celwen's weird black wetsuit and grey skin, but Teg had a more urgent use for it than disguising her Night Gen identity. He threw the jacket over the bladed wire that crowned the fence before leaping up and grabbing hold of the top. He held on with one hand while helping Celwen up with the other, and both of them peered over the top.

The yawning pit on the other side took up a third of the block. The side facing the Strand was a sheer bank four stories high.

A dirt ramp directly below sloped down to a large concrete slab. Halfway between the foot of the ramp and the east wall, a forest of thick metal rods grew up from the slab. A gridwork of bars perpendicular to the uprights gave the appearance of a pit half-filled with cages.

Two smaller slabs rested upon the cages against the far wall, granting a cutaway view of uncompleted basements stacked atop each other. Darkness prevailed within.

A familiar crack echoed in the street behind him, warning Teg that at least one of the spooks had a zephyr. He and Celwen briefly exchanged glances; then vaulted over the fence.

Teg hit slick mud and rolled several feet before sitting up to finish descending the ramp in a controlled slide. The smells of wet sand, rust, and hot concrete washed by rain surrounded him.

Celwen had somehow managed to stay on her feet. She skidded to a stop at the base of the ramp.

The forest of cages rose up ahead, covered in gloom that deepened to pitch blackness under the unfinished slabs.

"I can't see a thing in there," said Teg.

Celwen offered her hand. "I can."

Angry voices shouted from behind the fence. Teg grabbed hold of Celwen's hand. She helped him regain his feet and led him into the dark maze of dripping metal.

The two of them ran straight ahead for some distance before Celwen veered off to the right. Teg could see nothing beyond arm's length. The way back was lost behind a wall of overlapping metal lattices and rainy darkness.

"Does this ride ever stop?" he asked.

"I see a hiding place close by," Celwen said in a harsh whisper. "Keep quiet until we reach it."

After a few more twists and turns, Celwen brought them to a halt. Teg saw a concrete ledge jutting out from the wall that looked to be flush with the ground, but closer inspection revealed it as the lip of an overhang mostly covering a shallow pit. The babble of running water echoed from below.

"Good eyes," said Teg. "I never would've seen this."

Celwen got down on her stomach and rolled under the ledge. "The Night Tribe has spent millennia in the outer darkness," she said softly. "We need little light to see. Are you coming, or will you wait up there to meet the spooks?"

Teg crouched down and felt along the floor under the lip. He soon found that it slanted downward in a moderately steep concrete-lined slope. Squeezing under the ledge took some effort, but once his legs cleared the rim he easily made the descent.

The area under the ledge was a long narrow dugout deep enough to stand in. Rain and thin light trickled in through a metal grate in the ceiling. Water ran through a channel in the center of the concrete floor and spilled down a circular drain.

Celwen sat against the far wall facing the entrance, hugging her black-clad knees to her chest as dark hair spilled down her shoulders. Her relatively lighter hands and face seemed to float inside a Gen-shaped shadow.

Teg slid down beside her, leaving a muddy streak on the wall. He hadn't smoked in years, but the old urge sometimes came upon him. Digging through his pockets yielded a pack of matches, one of which he stuck between his teeth. The soft wood tasted faintly of peat moss.

"The water should hide our voices, so let's talk."

"Did you have a subject in mind?"

"A couple," said Teg. "Questions, mostly."

Celwen turned her ashen face toward him. "Ask, then."

"Those blobs that looked like the spawn of a puffer fish and a bundle of power conduits—what were they?"

"Anomians," Celwen spat. "They sought freedom through transessence but lost their souls. Now, if they can be said to live at all, it is only to absorb the qualities of other essences."

Teg nodded. "Parasites. A bit extreme, but they've got kindred spirits everywhere. Sounds like you've dealt with them before."

"My people fled into the dark and found them there waiting. After centuries of fighting the Guild, we spent centuries more driving back the Anomian threat. Now our pact with Shaiel brings us into alliance with our ancient foe."

"Is that why you jumped ship?" asked Teg.

Celwen was silent for a long moment before she answered. "It was the final insult. There are other reasons. Even after we fight his war, I do not think Shaiel will let us live in peace."

"Trust me," said Teg. "That bastard won't let anyone live, period."

Celwen was about to speak, but Teg thought he heard a noise outside the dugout and hushed her.

He listened. There was only the gurgle of draining water and below that, the faint patter of rain on metal.

At length, Teg risked another question, but he spoke in a low whisper. "Can you find the men who were following us?"

Celwen seemed to look—not *at* the paved slope, but *through* it. After a minute or two she said, "No. It is as if they vanished. But they were right behind us when we went over the fence. They could not have left the range of my sight so quickly."

"What if they were dead?"

Celwen's frown was audible. "I was searching for men. A corpse is a different being."

"Do you know the way to my ship?" asked Teg.

"I know where to find the gate that leads to your ship."

Teg stood. "That'll have to do. We need to head for the gate. You're on point. Ready?"

"Wait," said Celwen. She rose and clutched his arm. "I answered you; now answer me. What danger do we face?"

"I'm not a hundred percent sure," said Teg, "but I think it's a guy named Izlaril. He's Shaiel's Blade."

Fear and anger mingled on Celwen's face. "The Blade is wielded by Shaiel's Left Hand, Lykaon. If the weapon is anything like the wielder, we face a foe as deadly as he is hateful."

"Sounds about right. Can you get a fix on him?"

Celwen's eyes took on their eerie thousand-yard stare. Her brow furrowed.

"Did you see anything?' asked Teg.

She faced him. "I thought I did, but something distorted my nexic vision—like water bending light."

"He does that, too." Teg removed the matchstick from his mouth. "We can't see him, but he'll have a hard time seeing us in the dark."

"Unless his eyes are accustomed to it, like mine," Celwen said.

Teg conceded with a grunt. Izlaril's makers had bred him with a grab bag of weird, lethal tricks. Why couldn't seeing in the dark be one of them?

"There are two possibilities if we go out there," he said. "Either Shaiel's Blade finds us, or we make it to the gate free and clear."

Celwen nodded.

"Staying here also has two outcomes," Teg went on. "The backup spooks that are already on their way find us, or Izlaril does. Either one is pretty much certain if we wait till morning."

"Then let us go out there." Celwen turned and started up the slope.

"Decisive," Teg said as he climbed after her. "I like it."

Back in the cage forest, Teg kept Celwen from dashing ahead. He pressed a finger to his lips, and she nodded her assent.

The two of them crept along, led by Celwen's acute natural and nexic sight. Now and then some sound of stone or metal rising above the rainfall gave her a start, but Teg nudged her to go on. If Izlaril was stalking them, they wouldn't know it till he struck.

Teg tried to draw a mental map of the rambling path Celwen led him on, but he lost track in the damp steel labyrinth. The Gen ship's false lightning played across the tops of dark clouds far above.

Celwen spun and tackled Teg to the ground behind a metal cage. Something hit the bars with a resounding clang, striking sparks at what had been the level of their necks.

Teg picked Celwen up and ran.

Walls of metal bars loomed out of the dark, and Teg veered around them at random. More than once he skidded on the slick concrete and banged into a steel cage. The pain was nothing compared to the dread of knowing that each jangling impact would lead his enemy closer.

At last, Celwen squirmed out of Teg's arms and took his hand, pulling him back along the way they'd come and slightly to the right.

A couple of turns later, the path ahead vanished into total

blackness. Teg looked up and saw the leading edge of a concrete slab—the cutaway floor of the mid-basement level above. Celwen led him into the building's lowest depths, and blindness covered him like a shroud.

They turned one corner; then another, the sound of rain fading as their rapid breath echoed from close concrete walls. Celwen slowed and finally came to a stop.

Teg heard her slide down against a wall and sit back, panting. He followed suit. Running a hand over his wet head, he disentangled a broken chain segment from his hair.

So that's *what the bastard threw at us.*

"We shouldn't stick around here too long," he said when the burning in his lungs subsided.

"I cannot..." Celwen began, her breath still heaving. "I cannot see well enough to guide our way."

Teg's heart sank. He'd planned to circle around and sneak out of the maze, hopefully losing Izlaril in the process. He even had an idea of how to do it.

A lot of buildings on this part of the Strand were connected by old service tunnels. The men who'd turned a dockside fish market into a thriving hub of tourism had dug them to transport money from the gambling houses, bring women to entertainers in the hotels, and move contraband everywhere—leaving the tourists and the local authorities none the wiser.

Teg was pretty sure that a little searching would turn up an entrance to one of the old tunnels. From there they could get into a hotel. Though not impregnable, a VIP suite was far more defensible than a hole in the ground—especially if he could get in touch with Astlin.

The thought raised troubling questions. Why hadn't Astlin contacted him since she'd ditched him in the swamp? Where was she now? Was she in trouble?

"You felt it when I translated into the marsh," Teg said to Celwen. "Can you feel other nexists, too?"

"Not nexists; uses and concentrations of nexic power." Celwen's breathing had almost returned to normal. "The more nexism is used, the easier it is to detect. For example, I can sense the shield surrounding this sphere at all times, even though it is in orbit."

"Is that how you knew to hit the deck?"

"I was on guard against our enemy," Celwen said. "I acted on reflex when something warped my vision again."

"Good thing you did," said Teg. "Do you sense anything odd around us now?"

"No, but that is not a guarantee of safety."

"Nothing is." Teg stood and fished another match from his pocket. With the lack of fear that comes from a lack of choices, he struck the match head against the wall.

Celwen gasped as the orange-yellow flame's flickering glow pushed back the darkness. Even such a tiny light hurt Teg's eyes at first, and he squinted until his vision adjusted.

"What have you done?" Celwen hissed. "You will surely attract our enemy!"

"Yeah," said Teg. "We can't run from him, so when he gets here I'll kill him."

"Are you sure that you can?"

Teg held her in a piercing stare. His voice became somber. "I've run the ether from Keth to Crote, hell to Mithgar, and I've seen every law broken but one—anybody can kill anybody else."

The flame guttered and went out. A warm sulfur smell not unlike spent gunpowder filled Teg's nostrils. He lit another match and, facing in the opposite direction, saw what looked like a pillar half-hidden around a corner.

Teg strode toward the cylindrical object, which did in fact turn out to be a pillar carved from black marble veined with white.

Celwen ran up behind him. "Why did you leave me in the dark all alone?"

"This shouldn't be here." Teg held the match toward the pillar, which was fashioned in a style that he recognized from Stranosi ruins on Mithgar.

Immediately to the left of the pillar was a narrow section of dark grey stone that might have been basalt. This structure turned out to be a jamb framing a door made from wood so white that Teg was sure it had been painted until he ran his fingers across it and felt the bare grain.

The white door turned out to be half of a set of double doors, its mate having been carved from a glossy wood darker than ebony. The black door was also flanked by a basalt jamb and a second pillar of white marble with black veins.

Teg lit a fresh match and bent to study the intricate carvings that covered the doors. The stern, half black and half white face of a man glowered where both sections met. He didn't recognize the image, but a nagging feeling told him that he should. Twelve panels, six on each door, surrounded the face.

One panel featured a youth—the relief was detailed enough to show that he was a Gen—standing amid a besieged port. The only unrealistic element was a sun, many times larger than normal, filling the center of the sky. An arm was reaching down from the sun to hand the young Gen a bow. Though it appeared on the white door, the bow was jet black.

On another panel farther down, a regal man whose scholarly face fit the thick book in his hand descended from what looked like a giant opal lozenge. Teg would have thought it was an ether-runner if the scholar's breastplate and the even more primitive dress of the awestruck crowd below him didn't predate the dawn of ether travel.

Those barbarians look like ancient Kethans…

A panel on the black door drew Teg's eye. His heart pounded when he saw the image of a huge rat. It stood upright like a man, raising its clawed hands to a flame rising from the floor of what looked like a crumbling tomb. Teg recognized the rat-thing. He also recognized its posture from his long dead mother's illegal prayer meetings.

The rat was calling to something monstrous in the fire—something that answered.

Celwen's shriek from the darkness to Teg's left warned him that she'd wandered off. His match went out as he rushed toward the cry's point of origin, so it wasn't until he lit a new one that he saw the body.

Celwen was still as a rock. She stood looking down at a man in a dark blue suit who sat slumped against the wall. His skin was more ashen than hers, and his head lolled at an odd angle.

"One of the spooks who was tailing us," said Teg. "Looks like Izlaril found him first."

Celwen let out a ragged breath and bolted into the dark.

Teg heard a door bang open. He hurried toward the noise, taking care not to let the match go out, and saw the nearer door—the black one—standing open.

"That's not how this works," he called into the darkness beyond the door. "You really need to check before barging in."

Teg considered subjecting both doors to the Formula's full scrutiny, but with a stealth killing machine on the loose and his sole ally lost in an abandoned tunnel under enemy territory—though he wasn't sure they were even on Temil anymore—Teg said "Screw it," threw both doors wide open, and marched straight through the middle.

19

The air on the other side was dry, cold, and uncomfortably still. The loudest sound was Teg's own breathing.

In the dim light he saw a square hallway running out of sight to his right and left. The walls weren't concrete but some kind of dark brown stone. As far as he could see the walls, floor, and ceiling were one continuous piece. That meant he was in a tunnel dug through solid rock, though there were no visible tool marks.

There was no telling how far the tunnel went or where either branch led, so Teg stood in place just past the threshold. Listening carefully, he heard the faint sound of breathing down the hall to his right.

Teg snuffed the match. The resulting darkness smothered his sight like a black velvet blindfold. Good. He couldn't see in total darkness, but neither could anyone else. He snuck down the tunnel with one hand pressed to the rough stone wall, guided by the rhythmic whisper of soft breathing.

The deep, steady breaths grew louder until they suddenly rose to a frightened gasp. Teg heard panicked movements in the dark.

"It's me," he said. "Calm down."

"Show me," said a voice that was probably Celwen's.

Teg rummaged in his pocket for another match—the second to last—and struck it against the stone. After walking in utter darkness, the pea-sized flame seemed impossibly bright.

Celwen sat curled up against the wall on his right. Her grey face and green eyes held a mixture of relief, fear, and shame.

"I ran," she said.

"Yeah, I noticed."

"I do not know why."

"You panicked," said Teg. "It happens under stress. I've known seasoned pros who kept their cool through day-long firefights; then snapped when somebody dropped a mess tray back at camp. No shame in it."

"Teg, what are you really after?"

"I told you. They stole my ship." At length, Teg sighed. "They also kidnapped the husband of an old friend—I guess sticking my neck out like this makes him my friend, too."

He offered Celwen his free hand. "Two necks are better than one."

Celwen studied his dirty callused hand before taking it in her soft slender grip. Teg pulled her up and set her on her feet.

"Which way now?" she asked.

"You're the one who said there's a gate leading to my ship. I take it that was the door?"

"Yes," Celwen said. "We left Temil when we passed through."

Teg glanced around the bare tunnel. "Any clue where we are?"

"If I had to guess, I would say that this is the Stone Stratum."

She was probably right, which Teg didn't find comforting. What little he knew of the Stone Stratum came from tales of mining companies a hundred men strong vanishing without a trace between weekly supply runs.

The whole place was supposedly an infinite mass of solid rock, except for manmade tunnels like this one. Visitors from the Middle Stratum had been digging around the Stone Stratum in search of precious minerals for ages, and there were stories of strange tunnels dug by visitors from elsewhere. He'd have bet real money back in Vigh that this tunnel was one of the latter.

Teg recalled that this was the last Stratum before the Void. He wondered how close he was to hell, and shivered.

"I don't suppose your nexism could scout out where the tunnel leads?"

Celwen's face conveyed deep concentration. Silence fell, and it was more than a minute before she cried out, her eyes wide.

"Come on," she said, gesturing urgently down the hall to the right. "Quickly!"

She and Teg were still holding hands, so he managed to rein her in.

"Panic is understandable," he said. "Rashness is plain stupid. Some of these tunnel systems run for hundreds of miles."

"This hallway leads to a large chamber about a quarter of a mile straight ahead," Celwen assured him. "It is lighted, and people are there. At least, one of them is a person. He may be two."

"Can you repeat what you just said in a way that makes sense?"

"No time!" Celwen broke into a run, nearly pulling Teg off

his feet. He caught his balance with an effort and ran with her.

The small fire died, bringing a total, oppressive blackout. But after a while Teg saw a somewhat lighter patch amid the absolute darkness.

At first he thought his starving eyes were playing tricks on him, but the slightly less dark patch slowly brightened to charcoal; then gradually lighter shades of grey, and finally resolved into a silver rectangle standing amid the black.

This welcome sight was soon joined by other sensations. Mechanical sounds echoed down the hall. Closer to the archway—which the silver rectangle turned out to be—Teg smelled the sharp scent of ether.

Teg signaled a halt by stretching his arm out in front of Celwen. She stopped, and he positioned himself in front of her, facing the light source. Then he drew his gun, checked to make sure all six chambers were loaded, and crept toward the open arch with his back pressed to the tunnel wall.

Whatever he'd been expecting, the sight waiting for him on the other side wasn't it. Teg stepped through the square arch and onto a metal platform anchored to the wall of a gigantic shaft.

Work lights fixed to the railing revealed the pit to be a hundred feet across, easy. The silver lamplight gave out before reaching a ceiling above or a floor below.

Teg fought the sudden urge to throw his last match into the hole. Reason prevailed. The damn thing might actually be infinite.

The industrial sounds were coming from an open archway directly across the shaft. A platform on the opposite side had its own work lights, plus an extendable bridge of metal struts and grills that was inconveniently retracted.

Teg motioned for Celwen to join him on the platform.

She sighed. "There is no way across."

"Yeah there is." All that stood between Teg and the abyss was an aluminum railing that he now climbed over. His heels landed on a narrow metal lip, and he cringed at the echo that redounded from the four sheer walls. The machine noises from the other side continued uninterrupted.

Celwen gripped the railing. "You cannot mean to climb across!"

"I've climbed worse. At least it's not snowing."

Sweat moistened Teg's palms as he felt the cool rock face. Finding a pair of likely handholds, he tightened his grip and swung his legs out over the pit. His right foot slipped off a small crease in the stone. His stomach lurched in anticipation of a fall, but his left foot found enough purchase to let him regain his footing.

Teg glanced at Celwen, who stood on the platform covering her mouth with her hand, eyes wide.

"This might be harder than I thought," he said between rapid breaths.

"What if we are discovered?" Celwen asked. "I am completely exposed here."

Teg nodded toward the wall. "You're welcome to join me."

She shook her head. "What if you fall?"

"Then just do whatever you want. It won't matter, anyway."

Teg inched along the wall. He realized with a sickening feeling that he was more out of practice than he'd thought. Less than halfway to the side wall, his fingers were already numb; his hands cramping.

But Celwen was right. Getting caught here meant certain death for both of them.

Teg pushed his burning muscles onward, counting on his unnaturally quick healing to cover the cost of overexerting himself.

Mostly to take his mind off the pain, but partly in the hope of an answer, Teg silently prayed.

You got me this far, he reminded Elena. *Anyway, I'm pretty sure it was you. Get me through this—get all of us through this—and I'll set you up like the old gods. Temples, worshipers, tax exemption; the works.*

The promise had come to Teg out of desperation. But the more he thought about it, the more right it seemed. The Guild had pulled down all the temples and banned the ancient faiths— and perhaps the old gods had earned it by deserting the world. But the Guild's failure to give people something else to believe in had clearly been a mistake.

Teg reached the right angle where the first and second walls met. A visual search turned up new hand and footholds, letting him traverse the corner. His infernal healing ability kept his body in equilibrium, so while the burning ache never went away, it didn't get any worse either.

Teg's spirits were actually rising until he came to the limit of the lights' range. A long stretch of sheer stone bathed in total darkness stood between him and the vertical pool of light cast from the far platform.

The lightless section spanned the middle third of the wall. Continuing on would mean going by feel alone.

With no other options, Teg eased his throbbing hand into

the shadows. His fingers met only smooth stone.

A moment's frantic thought reminded Teg of the short sword strapped to his left leg. He carefully released the blade from its bindings and drew it. Transferring the weapon to his right hand was a harrowing but ultimately successful exercise.

Using the blade to extend his reach, Teg found his next handhold. He slid the blade into his belt and blindly stretched his arm toward the narrow crevice in the stone. His left hand slid into the right's former position, and his aching arms bore his full weight while his feet probed the wall for support.

After several repetitions of this grueling process, Teg still hadn't escaped the darkness. He sucked in a couple of deep breaths to calm his nerves and reached out with the sword again.

This time the blade found no handhold. His anxiety rising to panic, he stretched his right arm till he feared it would pop out of its socket. The sword still scraped against bare stone.

Teg's left hand slipped. It reflexively sought a new handhold, but his sweaty fingers couldn't get traction. The half inch-wide ledge below couldn't support all his weight, and his feet shot out from under him.

The next instant of terrible weightlessness stretched into absurdity. Teg recalled his Mithgarder climbing instructor's stern warning that arresting a fall from a vertical surface was next to impossible.

His reflexes took charge again, making his arms and legs scrabble against the pitiless wall as he fell. In an act of final desperation Teg gripped the sword's hilt in both hands and stabbed the rock with strength amplified by mortal terror.

The blade sank into the stone. Teg's downward motion

ceased with a jarring suddenness that sent an agonized jolt through his upper body and scattered pebbles into the abyss. The sword bowed. It took all the strength of his arms and will to hold on.

"Teg!" Celwen cried. His name reverberated from the walls.

"Still here," grunted Teg. "Please shut up."

Teg's mind raced. He'd fallen even farther from the light, and now his best means of finding handholds was stuck in the wall.

There was only one way he knew he could climb—up.

Teg dangled from the sword hilt until the hellish pain in his shoulders had subsided to a burning ache. Then he let go with his left hand and carefully felt for a handhold, which he thankfully found.

Now came the risky part. Teg jammed his right hand into another fissure in the stone and hauled himself up. The sword still jutted from the rock below him, and he gingerly set first one foot; then another on its hilt.

Confident that the bending sword wouldn't break, Teg ran his hands over the wall above him until he found more secure handholds. He ascended, leaving the weapon that had saved his life.

Teg didn't know how long he'd climbed before the fear that had fueled his ascent wore off and he paused for a breather, but looking at the next wall showed him that he was level with the door again. The platform was tantalizingly close.

Seeing the retracted bridge and the lever that extended it gave Teg an idea. It was undoubtedly stupid, but it was his only way forward.

Teg continued up the wall until the stone became too smooth

to climb. He looked down at the bridge controls twenty feet down and perhaps twice that distance to his right.

The lever stood up from a metal box attached to the railing. It was thin, and he might miss. It might've had a hidden catch that locked it in place.

Teg ignored these disastrous possibilities, drew Scrope's knife, and threw.

For one gut-wrenching moment it looked as though Teg had aimed too high, but the knife struck the top of its target with the ring of steel on steel.

The lever moved a fraction of an inch and the knife clattered to the platform.

Resisting the urge to curse out loud demanded all of Teg's self-control. He took a few more deep breaths and thought again.

One idea kept popping into Teg's mind, and he forced it back down each time it surfaced. But the jagged crevices to which he clung bit into his fingers. His hands were slick with perspiration. He only had one more shot.

Actually, if he went through with this he'd have no more shots. But he would have a slim chance of living.

Teg pulled the gun from his pocket—but not to fire it, which would alert everyone for miles and probably jar him from his perch. Unloading the cylinder with one cramped hand, he tried to preserve the ammo. But four of the six cartridges fell through his fingers and into the pit. He never heard any impacts.

After stuffing the last two shells in his pocket, Teg flipped the cylinder back into place. A pang of shame assaulted him as he drew back his arm, took aim, and threw away his last weapon.

Teg's remorse turned to giddy relief when the gun banged

into the lever, throwing it flat against the box. His relief became dismay when the revolver bounced off the railing and joined the lost bullets in the endless depths of the shaft.

A low-pitched hum and regular metallic clanking announced the bridge's deployment.

Its painfully slow deployment.

Teg's grip was about to give out when the leading bridge segment reached the space perpendicular to and below him. He was already slipping when he let go, dug his feet into the rock, and sprang from the wall.

He would have backflipped into the hole, but a last second twist brought him around.

The bridge was too far away.

Without thinking, Teg yanked the belt from his waist and flailed at the bridge. The narrow metal gangplank had no railing, but there were hooks along the side to secure the bridge in place when it retracted.

The belt buckle latched onto a metal hook, and Teg swung beneath the extending span. His stomach turned somersaults as he pendulumed back toward the wall. He swung back just short of impact to dangle off the side of the bridge.

Hauling himself up took the last of Teg's strength. He lay on the extending bridge, letting the perforated metal dig into his back, until it carried him to the entrance platform where Celwen stood waiting.

Teg looked up at her. "Told you there's a way across."

"I can see that, yes." Her voice was flat, but Celwen's face betrayed her horror and relief.

He let her help him to his feet. After another moment's rest,

Teg put his belt back on and started across the bridge.

"You nearly died!" Celwen said. "Why rush back toward danger?"

Teg didn't look back. "Because I nearly died."

Celwen hurried after him. By the time he reached the other side his footsteps were sure and his pain was gone, replaced with renewed purpose. The knife was lying on the platform, and Teg retrieved it, taking care not to let his only weapon slip through the grate.

20

The arch leading off the platform gave on a square chamber about thirty feet across. Carved from the same dark stone as the rest of the tunnel system, it had a sunken floor that descended in three steps. The walls were carved, but with simple recessed panels nowhere near as complex as the black and white doors' reliefs.

Teg examined the open archway as thoroughly as he could. Nothing out of the ordinary, except for the uniform light in the room beyond that seemed to shine from nowhere.

"Wait here a second," Teg told Celwen. He stepped through the arch, knife in hand, and descended into the room. The steady thrum of heavy machinery emanating through the far door was as loud as a powerplant turbine. The sharp scent of ether, which Teg had noticed out in the hallway, was strong enough to sting his nose.

Do they have a ship's engine room down here?

A blow to the head set off bursts of red pain behind Teg's eyes and sent him reeling. Before he could recover something slammed into his stomach and drove the air from his lungs.

Habits learned by painful repetition moved Teg's back against the right wall. Gasping for air, he brought his arms up in a fighting stance and cast about for his attacker.

Besides Teg himself and a fading trace of ether, the room was empty.

Izlaril? he wondered, feeling a surge of fear for himself and Celwen.

As if in answer to his silent question, a fist hammered Teg's right kidney. He cried out and fell forward onto his hands and knees. Darting a quick glance behind him, he saw only a seamless wall. Shaiel's Blade was crafty, but to Teg's knowledge not even Izlaril could attack through solid stone.

Another whiff of ether, this time accompanied by a blur of motion to his left, gave Teg enough warning to brace himself. The kick would have shattered his ribs but merely cracked them instead. He rolled to the right and felt a blow from an entirely new direction pass over the back of his head.

There's more than one of them!

Teg sprang to his feet, wincing as his skull and ribs reknit themselves. This time he kept moving in a complex dance meant to maximize his awareness while minimizing his vulnerability.

Not that it would do much good if he was really fighting ghosts.

"There are two of them," Celwen shouted from the entrance. "In the ether!"

Teg turned to face Celwen right as a man-shaped haze appeared and punched her across the face. She fell to the platform.

Teg lunged at the rose-tinted apparition, which looked like a man dressed in short wool robes with his head wrapped in linen.

But the image faded and Teg struck empty air.

Correction—air mixed with a touch of ether.

Based on Teg's experience and Celwen's words, the guardians hid in the ether and emerged just long enough to make hit-and-run attacks on trespassers.

And they can see between dimensions like she can.

Out of the corner of his eye Teg caught a blur coinciding with a powerful kick that swept his right leg out from under him. While he struggled to regain his balance, a savage punch to the face sent him backpedaling with blood streaming from a cut above his left eye.

The pain focused Teg's mind. In search of a plan, he looked to the entry and exit arches but decided against making a run for it. There was no guarantee that the ethereal guardians couldn't follow, and he cringed at the thought of fighting them on a narrow bridge over an endless drop.

Teg caught another whiff of ether and ducked under another blow aimed at his head. This time he saw his opponent clearly. Besides his monkish robes, the guardian's bound head was encircled by a mirrored band. Similar plates reinforced his gauntlets. Teg's reflection in the pale metal was a lavender shadow.

Ether metal. Probably Worked to pierce the veil between Strata.

Time for a little test. When he smelled ether again a moment later, Teg flourished the knife; not intending to wound, but only to make contact. His experiment met with success when the blade rebounded from his foe's armored glove.

Teg backed his way up the steps to stand inside the entrance.

He wasn't counting on the arch to give him any cover; just a quick escape.

Shoving his right hand into his pants pocket, Teg released the knife and fished around until his fingers touched the slim wooden shaft of his last matchstick.

The guardians' attacks indicated that one took point to lower an opponent's defenses while the other waited nearby to exploit the opening. Teg counted on them sticking to the same pattern, and on the first attack coming through the stone on his right.

Teg struck at the first hint of ether. True to form, a blurry gauntleted fist emerged from the arch's right side. Teg grabbed his attacker by the wrist and struck the match on the armored glove. The trace of ether in the air made the tiny flame blaze to twice its normal size.

Teg flicked the match onto the guardian's woolen sleeve. He didn't wait to see what happened next.

Falling prone onto the bridge didn't save Teg's back from the flames that shot through the arch, but he fared better than the two men whose screams rose above the roar of the blast furnace he'd made of the chamber.

Teg jumped to his feet as the screams drew closer. A pair of flame-wreathed figures; now fully materialized, judging by the smell of singed hair and burned meat, fled the inferno. They charged onto the bridge, threatening to run him down in their agony.

Instead of running, Teg sprang toward them and delivered a fierce kick that pushed the first flaming guardian into the one behind him. Both men lost their footing and toppled shrieking into the abyss like stars falling in the night.

Teg paused to stamp out his pants leg, which had caught fire from the guardian's burning robe, before moving back toward the chamber. Ether fires burned out fast. There was no sign that a raging blaze had just swept through the room except for faint smoke reeking of charred wool and flesh.

Celwen lay on the platform with her feet near the arch. Her dark hair was splayed across her back like a cloak. Her strange clinging suit seemed to have spared her legs from the fire, and besides an ugly bruise under her left eye, she seemed unhurt.

Normally Teg wouldn't have moved someone who'd been knocked unconscious in a fistfight. But leaving Celwen asleep on a small platform that clung to the wall of an infinitely deep shaft seemed like an even worse idea.

It was a good thing she didn't weight much. Carrying her into the smoky chamber only evoked slight protests from Teg's still mending muscles. The room's hidden light source must have been destroyed in the fire, because it was pitch black except for small pools of light at the entrance and exit arches.

Teg carried Celwen to the middle of the chamber and laid her on the steps running the length of the room. The dark gave her a little extra cover, and she could still see there, anyway.

With Celwen resting as comfortably as possible, Teg returned to the platform. It evoked recent memories that made his whole body ache, but retracting the bridge would foil most pursuit.

Teg raised the lever on the control box, and the segmented span whirred as it withdrew from the opposite side. He made sure the bridge locked into place. Then he stepped back through the arch, paused just long enough to hear Celwen's soft regular breathing, and crossed the darkened room.

215

21

The exit arch gave on an irregular space larger than the antechamber but cluttered with equipment. Metal plates inset with tracks partially covered the stone floor. Cables ran in parallel bundles along the tops of the walls out of a dark passage where unseen engines hummed. The cold air tasted of rust.

Teg saw no obvious hazards from the archway. He crept forward, taking care to walk on stone and not metal. Floodlights attached to the ceiling cast uneven cones of illumination. Randomly placed rock pillars rose to support the ceiling, and he took advantage of the concealment they offered.

A flurry of motion and a sound like someone dumping ball bearings onto the metal floor prompted Teg to duck behind a pillar. Pressing his burned back to the cold rock, he peered around the side to see the cause of the disturbance.

Two clusters of equipment stood along the far curve of a circular metal platform that all of the tracks and cables ran to. A shape—or a mass of shapes—flowed back and forth between machines with motions resembling a school of dark glossy fish.

The metal mass collected itself near the bank of hardware on the left. It bent over a long clear box that looked like a coffin filled with white light. The shadow of a hand resting against the inside of the box was the only sign that it was occupied.

Teg had no idea what the moving cluster of metal was, or whether it was hostile, friendly, or even intelligent at all. The best way to find out would be to move in for a closer look.

Stooping as low as he could, Teg emerged from hiding and stalked closer to the left cluster of machines. He carefully stepped around the conduits that snaked along the floor. The act recalled an old memory that made him smile despite himself.

A minecart stood against the platform, resting on its track. Crouching down behind it, Teg touched the side of the cart but reflexively withdrew his hand when he found the metal as cold as flagpole in winter.

The cart was filled with chunks of rock blacker than coal. Light only shone on half of the bin, and the rocks immersed in shadow gave off a faint blue glow.

Teg raised his eyes above the cart's rim for a look at the platform. The metal mass hovering next to the glowing box shifted toward a machine on its left, and Teg saw a hideous face come into view. Jaundiced and gaunt, the thing looked like the personification of famine from one of his mother's books.

Bony plates where lips should have been parted in a skull-like grin, and the face sank into the mass of what Teg now saw were thousands of small gears, surfacing on the other side a moment later.

Teg still didn't know what the creature was, but it felt strangely familiar. He watched transfixed as the main mass sprouted an array of tendrils made of gears that grew into complex tools.

One tentacle formed a clamp that held an egg-sized piece of the black rock. Another gear tendril opened a valve on a ceramic tank with a thick black hose running from it. Meanwhile, a third pseudopod deftly operated the hose head to release a single drop of liquid onto the stone. A sour odor stung Teg's nose as the droplet sizzled away, leaving the rock pristine.

The hose moved to a glass dish holding a few ounces of raw meat. The milky fluid poured in, dissolving the chunk of flesh like hot water poured on snow. The stench was incredible.

Teg knew that compound. It was a synthetic version of a chemical secreted by a rare species of snail. The Bifron shipwrights had used the stuff in the construction of the *Exodus*. He'd only seen one substance that was more corrosive.

Teg's reminiscing was interrupted by a green-white light that suddenly blazed beyond the platform and a hum that rose above the machine sounds. He blinked to clear his vision and raised his head.

The light bathed the far passage, and two men strode out. One had short brown hair crowning a long face and a scrawny body robed in red silk as dark as Stranosi wine. The other wore sky blue robes and was bald except for an iron grey fringe of hair and a tidy beard.

Silk slippers whispered on steel as the men advanced along the walkway. Though their faces differed greatly, both had a look that Teg had come to loathe on flag officers from his navy days.

The silk-shod princes stepped onto the platform and faced the gear creature, their expressions impatient. It kept working, indifferent to their presence until the blue-robed dignitary spoke in a Mithgar accent that Teg had only heard from actors in historical dramas.

"Take heed, Smith. It is a poor guest who slights his patrons and protectors."

The many arms continued their work while the sallow face slid toward the robed men.

"Speak, Magists."

"Vilneus and I bring you a warning," said the blue-robed Magist. "Enemies walk within our walls. They have slain our agents and sentries."

Smith chuckled. "Tell me why I should care."

"Both intruders pose a serious threat." The Magist swept his blue-sleeved arm toward the passage where the green light had gone out. "In accord with our brothers, we have deemed it wise to provide you with more secure accommodations."

Smith's metal claw rummaged through strange instruments cluttering a steel table and came up with a rod made of polished lavender crystal. He pointed it at the shadowy figure in the box.

"Forget it. My work is at a crucial juncture!"

The bald, blue-robed Magist folded his arms. "All the more reason to safeguard what you have thus far accomplished. Much is at stake."

A metallic grunt escaped Smith's beak. "Merging a Stratum with a living soul via transessence and nexism is well-documented. However, the subject poses a number of obstacles, primarily his status as the projection of a soul that transcends our cosmos, and whose material proxy is infested by a native deity."

Teg had almost forgotten about the Magist in the wine-colored robe. Now he noticed a distant look on Vilneus' long face that he'd seen before on Celwen's.

Thanks to another associate—the late Deim Cursorunda—

Teg recognized Vilneus' intricate hand motions as the start of a Working.

Uh-oh. They saw me.

Diving backwards as far as his legs could push him didn't get Teg out of the blast radius when the mine cart exploded. Lying on the hard stone, he felt his ears pop, his guts shudder, and his bones rattle as a spray of ice cold gravel bit into his back.

It took a moment for Teg's hearing to return. When it did, the first thing he heard was his own agonized groaning. The second was Smith and the Magists bickering.

"...could have damaged the prana tank!" Screeched Smith.

"I shaped the blast to avoid anything vital, of course," someone—probably Vilneus—said in a slightly less archaic Mithgar accent. "Besides, Rathimus and I were in mental contact. He erected the proper defenses before I loosed the Working."

With an effort Teg rolled over onto his back and winced as icy stone fragments sank deeper into his flesh. Black gravel mixed with twisted shards of the mine cart littered the floor around him. Up on the platform, Smith jabbed a claw at Vilneus.

"Keep being so rash, and you'll learn the limits of your defenses. Don't presume to know how the subject will respond if containment is breached!"

"Lord Shaiel will swiftly punish those who dare to confine his host," a deep airy voice spoke from the direction of the prana tank.

Teg's eyes darted toward the glowing box and saw what looked like a man-sized patch of warped space, except for a thin diagonal line dotted with puckered wounds on its side.

"Izlaril," he grumbled.

Rending noises and electrical crackling echoed across the room as the white light inside the box went out. A severed power cable seemed to hang in midair, shedding a few final sparks that danced like fireflies.

The tank filled with sickly golden light. Gears rippled as Smith scuttled to the other side of the platform. His wide eyes with their cog-shaped irises stared from his corpselike face.

"Destroy it!" he screamed.

Rathimus threw his blue-sleeved arms forward, and the tank hurtled across the room to land upright against a stone pillar. A split second later Vilneus loosed a Working that shattered the box and the pillar behind it, causing a cave-in that buried a quarter of the room under tons of broken rock. Mortal terror overcame Teg's pain, and he narrowly rolled clear of the cave-in.

Up on the platform, both Magists hurried through the motions of fashioning while Smith's self-assembling tendrils ransacked the table. At last he found what he was after and held it to his greedy eye.

Teg recognized the large, many-faceted ruby in Smith's grasp. A wave of revulsion dredged up unpleasant memories.

I've seen that gem before.

A rose-colored flash drew Teg's attention back to the Magists, who'd raised their arms as if shielding themselves from a fire.

"The ether is disturbed," Vilneus told Smith. "Quickly! Abandon your work and flee through the gate."

The Magists turned to run, but Izlaril's unsightly naked form appeared at the head of the walkway, cutting them off.

"Why would you flee from justice?" he asked, sounding genuinely baffled.

Vilneus thrust his hand toward Shaiel's Blade in the accusing gesture that Factors used to release Workings. Izlaril's arm blurred, and Vilneus' seemed to vanish from the elbow down. The Magist didn't scream until a moment after his amputated limb hit the steel plate with a limp slap. The severed end was blackened as if it had been cauterized.

No, Teg corrected himself. *Frostbitten.*

Izlaril stood rooted in place, his charred hand holding a dagger-like plane of black rock. The Magist's blood blackened and flaked on its rough edge.

Rathimus gathered up his sky blue robes and bolted.

"Open the way to Kairos!" he begged Smith, who hadn't moved from the table. "Shaiel's minions will not harm his kin. Grant me sanctuary within your soul."

Smith's cadaverous face swiveled to leer at him. "Make it worth my while."

Rathimus cast a harried look at his fellow Magist, who'd fallen to his knees, clutching his stump and wailing. He turned back to Smith and licked his lips.

"I know the nine forbidden Mysteries, where the prison of the Nahash lies, and how to open it. I know the lost oracles of the Burned Book and how to trade the fate of man for life everlasting."

Smith sneered. "Do I look like a man to you? Not even forged ether can cut my life cord."

"Not so!" Rathimus said, almost giddily. "One blade can sunder your tie to the Nexus. You know its name. Admit me to the intersection of all times, and I will deliver it into your hands."

Smith's eyes narrowed, but his face rose above the Magist's

head as his body formed itself into a rectangular frame. Through the gate Teg could see an endless expanse of clockwork towers as large as cities divided by deep canyons.

Rathimus spared a final glance at Izlaril. Shaiel's Blade didn't even shift his weight as the Magist darted toward Smith's portal.

The mountains and valleys of gears vanished. Now the frame gave on a vast plain under black skies with only a line of sickly golden light to mark the horizon. Cold that Teg had only felt once poured through the gate, and the rock fragments burned like dry ice under his skin.

Xander appeared in the gateway, his face still hidden behind Vaun's emotionless white mask. He threw his cloth-wrapped arms wide as he exited the gate, and the frame shattered in a golden flash. Frozen gears clattered to the floor like hailstones on a tin roof.

The blank white face regarded the sallow corpselike one that soundlessly worked its bony beak amid a pile of gears on the ground.

"Kairos belongs to Zadok, my willful brother," Xander said in a voice colder than the stone chips embedded in Teg's flesh. "He does not treat gently with trespassers. You are fortunate that the *vas* in your possession allowed me to preempt your crime."

Rathimus' eyes darted back and forth over the platform. They soon fixed themselves on something lying among the scattered gears, and in an instant the ruby was flying toward his outstretched hand.

At a slight motion of Xander's forefinger, a torrent of gears, metal shards, and stone fragments swirled into the air. Rathimus' scream cut off as the rasping torrent scoured away his flesh, bones, and fine robes, leaving only a pair of feet clad in silk slippers.

The ruby floated serenely in midair, new facets catching the light as it turned. It might have been his ears healing from the blast, but Teg thought he heard distant screams coming from the gem.

Xander strode forward and plucked the ruby from the air. The crystal rod flew from the ground into his outstretched left hand. He walked up behind Vilneus and paused.

"Do you remember me?" Vaun asked through Xander.

Vilneus only whimpered.

Xander stepped around to face the Magist. The impassive mask stared down at him.

"I wore another body when last we met—one that you warped and tortured. Worse, you marred my soul. It is only just that I deal with you in kind."

Seeing Xander point the crystal rod at him loosened Vilneus' tongue. The Magist said only one word, "No", over and over; rising in volume each time.

Teg couldn't tell if the rod had done anything, but Vilneus suddenly went quiet. Xander held the ruby out, and a streak of silver light shot into it from Vilneus' heart. A golden glow shone through his wine-colored robe.

The light spread from Vilneus' chest to his extremities, and he started folding in on himself with sharp cracking sounds like ice in the sun. He imploded with a final inhuman scream. The shivering ball of golden light that hovered over the spot where he'd been kneeling gave off a bone-numbing chill just like the portal Xander had stepped through, and Teg's pierced flesh ached.

"For a century I carried such a wound in my soul," said Vaun. "It would be just to let you suffer as long. But your flawed designs led to my ascent, so I grant you mercy."

Xander pressed the ruby to the forehead of Vaun's mask. There was a glint of blood red light, and when he released the gem it stayed in place on the white porcelain. With a wave of Xander's hand, the ball of yellow light died.

Teg was pretty sure that everyone had forgotten about him, so he cautiously rose onto one knee. His shredded flesh pained him, and the disturbing realization dawned that his wounds weren't healing.

Xander's free hand reached for Smith's face, toward which streams of gears ran like columns of dark metallic ants. The face flew to Xander, who took hold of the gear tendrils trailing behind it as he marched across the platform.

"I will obtain transportation for the three of us."

Izlaril stepped aside, clearing the way to the exit.

Xander paused beside the Blade. "Master Cross has outstayed his welcome, if not as long as the Shadow Caste. Tradition affords a god one chance to slay a mortal. I leave his execution to you."

Izlaril bowed. His master continued down the path to the gate where the Magists had entered.

It's nice to be remembered, Teg thought. He weighed his options and decided that following Xander was pointless with Izlaril in the way. So he stood on the debris-strewn ground and brandished his knife as Shaiel's Blade advanced on him, stone dagger in hand.

"Tell me where my ship is, get Vaun's mask off of my friend, and you can walk out of here," said Teg.

Izlaril actually grinned. "Your threats are empty."

"Mine? Possibly." Teg pointed at Xander's retreating back. "But that guy's wife would upend the Strata to get him back, and you do *not* want to piss her off!"

"The female Zadokim offered little resistance."

"She got distracted," said Teg. "Trust me. We wouldn't be talking if you'd had her full attention."

Izlaril veered off to the left, circling around Teg as he spoke. "Trust you? Like the Gen woman you led to her doom?"

Teg thought he felt the ground shift. He resisted the urge to look into the chamber where he'd left Celwen and focused on his foe.

"If you hurt her, not only will I give you *my* full attention, I'll get creative about it."

"No need," Izlaril said. "She opened Bifron's door—the black one—and entered. You passed through both."

"Bifron," said Teg. "I've been there. Not exactly a vacation spot."

Izlaril fell into an attack stance but kept circling. "Not the broken sphere; the god of prophecy who lent the sphere its name. Only a duly consecrated priest may open the doors of fate. Thank you both for opening the way; for discharging Bifron's curse and blessing."

"In case you didn't notice," said Teg, "Bifron's gone."

He lunged at Izlaril, jabbing at the man's ugly face with his left hand while slashing at his midsection with the knife in his right. Izlaril tilted his head just enough to avoid the feint and caught Teg's knife hand by the wrist.

Muscles squirmed strangely under the scarred skin of Izlaril's palm. He yanked on Teg's arm, pulling him into the thrust of his own black blade. Teg's left arm reflexively dropped to intercept the jagged rock shard. His left hand gripped Izlaril's right just below the improvised dagger's blade. Its rough edge cut into the web of skin between Teg's thumb and forefinger. Biting cold radiated through his hand.

"Tethite," Izlaril said in his irritatingly calm voice. "They mine it where the Stone Stratum touches the Void. It is death made solid. Even you cannot heal from its wounds."

The chill spread up Teg's arm and resonated with his mauled back. The cold sapped his strength, and Izlaril's tethite blade inched closer to his ribs.

Teg bent his left knee, pushed with his right leg, and threw all his weight into a controlled fall to the left. He used the remaining strength of his left hand to twist Izlaril's dagger toward the ground.

Striking the rock floor under the weight of two men snapped the stone blade—but not before it cut a deep gash in Teg's hand. He ignored its icy bite and angled his own knife to slice Izlaril's left forearm. His foe's grip relaxed enough for Teg to slip free. Releasing Izlaril's left hand, he rolled away across cold gears and gravel.

As soon as he felt that he'd gained enough distance, Teg leapt to his feet. He swept his eyes over the place where Izlaril had fallen and saw only a few drops of fresh blood on the stone floor.

Teg didn't waste time searching for Shaiel's Blade. Instead he turned and dashed back to the platform where the banks of machinery stood. Most of the equipment was ruined, but not all.

Smith's tools lay on the table amid a shambles of stone chips and dark oily gears.

Teg stood and waited, trying to slow his breathing as he shot wild glances about the room. Nothing stirred.

"Vaun told you to kill me." Teg's challenge echoed between the stone pillars. "Did you just stop kissing his ass?"

A slender tethite shard flew out of the shadows between two pillars and embedded itself where Teg's neck met his shoulder. A second shard only missed his head because the shock made Teg's knees buckle. He fell, pulling the table down with him. Arcane instruments skittered across the steel floor.

Not all of Smith's tools were scattered. Teg dropped his knife and grabbed the thick black hose connected to the ceramic tank. He opened the valve on the hose's head and sprayed a stream of white fluid toward the shards' point of origin.

The caustic flow spattered bare stone, sending up a vapor that made Teg's eyes water. Through his tears he saw a warped area of space fleeing from between the pillars, a diagonal wound still visible on its side.

Hitting a moving target with a chemical stream proved harder than Teg had expected. He tried to lead his target, but Izlaril turned and started retreating farther away. Worse, the stream's pressure ebbed as the small tank emptied.

In desperation, Teg lunged forward, stretching the hose as far as it would reach. The fluid still sprayed uselessly onto the floor, but a final tug pulled the tank free of its stand.

Teg burned and froze as the contents of the shattered tank splashed his tortured back. He screamed, but a second voice joined his in an agonized duet.

Coughing as he crawled from the ruined platform, Teg looked across the chamber and saw a leg, an arm, and half of a human face shifting through a rainbow of pain.

Izlaril faced Teg. Shaiel's Blade was fully visible now; his left arm and leg and the left side of his face raw with chemical burns. A scowl replaced his normally placid expression.

Teg stood. The stone chips under his skin kept his own burns from healing, but he smiled.

"If you were saving up for plastic surgery," he said to Izlaril, "you might as well blow it on booze."

Shaiel's Blade glared at him with unbridled hatred.

"We can go another round and get even uglier," said Teg. "Or you can get that mask off my friend and point us to my ship. Your call."

Izlaril charged with a visceral snarl.

Teg assumed a ready stance. "Okay."

The force of his enemy's impact drove Teg back several steps. He'd learned better than to try reading Izlaril's unpredictable attacks, so Teg abandoned any thought of defense and laid into Shaiel's Blade with everything he had.

The one corner of Teg's mind not devoted to murdering his enemy realized that Izlaril's musculature, skeletal structure, and nervous system couldn't be human. His speed was uncanny, and speed translated to power. A nearly simultaneous chain of blows pulverized Teg's ribs and drove the wind from his lungs.

Not pausing to catch his breath, Teg threw a barrage of kicks and punches at his foe's vital areas until blackness clouded the edges of his vision. Few of his attacks bypassed Izlaril's defenses; and muscles, bones, and organs shifted away from those that did.

Teg had spent a lifetime learning to kill with precision, but now he found himself without a map in unknown territory. Izlaril was as slippery as a slime eel and faster than a mantis, but Teg was healing as quickly as the Blade could hurt him.

We're at a standstill, Teg thought. That was bad. The longer a fight went on, the greater his risk of serious injury or death.

So what? asked a voice from the darker reaches of Teg's soul. *You're a remnant of a bygone time who's outlived everything he knew—even his own home world. What do you have to live for, much less fight for?*

Izlaril's elbow pistoned into Teg's face, fracturing his jaw with a jolt of pain. A knee to his midsection followed, and it took all of Teg's willpower to keep from vomiting.

"Solitary existence is torment," preached Shaiel's Blade. "Dissolve into oneness with all."

Now Teg knew what he had to live for—not letting a soulless scut like Izlaril be the one to kill him. Besides, dying would seriously complicate Teg's plans to get even with Vaun.

Unpleasant as it was, Teg listened to what his body was trying to tell him. Currently his back was screaming about icy rock fragments and deep tissue burns, while three ribs and his jaw pouted as they healed. Then there was the numbing cold at the angle of his neck and shoulder.

Izlaril's foot shattered Teg's kneecap just as Teg pulled the five-inch tethite fragment from his own shoulder. He wobbled and fell forward as Shaiel's Blade danced aside. Teg twisted in mid-fall and agony coursed through him as his back hit the floor. Izlaril's bare foot was already bearing down on his throat when Teg drove the freezing stone shard upward with both hands, slicing Izlaril's leg from ankle to calf.

Teg rolled backward, savoring his wounded enemy's scream. He rose into a crouch, favoring his rapidly mending knee. The stone shard's intense cold finally forced him to drop it.

Izlaril paused for a moment as his muscles compressed his leg wound to a thin crease. His bleeding slowed to a trickle and then stopped. It was only with a slight limp that he advanced again.

Teg stood and rejoined the fight with new confidence. He'd done lasting damage to Shaiel's Blade, while the wounds inflicted by his enemy were steadily healing.

But within the opening moments of Izlaril's renewed attack, during which Teg suffered a ruptured kidney, a cracked sternum, and a skull fracture without connecting once in return, a sickening awareness dawned.

Izlaril was now causing damage faster than Teg could heal it.

Teg willed himself to remain calm and focus on dealing out punishment. His persistence paid off when he caught Izlaril with a fierce right hook and felt teeth shatter under his fist. Teg's burst of elation died when Shaiel's Blade shrugged off the blow and drove his knuckles into the ribs under his foe's armpit, sending splintered bone tearing through Teg's skin.

Through the fog of pain, Teg realized that Izlaril was copying his strategy of relentless attack. A second punch streaked through Teg's flagging defense to hammer his chest; then a third, followed by a crushing elbow to the same spot that caved in his ribs. Bone grated against bone whenever Teg took a labored breath.

Teg poured the last of his failing strength into a wild, desperate punch. Izlaril trapped Teg's arm between his own forearm and biceps and wrenched upward.

The pain of having his elbow broken paled in comparison to what followed when Izlaril pressed his thumb deep into Teg's left eye. Teg backpedaled while beating against the arm of the hand that gouged him, but Izlaril kept both his pace and his hold.

Teg's heel struck something unyielding, and he fell backwards in blind agony. His head slammed down on hard steel, and pulsing lights filled the blackness that had swallowed his world. Izlaril was on top of him, raining a barrage of merciless blows on Teg's already open wounds.

Teg's body could no long answer his mind's increasingly feeble urge to save itself. His struggle ended.

22

Astlin sat at table with the Shadow Caste for hours, suffering through their veiled threats against Xander as her rage grew. They gloated constantly about their plan to revive Thera, until a sudden silence hinted that something had gone wrong.

One of the uniformed servants who brought in platters of rich food, cleared empty plates, and freshened drinks whispered something in Kelgrun's ear. The smug blustering between him and the other three Magists turned into furtive, hushed comments.

Astlin hadn't heard what was said, besides Kelgrun muttering that Zoanthus was now the last light of Mithgar, but she doubted it was a coincidence that Magists Vilneus and Rathimus had been sent on some secret errand a few minutes earlier. Their absence left her with yellow-robed Belar, dark blue-robed Zoanthus, veiled and wild-eyed Gien—who'd been the only one not to speak—and worst of all, Kelgrun.

And it couldn't be good that Vilneus and Rathimus had left the golden marble hall shortly after she'd lost track of Teg.

The remaining Magists fell quiet. It didn't take nexism to know that they were communicating telepathically. Astlin yearned to eavesdrop on their mental conversation, but the risk was too great while the Shadow Caste held Xander hostage.

Gien's ice-blue eyes suddenly snapped into focus on her. His gaze lingered expectantly.

"Anything I can help you with?" she asked her conspiring hosts.

The frown beneath Kelgrun's beard made his whole face sag. "Nothing remotely within your aptitude or experience."

"Or anyone else's?" Astlin said in a flat tone. "Don't you have people running the sphere for you?"

"Matters sometimes arise which require our personal attention," Zoanthus said.

Astlin pointed upward. "Like a Night Gen invasion?"

Belar inclined his bald head toward the ceiling. "Our shield is impregnable. No Night Gen will set foot here against our will."

A Night Gen stepped out from behind the wine-red banner through which Vilneus had exited earlier. Her black hair fell past shoulders clad in a suit of sharkskin-like fabric. Her emerald eyes betrayed desperation as they searched the room and fixed themselves on Gien.

"The rumors were true," she all but whispered in an accent that reminded Astlin of Szodrin's. "You have not changed in almost a century."

"No, I still contain multitudes," Gien argued before agreeing, "Yes, they have grown."

Kelgrun, Zoanthus, and Belar exchanged looks that ranged from startled to grave. The nexic waves of their wordless conversation washed over the room.

Astlin took advantage of her captors' divided attention to

make contact with the gatecrashing Night Gen's mind.

The woman's green eyes darted from Magist Gien to her.

You are a telepath! the Gen woman, whom Astlin gathered was named Celwen, silently exclaimed. *I thought that nexism was all but unknown among the clay tribe.*

Astlin reminded herself that Celwen's ability to detect telepathic probing shouldn't have been a surprise. After all, Szodrin had credited his skill at seeing through her illusions to Night Gen training. It made sense that Celwen had learned similar defenses.

Yes, I'm a telepath, Astlin confirmed. *We can talk about why later. Right now I'm more concerned with why you barged in on a secret meeting of the evil cabal that's holding my husband hostage.*

Husband? Celwen's grey face brightened with recognition. *Do you know a man named Teg Cross?*

Only the knowledge that jumping up from her seat would draw the Shadow Caste's attention gave Astlin the strength to keep still. She chose her thoughts carefully.

Yes. Teg is my friend. He was looking for my husband, Xander. If you want to leave this room alive, drop your defenses and show me everything you know.

Kelgrun's eyes fluttered as he surfaced from the telepathic link. "Dearest Celwen, Magist Gien has informed us of your sterling service in acquiring Thera's fragments."

He motioned from her to Astlin. "Please join our gathering, which happens to include one of her former hosts."

By the time Kelgrun finished speaking, Astlin had absorbed Celwen's memories of her and Teg's harrowing descent into Vigh's underworld, their battle with ethereal guardians, and her awakening afterward to find Teg horribly beaten.

There is a gate in a passage off the Stone Stratum chamber, Celwen explained as she cautiously approached Astlin. *I came through it seeking help for Teg. He is dying!*

Astlin barely registered Celwen's plea under the deluge of other, more disturbing memories that flowed from her unguarded mind. Few events from Astlin's fist life were as painful as her death at the hands of Zan, the souldancer of air. But she was enraged and disgusted to learn that Zan had been betrayed by Celwen, his own daughter.

This time Astlin did stand, but she wasn't alone, as Zoanthus sprang to his feet and stabbed a finger at Celwen.

"The Gen bitch conspires with the Zadokim!"

Acting on impulse, Astlin gripped the edge of the table and heaved. The stout hardwood disc pitched forward with a clash of silver plates. Zoanthus jumped clear and Belar toppled backward, but Kelgrun screamed as the table's far edge crashed down, splintering his chair and pinning his legs against the marble floor.

"Dinner's over," Astlin said.

A telepathic warning from Celwen alerted her to Zoanthus. His dark blue, star-flecked robes flowed as he finished the Steersman's Compass and thrust his arms across the upended table toward Astlin.

The flaming torrent that leapt from Zoanthus' hands gave Astlin no time to move. She wasn't an expert with Workings, but she knew fire intimately. She let her stars shine and willed the orange flame back from their sapphire light.

The jet of fire streaked halfway from the Magist to Astlin. It burned the overturned table, sending up thick sweet smoke, but refused to approach closer.

I wasn't sure that would work! Astlin thought with heartfelt relief.

Xander could make prana around him form itself into shapes and materials he understood. Astlin had tried making a spear like his without success. Now she was encouraged to revisit the idea.

It would have to wait though, because Belar had struggled to his feet and was fashioning his own Working.

Just before the moment of release, Astlin rammed through Zoanthus and Belar's telepathic resistance and took hold of their minds. Both Magists turned toward each other as Astlin hid her light. Zoanthus' flame surged to its full extent, bathing Belar with fire. At the same time, a lumpy block of stone engulfed Zoanthus' head. A few wisps of dark hair were all that escaped the rough brown chunk of rock.

Zoanthus teetered, arms flailing, as he tried to support the crushing burden suddenly laid on his neck. After a brief struggle he lurched forward. The stone encasing his head hit the table's edge with a loud thud and a crunch that made Astlin wince. Then it struck the floor with the sound of a stone coffin slamming shut.

Stabbing pain fixed Astlin's eyes on her right leg, where a large carving knife jutted from her calf. A hoarse cry of triumph rose up from the table's lower right edge.

Belar lay propped up on his left arm. His mustard-colored robe was immaculate, but his face was a smoldering ruin. A serving fork floated before his blistered right hand.

He has Xander's gift. Astlin's brief look into Belar's mind had revealed that the gift was stolen.

As if to avenge the ancient Gen whose life had been taken to extend Belar's, Celwen pounced on the Magist and slid a horn-handled pocket knife across this throat. The fork dropped into a spreading pool of blood as the last sputtering breaths escaped Belar's mouth.

Celwen looked to Astlin but quickly averted her eyes. "Are you all right?" the Night Gen asked between heaving breaths.

Astlin focused, willing her body to match the pattern of her soul. The pain in her leg faded, and a clear note rang out as the knife fell to the floor.

"I'm okay," she said, "but my dress has a knife cut to go with Teg's bullet hole."

"Teg shot you?" Celwen said incredulously.

"By accident."

Astlin stepped forward to peer over the fallen table. Kelgrun lay on his back atop the shattered remains of his chair. His clearly broken legs were still trapped under the heavy circle of wood. Taking satisfaction from death and maiming was wrong, but the Shadow Caste had caused so much of both that Astlin couldn't feel guilty about savoring their defeat.

"Speaking of Teg," she said to Celwen, "Keep an eye on the last Magist while I step out for a minute."

A smile twisted Kelgrun's sweat-streaked face. "Not the last," he wheezed.

Astlin turned to see Gien crouching beside a pillar at the edge of the room. His expression was unreadable behind the net covering his face.

Celwen rose from Belar's motionless body and fixed a predatory look on Gien. "They are monsters. Both of them deserve to die."

"So do you," said Astlin.

Celwen rounded on her, looking suddenly like a trapped animal.

Gien came skulking forward in weird spurts of motion. "I can help," he said in a thin whiny voice. "I can help guard Kelgrun."

Astlin looked into the veiled Magist's mind and instantly recoiled at the fevered chaos she saw there.

I was crazy, she thought. *This guy had a messy divorce from sanity, went back and burned the house down!*

"I didn't fight you," said Gien. "Let me help!"

"You're a whipped cur," Kelgrun spat at Gien. "Long since gone rabid. The Mithgarders would have put you down, but I stayed them."

Childlike wonder lit up Gien's face. "They're all dead."

Kelgrun lay back with a groan.

Leaving Celwen with Gien seemed like a questionable idea at best. But a sudden foreboding fanned Astlin's concern for Teg into a blaze. She pictured the deep chamber she'd seen in Celwen's mind and was there.

The cold dry air smelled of lye and blood. Astlin stood on a round platform covered with small dark gears.

Smith.

Could a souldancer lose so much of himself and survive? The absence of a screaming rift to Kairos argued that, at least in Smith's case, the answer was yes.

The skull-like face of the souldancer of Kairos was nowhere in sight. But Astlin wasn't inclined to look—especially since Teg lay on the cavern floor in a distressingly large, dark pool.

Instantly Astlin was kneeling beside him, her skirt soaked in blood that felt far too cold. Shadows mercifully hid the full horror of his wounds.

In that terrifying moment, Astlin realized that she had no idea what to do. She hesitated to touch him for fear of hurting him even worse. If only Tefler were there, he could channel prana and Teg would be healed. But Astlin didn't know how to reach him.

"Teg," Astlin said, her voice trembling. "I'm here. I'm sorry. Please say something."

There was only silence, deeper than any Astlin had known. Her mind reached out to Teg's and found nothing.

On the edge of panic, Astlin pierced the veil of the ether. The sight of a life cord, however faint, extending from Teg's body consoled her. But her comfort proved fleeting when she saw a hazy image of Teg racing along the dimming silver thread toward a colossal shape that loomed in the rose-colored mist like a black pyramid.

With a cry of defiance Astlin plunged fully into the ether, imposing herself between Teg's fleeing soul and the all-consuming Nexus.

"You took my whole family," she raged at Zadok. "You're not getting any more of my friends!"

The body that Astlin wore covered the light of her soul like a shroud. She tore the cover away.

23

Teg had fought.

He knew that much. Even when Izlaril had pinned him down and hammered him with inhuman ferocity, Teg had kept fighting through darkness and pain until the darkness parted and the pain vanished like a bad dream.

Now he was floating in a rosy fog. Or was he flying through it? His long experience with ether-runners informed him that this was the ether, but not how he'd gotten there.

Since everything seemed okay at the moment, Teg decided to relax and enjoy the ride. He wondered if this was what manning the Wheel felt like and made a mental note to ask Nakvin the next time he saw her.

Eventually—there was no way to tell time in an infinite featureless mist—a dark spot appeared. It gradually got bigger and bigger until Teg realized that the dark speck must actually be something really huge a great distance away.

He continued gliding toward the distant object, eyeing it with more curiosity than concern. When the speck resolved into a black triangle roughly the size of a guilder piece held at arm's length, something else appeared.

It hung in the ether between him and what was now clearly a pyramid. At first Teg thought it was a person. But that would be ridiculous. Nobody traveled through the ether without a ship—well, nobody *else* did.

Teg got confirmation that the new arrival wasn't human when it suddenly burst into brilliant blue light that turned his calm to sublime peace. His second theory identified the radiant object as a star. But that couldn't be it, either because the ether's flammability meant that a star appearing here would vaporize him and whatever Middle Stratum system was on the other side of the mist.

Besides, no star was this beautiful.

The black pyramid pulled Teg closer. The speed at which it grew to dominate his field of vision gave him some idea of how fast he was moving. The blue star stayed right there between him and the pyramid. Oddly enough, he had no trouble looking at it despite it being brighter than any light he'd ever seen.

And there was something familiar about it that Teg couldn't put his finger on.

He was racking his brain for a word that clung stubbornly to the tip of his tongue when the light called out to him.

The Nexus is pulling you in, Teg. You have to turn back!

The blue light's words were familiar, but not enough to make sense. While Teg mulled them over, he saw that the pyramid, which now filled the ether in front of him, wasn't actually black. It was really made up of countless intersecting and overlapping planes in every color he could imagine; and some he couldn't.

The pyramid's heart remained dark though, and Teg felt an

overwhelming urge to know what was in there.

Teg, no! You'll lose yourself unless you go back now!

The blue star was talking to him again. It was still there, infinitesimally small against the dazzling dark majesty of the Nexus.

Teg knew what waited inside the darkness, now—everything. The answers to every question he'd ever had and infinite others he'd never thought to ask. It was all right there at his fingertips. And the only way to get the answers was to let go and become the knowledge.

Damn it, Teg. I'm not losing you like I lost Cook. Wake up!

Who are you? Teg asked the tiny blue light. And finally he saw.

Unlike the black pyramid, which was really a labyrinth of prisms wrapped around the unknowable, the blue star turned out to be human after all.

In fact it was Astlin.

Now I remember where I saw that light, thought Teg. It was the same blue glow given off by the three luminous points that sometimes hovered above Astlin's forehead.

Except now there weren't three little balls of light, but a circlet that seemed to be carved from a single sapphire and set with three oval gems of the same type. Teg looked closer and saw that the crown didn't glow. It reflected a hidden source of light so incomprehensibly pure that he was both irresistibly drawn to it and repulsed by it with a terror he couldn't name.

Go back! Astlin pleaded.

Why? Teg wondered again. *There's nowhere to go back to. What's left for me now?*

Please. Astlin's outstretched hand touched his.

That was when he knew.

Zadok beckoned him with the answers to every question in the universe. But Astlin had just answered the only one that mattered, which the Nexus never could, because the answer was outside the universe.

Teg had watched the Guild march across the spheres despite all the resistance that the old faiths, the Gen, and finally Jaren's ragtag crew of pirates could muster. He'd heard his mother's prayers fall on deaf ears and had seen Deim's mad pilgrimage burn down the world, only for Vaun to plant his flag in the ashes.

Now Teg knew why every cause was lost, every movement doomed; every battle hopeless. He considered again the ancient philosophers' riddle of whether the White Well's emptying into the Void caused evil or if sin caused the dimming of the Well, and he laughed to see the question resolved.

The answer was yes. The game was rigged. Evil had its thumb on the scale.

Now Teg looked at Astlin and saw Good's little finger brushing the balance's other pan.

I thought I was looking for a home, Teg confessed to Astlin, *but I've really been looking for you.*

Teg's journey to the edge of the Nexus looked like a glacier's advance compared to his flight back along his silver cord.

Time lost all meaning while Astlin knelt beside Teg in the lonely chamber surrounded by endless miles of stone. His chest slowly rose and fell, signaling her victory over the Nexus for his soul.

Though she couldn't say how long it had been since she'd

hidden her light and left the ether, she was relieved to see that most of Teg's horrific wounds had healed—except for deep, frostbitten gouges in his hand and neck. And those were just the injuries she could see. Astlin still didn't dare turn him over.

At last she gathered the resolve to reach him telepathically.

Teg, it's Astlin. We're back in the Stone Stratum, but you're still hurt pretty bad. Please tell me what to do.

The only answer was a jumble of dream images—a banquet in the middle of an enormous white Guild hall where a wolf, a lion, a leopard, a rat, a bat, a walrus, and Gien sat feasting on Teg, whose constantly healing body lay on a golden table.

A winged woman whose hair looked jet black from one angle and ginger-brown from another floated overhead, declaring that this was her funeral feast and that others would take her place.

Astlin left Teg to his dreams and stood up. She didn't know why his body wasn't fully healing or why his mind was still dormant. She needed to go for help, but she hated the thought of leaving him comatose and alone.

An intense nexic impression made up Astlin's mind for her. *That was Gien—crying out in pain before something cut him off.*

With a thought, Astlin was back in the Magists' dining room. The massive table seemed to have disappeared until she saw its splinters flung across the gold marble floor. Kelgrun definitely was gone.

Astlin's heart raced as she searched the room. Her sudden glare startled a young man in dark pants and a white jacket who emerged from behind the yellow banner. The tray of shellfish he'd carried crashed to the floor like a cymbal.

"It's dangerous here," she told the servant, reinforcing her words telepathically. "Get back to the kitchen and close the gate."

The serving man did as he was told, but Astlin doubted that she'd remain undisturbed for long. The Shadow Caste—known to the people of Temil as the Magisterium—were actually the sphere's secret rulers. The local puppet government would notice their absence soon.

A whimper reached Astlin's ears from beyond the room's only set of doors. She hurried toward the sound and saw that one section of the left door's intricate glasswork had been smashed out. Cool night air carrying a hint of salt wafted in through the broken frame.

Outside, the sea below the clifftop was a shadowy abyss. Grey clouds racked by green-white lightning hid the sky. All around her an orchestra of chirping insects played.

The whimpering was coming from beside the door. Astlin turned to find Celwen and Gien huddled in the manicured bushes growing next to the outside wall. It was the Magist who sniveled as he clutched his left wrist, which had a large splinter driven through it. Blood dripped onto—and ran ran off—his green robe.

"What happened?" asked Astlin.

Celwen rose and answered. "Kelgrun shattered the table with some kind of Working. He must have mended his legs too, because he fled through one of the gates."

Astlin studied Celwen, who looked shaken but unhurt. "Are you okay?"

The Night Gen gave a curt nod and looked down at Gien. "He dove through the window and took me with him. I was

246

shielded from harm, but he was less fortunate."

Both women helped Gien to his feet. "Let's get you a medic," Astlin told him.

"No time," the Magist said. "Pull it out."

Astlin had no objections to yanking the finger-sized splinter out of Gien's wrist. She felt a burst of nexic power and saw the puncture wound shrink until not even a scar remained.

"You can heal with nexism?" Astlin marveled.

Gien sniffed.

"He uses metasomatic tissue regeneration," Celwen explained. "It is similar to Teg's. Speaking of whom, I assume that is where you disappeared to. How is he?"

Astlin frowned. "He's in some kind of coma. We need to find him some help. And we need to get off Temil before we're found out. Kelgrun probably went for reinforcements."

"He fled to the Guild house dock," said Celwen, "in pursuit of a bald man in a mask."

Astlin's eyes widened. "Show me."

A vision of walls like slabs cut from white mountains came to Astlin through Celwen's mind. Hundreds of ships were attached to a network of pipes and scaffolds that hung from the ceiling.

Xander was striding down a catwalk leading from a gate to the familiar three-bladed hull of the *Kerioth*. A blurry form limped behind him—probably Izlaril. Kelgrun had just stormed through the gate behind them a moment ago.

"I'm going after them," Astlin told the Night Gen and the rogue Magist. "Take a gate and meet me there."

She pictured the dock. It was a substratum within Vigh's Guild house, but as long as Astlin could see her destination, she could will herself there. She turned to Celwen.

"About what I said earlier…"

Celwen cut her off. "You were right." She bowed her head. "I deserve to die."

"If we all got what we deserved," Astlin said with a sad smile, "there'd be no one left."

Astlin's next thought took her to a catwalk suspended dizzyingly high above a pearl-tiled floor. The smell of heavy machinery and a faint sharp ether scent replaced the ocean air.

The sourceless light reflected from the white walls momentarily dazzled her, but Astlin's eyes soon adjusted enough to see Xander and Izlaril standing in front of the *Kerioth's* boarding hatch at the walkway's end.

Kelgrun stood midway between the nexus-runner and Astlin with the back of his orange-red robe turned toward her. The former head of the Shadow Caste faced Xander and spoke in a booming voice.

"Tainted soul of Vaun Mordechai, your maker commands you! Return with me and complete our great work."

Xander cocked his head. The expressionless mask on his face tilted, and the ruby on its brow glittered.

"Strange. I seem to recall Vilneus tainting my soul."

Kelgrun advanced a few steps. "He acted at my direction. I enabled your apotheosis. Yet your host absconds with Thera's *vas* and the rod of partition."

Xander held up a slim purple rod. Astlin's breath caught at the horrid sight.

It's the same one, she thought. *It tore my soul apart.*

"You mean this clever bauble?" Shaiel asked Kelgrun through

Xander. "Rest assured, I shall put it to far better use than your decrepit order could have dreamed."

"Xander!" Astlin shouted from the middle of the walkway. "I'm here to take you home."

"From what I've seen of this pretender's mind, you and he have no home."

Xander's mocking tone was a dagger in Astlin's heart, but she reminded herself that the words were Shaiel's.

"His home is with me," she said.

Astlin saw Izlaril break into a run before she noticed Kelgrun making the signs of the Steersman's Compass. Shaiel's Blade was fast, but not as fast as the Magist's Working.

Blue lightning sizzled from Kelgrun's hand to strike Izlaril, blasting him off his feet. The Blade of Shaiel lay groaning on the catwalk under a cloud of smoke that reeked of burned hair.

"We bred you for loyalty, Son of Haath," Kelgrun told Izlaril. "So I do not begrudge your devotion. But your choice of master casts doubt upon your judgment."

Xander advanced and held out his hand as if ordering Kelgrun to move back. Sickly golden light shone from his open palm. Frost formed where it touched the catwalk, but the air in front of Kelgrun scattered the freezing light like a prism. The distortion moved back along the beam and surrounded Xander.

Kelgrun raised his arms. "As I made you, souldancer of the Void, so do I unmake your host."

A cloud of fire swept across the catwalk , cutting of Astlin's view of everything beyond Kelgrun. Xander's scream rose above the roar of the flames.

Otherworldly heat radiated from the fiery curtain, and Astlin immediately knew its source.

Elemental fire.

Kelgrun was drawing much more from the Fire Stratum than Astlin had needed to incinerate Hazeroth. Not even Xander's idealized body could take that kind of heat for long.

Astlin dashed toward Kelgrun, but a wave of his hand sent a torrent of flame screaming across her path.

The same swirling fire storm that engulfed Xander now protected the man who was trying to murder him. Astlin willed herself inside the burning whirlwind. She stood face-to-face with Kelgrun, who only smiled when she rushed him. She felt his will assert itself, wrapping him in a bubble of nexic force that repelled her charge.

"Foolish child," he scolded her. "You think your borrowed light is truth? One abstract truth is nothing against the practical knowledge of a hundred lifetimes."

Kelgrun loosed a gout of fire at Astlin without warning. She reflexively held out her hands and called on her light to fend off the flames. Unlike Belar's Working, some of Kelgrun's fire managed to break through.

Astlin cried out as her hands blistered. She composed herself with an effort and focused on conforming her body to the ideal of her soul. The burns faded, but there was still pain in the little finger of her right hand. An orange-red band encircled it, and Astlin realized that it was Rosemy's ring, still glowing from the heat of Kelgrun's fire.

She looked at the ring. It was actually a washer; part of a game that the girl's father had made before he'd died. Astlin remembered her own father, gone these many years. She pictured her first life as an empty house—abandoned by everyone, including her. And now, as if recalling a childhood dream, she remembered what had drawn her back.

I'm going to save him; all of them. I'll take my family back from the Nexus.

Kelgrun's nexic shield kept her from approaching him, but it wasn't skintight. With a thought she was embracing him. The body under his splendid robes felt soft and frail. His eyes widened behind his square glasses, but the fire still raged.

"This is the truth," Astlin said. "You're just a dream, and so is everything you know."

Kelgrun smirked. "And yet I've won every round. What does that make you?"

"A dreamer."

Bringing someone else when she moved by thought didn't bode well for Astlin or her passengers. But this time Astlin didn't care what happened to her, and she sure as hell didn't care what happened to Kelgrun.

Astlin pictured a black pyramid larger than worlds surrounded by rose-colored mist. Projecting Kelgrun there with her was like holding onto the idea of being him and herself at the same time. The effort was nauseating, but Astlin kept it up until the universe conceded that she and Kelgrun were floating in each others' arms at the gates of the Nexus.

Astlin spun Kelgrun around to face the god monolith and let him go. "Look!" she said. "All the knowledge you could ever want, and more."

Kelgrun didn't say anything. At first Astlin thought she was seeing double, but it soon dawned on her that she really could see two Kelgruns—his empty body set adrift beside her, and his soul racing toward the Nexus along a silver cord.

Astlin didn't intervene as she had with Teg. She considered guiding Kelgrun through the Nexus to the light on the other side, or at least giving him directions. Instead she watched, silently and without remorse, as Zadok swallowed the tyrant whose secret reign had scarred countless souls, including her own.

Then her will broke like a frayed thread. She fell into a dreamless sleep.

24

Celwen led Gien back inside immediately after Astlin's departure. Her turbulent meeting with the strange woman had been unsettling, but Celwen hoped that her absence would be short.

One reason was Gien. He had been Celwen's overseer when she had betrayed her father to the Shadow Caste. Knowing that the Magist was responsible for his brutal torture and eventual death compounded her sense of guilt and deepened her hatred of him.

Another reason was the squad of soldiers waiting for her and Gien in the dining room.

The six men wore light blue uniforms with sidearms in white holsters at their hips. Two of them knelt beside the corpses of Zoanthus and Belar with disbelief etched on their faces, while three more stood guard.

A final soldier—the leader of the group, judging by his impatient demeanor and his position at the center of the room, rested a hand on the grip of his pistol and frowned at the two newcomers.

"Magist Gien," the squad leader said, "are you alright, sir?"

The other soldiers paused from their duties to stare at Celwen. Gien passed her on his way into the room. Broken glass crunched under his slippers.

"I'm a little hungry," the Magist said. "Had to leave dinner early. I hope you're well, Capgrave."

Capgrave's voice took on a practiced tone and meter, like one used to speaking with a flighty child.

"Thank you, sir, but frankly my men and I are concerned. Magists Vilneus, Rathimus, and Kelgrun are missing. Magists Zoanthus and Belar are dead. And now you return in the company of the enemy. It would set us—and all of your loyal initiates—at ease to learn precisely what happened."

Celwen stepped forward. "I also serve the Shadow Caste. Let me help you end the siege of your world."

The guards stationed between the gates drew their weapons and pointed them at Celwen. She froze in place.

Capgrave motioned for her to keep still with a raised hand. "I haven't asked you any questions, Miss, though we'll have time for that later. For now, consider yourself a prisoner of war. I'd keep quiet unless you want to be treated as a spy."

"It's okay," Gien said with a dismissive wave of his arm. "She's with us. Has been since before your grandpa was an itch in your great-grandpa's pants."

Capgrave raised a dark eyebrow. "Sir?"

"It doesn't really matter." Gien bent down, poked through the debris on the floor, and picked up a broken gold-rimmed wineglass. "The Shadow Caste is over."

An uneasy look passed between the soldiers who were examining the bodies. The men on guard fidgeted.

"What do you mean, 'over'?" Capgrave asked.

Gien let the glass fall from his fingers to shatter on the floor with a single crisp chime.

"I mean we're done. We failed to revive Thera. Then a Zadokim possessed by Shaiel broke loose and murdered everybody." He winked at Celwen through his veil. "She helped me get away."

Capgrave's face fell. He signaled for his men to holster their weapons, which they did with obvious reluctance.

"If the other Magists are dead, Even Renneker and his bootlickers will catch on eventually. We should enact emergency protocols."

"Yes. That's a good plan. Do that." Gien shuffled across the floor to stand beside Celwen. "We'll get out of your way."

Celwen suppressed a shiver as Gien took her arm and led her toward the dark green curtain. She balked at the thought of being alone with him but supposed that it was better than confinement in a stockade.

Capgrave fell in beside Gien. "Beg your pardon, sir, but you are the last living member of this sphere's ruling council. The elected government couldn't run a birdwatching club under the best circumstances, and this is wartime!"

"Absolutely," said Gien. "What's your point?"

Capgrave pinched the bridge of his nose and squeezed his eyes shut. "Don't you think it wise for you to remain under guard in the Magisterial Tower? What if we require your insight and direction?"

"I think you'll come through just fine on your own," said Gien, patting Capgrave's shoulder. "Besides, none of the policy stuff was mine. That was all the Mithgarders; sometimes Belar. They're dead now. Good luck!"

Gien swept the curtain aside and led Celwen into the marble passage beyond. The Short hallway seemed to reach a dead end, but just before she walked into the wall, Celwen found herself treading on plush white carpet.

"Where are we?" she asked, looking around what seemed to be a small amphitheater descending in three tiers to a circular floor below.

Already tromping down the stairs, Gien called back, "We used to meet here—the others and me. We talked about our plans."

Celwen waited near the stairs, gripping the low wall that encircled the top row. "Astlin told us to meet her at the dock."

"She's not there," said Gien. He tinkered with a console set into the room's back wall. "Look for yourself. You'll see."

Despite herself, Celwen started down the steps. "You know more than you let on."

Gien sighed. His shoulders sagged, and he suddenly seemed very old. "The others—mainly Kelgrun and the Mithgarders—they helped kill most of your people."

Celwen found herself on the lowest tier of seats. Surely being with Gien approximated the primitive idea of consorting with demons. She listened intently.

"They didn't start it," he said. "But they kept it going longer than it should have. Kelgrun learned a way to steal your people's lives; their powers, and add them to his. He shared it with a few others, like me."

Stepping onto the stage, Celwen stood behind Gien as he worked at the console.

"People don't change," said Gien. "You can predict how they'll act, if you study them long enough. Create situations where you know they'll act a certain way, and you can control them." He laughed. "It's funny. The Gen had all the time in the world, but they never tried to control humans."

"It is not our way," Celwen said. But the boast rang false, so she clarified, "The clay tribe's empires seemed to rise in the spring and fall by winter. We never took enough interest in their affairs to govern them. None foresaw that their final dominion would outlast us."

The console gave a synthetic trill, and the wall above it seemed to become a window into a grey infinity.

"We got control of the Guild," said Gien. "It took a while, but eventually we made it run by itself. The others liked to play with different political systems. Temil was the opposite of the Guild. It'll completely fall apart, now. That was the plan. After years and years of chasing power, in the end all we had was the plan."

Celwen couldn't bring herself to pity a man who'd helped exterminate most of her race and drive the rest into exile. But she could imagine the dreariness of secretly ruling a civilization that ceaselessly repeated the same patterns for millennia.

"Give me the nexic focus of your ship's telepathic command channel," said Gien.

The command shocked Celwen from her reverie. "What?"

"The ship in orbit. Give me its command channel so I can tell them we surrender."

The response stunned Celwen. She'd been sent to infiltrate the Shadow Caste and betray Temil to the Night Gen. Her superiors thought it was a suicide mission, but if Gien did as he said, total victory would fall into her lap.

"Are you serious?" she asked.

Gien stepped aside to make room for her at the controls. "Don't worry. The gate's the only way in here, and it's nexically keyed to me. No one else will know you told me. It'll be our secret."

Celwen approached the console as if sleepwalking. Just yesterday finding a nexic communications system on a clay tribe sphere would have surprised her. Now she mechanically keyed in the coordinates of Raig's priority comm node in the Nexus and watched as the grey expanse became a window onto the admiral's private quarters, where he sat meditating on a simple black mat.

This device can display telepathic impressions as images and sounds. Not even our next generation systems will duplicate this effect!

Night Gen comms were essentially artificial telepaths that connected two or more people mind-to-mind. Mediating telepathic conversations through an external display was revolutionary. How many other advancements had the Shadow Caste made in their restless centuries of stolen immortality? What else might they have accomplished if not for death's delayed intervention?

Celwen decided not to think about it.

"Can he see me?" she asked Gien.

"No," said the Magist, "but he can hear us."

Raig remained seated, his eyes closed, as he spoke. "Celwen?"

"Yes, admiral"

A half-smile turned up the corner of his mouth. "I thought I had heard the last of your surprises, but it seems you have prepared just one more. You must realize that no rescue party can be sent to extract you. However, I will listen if you wish to confess your crimes and clear your conscience before the Shadow Caste execute you."

"Most generous of you, sir," said Celwen, indulging in a smile of her own. "But I have not contacted you to report any crimes; only Temil's surrender."

Raig's blue-green eyes shot open. "I offer you a chance to make amends for your treason," he said, pronouncing each syllable with slow precision. "Answering with jests or ruses will not increase the esteem in which your memory is held."

"If you mistrust my word, then allow me to introduce Magist Gien, sole surviving member of Temil's ruling council."

Gien tilted his head toward the display. "Hello. Good evening, sir. Yes, we surrender."

By the time Astlin regained consciousness and returned to the Guild house dock, the *Kerioth* was gone—along with Xander and Izlaril. Only the catwalk, two of its sections scorched and twisted by elemental fire, gave any sign of the battle with Kelgrun.

What could she do now? Transporting herself onto the *Kerioth* with Shaiel and his Blade would be taking a huge risk. Boarding the ship alone would probably lead to her death—or worse, Xander's.

Astlin felt as if a crushing weight had landed on her back. She leaned on the railing and groaned, looking down on the maze of walkways, ductwork, and ships stacked in layers all the way to the white floor half a mile below.

I came here to find Xander, she thought, *but Shaiel just snatched him away from me again. And he's got Smith.* And *Teg's in a coma.*

Since her return to Zadok's domain, people had called Astlin a queen; even a demigod. All she felt like now was a bad wife and a worse friend.

At least the Shadow Caste can't hurt any more innocent people.

Green-white light flashed behind her, and Astlin turned to see Celwen striding through the gate, followed closely by Gien.

"I am sorry we kept you waiting," Celwen said, practically beaming.

Astlin waved off the apology. "I just got back a minute ago."

Celwen looked down at the first section of singed, warped steel. "You had nothing to do with this?"

"That was Kelgrun," Astlin said. When Celwen cast nervous glances around the dock, Astlin added, "He won't be a problem anymore."

"He wanted to die," said Gien, "so he got his wish. But he wanted to kill everyone else first, so he didn't get all of it."

Celwen looked to the end of the catwalk and frowned. "When you told us to meet here, I thought you would find us a ship."

"Our nexus-runner *was* here," Astlin said. She bit her lip. "But Shaiel got to it first. Sounds like we're all in a rush to leave."

"We're going up to the Night Gen ship so I can surrender," said Gien.

Astlin stared, wide-eyed, at the strange little man in his green robe, black cap, and veil. He seemed less like the ruler of a sphere and more like a clown.

A mad, potentially murderous clown.

Astlin pointed at Gien. "Is he serious?"

"That is what I asked him," Celwen said. "But yes, he has agreed to surrender Temil, and the fleet commander has called a tentative ceasefire. Gien has lowered the shield. We can depart the surface in a ship."

Celwen looked glumly at the ether-runners docked all around her. "But I can only fly nexus-runners."

"I can man the Wheel," said Gien. "I really can. Pick any ship you want, and I'll fly it."

Celwen's face fell. "I am not entirely comfortable with that idea." She looked hopefully at Astlin. "Teg mentioned that you are a pilot. Can you fly us to the *Sinamarg*?"

"Teg!" Astlin slapped herself on the forehead. "He's lying in some godforsaken hole on the Stone Stratum!"

Astlin turned to Gien. "Did the Shadow Caste have some kind of secret medical facility where I can take him?"

"I advise getting him off the sphere as soon as possible," said Celwen. "The occupation will begin shortly, and my people will hold him as a spy if he is found."

Astlin searched the dock as if seeking a sign and saw one in the form of three scrap metal pods joined at an angle by two long pylons.

"You two go ahead," she told Gien and Celwen with a smile. "I'll pick up Teg and take him back to the *Serapis*."

The Magist and the Night Gen started back along the catwalk, but Celwen paused and turned to face Astlin.

"There is something I feel I must say." Shame and resolve warred in Celwen's eyes. "I do not know why it feels right that I should say it to you. It just does."

Pity softened Astlin's heart and face. "Go on," she said. "If you want to."

A tear streamed down the Night Gen's ashen cheek. "I think you saw," she said, her voice starting to break. "When you said I deserve to—"

Astlin covered the rest of the distance to the other woman in a few brisk strides and hugged her. Celwen's body shook under her sharkskin garment.

"Zan was your father?"

Celwen nodded against Astlin's shoulder.

"He was my friend," Astlin said.

The Night Gen woman held Astlin in the emerald intensity of her eyes. "Do you know how he died?"

Astlin hesitated before saying "Yes."

"I would know how it happened."

"It won't be easy for you to see," Astlin warned.

Celwen's sorrow became determination. "Show me."

It only took a moment. Astlin impressed her memories of Zan—from their first meeting on the *Kerioth* to his deadly betrayal of their friendship on the *Serapis*. She filled in his body's destruction and his soul's return to the Nexus from Xander's accounts.

Celwen slowly pushed herself back from Astlin and stood on the dock with no expression on her face.

"Will you be alright?" Astlin asked.

"Tell me," said Celwen. "Are any people truly who they seem to be?"

"Everyone has secrets," said Astlin. "But people are who they are."

Celwen half turned away. She nodded to herself; then followed Gien back down the catwalk without a word.

25

Astlin stood at a wide oblong window looking in on the *Serapis'* infirmary, where the ship's surgeon dabbed his receding hairline with a hand towel after removing the last rock fragment from Teg's back.

The double handful of bloody gravel in the medic's pan didn't ease the worry that had nagged Astlin since she'd commandeered the *Theophilus*, picked up Teg on the Stone Stratum, and flown him beyond Temil's moon to the *Serapis*.

Because Teg's wounds still weren't healing. And he still lay unconscious, his breath hissing through a tube.

The chief medic removed his gloves, washed his hands, and stepped into the outer room with Astlin. The scent of antiseptic soap followed him. His friendly but tired face seemed to have gained some extra lines since she'd brought Teg in.

"How is he?" she asked.

"For a patient you say is pushing sixty, he has the muscle and bone mass of a man half his age."

Astlin gestured toward the operating room, where an assistant was helping the ship's only nurse load Teg's limp form onto a gurney.

"Never mind that. Why isn't he waking up?"

The medic sighed and laid a gentle hand on Astlin's shoulder. He turned with her to watch as Teg was prepped for transfer to a private bed.

"I'll level with you," he said. "That debris embedded in his skin caused some ugly looking wounds but didn't damage any major blood vessels or organs. Despite the beating he supposedly took, there's no sign of brain damage, and his bloodwork came back clean. If you're asking why he's in a coma, we just don't know."

"Mind if I take a stab at it?" asked a self-assured male voice.

Astlin turned and saw Jaren standing right behind her.

The medic gave a start. "And you are?"

The transformation that Jaren had undergone since she'd left made Astlin look twice. His thin angular face was now clean-shaven; his waist-length red hair tied with a cord at the nape of his neck. Before he'd looked like a feral castaway. Now he could've stepped from the pages of an adventure tale—a pirate captain right down to his naval uniform jacket and missing hand.

"He's Jaren Peregrine," Astlin said.

The medic turned pale. "The captain of the *Exodus*?"

Jaren's green eyes fixed themselves on the medic. "That's right. Until recently I was in pretty much the same shape as Teg."

"I'm not sure that qualifies you to diagnose my patient."

"Let's hear him out," Astlin said, admitting silently that she'd hear Shaiel out if he showed up with a theory on Teg's condition.

Jaren pointed through the window. "See that pile of black rocks?"

Astlin and the medic looked into the pan.

"Notice anything strange about them?"

Staring at the bloody pebbles gave Astlin no new insights, but the medic suddenly dashed back to the operating room. He picked up the pan and examined it closely for a moment before turning it upside down.

Only one or two rock fragments rattled down on the steel table. When the medic turned the pan toward the window, Astlin saw why.

The blood's frozen!

The medic set down the tray of pebbles cemented together with iced blood and returned to the outer room.

"Those rocks froze my patient's blood," he told Jaren in a serious tone. "Care to explain?"

"The rocks are cold," Jaren said matter-of-factly. "You didn't notice while you were taking them out?"

"I used forceps." It was hard to tell if the medic was more annoyed with Jaren or himself. "And I don't make a habit of touching foreign objects removed from patients' backsides. So let's skip to the follow up question. Why are the rocks cold?"

"A shady customer I did a job with carried a sword that was always cold. The blade was grey and gave off a dark blue glow."

"Sounds like a Lawbringer's sword," said Astlin.

Recognition dawned on the medic's face. "I'm an idiot. Shadow blades freeze the tissues they cut—just like Teg's wounds. I thought it was just frostbite from too much time on the Stone Stratum."

"You had no reason to expect it," said Jaren. "But I know swords, and I think the stuff you pried out of Teg is the ore that shadow blades are forged from. It's concentrated Void."

The medic rubbed his chin. "If you're right, then it's possible that Teg's been poisoned in a way we can't detect." He pointed to Astlin. "You told me when the patient was admitted that his body's recuperative powers have been enhanced."

"Yes," Astlin said. "I think it's caused by nexism."

"If the Void is really some sort of anti-life substance," said the medic, "then prolonged exposure to it might counteract even nexically accelerated healing."

"We need to neutralize the poison," Jaren said.

The medic held up his hands in a cautioning gesture. "That's outside my expertise. Keep in mind that I became ship's surgeon by default. Anyway, I meant *poison* in a metaphoric sense. If we are dealing with some kind of toxin, it works on a nonphysical level."

"How do you treat a spiritual poison?" Astlin wondered aloud.

Jaren looked her straight in the eye. "With prana".

"Much easier said than done," the medic warned. "The only reliable source of pure prana on board is the ship's fuel line. Exposing Teg to that would be like throwing a patient who needs more sun into a star."

A solution immediately came to Astlin's mind. "I know someone who can channel prana," she said. "Two people, in fact—Tefler and his mother, Thera."

Both men stared at Astlin as if she'd claimed to be friends with an invisible, wish-granting dragon.

"Tefler is Thera's son?" the medic repeated.

"Thera has a son?" marveled Jaren.

Astlin choked back a nervous laugh. "Yeah. She's the goddess of the White Well, and he's her priest. But there's another problem. They're both in Avalon."

"So is Nakvin," Jaren said. "No one's more qualified to treat Teg." He nodded to the *Serapis* medic. "No offense."

"None taken," the medic said. "But how do we get past that Night Gen warship?"

Jaren exchanged a look with Astlin. She knew what he was thinking without reading his mind.

"There's no way I'm doing that!" she protested.

A smile twisted Jaren's lip. "You got that nexus-runner through Temil's shield and flew the *Theophilus* to the Stone Stratum."

"Temil isn't protected by a devil queen who's expecting an attack from Shaiel," said Astlin.

"Nakvin's a queen," said Jaren. "Can't you overpower her? You're a demigod."

Astlin threw up her arms. "Her daughter's a full-fledged goddess!"

"Besides," said the medic, "Gid and the rest of the crew might not approve of trespassing in sovereign territory."

"Fine," Jaren said. "Let's ask permission to visit."

Astlin's mouth fell open. "I don't have Thera's contact information. Are you saying I should pray to her?"

Jaren rolled his eyes. "I shouldn't be the one who has to explain this. Look, you're a nexist, right?"

"Not exactly," said Astlin. "I'm not tied to a nexus, but I can talk directly to the shards' minds."

"Well, Thera *is* a nexus, right? Why can't you talk to the whole thing at once?"

Jaren's simple logic left Astlin dumbstruck.

"I never thought of that," she said at length.

"Why don't you give it a try?" suggested Jaren.

"There are lots of good reasons not to bother gods," Astlin said.

"True," said Jaren, "but one good reason to risk it is in a coma right now."

Astlin thought of Teg, lying hurt and unconscious because he'd tried to help her rescue Xander.

"Okay," she said softly. "I'll reach out to Thera—but the ship's passengers and crew have to agree."

"You've got my vote," the medic said as he exited into the outer hallway.

26

Celwen stepped from the airlock of Gien's stolen ether-runner and found Raig waiting for her with a squad of men in dark blue and black uniforms. Unlike most hallways aboard Night Gen ships, this one was fully lit; and besides Raig and his men it was empty.

"Admiral," Celwen greeted him. "Courteous of you to bring a security detail. I am sure that Magist Gien will appreciate the extra protection."

A glint of satisfaction broke through Raig's stern expression. "Not all of them are here for our esteemed guest's safety, Lieutenant." He motioned to three security officers on his left. "These men will escort you to the brig. You are hereby placed under arrest."

The arresting officers came forward just as Gien shuffled in through the airlock.

"That was fun!" the Magist said, adjusting the black cap over the netting that covered his face. "I missed flying. You're a good passenger, too. You only screamed a couple of times."

Raig's grey brow furrowed. "This is the man who will negotiate Temil's surrender?"

"Yes, sir," Celwen said. "This is Magist Gien, the de facto ruler of Temil."

"Let me remind you," Raig warned her, "to guard your comments. They may be entered as evidence at your court-martial."

Two members of the security team flanked Celwen while the third bound her hands behind her back.

She scoffed at Raig. "What happened to your concern for the crew's morale?"

Raig's emotionless façade cracked once again—this time in a faint smile. "Allayed by our recent victory."

"A victory I brought you," Celwen said.

"Pretension is an unbecoming trait," said Raig. "Better to take quiet solace in having made reparation for your crimes, the easier to face execution bravely."

Gien sidled up to the admiral. "What did she do?"

"It would be improper to discuss a subordinate's case with uninvolved parties."

The admiral never deigned to look at the Magist, but nodded to the other half of the security detail. "Let us speak no more of Lieutenant Celwen and instead prepare for the negotiations. These men will show you to your stateroom."

"I am involved, actually," said Gien. "You're arresting her for selling her father out, right? I'm the one she sold him out to."

Raig finally looked at Gien. The admiral's blue-green eyes widened but quickly narrowed again.

"I see that we have much to discuss," said Raig. "But a hallway is no place for sensitive conversation. We will adjourn for now and reconvene to address this subject later."

"We will address it now," a deep harsh voice said from down the hallway to the left.

Celwen turned toward the rough order's point of origin and saw a towering figure in a mix of archaic armors and wolf pelts approaching. Her hackles tried to rise under the high neck of her form-fitting suit.

Raig's aura of command vanished, replaced by nervous desperation. "Prince Lykaon! There is no need to trouble yourself, sir. The matter is well in hand."

Lykaon strode forward as if no one had spoken, preceded by a musky scent. As he approached, Celwen saw a repugnant hunched form slouching along behind him.

"The Anomian," she cursed aloud.

A thin, three-fingered hand emerged from beneath Liquid Sign's scaled membrane-cloak and waved in greeting.

"Hello, Celwen," the Anomian's smacking, sucking, and biting mouths said in concert. "I have been busy absorbing more qualities of your language and customs. Hopefully we can communicate better now."

Gien whirled to face Liquid Sign. "I've read about you!" said the beaming Magist. "*Elegy for the Locust* was a big influence on my order. It was inspiring how you pushed the boundaries of transessence."

The Anomian bowed its bulbous, stringy-skinned head. "You must be the Shadow Caste survivor. Praise from one who advanced our early work in such novel directions is an honor."

"Quiet," Lykaon growled beneath his horned helm. He pointed a thick hairy finger at Celwen but spoke to Raig.

"Here is the pilot you begged me to spare. Now you would

have others spill her blood? Even that coxcomb Hazeroth slew his own prey."

Raig's already ashen face paled. His mouth and eyes twitched.

The full weight of Lykaon's presence fell on Celwen. "Unlike Shaiel's former Blade, I quickly tire of games. Have out with it! Did you betray your sire to the princes of this world?"

The trials of the past several hours left Celwen emotionally numb. She looked into the dark slits of the demon's helm and said, "Yes. I did."

"You were warned," shouted Raig. "That confession is the final seal on your death warrant!"

Lykaon ignored the admiral and looked down at the Magist. "I smell your madness," he told Gien. "Know that I can also smell lies. What was your interest in this woman's father?"

"He had part of Thera in his soul," said Gien. "We wanted to take it out and put her back together. So we did, but not quite right. Some impurities got into the mix."

"Did you inflict the same wounds upon a man called Vaun Mordechai?" Lykaon asked.

Gien chewed on the end of his own thumb. "I think that was Vilneus, but we all pitched in on the project."

Raig scowled at Celwen. "What did they offer you? What was the price for betraying your own blood?"

The web of rationalizations that Celwen had spun over the years fell away, and she looked upon her own guilt.

"I wanted to be a pilot," she said. "My father objected. I wonder if he had some glimmer of nexic sight, because he saw war with the clay tribe coming. He feared for my safety. But living aboard ships on a voyage through empty darkness was like being caged from birth. I just wanted to fly."

The wall around Celwen's heart crumbled, and she wept. She nearly screamed when Lykaon's cold finger brushed a tear from her face.

"The tribunal is concluded," said Shaiel's Left Hand. "You have done my master a great service. Indeed, it is partly thanks to you that he was deified. I pardon you in Shaiel's name."

Celwen's numbness returned, spreading from her heart to her mind to her soul.

Raig quivered on the edge of fury but held his tongue. He turned and walked away alone.

"Shaiel's pardon extends to the Magist," Lykaon added, "if he swears not to rebel against creation's rightful lord."

"I do," said Gien. His robes fluttered as he raised his right hand. "I swear."

Lykaon bent closer to the Magist, and made snuffling sounds under his helmet.

"Shaiel's Law is satisfied," the Left Hand said. He turned on his heel and marched back the way he'd come, with the Anomian creeping along behind.

"Orders, Lieutenant?"

Celwen almost jumped out of her skintight suit at the question. Amid her introspection she'd forgotten about the security detail.

"Dismissed," she told the lower-ranking security officers. All six men saluted her, though she could see the reservations in their eyes. She returned the salute, and they quickly left.

Celwen found herself alone with Gien in the broad, black paneled hallway.

"That was great," the Magist said. "What should we do next?"

"I will arrange new quarters for you," Celwen said with a sigh. "Then I will return to my own, get out of these clothes, and take a wastefully long bath."

Astlin strode into the dim, spartan confines of the *Serapis'* backup bridge ahead of Jaren. The low chatter among the few hands present stopped as she and the Gen passed between stations.

Gid stood upon the Wheel, looking haggard in his rumpled grey uniform. He turned to face Astlin and Jaren as they approached.

"The two of you are up to something."

Astlin cleared her throat before speaking. "We need to go somewhere else."

Gid grimaced. "No kidding. There's nothing but an oversized chunk of rock between us and that Night Gen leviathan, and I don't want to be anywhere near her when she's done with Temil. The problem is, we're fresh out of places to go."

"I was in the same pinch a while back," Jaren said. "Wherever I went, the Guild was already there—until I signed on to the *Exodus.*"

Gid's face fell. "Please don't say what I think you're about to say."

"We can take the ship to Avalon," said Astlin.

"That was it." Gid removed his glasses and rubbed his eyes.

Astlin reached up and gripped the Wheel's railing. "Gid," she said, "Teg's been poisoned. Avalon might have a cure."

"And it's tactically sound," said Jaren. "Nakvin and Thera have the realm sealed off. Shaiel and the Night Gen won't be able to follow us."

"That sounds perfect," said Gid, "except for one small detail. If the whole place is sealed off, how do we get there?"

Jaren looked to Astlin. "She's our ticket in."

"You plan to bust down a goddess' door?" said Gid.

Astlin raised her hands in a defensive gesture. "No. I'll ask her to open it."

"Supposing she agrees," said Gid, "What then? This ship wasn't designed for inter-strata travel."

This was the part Astlin felt the least sure about, so she hesitated before answering. "I can travel between Strata at will. It should be possible to bring the *Serapis* with me—if I take the Wheel."

"I recall a similar discussion from before." Gid crossed his arms. "You said that trying it with the *Serapis* would be too risky."

"She's had two successful test runs since then," Jaren said. "It's a proven concept."

Gid frowned at Astlin. "Don't you need to have visited Avalon for this to work?"

"A secondhand memory from someone else will work," said Astlin. "I could've pulled the image from Teg, but his mind is stuck in some weird dream."

She looked hopefully at Jaren. "Haven't you been to Avalon?"

"That's what they tell me," Jaren said, tapping his temple. "Not that I remember."

"What if your memories aren't gone," said Astlin, "just

hidden? Maybe I can help you remember."

Jaren's mouth bent in bittersweet grin. "I've led a pretty brutal life. The little I do remember makes it hard enough to sleep at night. There are plenty of memories I'd like to have back besides my trip to Avalon—my dad's face; more of my time with Nakvin—but there are things I'd rather not know. And frankly, I'd rather you didn't know them, either."

Astlin saw flashes of her own shameful past. "I understand," she said softly.

"We're right back where we started," said Gid.

"Not necessarily," Jaren said. He put his hand on Astlin's shoulder. "Thera's in Avalon. Just have her send you a mental picture."

Astlin smiled. "That should work. Now all I have to do is take the Wheel."

"I'm still not a hundred percent on this," said Gid.

"Don't be stupid," Jaren said. "You've spent how many hours on the Wheel in the past week? You're asking for ERIS if you don't take a break. And whether or not Astlin can get us to Avalon, she's the only one qualified to relieve you."

Gid leaned against the railing and sighed. Then he stood up, straightened his jacket, and stepped down from the Wheel. The raised disc that had glowed white while he'd stood on it went dark.

"All yours." Gid motioned from Astlin to the steps leading up to the Wheel.

Astlin looked over the expectant faces of Gid, Jaren, and the bridge crew.

I'm about to take control of a warship and ask a goddess if I can bring it to her mother's hidden kingdom. Nothing to be afraid of.

Except for the fact that piloting this same ship had gotten Zan possessed by the trapped soul of the former captain—who'd then proceeded to murder her.

But what were the odds of that happening again?

Astlin ascended to the Wheel. Standing atop it made her even more aware that everyone was looking at her. She took her mind off it by running through a quick inspection of the Wheel's surface and the instruments attached to the railing.

Everything looked fine as far as she could tell. At that point a fully trained steersman would have used the Workings that linked a pilot's mind and senses to the ship. Astlin had never learned them, relying instead on her father or emergency backup systems to connect with the Wheel.

Xander didn't know those Workings, either, but he'd been able to fly the *Theophilus* by willing his consciousness to extend itself over the ship. Astlin concentrated on joining herself to the *Serapis*, and the Wheel glowed bright white beneath her.

Astlin got the strange yet familiar feeling of having two bodies— her own standing on the Wheel, and the massive hull of the *Serapis*. The unrepaired damage from recent battles still smarted, but paled next to her sense of the warship's barely restrained power.

To her relief, there was no evil presence haunting the connection like a spirit in a golden flask.

But the sooner she got this over with, the better.

"Hello, everyone," Astlin said through the intercom. The ship's internal vision showed her passengers and crew; even the Nesshin camping out around the observation deck tree, pausing to listen.

"I took the Wheel so Gid can rest," she continued, "and for another important reason. The Night Gen have conquered Temil, so we can't stay here.

"But there's one last place free of Shaiel's control—Avalon, the home of the Light Gen. It's protected by Queen Nakvin and her daughter Thera. If you want me to, I can ask them to let us in."

"A word of advice from one captain to another," said Gid. "Give them a voting deadline."

"Since there's probably not much time until the Night Gen find us," Astlin sent out to the ship, "please take a vote within three hours and send someone to the backup bridge with the result. Thank you."

"Not bad," said Gid. "That should be plenty of time to reach a consensus—provided the Night Gen leave us alone for the next three hours."

Astlin only half-heard what Gid said, because through the ship's magnified vision she caught sight of several objects glittering in space around the moon's curved horizon. She felt as if she were sinking into the Wheel when she realized that the angular, glossy shapes were speeding toward her.

"We don't have three hours," Astlin said, trying to keep her voice calm. "Three minutes might be pushing it."

"What's wrong?" asked Jaren.

Saba, a Nesshin who'd been trained in ether-running by the late steersman of the *Theophilus*, reported from a sensor station.

"I'm picking up several small, fast-moving craft in our orbit. Their drives aren't prana-based—probably nexus-runners. They'll be on us in thirty seconds."

Astlin recognized the obsidian spear points as the same kind of nexus-runner she'd flown to Temil. She made telepathic contact a Night Gen pilot.

I'm the steersman of the Serapis, Astlin informed him. *We're not interfering with you. What do you want?"*

You already have interfered, the nexus-runner pilot replied. *The sole survivor of Temil's ruling cabal has informed us of your role in murdering his co-conspirators. We claim jurisdiction over perpetrators of the Guild's Purges. As such, you are guilty of frustrating Gen justice. Surrender your ship. All passengers and crew will be taken into custody.*

The Magists wanted to slaughter everyone, Astlin argued. *I was defending myself and one of your people.*

Tell Admiral Raig at your interrogation, the pilot said.

Gid's voice called Astlin's focus back to the bridge. "Can anyone explain why we're about to be shot down?"

"The Night Gen commander was itching to kill Temil's leaders, and he's upset that I beat him to it," Astlin said. "He wants the *Serapis* seized and us arrested."

"He'll get what he wants if we're still here in ten seconds," said Gid. "Democracy is nice, but it's time to make an executive decision."

"I second that motion," Jaren agreed.

Astlin peered into the ether's farthest heights. A familiar black pyramid basked in the light of the White Well. But she wasn't interested in Zadok's Nexus. Two other divine souls—one in the form of a cube; the other a diamond—loomed to the pyramid's left and right.

The nexuses were as far apart as neighboring star systems, but from Astlin's perspective they formed a black constellation.

Hello? Greeting the black diamond felt oddly like talking to herself. *I'm Astlin. We met once in Kairos.*

The answer was startlingly prompt and blunt. *I know who you are and who's aboard your ship,* said Thera. *What do you want?*

The corner of Astlin's mind tasked with watching the incoming nexus-runners cried out in panic when they swarmed into firing range of the *Serapis*.

Red lights flashed and alarms blared on the bridge. "Fifty ships off the starboard bow!" Saba yelled. "They're fanning out to surround us."

We're under attack! Astlin told Thera. *Let us in to Avalon.*

I'll have to ask permission, Thera said.

Green-white light flashed from the points of a dozen attacking ships, and Astlin felt a dozen wounds burned into her ship's hull.

Gid ran to a crew station. "Let's get some weapons online!"

"I'm trying," Jaren called from another post. "I've only got one arm."

We have to get out of here now! Astlin thought. She couldn't move the ship to Avalon, but then again she didn't have to. Picturing Keth's fiery sphere, she willed herself and the *Serapis* into orbit above it.

"My screen is clear," Saba marveled. "The moon's gone. Where are we?"

"Keth," said Gid. "He turned and smiled up at Astlin. "If we weren't sure that our steersman could move the whole ship, we are now."

"Nakvin is the best pilot I've ever known," Jaren said. "She'd be proud."

Astlin tried not to grin. "We're not out of trouble yet. The Night Gen can track us nexically. This just bought us—"

Dark, formless thoughts; sharp impressions of agony, called to Astlin's soul. For a moment she feared that the presence once trapped in the *Serapis* had returned. But the incoherent yearnings weren't coming from the Wheel; not directly.

Through the ship's magnified sight, Astlin saw a swirling disc of clouds hovering over the burning sphere. Lightning flashed between the spiraling arms, coloring the storm a faint electric blue.

The lightning and the silent wind spoke to her in voices filled with chaos and pain. The storm screamed in mindless torment, but Astlin understood.

It was calling her closer.

"What is it?" asked Gid.

"Zan," Astlin thought aloud.

"I'm detecting an ethereal disturbance in high orbit," Saba said. "It's the Air Stratum rift the *Theophilus* went through. We're turning toward it."

"The Night Gen probably won't follow us," said Jaren, "but trust me, Astlin, you don't want to go in there."

Astlin heard what Jaren said, but fascination with the storm held her will captive. Something in the rift was contacting her through her connection to the Wheel, and it knew that connection well enough to turn her bond with the ship into shackles for her mind.

Sorry for making you wait, Thera's nexus said. *There were complications I had to sort out. You can bring the ship through now.*

An image of rolling green hills under a clear blue sky drove away the storm that had raged in Astlin's mind. She grabbed hold of the beautiful scene and willed herself into it.

The emerald hills of Avalon reminded Astlin of her life beyond the Nexus. But the faint memories fled when a rumbling masculine voice came over the *Serapis'* sending.

"This is Captain Anris of Her Majesty's Army. On behalf of Queen Nakvin, I welcome you to Avalon."

Astlin's smile colored her voice as cheers went up from the handful of men stationed around her.

"Thanks for the warm welcome, Captain. We have injured in need of medical help and passengers the queen will want to see. Is there anyplace to land this thing?"

Anris gave a deep, rich laugh. "It's been years since a vessel your size came into port, but we can accommodate you. I'm sending directions now."

The dock where Astlin landed had been created by removing the southern half of a hilltop. Towers and cranes stood atop the resulting cliff.

Despite what Anris had said, Astlin worried at first that there wouldn't be enough room for the massive warship. But she soon found that the dock could have held a vessel even bigger than the *Serapis*.

Astlin felt relieved to get off the Wheel—though probably not as relieved as Gid, who'd flown the *Serapis* most of the way from Keth. At Saba's request she went to round up the other Nesshin.

She found all eight of them on the observation deck standing beyond the room's central tree. Three men, one woman, and four children stared through the broad window at a land that rose and fell like waves of a green sea.

Astlin stood beside the stout, spreading tree. "You had such a long journey," she said to the Nesshin. "I can't imagine what this is like for you."

Some of them turned to face her, their eyes glistening with an emotion that she had no name for. But there were traces of pride and gratitude; sadness and even fear.

"Astlin!" Rosemy ran toward Astlin, who caught the small girl up in her arms and kissed her on the cheek. Her dark hair had been braided, and her joyous warmth spread through Astlin's chest.

"Is it true?" Rosemy asked. "Did you bring us here?"

"With lots of help from lots of other people," Astlin said.

Zay, the short-haired boy with a serious look, turned from the window and asked, "Are we really in hell?"

"Mind yourself, boy." Marse, the only other grown woman present, swatted the back of Zay's bristly head. "You're too young to remember Tharis. If this is hell, I'll take it over that blasted ash heap!"

Astlin set Rosemy down and spoke to the Nesshin as a group. "This is just a dock out in the countryside. A transport is coming to take us to Seele, the city where the queen lives."

"Can they help Teg there?" asked Marse.

"I hope so," Astlin said, trying to hide her fear. The ship's medical staff had done all they could for him, but Teg remained in a coma.

"We'll pack up our things and get ready to disembark," said a stocky bald man named Hez.

"Good," said Astlin, suppressing a painful longing for

Xander. "We'll leave from the hangar in an hour." She forced herself to give the Nesshin a parting smile. Then she turned and walked briskly from the room.

27

The airdrifter sent from Seele touched down in the hangar with a whisper of engines and a grace that followed its design. The vehicle's white hull was a series of gentle curves flowing into each other with no hard edges. Though dwarfed by the ether-runner within which it docked, the transport took on everyone from the *Serapis*.

Astlin stood on the floor that still showed burn marks from her fight with the kost days and decades ago. She watched the Mithgarders and Nesshin board the transport with their few belongings while Light Gen in green, gold, and brown uniforms helped the medical staff load Teg's hospital bed.

Tharis and Keth are dead, Astlin recalled as a grey cloud darkened her thoughts. *The Night Gen took Mithgar, and now—with help from me—Temil.*

That wasn't really fair. She'd been trying to save Xander, and Shaiel had used her—just like he'd used the Night Gen's thirst for vengeance. She'd gotten revenge too, but Shaiel had taken her husband.

And what Shaiel took, he never gave back.

The approach of an awe-inspiring figure jarred Astlin out of her brooding. His armor of overlapping leather bands covered lavender skin stretched over lean muscles. Short hair as white as summer clouds crowned an almost boyish face and matched the feathered wings folded against his back.

The hangar's huge size obscured the winged man's stature at first, but even before he towered over Astlin she realized that he was a giant. The hooked blade at his side could have been a two-handed scythe. His light brown, almost yellow, eyes shone down on her.

"You must be Astlin." His voice boomed like approaching thunder. "I thought it well to introduce myself in person. Captain Anris, at your service."

Anris' hand was slender and nimble, but it still engulfed hers. Astlin found it impossible not to smile.

"Thank you," she said. "I'm honored. And all of us are grateful to your queen for taking us in."

Anris returned her smile, banishing all but a trace of the shadow on her soul. "She will be glad to hear that." The giant fell in beside Astlin and placed a guiding hand on her back. "Come! Hearing it from your lips will increase her gladness."

Astlin joined Anris in the transport's spacious cockpit, where Jaren and Gid were already seated. She sat down in a plush red chair while Anris, who remained standing, informed the Gen pilot that they were ready for takeoff.

Early into the flight over marching rows of forested ridges, Jaren raised his eyes to Anris. "I don't think anyone will object to me pointing out you're not a Gen."

Jaren's almost accusing tone struck a sour note with Astlin.

"You could be a little more polite," she said.

Anris waved her objection away. "Captain Peregrine's curiosity gives no offense. I am a malakh—one of several peoples that stand between his race and the gods."

Astlin looked at Anris with newfound wonder. Xander's friend Nahel had been a malakh, so she'd known that they existed. But Nahel's death had kept her from getting to know him or his people.

He died trying to rescue Xander, she recalled. *From* me.

The shadow came rushing back, pressing down on Astlin's soul as if it had physical weight. She silently pledged to follow Nahel's example if necessary.

"That's an interesting accent," Jaren told Anris. "Are you Thysian?"

Anris drew himself up, and Astlin worried at first that his head would scrape the white carpeted ceiling.

"I served as messenger to the pantheon of Khemet," he said with pride. "It was once my honor to carry petitions from the commanders of our armies to the gods, and to deliver victory from the gods to our armies."

The malakh's bright face darkened. "But a day came when there were no answers to deliver; and soon thereafter, no more petitions. For many years I wandered, lost."

Anris' expression changed again, this time to the stern look of a penitent.

"I was a shell of myself, little more than a beast, when he found me," said Anris, his voice rising. "Almeth Elocine. Almeth Blackbow. Favored of Midras. The last god."

Anris shook his head. "Many a blow we dealt to the Guild when we fought side by side, but defeat had the final word. No matter. I swore to guard his people, and my vow has passed to Queen Nakvin. I shall serve her until the Gen need no longer fear any foe, or until another succeeds her."

"It says a lot about the Light Gen that they're ruled by a half-demon and protected by a malakh," Jaren said.

"Do you take offense at my presence?" Anris asked.

Gid spoke up. "Having captained a crew of weirdos and outcasts, I can say for a fact that you fit right in."

Silence fell as the airdrifter soared through the open sky. Soon a prominent peak appeared on the horizon, taller than any hill that Astlin had seen in Avalon, but not quite a mountain. Small towns nestled inside clearings on its forested slopes. The very top was crowned with a city built in harmony with the trees growing around and throughout it.

"Seele," Anris announced, "the royal hill, city, and court of Avalon. The Gen of old paid a terrible price to raise it, and the Light Gen recently paid dearly in blood to free themselves from that tithe. Her Majesty will receive you there."

The transport descended in a gentle spiral over the city and landed on a lower summit that had been leveled off and paved with white stone. Through the right hand window Astlin saw a retaining wall that sloped away from the landing pad to blend with the green hillside.

The airdrifter landed as softly as a fallen leaf, and Anris motioned to the cockpit door.

"I welcome you as an officer of the court of Seele," he said. "Go freely under our hospitality and protection."

Astlin inclined her head toward him and rose from her chair. "Thanks, Anris."

"We'll find out what their protection's worth when Shaiel comes knocking," Jaren said.

"Call me an ingrate," said Gid, "but I'm with Peregrine. Swords and armor won't do much good against corvettes and nexus-runners. Does Avalon have any other aircraft?"

"We may appear defenseless," Anris said, "but appearances can deceive. Our last war was a struggle for the conquest of hell fought across all types of infernal terrain. Air power was of little use in a campaign to take and hold ground, so we devised other innovations."

Unsettled by the talk of war, Astlin left Gid, Jaren, and Anris and joined the *Serapis* refugees on the landing pad. The Nesshin children laughed as they chased each other around the narrow lawn that encircled it.

A breeze blew in from the left, perfumed with tree blossoms, pine needles, and clover. Astlin turned into the sweet wind and saw a delicate-looking bridge of pale stone and metal spanning a deep ravine from which the sound of rushing water rose.

The bridge vanished into the trees on the other side, and while she tried to puzzle out how the natural and artificial beauty complimented each other, Astlin saw a line of figures emerging from the tree line to file across the bridge.

Leading the procession was a woman of stunning beauty whose raven black hair, gathered in a complex arrangement at the top and back of her head, defied the wind. The breeze did ripple the snowy silk of her Steersman's robe and made the golden Master's pattern at its hem shimmer.

Next came a willowy young woman who, like Astlin, seemed to be in her late teens. Light brown waves of hair fell to the waist of her white dress' skirt. Her sharp-featured face resembled the first woman's so closely that the two of them had to be related.

Thera. Never thought I'd meet you again so soon.

A pair of soldiers in green and gold uniforms under silver armor marched behind the two women. The men faced straight ahead, but their eyes constantly scanned their surroundings.

Anris stood at attention beside the bridge's near end. Just before the dark-haired woman crossed onto the platform, he called out, "It is my honor to present Nakvin, by Faerda's Favor, of Seele, Avalon, and all the Nine Circles, Queen and Protector."

Nakvin looked over the newly arrived crowd and gave Astlin a warm smile that showed small sharp fangs. But in the next moment her silver eyes widened, and she brushed by Astlin heading for Teg's bed, which was being wheeled out of the transport.

"Talk to me, gentlemen," the queen said to the medics hovering over Teg. "What's his condition?"

"The patient's in a deep coma," said the ship's surgeon from the *Serapis*. "Our working theory right now is tethite poisoning."

Nakvin looked down at Teg's sleeping face. She bit her lip in what Astlin perceived as an attempt to keep her composure.

"Get him to Faerda's temple," Nakvin ordered the medics. "I'll show you the way."

The *Serapis'* chief surgeon frowned. "I was expecting unorthodox treatment, but not slaughtering goats and burning incense."

Silver fire flashed in Nakvin's eyes. "The first hospitals started as religious institutions. But you can relax. This one's the royal infirmary. It hasn't been used for worship in centuries. Now shut up and follow…"

Nakvin's voice trailed off as she saw Jaren stepping down from the cockpit. Both of them stared at each other for a long moment.

"Jaren?" the queen asked in a near-whisper.

"Nakvin. It's been a while." Jaren nodded at Thera. "Elena."

"I have to get Teg to the infirmary." Nakvin made it sound like a dismissal and an apology at the same time.

Jaren raised his only hand in surrender. "Don't let me keep you. We need every man in fighting shape. But it's good to see you've done well for yourself."

Thera—or Elena, as Jaren called her—approached Teg's bedside and spoke to Nakvin.

"Teg is my responsibility, mother. Let me see to him."

Nakvin glanced at her daughter before facing Jaren again. "Looks like my schedule's opened up. If you want, we can have lunch in the council hall."

"How about somewhere more private?" asked Jaren.

"Whatever." Nakvin threw her arms around him. Her musical voice started to break. "I'm just glad you made it back alive."

Jaren returned her embrace and planted a small kiss on her lips. "Me too," he said, sounding equally tired and relieved. "It was a strange hard road, but you're worth the trip."

"Anris?" Nakvin waved the malakh toward her. He covered the distance in a few great strides while Elena and the medics took Teg across the bridge.

"Have someone find Jaren a room," Nakvin continued. "He'll also need new clothes.

Anris bowed the way an oak tree might. "I shall see to it myself, Your Majesty."

"Thanks," Nakvin told him with a smile. "One last thing—can you make sure Jaren finds his way to my apartments once he's freshened up?"

"You may depend on it," Anris said. He nodded to Jaren. "Captain Peregrine, if you will follow me, sir."

Anris and Jaren filed toward the bridge. Just before he set foot on the fragile-looking span, Jaren looked back over his shoulder.

"I hope this meeting with Avalon's monarch goes better than my last one," he said to Nakvin with a wink. Then he turned and followed Anris across the ravine.

"Please excuse the wait," Nakvin said to the remaining *Serapis* crew and passengers on the landing pad. "I know some of you from my short visit to your ship. For those I haven't gotten to know yet, my daughter explained that you're Shaiel's enemies, which is good enough for me.

"That's my way of saying welcome to Seele. Following the nine foot purple guy will get you to the palace, where my staff will help you settle in. If there's anything you need, just ask one of them. If you need something only I can help you with, I hold court every day. Feel free to drop in."

Gid stepped to the head of the murmuring crowd and raised his voice. "Okay. You heard the lady. We're guests in her house, so don't carry on like idiots. Everybody grab your gear and catch up to the big guy."

The platform emptied amid a chorus of excited chatter, thudding luggage, and footsteps clattering on stone.

It was only a matter of minutes until Astlin stood alone beside the parapet, looking out over Avalon's hills. Jaren and Nakvin clearly meant a lot to each other, and Astlin's heart had leapt to see them reunited. Now it ached in sharp awareness of Xander's absence.

This is selfish, Astlin thought. *Nakvin took me into her home. I should be as happy for her as I would be if Xander were back.*

In truth, she was happy for her friends. But the gloom wouldn't lift from her soul while her husband was Shaiel's captive.

"You're not cut out to be a tragic loner," a melodic female voice said from behind her. "I think it's the hair. Really makes you stand out."

Nakvin stepped up to the wall. She briefly surveyed her realm before turning to Astlin.

"I'm sorry," said the queen.

Astlin met her silver eyes. "For what?"

"For ignoring you."

Uncomfortable warmth radiated through Astlin's face. "It's okay. Really. You just saw your oldest friends for the first time in years."

"I've been waiting even longer for you," Nakvin said softly.

The queen's words gave Astlin a start. "For me? I've never met you before."

Nakvin took Astlin's hands in hers. "But I met you—before the Cataclysm, aboard the *Exodus*. Fire and wind helped me save my daughter that day. You were the fire."

Astlin looked away. "That was another life. One I'm not very proud of."

"Then be proud you brought my friends back to me in this one," Nakvin said. "I am. I wanted—*needed* to thank you. Don't you know who you are, Astlin?"

Numbing cold replaced the ache in Astlin's heart. "Someone who couldn't help the man who means more to her than anyone."

Nakvin lowered her hands and smoothed her robes. "Well, custom says that petitions are supposed to wait for tomorrow's audience, but cases like this warrant invoking my royal prerogative. Elena told me about Xander. I don't play the gods' games, but I'll do everything in my power to break Vaun's hold on your husband."

The ice encasing Astlin's heart shattered. Warm moisture filled her eyes. "Nakvin, I—I don't know how to thank you."

"I already granted your petition," Nakvin said with a smile, "but I want you at the audience tomorrow, anyway."

Astlin blinked. "You're summoning me to court?"

"Not exactly. I'm asking you to hold court with me and Elena."

Astlin had no words.

Nakvin snagged the bullet hole in Astlin's dress with her fingernail. "You'll need some new clothes, too. Come on. I know a good tailor."

Nakvin's plan to leave her guest in the royal tailor's expert care turned into a lengthy collaboration on Astlin's new dress. Nakvin insisted on making her a gift of the garment, and when Astlin mentioned having her last several outfits ruined in combat, the queen ordered the dress to be Worked using the same process that made her own Steersman's robe nearly indestructible.

After failing to argue Astlin out of a mostly black color scheme, but winning her agreement on fine velvet and silk fabrics, Nakvin hurried back to the royal apartments. She scolded herself for losing track of time while admitting a strong affection for the earnest young woman.

The guard outside her gold and ivory doors informed Nakvin that Anris had already shown Jaren in and departed. She rushed inside, her pulse pounding with anticipation and her stomach fluttering with uncertainty all the way down the sweet-smelling cherry wood hallway.

As she touched the inner door's handle, the sudden fear came over Nakvin that Jaren wasn't really there. Her fleeting conversation with him on the landing pad had only been an illusion or a dream. Now she would enter and find the room empty.

Nakvin opened the door and there he sat—waiting for her on the couch. His fiery hair was freshly washed, combed, and tied back. He wore the uniform and insignia of a Gen privateer captain. The green jacket with gold piping was open, showing the white shirt beneath. One of his booted feet rested on the low table in front of the couch.

"What kept you?" Jaren asked.

Nakvin slipped inside like a teenager coming home late and shut the door behind her. "Sorry. The time got away from me. I was helping Astlin."

"Good for both of you," Jaren said. "That girl's been to hell and back. I should know."

"The last time I saw you," Nakvin said, taking a seat on the opposite couch, "you vanished in a big ball of light. What happened to you? How did you get back?"

Jaren's smile failed to hide his pain. "I just remember bits and pieces of the last, what, twenty years?" A rueful laugh escaped his chest. "All I know for sure is that I ended up on Crote, scratching out a living like a starved beast. I'm not sure how much longer I'd have held out if Teg's people hadn't found me."

Nakvin didn't know whether to laugh or weep. "And here you are."

"Here I am." Jaren put his foot down on the carpet and leaned forward. "Now you get to tell me how you came into all of this." His emerald eyes looked over the room.

Nakvin sighed. Compared to the squalor that Jaren had been mired in, contemplating her own rise in station almost made her feel guilty.

"Elena sent me through a door in Tzimtzum that led to the Fourth Circle," she said. "The place was pretty fireproof, so it weathered the Cataclysm okay.

"Some emissaries from Avalon caught up with me at the Freehold. They confirmed the old king's death, courtesy of Fallon, and revealed that he'd left no heirs."

Jaren's eyes glinted with keen interest. "Not surprising, since the Well was too dry for him to sire kids. Where do you come in?"

Mentioning her parentage made Nakvin's skin crawl, but Jaren had told his story, so she owed him hers.

"The Light Gen king technically held Avalon as a vassal of Mephistophilis," she explained. "When you killed him, the deed passed to his consort, Zebel. She'd already fled the Circles, which the Gen court ruled abdication.

"I'm her only known living issue. The court legitimized me and upheld my claim to Avalon's throne."

"That was generous of them," Jaren said. "And unambitious. Why didn't some other Gen noble claim the throne?"

Nakvin's voice became flat. "Because none of them can shape the Circles by will alone, I can, and only I was in a position to let them out of the tithe."

"Smart," said Jaren. "If they'd tried to go it alone, another baal could've barged in and taken over. But giving the throne to Zebel's heir let them renegotiate the rent and gave them insurance on the deal."

"You guessed it," Nakvin said. "Of course, nothing is ever that simple. The baals have been vying for power down here since forever. Every surviving power made a play for Avalon—or was planning one."

She shivered. "It took years of bloody war, but we finally threw down the baals. I absorbed their domains into Avalon as they fell. Now the Gen homeland fills every Circle."

Except for one...

"The Gen homeland seems to have a lot of non-Gen living in it," said Jaren.

Nakvin tried to keep her voice free of umbrage. "It was six against one. We needed all the warm bodies we could get. Some were former prisoners or servants of the baals who swore loyalty to me. Some rallied to my banner from outside—Anris, for one. Others were mercenaries, or outcasts with nowhere else to go."

Jaren raised an eyebrow. "Which category does Elena fall into?"

Nakvin's anger boiled over. She leapt to her feet. "Elena is my daughter. That's all the explanation you'd need if you had any concept of love. All you know is what you can use!"

In an instant, Jaren was standing before her. His callused fingers took her hand.

"I use most people," he said. "But not you."

His lips met hers faster than she could think. Nakvin's first impulse was to pull back, but the feel, scent, and taste of Jaren's closeness reawakened her long dormant yearning for it.

Her starving heart fed on his presence and gave back redoubled affection.

What am I doing? asked a small echo of her own voice. *We've been apart for twenty years. And he's like a brother. I shouldn't rush this.*

But reason yielded to passion.

28

Astlin had never experienced comforts like the palace of Seele offered. Her rooms were larger than her family's apartment but free of big city noise. Yet she tossed and turned in the large soft bed despite her soul-deep weariness.

Blacking out after taking Kelgrun to the Nexus had been the last time she'd slept, and it had been a short, restless sleep. Still, every time Astlin was about to drift off, thoughts of Xander screaming in torment shocked her awake.

It won't be long till he's free, Astlin told herself. *Nakvin said she'd help. So will Teg, just as soon as he's healed.*

Astlin must have dozed off, because a sudden noise startled her awake. The mid-evening light that had filtered through the gauzy curtains had given way to a moonless night, covering the room in shadow.

Her heartbeat drowning out all other sound, Astlin sat up and surveyed the pitch black chamber. Not for the first time, she missed being able to see in the dark.

That was alright. Astlin couldn't see hidden strangers by their body heat, but she could see their silver cords.

Astlin looked into the ether. The rosy mist was thin and stagnant in Avalon, as if it were cut off from the rest of the ethereal sea. She searched the local ether, seeking peace of mind.

Instead she found a silver cord ending at the foot of her bed with a thread of sickly gold strung beside it.

By reflex, Astlin uncovered her crown. Clear sapphire light melted the shadows to reveal a boy standing in the middle of the floor.

"Zay," she said, "wake up!"

Astlin instantly saw that she'd misspoken. The boy wasn't sleepwalking. His dark eyes were wide. The skinny chest beneath his new linen shirt rose and fell in time with his quick deep breaths.

Covering her black shorts and sleeveless undershirt in a blanket, Astlin swung her legs over the right side of the bed and stood up.

"What are you doing here?" she asked, trying to slow her breathing.

"He's taken my king," the boy said. "I don't know where, but he's gone."

"Who's gone? Who took him?" Astlin inched closer.

Zay spoke again, stopping her in her tracks. "Serieigna? I cannot see. No matter what he promises, don't listen!"

Astlin's breath caught in her throat but finally burst forth in a pleading cry. "Xander!"

A chill settled over the room, too fast and deep to be natural. Astlin shivered under her blanket. The next words from Zay's mouth weren't Xander's. The cold itself somehow spoke.

"There is no escape. Nowhere my judgment cannot find you.

Many times I offered the kinship that you crave, but you struck my open hand. No more. I have put away patience and mercy."

Astlin tried to speak firmly despite the fear clutching her heart. "Let the boy go."

"Have I bid you pluck a single hair from your head? The boy is even less to me, though a part of my godhead. I know your foolish design, and I tell you that all of my members are numbered. I shall part with not a one. All are mine to keep."

"Xander isn't yours," Astlin said. "Let him go."

"What ransom do you offer?" Shaiel asked through his fragment. "Or will you challenge me for his freedom? Come to the Void, if you think yourself strong enough. My gates stand open, unlike the cellar where the harpy cowers with her rats."

"If you're playing on my pride," said Astlin, "then you don't know me as well as you thought."

"Tell the harpy to open her gates for my emissary, who comes to deliver terms of peace."

Astlin drew the blanket tighter around herself. "Why should I do a damn thing for you?"

Zay's face twisted into an expression so hideous that it stole her breath.

"I have many servants," said Shaiel. "But to Avalon I send your husband. He shall instruct the harpy in my will. If all is done as he advises, the pain of my Law shall rest lightly on her people. Defiance—including failure to admit my emissary—will call down such punishments as were undreamt of even in hell."

Hope glimmered within Astlin's fear. "What about Xander? Will you release him once he delivers your message?"

"My eyes are fixed on Avalon's gate," Shaiel said. "If it

remains unopened six days hence, I shall consider the harpy's defiance an act of war. "All my armies shall besiege Avalon from all sides until the Well runs dry. No quarter will be given; no pleas for parley heeded. Tell her."

Astlin's light burned brighter. "Not until you tell me what happens to Xander!"

"All captives shall be mine to dispose of at my whim. Now, quench your filthy light and tell her!"

The silver cord wending through the ether pulled away from the back of Zay's neck. As it retreated through the mist, the remaining gold cord pumped sallow light into his soul. The boy's skin paled, and his already lean form became hollow and emaciated, as if the golden light were eating him from the inside.

"Stop!" Astlin cried. She rushed toward Zay. His skin was blackening and pulling away from his bones as she reached him. With a faint whimper, he collapsed into a pile of cold ash on the white carpet.

Astlin's cry became a scream when the black cube pulled Zay's golden cord free of his ashes and whipped it across her face. Pain like an icy razor slashing her eyes plunged the world back into darkness. Astlin fell in after it.

Enthroned by herself on the council hall dais, Nakvin didn't mind that her two other tribunal members were late. After the night that she and Jaren had spent together, she felt better than she had in years.

Nakvin scanned the crowd gathered between the hall's double row of pillars but didn't see Jaren's face. She wasn't surprised. Though he'd tacitly accepted her offer to attend the morning audience, Jaren hated pomp and formality.

With court already half an hour behind schedule, the nobles and commoners were fidgeting, and the court officers were shifting their feet. The susurrus of conversation hovering under the high rafters gradually rose in volume.

Elena and Astlin would have to jump in mid-session. It was time to get started.

"This general audience is now convened," Nakvin announced over the din.

When the crowd had quieted down, she turned to the officer in charge of petitioners.

"Who's first?"

The uniformed Gen escorted a thin woman to the foot of the dais. Nakvin recognized her ruddy complexion and the brown hair she'd gathered up in a bun.

She's one of the Nesshin who landed yesterday.

"Please state your name," the officer said.

"Marse of Clan Rix," the woman said, her eyes darting around the hall.

"Welcome to the court of Seele, Marse," said Nakvin. "Do you have a request for me?"

Marse wrung her hands. "Yes, ma'am. I don't want to sound ungrateful for the lovely rooms you gave us, but my boy Zay wasn't in his bed this morning. The guard said he'd keep an eye out but thinks my son's off playing. That isn't like Zay, so I thought I'd bring it to you."

The great doors at the back of the hall slammed open. Several people in the court gasped, including Nakvin. She rose to look over the startled crowd and saw Astlin storming in followed by two guards. The black skirt of her new silk and velvet dress fluttered in her wake.

What she lacks in manners she makes up for in boldness, Nakvin thought. But something about the Zadokim's entrance troubled her.

"Come and join me, Astlin," Nakvin said, patting the scarlet backrest of the gilded throne on her left. "I saved you a seat."

Instead of climbing the dais, Astlin drew Marse aside. No words passed between them.

She's using telepathy.

Finally, Astlin spoke in a voice shaking with anger and dread. "I'm sorry, Marse."

Tears flowed freely down Marse's red cheeks. She pressed both hands to her mouth to stifle a wail. Astlin wrapped her arms around the Nesshin woman and held her as she wept.

A number of nobles stood to demand explanations. The agitated crowd threatened to become an outraged mob.

"Quiet!" Nakvin shouted, lacing the command with a Working. The hall fell silent.

"Tell me what happened," she said to Astlin in a gentle but firm voice.

Astlin faced Nakvin with a look so intense that her blue eyes seemed to shine with their own internal light.

Zay came to my room last night with a message from Shaiel, she told the queen telepathically. *He died when he'd delivered it.*

The cold fear evident on Astlin's face poured into Nakvin's heart. *It can't be Shaiel! How could he get past me* and *Elena?*

"Change of plans," Nakvin announced. "Court is adjourned until further notice."

She descended the steps and turned to one of the guards who'd escorted Astlin up the aisle. "Show our friend Marse to a safe comfortable room. Take her statement when she feels up to it."

To the other guard she said, "Find Elena, Anris, and Jaren. Tell them we're meeting in my private dining room."

Finally, she motioned for Astlin to follow her. "You're with me."

Nakvin headed for the door without waiting for an answer. When she exited into the hallway, she was glad to hear Astlin speak up.

"Thanks for taking this seriously. Anyone else would think I'm crazy."

"Crazy or not," Nakvin said, "you're worth taking seriously."

29

Astlin sat at a long table of red mahogany beside Jaren, who looked mildly puzzled but relaxed. Seated immediately to Jaren's right at table's head, Nakvin kept glancing at the door, where Anris stood waiting on the others.

Astlin's eyes wandered over the royal dining room and lingered on hunting scenes adorning dark wood walls. A brass chandelier hung from the low ceiling and shed warm light from Worked fixtures. An unlit brick fireplace fronted with richly carved paneling dominated the wall behind Nakvin. A trace of pipe smoke haunted the air.

The room's luxuries didn't loosen the knot in Astlin's stomach. She turned her mind to her new dress.

Astlin hated wearing formal clothes in any life. But even though her new gown definitely qualified, it was also the most comfortable garment she'd ever owned. Somehow the long skirt didn't restrict her movements, and she remained cool despite its high neck and long sleeves.

And according to the royal dressmaker, the gold, dark purple, and wine-colored embellishments held Workings that made the fabric almost indestructible. That didn't mean she could safely walk into a burning house or shrug off bullets, but at least her clothes would hardly ever need repairs.

The sound of a door opening called Astlin's attention to the far wall, where a young girl in a green velvet dress slipped through an entrance hidden behind the panels. The white silk ribbon in her brown hair bobbed as she carried a silver tray of wineglasses to the table.

"Thanks, Ydahl," Nakvin said as she took a glass from the tray. Jaren also helped himself but didn't acknowledge the girl's presence.

Ydahl skittishly approached Astlin. "Care for some refreshments, Your Majesty?"

Having assumed that the girl was speaking to Nakvin, Astlin had to look twice before she realized that Ydahl was addressing her.

"Hi," she said, taking a glass from the tray. "You can call me Astlin."

Ydahl's eyes grew wide as saucers. "Oh! I could never be so familiar with royalty, mum. I still don't use my queen's given name, even after twenty years."

Astlin pondered the girl's words while raising the apple-scented glass to her lips. "Are you from Temil? They thought I was a queen there, too. And you look a lot younger than twenty."

Ydahl studied the tray in her hands. "I hate to differ with you, but I'm from Mithgar and much older than twenty. The dead stop aging when we come here."

Astlin quickly set down her glass, spilling amber wine on the table. She shot a questioning look at Nakvin.

"This place used to be hell, remember?" Nakvin said. "What was I supposed to do with the damned, evict them?" She took a sip of wine. "Besides, I needed the help."

Astlin turned back to Ydahl. "You died, and came here, and never saw the Nexus?"

The girl nodded without meeting Astlin's eye.

"How long have you been here?"

"Time works differently here, mum," said Ydahl. "Folks who came after me hadn't even heard of Almeth Elocine, or thought he was made up. But when I was little they taught us he was real."

Astlin did some quick calculations based on her sparse knowledge of history. *She might've been here for centuries!*

"Hell was built by ancient gods to trap souls," said Jaren. "Ydahl is one of the later arrivals. I've met beings who'd been here for eons." He drained his glass. "Before I killed them."

A prison full of souls who've never been to the Nexus. The implications fascinated Astlin.

Once again, the opening of a door broke Astlin's train of thought. This time the source of the distraction was the main entrance, where Anris ushered in a lanky figure with sandy hair whose new brown jacket and tan pants already looked rumpled.

Ydahl set down her tray so fast that more wine splashed the table. "Mister Teg!" she squealed as she ran to him and threw her small arms around his waist.

"Hey, kid," Teg said as he ruffled her hair.

Astlin motioned from Teg to Ydahl. "You two know each other?"

"Yeah," said Teg, hoisting Ydahl up to sit in the crook of his arm. "I shot her. You don't forget people you shot."

"*You're* the reason she's here?" Astlin nearly jumped out of her chair.

"He shot her *after* she was dead," Nakvin explained.

Teg pulled a long sharp hatpin from Ydahl's hair. He patted down her dress and came up with half a pair of scissors and a small sharpened screwdriver.

"Also," he added, "she was trying to stab my friend at the time."

Ydahl giggled.

Teg carried the girl to the table and set her down on the edge. "You get these back when we're done," he said, pocketing the assorted sharp objects before taking the seat across from Astlin.

With a start, Astlin realized how callous she'd been. "It's great to have you back, Teg. Are you all healed up?"

"Good as new," said Teg. "Thanks to you guys, and another special lady who should be coming in right behind me."

Everyone looked to the door where, as if at Teg's signal, Elena glided into the room. Her dress was the reverse of Astlin's—white instead of black but with a lower neckline. Anris seated her on her mother's right, directly across from Jaren.

"I'm glad you two could make it," Nakvin said. "If I'd known Teg was awake, I'd have sent for him. Now let's get down to—"

"Neither of you have silver cords," said Elena, her rose-colored eyes looking from Jaren to Astlin.

The abrupt statement startled Astlin. She sat speechless while looking into the ether. *Elena's right. Jaren's not connected to the Nexus.*

"Why didn't someone tell me Astlin's here?" a familiar voice called from the servants' entrance. The secret panel had swung open again, admitting a young man with light brown hair and strange eyes that glinted with many colors.

Astlin's greeting died on her lips when she saw not only a silver cord, but a golden one, trailing through the ether from Tefler's neck. Zay's death flashed before her eyes.

"No offense, Tefler," said Nakvin, "but I didn't invite you. Who told you about this meeting?"

Tefler took off his grey riding jacket and hung it on the back of a chair. His white shirt's top button was undone.

"What meeting?" he asked.

With a sigh, Nakvin waved her hand at Tefler. "I won't ask how you wandered past the guards. Go ahead and sit down."

Tefler sat at the foot of the table. After a moment he leaned toward Ydahl and spoke in a loud whisper.

"Can you pass me a drink?"

The girl hopped down from the table, picked up a wine glass and handed it to Tefler, who took a long swig.

"Thanks," he said, slightly out of breath. "While you're up, would bring me a ham on rye?"

Ydahl turned to leave but, Tefler grabbed her wrist. "And pickles. Actually, just bring the jar."

Teg held up Ydahl's screwdriver. "Do you want this back now?"

Ydahl grinned.

Tefler gave Teg an exaggerated frown. "Are you offering the Gouger a shiv?"

"Well," Teg said casually, "It *is* hers."

Keeping his eyes on Teg, Tefler pointed to Elena. "You're

gonna sit there in front of my mother and tell a known psychopath to shiv me?"

Teg's eyes widened. He joined Tefler in pointing at Elena. "She's your *mother*?"

Nakvin slapped her hands down on the table. "Nobody's shivving anyone! Now, if we're done ordering lunch and conspiring to commit armed assault, there's important business to discuss!"

"Jaren and Astlin not having silver cords is important," Elena said.

"Ydahl doesn't have one either," Astlin noted as she studied the empty ether around the girl. "Tefler has two—one gold and one silver."

"If you're his mom," Teg said to Elena, "who's the father?"

"Deim," she said.

Teg pressed both hands to his eyes, leaned back in his chair, and groaned.

"If I'd ever met my dad, I might be insulted," Tefler said. "Right now, I'm too hungry to care." With a gentle shove, he sent Ydahl hurrying back through the servants' door.

Concern replaced the anger in Nakvin's voice. "Elena, are you saying Jaren's dead?"

Jaren's face fell. "It's possible."

A thought occurred to Astlin. "Could he be like I am?"

"The last time I saw you before Crote," Teg said to Jaren, "you were in Tzimtzum pulling the trigger on a frontloaded rodcaster."

"Yeah," said Tefler. "That'll kill you."

Jaren held up a finger. "One problem. The damned get new

bodies. But I didn't die in hell, and I didn't end up here afterward."

"But the gate to the Middle Stratum was open," Nakvin said. "And we'd just come through another gate from the Ninth Circle."

"Frontloaded rodcasters can blow people into other Strata," Tefler said.

Nakvin looked to Elena. "Could the rodcaster have shot Jaren out of Tzimtzum, through hell, and back to the Middle Stratum? If he died along the way, could he have ended up like the Freeholders the *Exodus* took on?"

"It's possible," said Elena, "but highly unlikely."

Jaren folded his arms. "What are you saying?"

Tefler answered. "That you probably shouldn't be at a secret meeting if we don't know what you are."

"Ask your grandmother," Jaren said. "She'll tell you who I am."

"I said *what*, not *who*," Tefler corrected him.

"Jaren," Astlin said, "I know you don't like the idea, but there's a chance we can clear everything up if you let me search your memories."

"Don't bother," said Elena. "I already tried."

Nakvin stared at her daughter. "And? What did you find out?"

"Nothing," Elena admitted. "I couldn't read him telepathically."

"Then Jaren *is* like me?" said Astlin.

Elena extended a finger toward a point in space below the chandelier. A small black cube appeared. Floating in midair under one of the Worked lights, it cast a square shadow on the table.

"Mortal beings are like two-dimensional shadows cast by a nexus in the light of the Well," Elena said, pointing at the square patch of darkness on the tabletop. "Even the cube is just a three-dimensional shadow of a hypercube—the real nexus."

"You're gonna need to dumb that down a few grades," said Teg.

"You're a flat shadow." Elena pressed a hand to her chest. "I'm the three-dimensional shadow of my nexus. Astlin is like me, except her soul is outside the universe. Even though she doesn't have a nexus here, our souls can interact with each other through the bodies they inform. We can read the dead because their souls are frozen inside provisional bodies."

"What of Captain Peregrine?" asked Anris.

Astlin turned her head to look at the malakh, who could be pretty discreet even though he was nine feet tall and purple. With the way everyone else was staring, they must have forgotten about him, too.

"I'm still not sure," Elena said. "It's as if he's a physical body modeled after a soul, but not tethered to or containing one."

Jaren looked as if someone had walked over his grave while he was lying in it. "I don't have a soul?"

"Elena said she's not sure," Nakvin reminded him. "The Cataclysm turned everything upside down, and you had front row seats. Who knows what kinds of weird cosmic forces you were exposed to?"

"Even so," said Anris. "I strongly suggest that Captain Peregrine be excused from these counsels until the nature of his condition is known."

"What?" Jaren snorted. "Do you think Vaun's spying on us through me? Did he dump me on Crote, figuring that Teg would pick me up and Astlin would bring me here? Vaun was always too smart for his own good, but can he see the future?"

Elena shook her head. "No. His intellect is far beyond anything human, and his perceptions extend into higher dimensions, but Szodrin has shut Vaun and me out of Kairos."

"And Jaren doesn't have a golden cord," said Astlin. "But Tefler does."

Ydahl must have brought Tefler's food in while no one was looking, because he was too busy chewing a large mouthful of meat and bread to respond.

"Tefler's golden cord isn't from Shaiel," Elena said. "Like all priests of Thera, he inherited it from his father."

"Deim was a priest of Thera," Teg said more to himself than the others. "That makes an extra scary kind of sense."

Anris raised his hands in a placating gesture. "I do not accuse Mr. Peregrine of spying. But as one captain to another, I urge him to consider the welfare of those under his protection. Shaiel is not the only evil in this world."

"We all appreciate your concerns, Anris," Nakvin said. "But two goddesses just vouched for Jaren. He's one of the best strategists alive, and he knows Vaun better than almost anybody. I need him."

Jaren pushed back from the table. "Sorry," he said with resignation in his voice and a half-grin on his face, "but Anris is right. You want my strategic advice? Now is not the time to deal with unknown quantities."

Nakvin's face fell. "Are you sure, Jaren?"

"It's the smart move," Jaren said, "at least until we know more." He stood and gave Anris a ghost salute with his missing right hand. The malakh returned the salute and escorted Jaren out of the room.

Tefler's loudly squeaking chair broke the uneasy silence as he got up from the table.

Nakvin glowered at her grandson. "Where do you think you're going?"

"I just came to eat," said Tefler, spreading his arms wide. "I'm done now."

"Sit down," the queen said through clenched teeth.

"I should've let your imp kill Sulaiman," Tefler said. "Then there'd have been this weird time paradox where I'd probably never have existed, but at least I wouldn't have to put up with your tyrannical dining etiquette." He sat down heavily and crossed his arms.

Nakvin set her elbows on the table and buried her face in her hands. Teg stared wide-eyed at Tefler. Elena destroyed her cube with a dismissive gesture. Anris returned and stood quietly beside the door.

"Sulaiman died anyway, didn't he?" Astlin said sadly.

"Yes," said Nakvin. "He went back to kill Elena aboard the *Exodus*."

"But Vaun killed him first," Teg finished for her, looking as if he'd found the last piece of a fiendish puzzle.

Sorrow and anger warred in Astlin's heart. "Death is Vaun's Fire."

When Astlin saw everyone looking at her, she explained, "When I was a souldancer, the fire in my soul wanted to consume everything around me. Vaun was the souldancer of the Void. His power has grown, but the connection's still there. He killed my friends. Now he's killed an innocent boy."

Teg raised his hand. "As someone he killed, I can vouch for your theory. It doesn't matter if they're souldancers, gods, or men. Vaun's kind bring death, and they don't stop unless you put them down."

Astlin felt a delicate yet strong hand take hers. She looked at the table's head and saw that Nakvin had joined hands with her and Elena.

"Tell us what happened last night, Astlin," Nakvin said.

"Zay—one of the Nesshin children—woke me up in the middle of the night." Astlin fought to keep her voice even and partially succeeded. "I saw that he had two life cords. One was gold. He spoke to me. Then Xander spoke through him; then Shaiel."

Nakvin leaned forward. Her silver eyes gleamed as they came under the lights. "What did they say?"

"Zay said that someone had taken his king." Astlin shook her head in frustration. "Then I heard Xander. He warned me not to listen; no matter what Shaiel promised."

"Vaun made you a promise?" asked Nakvin.

Astlin looked around a room filled with people she couldn't bear to lose. "He said someone's coming to negotiate our surrender. He promised to destroy Avalon if the gate's not open in six days. Then he killed Zay to make his point."

"He was a good kid," said Teg. "Wanted to be a steersman. The last thing he'd want is us caving to Vaun's empty threats."

Nakvin squeezed Astlin's hand. "Who is Vaun sending, Astlin?"

"Xander," Astlin said, her voice trembling.

"Why is Xander working for Shaiel?" asked Tefler. "He hates him more than I do."

Teg rubbed the side of his neck. "Izlaril—the psycho nudist who murdered Cook and almost got me—slapped Vaun's old mask on Xander's face. Apparently he's possessed now."

For the first time since he'd joined them, the flippant look drained from Tefler's face. "Cook is dead? That Izlaril guy killed Cook?"

Astlin bowed her head. "Tefler, I'm sorry. I was there, but I couldn't save him."

"Hey," Teg said with iron conviction, "it wasn't your fault. Izlaril did the job, and at the end of the day, he's Shaiel's Blade. Like you said, Vaun spreads death like a plague rat."

Tefler rose from the table. "Shaiel's dead," he vowed as he stormed out of the room.

Nakvin didn't try to stop him. She released Astlin and Elena's hands and looked to her captain.

"Anris, how do our forces match up against Shaiel's?"

"We are no match, I'm afraid," said Anris. "Shaiel controls all three inhabited Cardinal Spheres, either directly or through his allies. The strongest of those are the Night Gen, whose fleet has conquered Mithgar and now Temil. Meanwhile, Shaiel's fleet at Cadrys wields a remnant of the Guild's old might.

"By comparison," Anris continued, "our numbers are a fraction of Shaiel's alone, and our army is trained and equipped to fight a ground war. The capital's air defenses notwithstanding, we are ill-prepared to repel an ether-runner assault."

"It's a good thing Nakvin and Elena can stop an invasion before it starts," said Teg.

Nakvin spoke gently to Astlin. "If I don't let Xander in, do you think Vaun will hurt him?"

The room seemed to tilt. "I think he already is," Astlin said in a near-whisper.

"Something's wrong here," said Teg. "If Vaun could talk through the kid, why send Xander?"

"The boy was only a facet of Shaiel," said Elena. "Vaun could see and speak through him, but Xander makes a far more useful tool."

Elena's words recalled a fearful memory to Astlin's mind. "He had the crystal rod," she said. "And the ruby—the tools Kelgrun used to cut out a piece of my soul."

"Yeah," said Teg, "Xander took Smith and a couple of Magists apart for those rocks. What are they?"

"The stone that looks like a ruby is Thera's *vas*," Elena said. "It holds the fragments that were cut from other souldancers to make me. The rod is a nexic device powerful enough to partition aspects of a soul. It's how the Shadow Caste isolated parts for removal."

Astlin's fear turned to cold terror. "Shaiel was hunting Smith to make more souldancers. Now he has everything he needs."

"That sounds bad," said Teg, "but judging by the look on your face, it's even worse than I think."

"Souldancers are living gates to other Strata," Nakvin said. "If Vaun makes new souldancers for each Stratum and gives them golden cords, they'll taint the cosmos with Void."

Astlin looked over her friends' troubled faces. "It's worse than that. I found out the hard way that putting the missing piece back in doesn't make a souldancer human again. Instead the soul perfectly merges with the Stratum. Vaun would have all of the soul fragments. He could make a souldancer and immediately perfect it. If the souldancer has a golden cord…"

"The associated Stratum instantly becomes an extension of the Void," Elena said.

A sharp exhale passed Teg's lips. "Sometimes I hate being right."

"That still leaves the question of why Vaun is sending Xander," said Nakvin. "If he needs the *vas* and the rod to make souldancers, it's a safe bet that Xander doesn't have them."

Elena's rose-colored eyes looked up and to the left for a second. "The *vas* is stationary on Cadrys. Xander isn't near any of my facets, but if Shaiel plans on sending him here, he's probably waiting in the ether for Avalon's gate to open."

"Could the ultimatum Vaun gave Astlin just be a diversion?" Nakvin asked.

"That's doubtful," said Elena. "Vaun most likely believes that he's trapped us in a lose-lose scenario. Letting Xander in gives him a foothold here, but ignoring the ultimatum gives him more freedom to create tainted souldancers and a pretext to use them."

Nakvin set her elbows on the table and rested her chin in her hands. "It sounds like Vaun is right."

"Perhaps," said Anris, "but he is also overextended."

Teg's eyes lit up. "Remember that con Malachi pulled on us?" he asked Nakvin.

The queen gave a dry chuckle. "Which one?"

"The time when he lured you and Jaren to that empty asteroid and raided Melanoros," said Teg. "That little gambit drove us off Tharis for good."

"If you're trying to reassure me," said Nakvin, "that didn't do the trick."

Anris strode up to Nakvin's side. "If I may, Your Majesty, I believe that Mr. Cross is suggesting a raid on Cadrys."

"That's crazy!" Nakvin said. "The gate's either open or closed, so sending a raid out means letting Vaun in."

Teg leaned toward her. "Even before he became a god, Vaun thought he was the smartest kid in school. We expect him to sneak a nasty surprise in with Xander, but he won't expect us to try the same thing."

"Because it's suicidal," said Nakvin. "Sending a big enough force to do any damage on Cadrys would leave us vulnerable to whatever Vaun sends here."

"Who said anything about sending a force?" asked Teg. "I plan on doing this alone."

Nakvin scoffed. "Now that's just silly." She took another sip of wine.

"It's our best option," said Teg. "I'm not a frontline soldier. If Vaun brings the kind of air and ground war we expect, you won't even notice I'm gone. What I do specialize in is sneaking around and taking things unnoticed."

A smile brightened Anris' lavender face. "You intend to steal Thera's *vas* and the rod of partition."

"That's just the warmup," said Teg. "For the main event, I'll extract Smith to Avalon."

Elena looked thoughtful. "The *vas* contains a fragment of Vaun's soul. I should be able to strike at him through the gem if Teg succeeds."

"And when Teg's pulled that off," said Nakvin, "he can go to the ether and practice fire eating!"

"You're the leader of a country facing invasion," Teg told her. "Part of your job will be making decisions that get people killed. I'm comfortable with the idea that I could be one of them. If you're not, step down and let someone else run this war."

Nakvin's expression softened as her eyes met Teg's. "I spent years getting comfortable with the idea that you already were," she said. "How am I supposed to do it again?"

"Look," said Teg, "I have contacts inside Vaun's organization. He'll have his eyes on Avalon, and I can arrange a diversion for his people on Cadrys. Worst case scenario, I can deal with anyone who becomes a problem."

The image of Teg lying cold and bloody on the floor of a cave sent a chill down Astlin's spine.

"What about Izlaril?" she asked.

Teg faced her, his eyes and voice steady. "If Izlaril's there and he gets in my way, I'll kill him."

"Didn't he almost kill *you*?" asked Nakvin.

Teg sat back and looked at the chandelier. "Yes he did, and he knows that *almost* doesn't count. That leaves us tied at zero after round two. If there's a round three, he'll go into it knowing that his best shot wasn't enough. And he still hasn't seen *my* best."

Nakvin sighed. "At least let me send some of my stalkers with you."

"If I thought they'd be any help in urban operations, I'd take you up on that," said Teg. "Besides, if they're still half as good as the one who shot me in the *Exodus'* hangar, they'll be plenty of use to you here."

"I should know better than to argue tactics with you," Nakvin said. "I'll approve the operation on two conditions. First, we wait the full six days before I let Xander in."

She gestured from Teg to Astlin. "Second, both of you will spend that time in training. If anyone can whip you into fighting form, it's Anris."

Astlin stared at the smiling purple giant. "I don't doubt Anris," she said, "but how much can he teach us in six days?"

Nakvin finished her wine. "A lot, considering I'll be stretching each of those days into a month."

"Can you really do that?" asked Astlin.

"Making Zebel's daughter their queen wasn't just a matter of legality for the Light Gen," said Nakvin. "Hell is a machine that responds to a certain type of user. I can control it just like the baals."

"Maintaining that degree of time dilation won't leave you enough strength to hold the gate closed," Elena warned.

"You're right," said Nakvin. "Think you can keep out the undesirables all by yourself?"

Elena laced her fingers. "Shaiel and I are equal in power, but my presence here gives me an advantage. I should be able to deny him entry."

"Sounds like we have a plan," said Teg. "We prep for six months, which will be six days to Vaun. After that Elena and Nakvin open the gate. Xander comes in, and I go out. While you're keeping Vaun's messenger busy, I steal his toys behind his back. Elena hits him in the family jewel, and we win."

Nakvin turned to Elena. "Couldn't Vaun attack *you* through the *vas*?"

"Yes," Elena said. "The fact that he hasn't suggests three possibilities—he's unaware of that option, he is aware but doesn't know how to implement it, or he's fully capable but is holding it in reserve to coerce me. In any event, retrieving the *vas* is the only way to keep Shaiel from using it against me while letting us use it against him."

Astlin had been grappling with a dilemma throughout the conversation. Now she made a decision.

"You should all know that I won't leave Xander at Shaiel's mercy," she said. "No matter what happens, I'll do whatever I can to free him."

Elena's eyes, like circles of rose quartz, seemed to pierce Astlin's soul. "Shaiel is more than a match for you alone," Elena said, "and he can turn Xander's strength against you."

The words hit Astlin like a slap across the face, but she stood her ground. "Impossible odds never stopped me before."

A slight smile brightened Elena's face. "Defeat isn't certain. If I join my power to yours, the odds will be even."

Astlin felt suddenly light, as if she'd been carrying a burden that Elena now shared.

"I was angry with you for a long time," Astlin confessed to Elena. "Because they hurt me to make you. But if I had to go through all of that torture again just so you could live, I would."

Elena rose from her chair. Astlin couldn't read her expression as she spoke. "Thera was supposed to return and unmake creation. Do you know what stopped me from being her?"

"No," Astlin said softly.

"The people at this table," said Elena. "Especially you and my mother. What little room my heart has for others comes from you two. It's only right that you both have a place in it."

Elena exited the room. Anris stood and watched her leave in awed silence.

Astlin's certainty that Elena could help her free Xander gave her comfort, but a troubling question remained.

Who can help Elena?

A tap on her shoulder snapped Astlin out of her dark meditation. She looked up and to the right to see Teg standing beside her.

"I didn't mean to brush you off earlier," he said. "It's good to know somebody cares if I live or die."

"I'm not the only one," said Astlin. "We all hope you come back safe from Cadrys."

Teg put his arm around her. "How'd you like to help make sure that happens?"

30

After spending five hours up her to elbows in the *Aqrab*-class nexus-runner's control dais, Celwen was no closer to finding the source of the distortion in the ship's sympathetic interface.

Not that she minded. Isolating the problem could take another five hours for all she cared.

Celwen pulled herself out of the service hatch that exposed the control system's guts and sat on the steps leading up to the dais. Her grey hands were covered with a sooty residue left by the fungi that wove microbial networks through the ship's organic crystal brain. She looked for her hand towel and muttered a curse when she realized that she'd left it in her uniform jacket.

Taking care to make as little contact with the matte silver jacket as possible, Celwen removed the washcloth from the breast pocket and mopped her sweaty brow; then cleaned her hands as much as possible. The last vestiges of soot she wiped on her black undershirt. After all, it wasn't as if anyone would see it.

Celwen threw down the dirty towel and lay back on the steps with a sigh. Had she been assigned to repair the mid-sized vessel, she never would have been so lax. But this was a personal project taken on by choice in the absence of anything better to do.

She almost wished that Raig had arrested her and been done with it. Instead, she'd ended up on *mandatory recreational leave*, ostensibly to relieve the stress of her ordeal on Temil. Idleness was close to torture for someone who derived meaning from her work, but even worse was having to endure her shipmates' whispers and averted eyes as word of her treason spread.

Celwen took a deep breath of stuffy air that tasted faintly of rotten fruit. The act failed to calm her mind. Instead her thoughts returned to the vanquished sphere below, where the political machinery that the Magists had built was being used to relocate the human populace to small islands in less hospitable climates.

Behold my glorious triumph!

Suddenly, another voice joined Celwen's inner monologue.

Celwen, the masculine presence said. *It's Teg.*

Teg? Celwen sat bolt upright. *Are you alright? How are you talking to me?*

Through a certain red-headed nexist, Teg explained. *And I'm fine, thanks in part to you.*

I am glad you are well, said Celwen. *The last few days could have gone worse for me. Then again, things could be better.*

Funny you should say that. I'm in a bit of a bind myself, and I was wondering if you could lend a hand.

Sure, Celwen said. *What kind of a bind are you in?*

I'm gonna sneak onto Cadrys and steal some stuff.

Teg's pronouncement made Celwen's breath catch in her throat. *Cadrys is Shaiel's greatest Middle Stratum stronghold! The sphere is guarded by a fleet of recommissioned Guild vessels and a fanatical army of Lawbringers. Evil that has never been human oversees the House of Law.*

That's why I need you to create a diversion, said Teg. *I'll be in the Desolation six days from now. You have till then to get the navy and the Lawbringers looking the other way.*

Celwen paused to let the enormity of Teg's request sink in. The scope of the betrayal terrified her, but the challenge beckoned.

I have an idea, she said. *There are no guarantees, but the kind of diversion you need should be feasible.*

That's what I like to hear, said Teg. Celwen could almost see his roguish grin.

Celwen snatched up her jacket and headed for the exit hatch at a brisk stride. Gien had been sequestered by Lykaon's bestial lieutenants, but there were ways to get to anyone.

The path that Astlin had been told to climb ended in a steep flight of stairs carved into a rocky lesser summit of Seele. She paused on the first step to take in the dizzying view. The bare red-brown stone gave way to sheer green hillsides far below, while thick mists wreathed the upper slopes, hiding the main peak from sight.

Anris told me to meet him here in an hour, Astlin thought, remembering the captain's instructions to her after their meeting with Teg, Jaren, and Avalon's royal family. Unable to visualize herself into a place she'd never seen, she'd taken a few wrong turns in the woods. Now she hoped her hour wasn't up. It didn't seem smart to keep a malakh waiting.

The spectacle that greeted Astlin at the top of the stairs put the lower slopes' grandeur to shame. She stood upon a stone platform no wider than the stairway itself that was one segment of a broken rock rim. Other sections rose to her left and right like jagged horns crowning the head of some colossal beast.

In front of Astlin, another set of stairs plunged into a depression shaped like a shattered bowl. More stairways descended from some of the surrounding rim sections, while narrow platforms ending in vertical cliffs capped other segments.

The center of the depression was a solid circle sixty feet across whose smooth white stone matched the platforms above. Five sets of stairs, including the one before Astlin, rose from the circle to the rim. Past the circle's edge, and between the cliffs that formed the sides of each stairway, yawned a fog-shrouded abyss.

Men's voices echoed among the rocks. Astlin looked down and saw that they belonged to Anris and Teg, who sat at the feet of adjoining stairways, carrying on a lively conversation.

"…just about tripped over the cords," Teg said to Anris. "They're holding the door open. I look in and see her asleep in his bed while he's passed out on the floor."

Anris' light brown eyes widened. Then he threw back his lavender head and laughed so loudly that Astlin feared a rockslide.

"It is good to know that my queen's daughter conceived her son out of love," Anris said.

Teg scratched his goateed chin. "That's not what I took away from that scene, but you're a lot less cynical than me."

"Should you two really be discussing that?" Astlin called down to them.

Anris looked up at her and smiled. "The Zadokim is right. It is a poor thing to gossip about one's friends; especially those who can no longer defend their honor."

"The Magists called me a Zadokim," said Astlin. "What does it mean?"

"Ancient legends tell of those who stand before the gods on behalf of men," Anris explained. "They are set apart to make the final choice for good or evil. Those who choose for good are called the Righteous—*Zadokim* in Nesshin. You interceded for all before Zadok, so the title is doubly apt. Now, My Lady, please join us."

Astlin's palms prickled as she faced the sheer descent, but she put aside her fear and soon stood within the stone circle. A not unpleasant odor of sweat lingered on the cool air.

Both men rose to meet her. "We've been waiting for a while," said Teg. "Did you get lost?"

Embarrassment warmed Astlin's face, but thankfully Anris changed the subject.

"Her Majesty commands that I prepare both of you for the battles ahead. Your recent deeds against the enemy leave no doubts of your strength in mind and spirit. However, force of arms will also be needed to defeat our common foe."

Anris gave the impression of an agile predator from arid grasslands as he moved from Teg's side to stand over Astlin.

"I have already sparred with Mr. Cross," the malakh said. "He shows superior ability for a human his age. There is yet hope of making him equal to his chosen task."

For the first time, Astlin noticed the darker swathes of fabric around the neck of Teg's grey shirt and the sweat that plastered his hair to his forehead. Anris showed no signs of exertion. The contrast made her vaguely nervous.

Anris continued. "I have never faced a Zadokim in battle. Forgive my discourtesy in saying that the prospect intrigues me."

This guy is the head of Nakvin's army, thought Astlin. *Before that he was a Guardian of Almeth Elocine, and he was an angel of war before that.* Racking her brain for a way to gauge Anris' strength without betraying her unease, Astlin found a likely benchmark.

"My husband was good friends with a malakh from Avalon," said Astlin. "Did you know Nahel?"

A grim look came over Anris' face. "That one's name is held in high honor. He was my...what is the human term?"

"Lieutenant?" suggested Teg.

"Friend?" offered Astlin.

Anris' eyes gleamed with sudden remembrance. "Pet!"

Astlin felt as if the rock under her feet had turned to mud. "Nahel was your *pet?*"

Anris frowned. "Is that what you folk call your hunting hounds? Nahel served me in a similar capacity. But you must understand that each malakh differs from another as greatly as two mortal species differ from each other. Our relationships are difficult to describe."

"I think I've got the idea," Astlin said, forcing a smile. "You know I killed Hazeroth and Shaiel's Will, right? Can't we call that good enough?"

"Lykaon, Shaiel's captain, is greater than Hazeroth," Anris said. "As for the Will of Shaiel, a kost is not so easily killed. His soul flees to a specially prepared vessel if his body is slain, and he may return in other forms unless his *vas* is destroyed."

"You tangled with a kost and won?" Teg raised his eyebrows and pursed his lips in a silent whistle.

"Actually," said Astlin, her voice somber, "there were two. I got one. The other got me." She turned back to Anris and said, "If it'll improve my track record, then let's get started. What do you need from me?"

"What is your preferred weapon?" Anris asked.

Her lack of a ready answer frustrated Astlin. She cast about for a better response than *superheated metal hands* or *other people's minds.*

A tall rack standing between two stairways on Astlin's right caught her eye. Several hand weapons hung there, including a steel-tipped wooden spear.

Just like Xander used to carry.

"Let me see that spear," Astlin said.

Anris strode over to the rack and picked up the spear, which looked like a showman's cane in his massive hand. He walked to the center of the circle and tossed the weapon to Astlin. She easily caught its light slender shaft.

"Show me the ways of battle you have learned," said Anris, beckoning to her with his hand.

"What about your weapon?" she asked.

Anris patted the sickle-sword at his hip. "My steel shall meet yours if need be. First, see to yourself, and strike."

Astlin still disliked the thought of fighting Anris, but she needed his training for Xander's sake. She charged the malakh and swung at his side. The spear hummed as it cut the air, but Anris' leather-wrapped forearm intercepted the shaft with a tremor that jarred Astlin's shoulder.

"I could barely follow that," Teg said from the sidelines His awe should have encouraged Astlin, but the ease with which Anris had blocked her attack left her frozen with indecision.

The spear still rested against Anris' upraised arm. His face was unreadable as he said, "Your strength and swiftness far surpass those of normal humans, but these alone will not ensure victory."

Anris turned his wrist faster than Astlin could pull the spear away. He plucked the weapon from her grasp and swung it in a blurring arc that barely missed her head as she fell to her knees.

"If your opponent gains control of your weapon, he gains control of the battle," Anris warned. "Never open yourself to such a grave disadvantage."

That wouldn't be a problem if I could make a spear like Xander can.

Astlin recalled Xander's explanation of how he commanded the prana and elements around him to become a weapon. She concentrated on the stone beneath her feet, the mist and the air, the fire in the daylight beating down on her, and the prana coursing through everything. Then she willed them into the shape of a spear.

Pins and needles played across Astlin's palm. A hazy line extended from either side of her closed fist. Feeling her concentration slip, she partially uncovered her light. The ghostly spear solidified in the sapphire glow, becoming more and more substantial until Astlin could feel the wood grain in her hand. She stood, raising her new weapon in triumph.

The spear exploded. Wood fragments flew across the arena, sending Anris and Teg diving for cover.

Anris climbed to his feet. "Now there is a wonder."

"There is an eye hazard," said Teg, dusting himself off.

Astlin didn't try to hide her near-panic. "Are you guys okay!?"

"I'm fine," said Teg. "Your hand looks like a toothpick factory accident."

Only then did Astlin notice the throbbing pain in her right hand. Closer inspection proved Teg right. Several wooden splinters had embedded themselves in her bloody palm and fingers. Focusing enough to fix her hand took a long moment.

"I heard shouting. Is Anris playing too rough?"

Astlin recognized the musical feminine voice before she turned and saw Nakvin descending the stairs. The queen carried a slim box of lacquered wood in both hands.

"A little," said Teg, "but she got the worst of it."

"Sounds like it's time for a break." Nakvin turned to Astlin and said, "You need to lighten up."

Astlin hung her head with a heavy sigh.

"You're gonna make us ask what's in the box," said Teg, "aren't you?"

Nakvin marched up to Teg and thrust the case against his chest. "See for yourself."

Teg carefully took the box and spent a moment looking it over. "Walnut," he said approvingly.

"Just open it!" said Nakvin, rolling her eyes. "I promise it won't explode."

"That'll be nice for a change," Teg said as he popped the latch.

"Sorry," Astlin muttered under her breath.

Teg stared into the box at length, the open lid hiding his expression.

"Why don't you show the rest of us?" Nakvin suggested with a satisfied smile.

Anris held the case as Teg lifted a gleaming pistol from its black velvet lining. Astlin saw that a matching piece still lay inside. She didn't know much about guns, but she recognized the white metal in which Teg's hands cast blurry purple reflections.

"Are these what I think they are?" Teg asked.

Nakvin rested her hands on her white-robed hips. "Fifty caliber Worked pneumatic pistols—forged from ether metal."

Astlin had seen Teg fight a swarm of his dead neighbors and face down Shaiel's Blade, but she'd never seen him this surprised.

"You made zephyrs out of ether metal?" he said.

"No," Nakvin corrected him. "Zephyrs are Worked, but their ammo isn't. These not only have air elementals bound to them, they have direct lines to the White Well—tiny versions of the kind that fuel ether-runner engines. Pulling the trigger charges each round with prana as it's fired—a deadly little surprise for targets that normally shrug off bullets."

"You're a genius," said Teg.

"With the paperwork to prove it," Nakvin said, "but the automatic ammo charging was Elena's idea. In fact, she put in the prana lines herself. That time you spent with her in the *Exodus'* armory paid off."

"She's getting a new shrine for this." Teg gently laid the pistol back in its case and closed the lid. "No—a temple."

"I did add a few finishing touches," said Nakvin, "improved noise and recoil reduction, mostly. Emptying a mag sounds like popping bubble wrap."

Teg carefully; *lovingly* tucked the case under his arm while steadying it with both hands.

"I won't hug you," he said to Nakvin, "but I really want to."

Nakvin folded her arms. "You're welcome. Just make sure to kill enough of Vaun's lackeys to make it worth my while."

Teg rushed past Nakvin like a kid hurrying home to play with a new toy. "If anybody needs me, I'll be at the range for the next six months," he called back down the stairs.

Nakvin turned to Astlin. "How do you like working with Anris?" asked the queen.

"It's really testing my limits," Astlin said sheepishly.

"That is the only way they are known," said Anris, "and perhaps overcome. If I may say so, Your Majesty, the Zadokim's potential befits her exalted station."

"Vaun will do whatever it takes to get what he wants out of Xander," Nakvin said. "Will she be ready when he gets here?"

Imagining the torment that Xander must be suffering at Shaiel's hands kindled Astlin's resolve. "I will," she promised.

"Good," said Nakvin. "Because you might have to kill him."

31

Finding Gien was simple for a clairsentient like Celwen. Getting him alone was another matter.

Still, arranging a private conversation with Gien was a technical problem with a technical solution.

Celwen's father had often told her stories of his days fighting the Guild in the Gen Resistance. More than one of those tales had mentioned the communications abilities of guildsmen's robes.

Sneaking onto Gien's commandeered ether-runner proved far easier than infiltrating his quarters. Using the ship's sending to transmit a message to his robe depended on more than a little luck—and the assumption that Magists' robes were Worked like Steersmen's.

Largely due to their blood-soaked history with the Guild, the Night Gen relied on nexism more than Workings. That was no guarantee against detection—especially with Shaiel's minions aboard—so Celwen sent only a short message imploring Gien to meet her in secret.

Her mutinous deed done, Celwen sat back in the comm

station chair. A deep breath she didn't remember taking forced its way out of her lungs.

The rest is up to Gien.

The irony of trusting her people's fate to the man who'd tortured her father wasn't lost on Celwen. But to be honest with herself, she'd come to appreciate the symmetry.

With each step along the graceful bridge leading from the palace to the landing pad, Astlin recounted one day of grueling preparation for this one. She'd spent every hour of the past six months longing for Xander. Now, as she marched out of the sweet-smelling trees and onto the paved hilltop that would be the site of his return, she found herself dreading it.

Anris, Nakvin, and Elena walked before her, with Teg following behind. The queen had dismissed her guards, who would have been in greater danger than anyone under their protection.

The sky was overcast, and the birds that normally filled Seele's woods with song were strangely silent. But as the group neared the band of grass encircling the stone landing pad, Astlin noticed a low roar. She mistook it for the stream rushing under the bridge at first, but soon she realized that the deep rumbling was coming from in front of her.

"What's that noise?" asked Astlin.

Anris extended his arm toward the low wall at the platform's edge. "See for yourself," he said with a smile.

Astlin cautiously approached the retaining wall and stared, awestruck, at what she saw below. Thousands of men—tens of thousands—stood on the field at the hill's foot, arranged in tight rectangular formations. Their green, gold, and brown uniforms made Astlin think of fall leaves on grass. The deep roar was the army chanting with one voice.

"Are they praying?" she asked.

"They renew their oaths to family, tribe, queen, and country," said Anris.

Astlin felt new respect for the Light Gen army, but also deep sadness. "Those things won't help the ones who die."

"Those who live in hell may despair of a life beyond it," Anris said.

Teg stepped up to Astlin's right and leaned over the wall. "I used to be just like those guys down there," he said. "I even died in hell, but that didn't change anything."

"What did?" she asked him.

Teg fixed his eyes on Astlin. "You."

"Me?"

"No lie," said Teg. "These last few years gave me lots of time to think. The old gods conned everybody and walked out on the world. The Guild ran it into the ground. Now Shaiel's picking up where the Guild left off while Zadok plays watchmaker."

"What about Elena?" asked Astlin.

Teg turned to face her. "Elena's a good kid, but she'd be the first to say she doesn't want the job. She just wants to be left alone. We need gods who actually care. We need more like you."

Astlin's mouth hung open. "I'm not a god!"

"You could be," Teg said like a mechanic diagnosing engine trouble. "Elena, Vaun, and Zadok aren't real gods anyway. They just go along with people treating them like they are. Maybe what we need are gods who know what it's like to be human."

"Shaiel used to be human," Astlin said.

"But he's always been a prick," said Teg. "The point is, people are going to follow you whether you like it or not, so you'd better lead them someplace worth going."

Teg waved his arm over the soldiers gathered below. "You want to save everybody from the Nexus? Most of those men down there could be dead in a few hours. You could pass up your only chance to tell them how to escape this flytrap world, but I can't imagine you hating them that much."

Nakvin and Elena strode across the circular lawn, their white garments rippling in the cool breeze. Though one had night black hair and the other light brown, Astlin couldn't help noticing how closely they resembled each other.

"It's almost time," Nakvin said. She nodded to Teg. "You don't have to go through with this."

Teg opened his brown jacket. He checked the mirrored white pistols in their shoulder holsters and the protective aura generator clipped to his belt before fastening the jacket closed again.

"I'm all dressed for the ball," he said. "Might as well dance. Besides, my date will be pissed if I stand her up." He winked at Astlin.

I hope Celwen comes through for him, she thought.

"When everyone is in position, Mother will synchronize the local flow of time with the Middle Stratum," Elena said. "We'll open the gate, and I'll instantly transport Teg to Cadrys."

"You know the insertion point?" Teg asked.

Elena nodded.

"Vaun should send Xander through at almost the same time," said Nakvin.

Butterflies swarmed in Astlin's stomach. "What do you think he'll do?"

"Unless godhood has mellowed Vaun out," said Nakvin, "I expect a lot of blustering, threats, and arrogant demands. But the fact is, we really don't know what he has planned. That's why I wore myself out stretching time. Speaking of which, Anris, how's your star pupil?"

Anris' huge hand patted Astlin's back. She stepped forward to keep from falling down.

"She is formidable," Anris said. "I almost pity any foe foolish enough to invade your kingdom, Majesty."

Astlin could feel herself blushing. "I'll do my best."

"Good," Nakvin told her. "You're up here with Elena and me. As for Anris, I think you have an army to lead."

The malakh bowed deeply to his queen. "As Your Majesty commands."

To Astlin's amazement, Anris leapt into the air. It was the first time she'd seen him spread his wings. The cloudy sky gave their white feathers a silver sheen as he spun in midair and glided down to the field below.

"That's my cue," said Teg. He started toward the edge of the platform.

"Okay," Nakvin told the other two women. "Let's line up on the walk leading to the platform. Vaun might not send a ship, but if he does, opening the gate here should coax him into landing instead of opening fire. And if he gets cute, we can take the ship down without collateral damage."

Teg's words, which Astlin had been grappling with, finally moved her to make a decision.

"Wait," said Astlin. "I need to say something—something I should've said months ago."

Nakvin smiled. "It's not like Anris gave you much time to make speeches. Go ahead. What's on your mind?"

"I need to tell everyone," Astlin said.

Nakvin's brow furrowed. "Define *everyone*."

"All of the people who might die today," said Astlin.

"Yeah, that's everyone," Nakvin said. "Go for it. But remember, we're short on time."

Astlin faced the parapet and the broad field below. She closed her eyes, feeling the wind tousle her hair and her long silk skirt, and concentrated. She sensed Nakvin and Teg's minds and Elena's towering soul. Her awareness expanded, touching an unseen presence nearby, and casting itself over the palace, city, and hill of Seele before spreading over the plains.

In telepathic contact with every soul for miles, Astlin's words deserted her. She nearly faltered, but a feeling of calm reassurance radiated from Teg.

Just show them, he urged her.

As if she and Avalon's people were joined in a dream, Astlin showed them the stark glory of the Nexus—the countless silver cords streaking through the ether; tethering each man, woman, and child to Zadok's soul.

With every mind enrapt in wonder, Astlin gave them a vision she'd shared with only Xander. She took the teeming crowds through the black walls, past world-sized crystal planes in every known color and many colors none of them had seen, to the heart of the Nexus. The inability of Gen and human minds to know Zadok as he truly was left all of them in total, silent, darkness.

Unease flowed back to Astlin through the telepathic bond, threatening the onset of panic. But she didn't fear the dark and couldn't fear what came after.

A light appeared beyond the darkness. It looked small, but it shone as if no man, Gen, or malakh had seen light shining or felt the sun's warmth before; as if the White Well was a cool distant star preceding the sunrise on the day of a wedding feast.

The growing splendor contained everything—every light, every sound; all life and all joys—without mixture or confusion. The light of all welcomed all souls to take part in its boundless life; not by losing themselves, but by letting it make them what they truly were.

Astlin showed the others the irrevocable choice she'd made—accepting the light's invitation to live in it; for and of herself. Every mind in Seele delved into the captivating radiance until it became as darkness, revealing the awful shroud of unknowing in Zadok's heart as a pale imitation.

The perfect serene darkness wouldn't let her look beyond it unless she passed back through herself, so Astlin ended the vision with a final plea.

The Nexus will try to take some of you soon. Remember the way through, and you can keep yourselves!

Utter silence seemed to have spilled out of Astlin's vision and into the world. She turned to see Teg and Nakvin—along with Ydahl, who'd been the unknown presence lurking nearby—giving her unsettling stares. Elena looked troubled.

Teg's eyes moved from Astlin to Elena. "I'm pretty sure you're not God."

"Not even close," Astlin agreed.

Ydahl staggered onto the grass, knelt down before Astlin, and fell on her face.

"I don't think Ydahl's convinced," said Nakvin.

Astlin bent down. "Ydahl honey, please get up. There's nothing to be scared of."

When she raised her head, Ydahl's eyes held no fear; just yearning. "What you showed us," she said as Astlin helped her up, "Was it true?"

Astlin brushed the grass from Ydahl's green dress. "You saw my memories."

The girl opened her mouth, but bit her finger as if afraid to speak.

"What is it, Ydahl?" asked Astlin.

Ydahl's face fell. Suddenly she didn't look like a girl anymore, but something unspeakably old and weary in a child's skin.

"Is it really like I saw?" asked Ydahl. "No more being lonely and afraid? Do they really not care about the bad things I did?"

Astlin cupped Ydahl's face in her hand. "We're a lot alike. I lost my family, and did bad things, too. After leaving the Nexus I found out I was just a shadow. To the light, I hadn't done anything at all. But the light made me real, and anything I do from now on could mean staying in the light forever or being cast out of it forever. Do you understand?"

"Does everyone who gets out come back here?" Ydahl asked.

"No," said Astlin. "Just me and Xander so far, and only because we had something important to come back for."

Ydahl sniffled and cleared her throat. "Will...will you send me there?"

"No—" Nakvin started to object as she stepped forward, but

Elena held her back with an outstretched arm.

"Are you sure?" Astlin asked Ydahl. "The light will give you a second chance. But if you don't change, you could end up far worse off than you've got it here."

The life seemed to leave Ydahl's eyes. "I don't want to be here anymore."

"Remember what I showed you," said Astlin. "Follow the memory." She cradled the girl's face in both hands.

"Good luck, kid," said Teg.

Ydahl glanced at Nakvin. "Thank you."

Nakvin covered her mouth.

Astlin searched Ydahl's soul. The dead girl didn't have a silver cord. Instead, her body was a simple container for her shard of the Nexus. The artificial ties that bound Ydahl's soul within her body yielded to Astlin's will. Without a spirit to give it form, the girl's body crumbled to ash that blew away in a black stream over the hill and the field below.

Teg was the first to ask the question on everyone's mind. "Did she make it?"

Astlin had followed the tiny soul's flight through the ether. For one terrible moment it had begun sinking into the jaws of the Void, but a sudden burst of prana had sent Ydahl's fragment soaring toward the Nexus—another cosmic beast seeking to devour the child.

Ydahl's soul passed through the onyx walls of the Nexus; sped toward its black heart…

Astlin fought for breath like a pearl diver surfacing for air. Her emotions ran wild, making her body tremble.

"She made it," Astlin said in a voice halfway between laughter and weeping.

A sharp exhale passed Teg's lips. Nakvin did shed tears, but she quickly composed herself.

"We're one down Astlin," Nakvin said. "You'd better make up for it."

Astlin couldn't hold back a relieved laugh as she nodded.

But where did that burst of prana come from? Astlin looked at Elena, who stood quietly beside her mother.

"I hate to kill the mood," Teg called from the platform's edge, "but if I don't raid Cadrys soon, it won't get done."

Nakvin motioned to Astlin, who joined her and Elena on the walkway leading to the landing pad.

"We're about to open the gate, but first things first." Nakvin turned to her daughter. "Elena?"

The goddess of the Well pointed at Teg. "Done," she said.

Teg rubbed the back of his neck. "Do you have wasps around here?" I think something stung me."

"I attached a prana thread," said Elena. "You're now a pseudo facet of my nexus."

"I guess Vaun isn't the only one who can hand out extra life cords," said Teg. "Can you give me a dozen as insurance?"

"It doesn't work that way," Nakvin said. "Elena will be keeping an eye on you through the cord. When you've got Smith and his toys, or if you need to be pulled out before that, just think it, and she'll reel you in."

"Beats riding the bus," said Teg.

"Everyone ready?" asked Nakvin.

"I'd ask all of you to pray for me," Teg said, "but why add an extra step?" He looked to Elena. "Don't let me die."

Nakvin pressed her hands to her temples. Nothing seemed to

change. "Alright. Local time is back in synch with the Middle Stratum. Let's get this over with."

"Teg!" Astlin called out. "Good luck."

The only other living Kethan gave Astlin a casual salute and vanished.

"Did he get to Cadrys in one piece?" Nakvin asked Elena.

Astlin never heard the answer. A bone-shaking hum split the air and set Astlin's teeth on edge. Waves of nexic force pulsed through the sky before a black, three-pointed shape appeared.

The Kerioth!

The nexus-runner overshadowed the landing pad like a storm cloud. The deafening hum ceased. And suddenly, for the first time in months, Astlin felt a familiar presence.

"Xander is on that ship," Astlin said.

"He's not alone," said Elena.

32

Celwen was in the *Aqrab*-class ship's engine room rechecking the propulsion systems when she realized she wasn't alone.

It wasn't just the sound of soft footsteps on the deck grating that made her turn from the engine with a gasp. It was the failure of all the ship's alarms and her own nexic senses to warn of the intrusion.

Celwen's racing heart nearly stopped when she saw a masked, robed figure standing in the dim emerald light behind her. But she breathed a relieved laugh when she saw it was Gien.

"I'm here," the Magist said. "I got your message and I came."

Celwen closed the engine access panel; reducing, the compound odor of an infirmary and a brewery.

"You took your time about it," she said. "I had given up waiting."

Gien held up his right hand, fingers splayed, and the index finger of his left hand. The tips of all were crusted with scabs.

"Your message said we had to meet within six days. This is day six."

Celwen shook her head. "How did you get in here, anyway?

347

None of the sensors were tripped, and I would have felt nexic translation."

"I used velocitation; not translation," Gien said with a crooked grin.

Impressive, Celwen thought. Unlike translation, which shot a subject through space as a prana stream, velocitation reduced the distance between two points. Power was only expended at the starting point, which explained why Celwen had failed to sense Gien.

"There is little time left," Celwen said. "We may already be too late, so I will speak quickly."

Gien looked at her attentively while chewing on the tip of his left thumb.

"Today," Celwen said, "possibly at this moment, my friend is attempting to infiltrate the House of Law on Cadrys. He plans to recover certain items and prevent Shaiel's conquest of the universe. I need your help to distract the Lawbringers and the Cadrys Navy."

Looking up and to the right at something invisible, Gien licked his bloodied lips. "You're special. I should be you."

The compliment—if it could be called one—took Celwen aback. "Thank you?"

Gien turned and shuffled out of the engine room into the dim corridor beyond.

"Are you going to help me?' asked Celwen, following after him.

"Sure!" said Gien. "I always help myself."

Xander, Astlin projected at the *Kerioth* as its black trefoil hull landed at the center of the white stone circle. *If you're hearing this, please answer me!*

The lack of a response dismayed Astlin, but it didn't surprise her. The ship's nexic shields were up, making it impossible to reach the mind of anyone aboard.

But Astlin had senses beyond nexism, and they told her that Xander was aboard the *Kerioth*. Feeling his presence gave her comfort. Elena's warning that he wasn't alone instilled equal fear.

Astlin's anxious hope lingered as she stood at Nakvin's left facing the landing pad. The birds in the trees behind them remained silent. The soldiers on the field below had stopped their chanting. Even Elena, who studied the ship from her place at Nakvin's right, held her peace.

I should just go in there and find him myself, Astlin thought. She knew the *Kerioth's* interior well, and nexic shields couldn't keep her out.

Astlin formed a mental picture of the nexus-runner's bridge, but before she could will herself aboard, Xander appeared.

He stood on the landing pad under the ship's dagger-sharp bow, dressed in a short robe of umber-colored wool over light grey arm and leg wrappings. The awful white mask still covered the face below his shaved scalp. But Astlin noticed a change.

The ruby's gone!

Elena was right. Shaiel had removed the Souldancer's *vas* from the mask and left it on Cadrys. Which meant that Teg's mission had a chance.

Nakvin stepped forward with a slight shiver. "You came to deliver a message," she said to Xander. "So talk."

Dark eyes regarded Nakvin from behind the mask. Astlin stifled a cry when she saw they weren't Xander's. Instead of a lively light grey, these were the dead color of frosted flint.

The voice that spoke likewise resembled yet corrupted Xander's. "Your hospitality is noted, my dear harpy. I note also that you exhausted nearly all of my forbearance before opening your gate."

"I don't rush decisions," Nakvin said.

Elena surprised Astlin by speaking up. "Your host is still inside the ship's nexism-occluding shield. What are you hiding?"

"A question better addressed to you from your harpy of a mother," Shaiel said through Xander. "Temil was a toothsome foretaste of my final victory in our game. Now, thanks to your sentimentality toward Peregrine's swordarm, I claim the rest of the spoils."

Nakvin rounded on her daughter. "What does he mean *your game*? How is Teg involved?"

For a moment, Elena looked less like a goddess and more like a teenage girl caught in a lie.

"Teg was going to burn up over Keth," Elena said. "Shaiel was the only one in a position to help."

Nakvin's silver eyes blazed. "So you made some kind of deal with him?"

"I arranged for Teg to reunite with Astlin, and for both of them to remove the Shadow Caste."

"You handed a whole sphere over to Vaun?"

Elena stood her ground. "He and his Blade did most of the work. There was also a Night Gen spy. I saw her through the eyes of a crab cake vendor."

"Give yourself due credit," said Xander's stolen voice. "If not for you sister, my Blade would not have recovered my mask; nor acquired this most useful host. And had those events not transpired, I would not be standing where I most desired to plant my banner."

Astlin couldn't hold back her growing frustration. "You're not standing here," she said. "Xander is! Why do you keep possessing my family members?"

"It was my Will alone who inhabited your sister," said the voice from the mask. "He offered her as honey to lure you into our fold." Xander pointed at his masked face. "This, in part, is your punishment for spurning my friendship—and only a sample of your coming woe."

Anger and sorrow left Astlin speechless, but Nakvin faced Xander again.

"Enough bragging about your convoluted plans. You want to claim my kingdom? There's just one way to take it, and that's by killing me right here and now." Nakvin hooked her thumb back over her shoulder. "But if you'd rather go on posturing, we can do that inside."

Three silver stars burst to life over Xander's brow. Nakvin raised an arm to shield her eyes and stepped back from the terrible radiance.

Horror crushed Astlin's other warring emotions. Shaiel's control was complete enough to make Xander unveil his light.

"I will speak as I wish, where I wish," Xander said for Shaiel. "My terms are these—the bastard of my Right Hand will relinquish her throne and dominions to my host. She will dismiss her army and grant my forces safe entry into and free movement throughout Avalon. She will surrender herself into my servants' custody in advance of her trial for rebellion against my rightful rule."

"You left me out of your equation," Elena said.

The silver stars died. The dead eyes behind the mask turned to Elena. "I needn't account for what is unworthy of consideration. You are beaten, my sister. You were beaten the moment you begged me to save Cross' life. I revoke my offer of alliance and renounce our kinship. Your only choices now are to resist me and die, or to flee the dawn of my perfect order. I care not which corner of my world you choose for your cloister, so long as it is sufficiently remote."

Anger burned through Astlin's fear. "You already disowned me. Do I get a show trial and a cell, too?"

Xander stabbed an accusing finger at Astlin as Shaiel spoke. "You are an interloper with no further claim on this world. Zadok was a fool to permit your meddling. It will be his undoing, for he shall be the last obstacle removed. You who bear his name shall quit my world forever—by one means or another."

"And Xander?"

"I have broken him. He will serve as my host for as long as it pleases me. Perhaps when his usefulness is done, I shall send what is left of him back to you."

"Or what?" Nakvin asked. "Extravagant demands like that always come with an 'or else'. What will you do if we don't fold like laundry maids?"

A joyless laugh sounded from under the mask. "You live in hell in the company of a goddess. Need I elaborate on the penalties of defiance? You and all your people will know torments beyond what mortal souls were heretofore thought capable of enduring."

"I just wanted to make sure," Nakvin said. She thrust her open hand toward Xander.

Astlin heard a sound like a rush of air and felt sudden pressure emanating from the landing pad, as if a tidal wave were confined within the stone circle.

Xander didn't move.

"I'm reweaving space to hold him," Nakvin said, her voice strained. "You two drive Shaiel out!"

Astlin exchanged a look with Elena. Then she turned the full brilliance of her light on Xander while Elena filled the platform with a pillar of prana that rose beyond sight into the sky.

I love you, Xander. Astlin's light carried the fire of her longing. *I won't let Shaiel keep us apart!*

Though nothing moved on the platform, golden light that made Astlin feel sick just looking at it flared, rising up through the prana column. The white and gold lights never mixed, but intertwined like wrestling serpents. The winner would claim all of Avalon.

At the pillar's base, silver light shone out of the gold, pushing back Astlin's sapphire glow and answering her love with rage that strove to crush her spirit.

Once more, passion leads reason astray! The cold vengeful thoughts could only be Shaiel's. *You were already lost. This vain disobedience will only magnify your suffering.*

"I can work with suffering," Astlin said aloud.

She embraced the pain and loss of Xander's captivity, offering it to the light beyond the world that had burned away the shadow of her sin. She reflected that pure radiance onto Shaiel's corruption.

The tainted stars' silver rays had almost reached Astlin. Now the brilliance of her sapphire crown pushed them back. But her light's advance met immovable resistance halfway to the landing pad. Silver and blue strove for dominance; neither able to take ground from the other.

Nakvin has Xander's body trapped, thought Astlin, *and I've got his power in check. Then again, he's canceling out mine. It's up to Elena to drive out Shaiel.*

Astlin spared a quick glance to her right and immediately wished she hadn't.

There, on Elena's normally placid face, she saw fear.

Shouts went up from the army at the base of the hill. What started with a few voices raised in alarm quickly became a massive uproar.

Astlin risked looking over her shoulder. The sky over the plain seemed to be boiling, as if dozens of bubbling plastic sheets had been hung in the clouds. The warped patches of sky bowed outward as invisible misshapen forms pushed through from a realm of pure chaos.

Oh no, Astlin thought, and Xander's stolen light took back the ground it had lost.

The plastic bubble masses took on textures and colors that blended those of animals, plants, and machinery. Astlin had seen them before, but she still had no better way to describe them than flying jellyfish stricken with some kind of metallic cancer. These dwarfed the blobs she'd seen on Temil, and their bloated sacs drifted toward Seele trailing forests of ropy tentacles.

"We've got to get rid of those things!" shouted Astlin.

"I'm a little busy," Nakvin said through gritted teeth, both arms stretching toward the writhing white and gold pillar. "Elena, close the gate!"

"I did," the goddess said. "Every quality of these anomalies is undefined—including location. *Inside* and *outside* are the same to them."

As a mercy, I offered you death or banishment, Shaiel projected. Astlin knew from the other women's groans that they'd heard him, too.

But out of pride, he accused, *you clung to this realm. Now you will subsist forever within a vile confusion of living and inanimate states. Now the Anomians refashion Avalon into a hell worthy of the name!*

33

The biggest obstacle Teg faced on Cadrys wasn't the greycloaks patrolling the streets, the ships patrolling the system, or even the unmentionable horrors haunting the House of Law. It was the fact that everyone on the whole sphere was effectively a spy for the tyrannical god he'd come to rob.

Elena had warned him that Cadrys was Shaiel's sphere in every sense of the term. Vaun made sure the place was populated solely by facets of his nexus. That meant he could see through anyone's eyes and hear through anyone's ears.

Teg had to laugh. He and Vaun were the only men in the world.

Luckily, Vaun's major advantage brought several disadvantages. Between the Cataclysm and the culling or exile of anyone not cut from Shaiel's cloth, the sphere's population was barely enough to support the old capital city of Serapium. That left Teg plenty of unguarded suburban real estate for a landing zone.

Things got even better from there. Cadrys had been settled by frontiersmen fleeing the rigid class systems, lack of upward mobility, or just plain monotony of Mithgar and Keth. Although Cadrys had no more mineral wealth than the other Cards, and a quirk of the atmosphere meant the sky stayed black around the clock, Serapium had enjoyed a respectable boom period that saw its growth explode.

The bust that followed had hit Cadrys hard, ending with Temil snatching Third Sphere status and bumping Cadrys down to Fourth. The locals had soldiered on as they always did—dour, fatalistic, and pragmatic to a fault. About the only thing Teg liked about Cadrisians was their dark sense of humor, but he doubted Vaun's rule had improved it much.

Come to think of it, nothing ever seemed to improve on Cadrys, which was why Teg found himself in the empty parking lot of an abandoned concrete warehouse deep inside the vast expanse of urban blight that locals called the Desolation.

The blacktop was more cracked than an aging Temilian waitress' face, and looked to have been superheated and cooled. The odor of sulfur and burning oil didn't so much hang in the air as cling to every surface, along with a dusting of soot. It was almost three in the afternoon, local time, and the stars were out.

Yep, thought Teg. *Elena got me to the right place.*

The people of Serapium had once flowed out from the city center in waves, building until the metropolitan area had expanded to three times its current size. The Desolation was what happened when the wave broke and receded, leaving the exposed wrecks of roads, homes, and factories.

Even before the Cataclysm the only ones left in the Desolation—ignoring tales of Gen from the Transessists' Mill escaping into the tunnels to become blind, mute cannibals stealing kids from basements—were old-timers holed up in crumbling homes, riffraff squatting in forsaken tenements, and smugglers like Teg's old crew.

Serapium had never had a Guild house. Word was the Transessists had warned the Steersman to stay clear of their order's headquarters, and the ether-jockeys were only too happy to oblige.

Guild Customs had to make due with operating out of the local spaceport. Most Enforcers avoided the city's outskirts unless someone important caught fire there, and smugglers had used the old rail tunnels to run contraband through the Desolation.

Like the tunnel under this warehouse.

Unless Vaun had devoted most of his manpower to sealing the vast warren of tunnels under a part of town that even the Guild had written off, Teg could walk right into the heart of the kingdom with no one the wiser.

The going was apt to get bumpy after that. Teg would almost certainly face increased security; probably active patrols, once he got near the House of Law.

That was where Celwen came in. Unfortunately, there'd been no sign of a major disturbance in orbit or among the stark steel and glass towers on the horizon. Hopefully she'd arrange one before the locals caught on to Teg's presence.

No use standing around all day. Teg walked along the warehouse's perimeter until he found a rolling steel door. Applying the Formula, he failed to tease any meaning from the decades of overlaid graffiti but saw to his approval that no new vandalism appeared above the Cataclysm-baked layers.

A steel plate set into the concrete threshold featured a sturdy ring that lined up with another bolted onto the door, but the broken padlock lay rusting on the asphalt nearby. Satisfied that the door was no more dangerous than could be expected, and taking one last look to make sure that no one was around, Teg squatted down, grabbed the lip of the door, and heaved.

The segmented shutter resisted at first, but as Teg steadily applied pressure it inched upward with a sharp squeal of corroded metal. The rolling door was a quarter of the way up when the door and its rollers snapped free of the ceiling and came crashing to the floor.

Teg waved away the resulting cloud of soot and rust. To get the matching taste out of his mouth, he took a swig from his plastic canteen and spat into the black doorway.

There were no alarms. No one cried out. The certainty of being utterly alone weighed down on Teg as if transessence had turned the air to lead.

The warehouse door yawned like the rotting mouth of some gigantic dead beast. Teg recalled having seen one of those years before and shuddered. He pulled a thumb-sized flashlight from his pocket and aimed it through the door.

Dust motes danced in the conical beam above the ruins of the door and its rollers. Otherwise, the rust-stained concrete floor looked clear. The stench of an old oven dumped in a junkyard seeped from the building.

Teg drew one of his pistols from its shoulder holster. The gun's ether metal construction nearly gave it the lightness of a toy, even though it was stronger than steel. He made sure there was a round in the chamber, activated the aura projector on his belt, and stepped into the dark.

Locked in a struggle of light and will against Xander and the wicked god controlling him, Astlin could only watch as the Anomian blobs swarmed around Seele. Their dangling tentacles descended upon the hill. Trees, buildings, and men gave up what they were to the hideous mass and became what it was—everything and nothing.

Avalon's army was rallying to Seele's defense. Anti-aircraft weapons hidden on its slopes and those of the surrounding hills flashed and boomed like thunderclouds, but the hovering jellyfish simply absorbed anything shot at them.

"We need to end this!" Astlin shouted to Nakvin and Elena, who stood with her a stone's throw from the pillar of prana and Void that filled the landing pad.

You may end this farce at your leisure, Shaiel mocked from inside the column of light. *Or persist in your obduracy. You will be executed for attempted deicide in the former case; subsumed by the Anomians in the latter. It is all one to me.*

"Speak for yourself," Nakvin called out. "I'd much rather be eaten by mutant space jellyfish than bow to you, Vaun!"

"No," Elena said with absolute authority. "Everyone, stop."

The prana vanished, briefly turning the pillar of light solid gold before it faded entirely. The *Kerioth's* black hull steamed with melting frost.

Like the nexus-runner above him, Xander stood unharmed upon flagstones cracked and buckled in strange swirling patterns. Silver radiance streamed from his masked brow to impact Astlin's sapphire light at arm's length from her face.

"Elena!" Astlin cried. "What are you doing? We can't hold him alone!"

"Mother, Astlin," Elena said calmly. "Release Xander."

Nakvin grumbled in disgust but lowered her arms. Xander raised his to the overcast sky and laughed.

It wasn't despair that convinced Astlin to cover her light then. It was an oddly calm sense of resignation.

Xander's silver stars faded, giving a clear view of Vaun's emotionless mask. "Well done, sister," he said with false praise. "I admit that you have surpassed me in one respect—convincing your harpy of a mother to quit her career as an irritant so she can accept her due punishment."

"That's not why we let you go," Elena corrected him. "This is."

Nakvin stepped aside to reveal Jaren, crouching on one knee; his left hand aiming a shiny rodcaster at Xander's head.

Shaiel could have willed Xander out of the way, but doing so required imagining him somewhere else. Astlin felt Xander's will surge, wresting control of his imagination from Shaiel's hands. For an instant she saw her husband's mind and the vivid mental image that rooted him where he stood.

There was a loud click as Jaren pulled the trigger and a sound like a swarm of bees. A tight cone of distortion resembling a heat haze streaked from the rodcaster's barrel and blasted into the white mask. Two voices cried out—one Xander's; the other what an arctic storm would sound like if it could hate—as Xander fell backward onto the scarred stones.

The need to be with Xander overpowered all of Astlin's other thoughts. In an instant she was kneeling beside him. Her heart leapt when she saw that he was still breathing, and without any concern for the possible dangers of touching Shaiel's relic, she tore off the cold porcelain mask.

He looks so peaceful, Astlin thought as she caressed her beloved's beautiful sleeping face.

Sensing a vast nexic power from Xander reminded Astlin that the *Kerioth's* shield wouldn't block her telepathy now that she was inside it. She delicately searched Xander's mind and rejoiced to find that he was alone.

Astlin was so caught up in the joy of Xander's rescue that she gave a small cry when someone stepped up to Xander's other side and crushed Shaiel's mask under a thick-soled boot.

"Sorry if I scared you," said Jaren. He returned his rodcaster to the oversized holster at the hip of his dark grey pants.

"No," Astlin said with a relieved laugh. "It's okay. Thank you for freeing my husband."

"My pleasure," Jaren said.

"It's just…" Astlin searched for a diplomatic way to ask her question. "How did you break Shaiel's hold on Xander when Elena, Nakvin, and I couldn't?"

Jaren crouched down and frisked Xander. Astlin was about to object, but the Gen pirate cut her off.

"It's all about having the right tool for the job," said Jaren. "You and Teg weren't the only ones getting ready for Vaun's visit. Me and Tefler rigged up a new rodcaster and some Malefaction disrupting ammo."

"So that's where you kept sneaking off to," Nakvin said.

Astlin glanced at Nakvin and saw Tefler standing a short distance behind her and Elena. He looked like an ancient soldier ready to fight a holy war in his white pants and shirt under steel armor and a red cloak. His multicolored eyes stared daggers at the shattered mask.

"When did you and Jaren get here?" Astlin asked him.

Tefler blinked as if roused from a daydream and smiled at her. "Right before you said, 'We need to end this'. Talk about convenient."

Astlin furrowed her brow. "You knew Jaren and Tefler were here," she said to Nakvin and Elena. "Why didn't you tell me?"

"Tefler is my priest," Elena said. "I learned of his plan through our special bond and telepathically informed Mother."

"We didn't tell you the plan because Shaiel might've overheard it through Xander's bond with you," added Nakvin. "And because it involved shooting Xander in the face."

"That was probably smart," Astlin said.

"What have we here?" Jaren wondered aloud as he drew a clear lavender rod from Xander's robe.

The sight of the hateful device made Astlin's blood boil. *That's the nexic power source I felt.*

"It's the partition rod," Astlin said darkly.

"Why would Vaun send Xander with the rod but leave the *vas* at home?" asked Nakvin.

Jaren stood and raised his eyes to the sky. "Let's save the speculation till after we deal with the big meat balloons."

Thinking back to the invasion of Temil gave Astlin an idea. "Anomians are held together with transessence." She pointed at Jaren's rodcaster. "If that thing could disrupt the work of a god, it should turn the blobs to puddles of black goo."

Jaren opened the left side of his green jacket, revealing three more gold rounds thicker than a man's thumb held in place by loops sewn into the lining.

"Transessence uses prana," he said. "These only disrupt

fashioned Void. I doubt they'd even tickle the jellyfish."

One of the giant Anomian blobs loomed up over the crest of the hill. A tentacle like a kite streamer—except made of flesh and taller than a skyscraper—oozed onto the bridge between the landing pad and the palace grounds. The tentacle's tip rapidly turned grey with a luster halfway between steel and stone while a section of the bridge took on the appearance of human skin, but instead of hair it sprouted metal wires that twitched like bug antennas.

A shadow fell over Astlin. She looked up to see another tentacle descending from the bloated mass above. The weird spectacle held her enrapt, but strong arms encircled her waist as she was pushed clear of the landing pad.

"We are living in strange times, Serieigna, "said Xander. "You'd do well to keep your wits about you."

Astlin found herself lying on the lawn surrounding the platform, looking up at Xander's smiling face. No other soul looked out from his clear grey eyes.

"Xander," she said softly. "You came back to me."

"No petty god of this world could keep me away." He kissed her, fervently and deeply. She pulled him closer, reveling as his pure light flowed into her.

"Move it, lovebirds!" Nakvin yelled.

Astlin looked past Xander to the giant tentacle, which lay draped across the *Kerioth* and was already taking on the glossy hardness of obsidian. The fleshy tip was questing toward them.

With a shared thought, Astlin and Xander were standing on the walkway with Elena, Jaren, Tefler, and Nakvin.

"This could get messy," said the queen. She finished a series of complex hand gestures and raised her arm toward the floating blob.

A haze like the one Jaren had fired from his rodcaster burst from Nakvin's hand. The humming blast hit the blob dead center, reducing it to a rain of thick tar. Xander raised a nexic shield to deflect the reeking mess that poured down from the sky.

Nakvin turned the roiling cone on the bridge. The weakened span groaned and tumbled into the ravine with the squeal of twisting metal and the rumble of falling rocks.

Jaren's eyes showed more white than green as he stared at Nakvin. "I thought you fashioned Workings with songs!"

Nakvin gave him a tired smile. "I can slow time. In the last twenty years I spent half a century learning the Compass."

"I need to get you Adept's robes," said Jaren.

"What were we worried about?" asked Tefler. "Grandma can just pop Shaiel's balloons."

Astlin looked to the blob-dotted sky. "Can one Factor take down all of those?"

Over the plain, a third of the sky warped and blistered. Astlin couldn't tell if the disgusting, tumor-riddled hulk that pushed through the wall between worlds was the same one she'd seen over Temil, but it was easily as huge.

"To answer your question," Nakvin said, "No, I'd burn out my life cord before I could disrupt them all. And I doubt I'd even put a dent in *that*."

"We should consider moving house," said Tefler. "This neighborhood's going downhill."

A deep rumbling shook the stone chips on the platform. Astlin heard the whine of a ship's drifters growing until it drowned out every other sound. The rising din reached its peak when the *Serapis* roared past the hilltop like a colossal curved spearhead. Its backswept port pylon passed so close that Astlin felt she could have reached out and touched it. The wind that followed in its wake whipped her skirt and hair.

"Lucky for us," Nakvin said, "I had the good sense to order the *Serapis* repaired."

"That improves our odds," said Jaren, "but she's fighting out of her weight class."

Astlin looked up. Though it stretched the limits of ether-runner size, the *Serapis* was overshadowed by the Anomian giant toward which it climbed.

Xander turned to Elena. "Surely a true goddess would intervene, or are you merely the Mother of Demons?"

"I'm bound to the White Well," said Elena. "The Anomians will just absorb prana or anything made from it, so I'm limited to disrupting their transessence and attacking them with nexism."

"Nexism?" Astlin thought aloud.

Elena nodded. "The Anomians spread by exchanging properties with matter and energy. Nexism is nonmaterial."

Astlin looked at the *Kerioth*—singed and dripping with slime. She joined her mind to Xander's.

Is our ship still intact?

Yes, Xander confirmed. *Shaiel protected it from Thera's onslaught.*

In a moment they were standing together on the nexus-runner's flattened white sphere of a bridge.

Astlin rushed to the top of the control dais and joined herself to the ship. *Do you trust me?*

Xander was already at the weapons station. *With all my soul.*
Alright, Astlin advised him, *I'm flying straight for the* Serapis.
Why not simply imagine us there and will it so? Xander asked.
So you can shoot down some blobs along the way.

Astlin felt the *Kerioth's* kinetic drives come online. At her
whim, the nexus-runner leapt skyward, slicing through the air
like a three-pronged obsidian dart. Directly ahead, the *Serapis*
had almost closed with the even larger Anomian. The vast blob
grew new blisters as the ether-runner's three turrets fed it a steady
stream of blazing amber ordnance.

A blob reared up in Astlin's path like a bubble rising through
water. Though smaller than the mother jellyfish, it was more
than big enough to swallow the *Kerioth*.

Searing green-white beams lanced out from the nexus-
runner's bow, leaving charred holes in the smaller blob's knobby
flesh. It started to fall, but not fast enough for Astlin to avoid a
collision.

Xander channeled the translator into the nexic field,
wrapping the *Kerioth* in a blinding green-white sphere. Astlin
urged the ship forward, eating through the blob, which
plummeted toward the ground. Her elation faded when she saw
the falling mass break up into a swarm of smaller blobs.

They're heading for Seele! Astlin's heart sank. There was no
way to keep the city from being overrun.

A cone of warped space shot out from the hilltop like a
lighthouse beam, sweeping over the swarm of tiny blobs and
turning them to black oily mist.

What was that? marveled Xander.

Astlin saw a small figure standing at the landing pad's

parapet, her white dress and light brown hair streaming behind her as destruction flowed from her outstretched hand.

The Mother of Demons intervened, Astlin informed him.

I am glad I suggested it to her, quipped Xander. *We've almost reached the* Serapis. *Bring us alongside her, and I will hail the bridge.*

Light filtered through the mother blob, turning the sky ahead the color of curdled blood. The *Serapis* slowly fell back as cancerous growths swelled toward the amber fire of its guns.

Astlin pulled up to the giant ether-runner's port side.

This is the Kerioth, Xander signaled to the *Serapis. We are here to assist you.*

Since it had served alongside Cadrys Navy ether-runners, the *Kerioth's* comm system could convert telepathy into sendings and vice versa. So the answer to Xander's hail came directly to Astlin's mind but carried the impression of Gid's crotchety voice.

We saw the fireworks, replied Gid. *These things look like the spawn of a medical waste dumpster and a scrap pile, but whatever they are, they sure don't like your ship's guns.*

You've got something even better, Astlin told Gid. *The blobs are using transessence to hold themselves together, so…*

The Working disruption field, Gid interrupted. *Let's see if the Gen crew Her Majesty stuck me with can operate it.*

The tumors that had been growing from the mother blob suddenly merged into a giant tentacle that lashed out—not at the *Serapis,* but at the *Kerioth.* Astlin's panicked mind couldn't will the ship to safety.

Xander cried out. Nexic bolts, unhindered by the anti-Working field, streamed from the *Kerioth's* bow to drill smoking holes through the onrushing tentacle, but the target was too big to destroy before impact.

We are too close to the Serapis, Xander warned. *I can't deploy the translation field!*

Astlin felt ants racing across her skin. The striking tentacle evaporated. It stump writhed about, crusted with tar.

Okay, Gid announced. *We got the disruption field working.*

The mother blob's slimy membrane quivered, sparkling with the rainbow glint of metal particles. Slowly the giant Anomian retreated from its smaller foes.

Astlin regained her wits. *Charge it!* She urged Gid.

Aye, Captain, Gid replied, his wry grin coming through loud and clear.

Astlin looked to Xander, who nodded from the weapons station. The *Kerioth's* magnified sight showed the *Serapis* advancing, and she matched its course, opening enough distance between both ships to give Xander full use of the nexic translator while staying within the Working disruption field.

The mother blob kept backing away, but the ships were faster. It recoiled helplessly as the invisible anti-Working field made contact, boiling away metal-laced flesh like a blow torch through lard.

Swarms of smaller blobs broke off from the wounded mother. Any that came within a keel-length of the *Serapis* melted instantly. But enough slipped by to endanger Seele, where Nakvin and Elena had their hands full against dozens of larger blobs.

Take out the stragglers, Astlin told Xander. Receiving his wordless assent, she flew the *Kerioth* in a close orbit around the

Serapis, never straying outside the disruption field. A barrage of green-white light streamed from the nexus-runner's midline, erasing all Anomian flesh they touched.

Suddenly the wall of metallic meat that filled Astlin's forward view parted to reveal an overcast sky.

I've never seen a prettier cloudy day, she thought.

Gid's thoughts came over the comm. *That takes care of the big one. Let's swing around and mop up.*

The *Serapis* turned with surprising grace for a ship its size and sped back toward Seele, where only Elena still fought to disrupt the larger Anomians and the breakaway schools of blobs. Astlin stayed in formation with the giant ether-runner while Xander opened fire.

Wounded sky jellyfish scattered into smaller blobs that burst against the disruption field. The *Serapis* skimmed low over valleys and hills, burning out the infection where it had taken root.

Between the *Serapis,* the *Kerioth*, and Elena, it only took three passes to clear the land and sky of Anomian corruption.

Not bad for amateurs, Gid congratulated Astlin and Xander.

Or for an overworked shipwright, Xander teased him back.

Well done, everyone, Astlin projected to her husband and the whole *Serapis* crew. A nagging doubt lifted when she searched Seele and found Elena, Jaren, Tefler, and Nakvin resting on the landing pad.

Astlin's thoughts went out to Nakvin. *Are you okay?*

Yeah, the queen replied. *I decided to pace myself. Plus Elena told me to take a break before I burned out my silver cord. By the way, nice flying. I definitely need an air force.*

One last concern haunted Astlin. *What about your army? Is Anris alright?*

He's fine. Nakvin's laugh came through the telepathic bond. *A good captain knows when* not *to fight. Anris pulled back as soon as he knew that swords, bows, and guns wouldn't be much help. Most of the troops made it behind cover before...*

Astlin felt Nakvin's grief and frustration at knowing that many good men had met horrific deaths. Most of all, she felt the queen's burning hatred for Vaun Mordechai.

Vaun tried to take everything from you, Astlin said. *Now Teg will turn the tables.*

34

Six months wasn't enough downtime between urban spelunking trips, Teg decided. In fact, he vowed that if he survived his trek through Serapium's tunnels, he would never again delve deeper than a basement.

The darkness swallowed any sense of time, but by Teg's count he'd been creeping through the cold labyrinth for miles. The only sounds were his own breathing, the occasional scrabble of crumbling brick sliding down a wall, and sometimes the drip of water leaking from above. There was no echo of footsteps. He was too careful for that.

The dry air reminded Teg of a defunct mechanic's shop—metal, dirt and oil with a hint of old cinders. He thought of Salorien under its pall of fire and wondered how Astlin was faring in Seele. If Avalon had fallen, Teg was the last one standing between Vaun and total victory.

Luckily, the new regime seemed even less interested in Serapium's underground than the Guild had been. As he moved out of the Desolation and under the city proper, Teg found abandoned rail lines that had been in service up until the

Cataclysm. His flashlight's narrow beam fell on tracks buried in dust or swamped by flooding. Whole stations stood empty; their glazed brick walls, brass fixtures, and leaded glass windows looking like tomb ornaments.

It was a while before the faint glow of distant lights and the rumble of trains passing above or beside him warned Teg that he was nearing active tunnels. Since the city had changed in the last twenty years, now was a good time to head up and get his bearings.

Surfacing wasn't without risks. Teg knew that anyone who saw him might be serving as Shaiel's eyes, so extreme caution was called for.

Teg took a slight detour down a service tunnel that had connected the sub-basements of various downtown businesses. Intermittent stations marked by solitary lights stood above the tracks. Teg used extra care when passing a platform that might serve an open establishment. Even that far underground, some of them might have installed security measures.

At last Teg came to a tunnel branch that had been closed for never-finished repairs. He slipped between orange and white signs warning of danger and picked his way over dusty sandbags and rubble to a small station devoid of light.

Teg climbed onto the concrete platform, where he discovered a door—long disused, judging by the undisturbed dust at its foot and the rust under its peeling grey paint. The Formula confirmed the door's abandonment, and the lock yielded to the tools secreted in Teg's hip pocket.

Warm air smelling of cold ashes poured through the rusty door as Teg eased it open. A steel and concrete stairwell rose before him, bending at right angles in an upward spiral. Sunlight filtered in from somewhere high above.

Teg switched off his flashlight and crept up the stairs. The ground floor landing was coated in soot and cordoned off with yellow tape. He ducked under the symbolic barricade and continued up to the higher floors.

The damage worsened the higher Teg went, until a collapsed wall ended his climb on the twenty-third floor. As part of his examination he pressed his ear to the singed metal door and heard a low roar like a packed stadium waiting for the games to begin.

Teg opened the door a crack and peeked through.

The area beyond was a forest of bare steel beams spanning between a blackened concrete floor and ceiling. Its floor space rivaled a grand ballroom, and where the right wall should have been was a long jagged hole. The long rent was covered with translucent plastic that expanded and contracted in the strong wind, giving Teg the odd notion of standing inside the lung of a colossal beast.

A beast that's also been a lifelong smoker, he mused, surveying the scars left by the fire.

Confident that the floor was empty, Teg stepped through the door and quietly shut it behind him. The rising din of an arena before a match drifted through the breach in the wall. He approached the obscuring plastic sheet.

Teg's twin ether metal guns weren't the only weapons he'd packed for this trip. He drew a splinterknife from the sheath strapped to his right boot and lay down on his stomach. Without activating the Working that made the blade oscillate, he cut a foot wide slit in the plastic at floor level.

Bright light shone through the opening. No matter how many visits he made to Cadrys, Teg never got used to the strange sight of a bright afternoon under a black sky. He blinked to clear his vision and looked out through the hole he'd made.

Teg's building looked down on a wide paved street empty of drifter or foot traffic. Closer to his position the road was flanked by burned-out towers, rubble mounds, and yawning foundations. The ruins gradually gave way to gleaming new construction that reached its peak in a cluster of tall proud buildings. But even those majestic towers stood back from the huge square at the street's end.

Looks like Serapium finally got its Guild house.

The thought was an exaggeration. All of the skyscrapers and the open area they bounded could have fit inside a corner of Ostrith's Guild house. But like the far larger Steersman's Square, the grand plaza below featured an imposing structure at its heart.

That has to be the House of Law.

Teg's view was partially blocked by the buildings on his right, but he saw that the mound of dark grey stone amid the square rose in nine tiers. The first three steps were relatively squat and ringed with squared pillars. The fourth section was the tallest, with sheer blank walls rising several stories to the next four tiers, each of which was shorter than the last and enclosed with balconies. A serrated spire topped the whole monstrosity.

The source of the noise was even easier to see. A vast crowd filled the square from its entrance to the House of Law's steps.

Actually, *crowd* was the wrong word. A mass of humanity— and possibly other things—stood in rigid formations. Most wore dark blue uniforms or grey cloaks. One rough company wore hardly anything over their ashen skin, which marked them as Night Gen. Teg could hear their howls over the general racket.

The noise stopped as if a switch had been thrown. Teg looked in the direction that everyone was facing and saw a gold-robed figure emerging from the House of Law. The distance obscured the robed man's words, but Teg felt the cold of his voice and remembered it. The speaker's face was likewise indiscernible, except where his eyes should have been were two shadowy pits darker than the black sky.

Fallon, Teg thought with a sneer. *Nakvin was right. Your body died, but your rancid soul escaped. If I were a betting man, I'd wager that your* vas *is somewhere in the House of Law.*

At length Fallon stopped talking. No cheers hailed the end of his speech. There was only the clatter of ten thousand sets of feet as every company turned at once.

The unease of knowing that Vaun's whole army was facing in his direction became horror when Teg saw Fallon's body twist and grow. His golden robe tore away as his skin hardened into dark scales while the flesh underneath rotted. Wings like giant skeletal hands webbed with tattered membranes burst from his back as he fell onto all fours. The long triangular head atop the serpentine neck still had black abysses for eyes.

The dead abomination that Fallon had become filled the landing at the head of the stairs. It was hard to tell for sure, but Teg would've wagered that a corvette could land in the same spot.

Fallon's massive head looked up the street, and a sense Teg couldn't name screamed that the empty black eyes were about to fall on him. He withdrew his hand, letting the slit in the plastic close, and pressed his face to the soot-stained floor. The pounding of his heart smothered all other sound.

Teg didn't know how long he lay shivering, breathing in the stench of burned wood, plastic, and more disturbing things. But eventually the paralyzing horror left him. Several moments passed before he worked up the courage to look through the cut again.

The sight that met Teg's eye convinced him that he'd finally gone mad. The black sky was gone, replaced with silver-grey clouds over a high hill. A foul tarlike substance had been splashed across the woods and towns on its slopes and the fields at its base.

That's Seele! Teg realized. He opened the hole wider and saw that the image of tarnished greenery stood amid the street like a living canvas ten stories tall. It reminded him of the gate between hell's Circles that Nakvin had made in the *Exodus'* hold.

Half the street was hidden from Teg's sight, but he saw that Vaun's troops had marched from the square to fill the road leading to the gate.

They're not moving, Teg noticed. He considered the possibility that the gate wasn't fully open. If that was true, then Fallon was probably still down there somewhere, his colossal rotten carcass hidden by the window into Nakvin's realm.

If you can hear this, Teg prayed to Elena, *big trouble's headed your way. Get ready.*

Teg felt a strong urge to call for Elena to pull him back. But reason overruled his emotions. Opening Avalon's gate; even just a sliver, might let the army at Seele's threshold get a foot in the door.

Defending Avalon was up to Nakvin, Elena, and Astlin. Teg had his own, arguably more important, mission. If he couldn't keep Vaun from making new souldancers, the bastard would flood the whole cosmos with Void; and it wouldn't matter if Avalon stood or fell.

But right now, Teg and Nakvin had the same problem. The army massed to invade her kingdom stood between him and his objective.

He looked to the starry afternoon sky. *If you've still got a card up your sleeve,* he silently implored Celwen, *now's the time to play it.*

35

Celwen lay on the smooth, jelly-like sleeping pad in the relative safety of her quarters, but physical distance didn't obstruct her nexic view of the *Sinamarg's* bridge.

The only real obstacles in her way had been other nexists keeping watch for spies. But Celwen's intimate knowledge of security protocol and the personnel who enforced it allowed her to evade their net.

Now she saw and heard everything on the bridge as if she were present—a vantage that Lykaon and Liquid Sign's entrance almost made her regret.

Shaiel's Left Hand stormed across the obsidian deck toward the dais, his armor ringing with each heavy step. Three of his similarly clad sycophants tagged along behind him. The Anomian kept pace with the two-legged wolves, his scaled mantle concealing whatever alien means of locomotion enabled him to simultaneously advance and grovel.

Even if they noticed Gien slipping in through the closing door, the wolves, the Anomian, and the Night Gen bridge crew paid no mind to him—or the hand gestures he made.

"My Prince," the myriad mouths in Liquid Sign's bulbous twine ball head pronounced, "They Who Exist have allied with Those That Do Not Exist to nullify all Anomian processes in Avalon. I am the last iteration."

"How do you know?" Lykaon snarled.

"There is no qualitative division between one Anomian iteration and another. Being informed is a quality shared by all."

Lykaon scoffed. "If you are all one being, the others' destruction would have destroyed you."

"That would be true if we shared one essence," Liquid Sign corrected him. "Instead we shared a lack of essence, but now I am alone."

"A worthy sacrifice in service to Shaiel," said Lykaon. "You will not lose your reward." Approaching the control dais, he commanded the pilot, "Prepare this ship and the fleet for an assault on Avalon."

"She Who Exists and The Queen That Does Not Exist are barring the gate," Liquid Sign objected.

Lykaon's bloodthirsty smile somehow radiated through the grill of his cruel helmet. "Shaiel's Right Hand already grasps the key. In a matter of moments the gate will open. Then we shall join with the army under Shaiel's Will, tear out the harpy's warbling throat, and feed her people's flesh to the dogs."

In the terror evoked by Lykaon's words, Celwen had lost track of Gien. Now she found him again, standing next to Liquid Sign.

"I heard you're the last of your kind," the Magist said. His bearded mouth frowned behind the net that covered his face. "I'm the last of my order, too."

Liquid Sign's multiple mismatched eyes regarded Gien. Besides the hideous smacking and sucking of his mouths, the Anomian remained silent.

"You know what's interesting about Anomians?" asked Gien. "They don't have minds. Yeah, they're really just meat machines that run on transessence. So if you know how, you can control them the same way."

Lykaon finally turned toward Gien, but too late. The Magist's hand was already on Liquid Sign's varicolored mantle, loosing the Working he'd fashioned on his way onto the bridge. Gien's skin from his gnawed fingers to his elbow sprouted colorful scales like butterflies' wings.

"Oath-breaker!" Lykaon growled. "You swore allegiance to Shaiel."

Gien's brow furrowed. "I did? Sorry. After a few centuries your memory starts to go."

Lykaon's men loped toward Gien but paused when Liquid Sign's mantle began to flutter. The strange flesh beneath swelled and bulged, shooting out pale waxy pseudopods that glinted like metal. One tendril engulfed the *Sinamarg's* pilot, whose scream was cut off with startling suddenness. The Anomian doubled in size as his body lost all definite shape.

Gien retreated from the chaos at a leisurely pace. His arm regained its normal appearance as alarms blared and the bridge crew scattered.

Lykaon took only a few steps back from the growing abomination. A sickly golden aura surrounded his armored form. With a disgusted grunt, he sank his thick fingers into the all-consuming mass.

Liquid Sign's flesh blackened and died where Shaiel's Left Hand touched it, but other tentacles whipped out and ensnared two more hapless crewmen. The Anomian's already wild growth exploded, forcing Lykaon back as Liquid Sign fed on the crystal and polymer substance of the bridge.

Celwen saw Lykaon's own flesh swelling, and she thought the Anomian had taken him until his skin split, revealing a thick coat of grey and brown fur over rippling muscles. His armor clattered to the deck, and over the heap of iron, bronze, and hides stood a wolf the size of a *Yeleq*-class boarding craft. Curving horns grew from his head, and his eyes were the same sallow hue as the nimbus that enveloped him.

With an earsplitting roar, the wolf sank teeth like short swords into the Anomian's spreading mass and tore out a chunk, leaving a black, ragged hole. His dagger-sized claws left wounds that did not heal.

Liquid Sign's tendrils froze and died when they touched the wolf's golden aura, so the Anomian drew additional mass from the deck. Lykaon's bodyguards had also shed their human guises for lupine forms. They growled and paced, shying toward the edges of the bridge as more and more of the deck became an amalgam of crystal and flesh.

Annoyed at his pack's cowardice, or perhaps just fighting fire with fire, Lykaon turned on his followers. His gaping maw snapped up first one lesser wolf; then another as they yelped in terror. With each act of cannibalism, the great wolf grew, until at last his jagged horns scraped the ceiling.

The Anomian corruption had spread most of the way from the control dais to the main door. Liquid Sign and Lykaon were the only beings left on the bridge. Like a sheet of melting plastic burdened with heavy stones, the deck sank and finally collapsed, plunging both monsters onto the level below. The hellish noise of their combat echoed up through the hole.

"Hey!" Someone called from a great distance. "Get up!"

Celwen sat upright with a start. She cast about her darkened chamber and saw Gien's robed form bent over her sleeping pad.

"I asked you to help me commandeer the ship," Celwen said as she rose, "not destroy it!"

Gien's shoulders slumped. "I *am* helping. How else did you expect me to get Lykaon out of the way?"

"Not like *that!*" said Celwen. "Besides, neither Lykaon nor the Anomian is out of the way. The last I saw, they were fighting tooth and nail in the service corridors."

"They're away from the bridge," said Gien.

Celwen straightened her pilot jumpsuit and ran a hand through her long black hair. "But closer to the auxiliary control station, which is where we must go now that the main dais is offline. Do you remember its location on the schematic I showed you?"

"Sure," said Gien. "I think so."

Celwen hesitated for only a moment before taking her place beside Gien. Velocitating into a wall was a more merciful fate than Lykaon or the Anomian offered.

"Take us there," Celwen told Gien.

Holding off Vaun's renewed attack on her gates was taking its toll on Nakvin.

Elena's help lightened the load enough to make the burden

bearable, and even gave Nakvin enough slack to make time pass at half speed compared to the Strata. Astlin and Xander were using the extra time to help look for survivors of the Anomian attack. Meanwhile, Tefler was back at the drydock helping the *Serapis* crew with repairs.

"Any minute now," Nakvin said between labored breaths, "Vaun will lose interest in us and go back to his decorative embalming."

Seated next to her mother on the palace's back patio, Elena stared through the lattice above them and into the overcast sky.

"No, he won't."

"That was a joke, dear." Nakvin's voice held more exasperation than she felt. The real division of labor was closer to Elena hauling a large bucket of water uphill while Nakvin lent a hand to steady it. If that simple effort was wearing her out, she couldn't imagine the strain her daughter must be feeling.

Like every other structure in Seele, the palace patio blended elegantly with its surroundings. What started near the building as smooth flagstones beneath wooden latticework supported by slender stone pillars gradually gave way to a carpet of lush grass under rows of young trees whose interwoven branches formed a green bower.

The sight of Jaren approaching between the stands of trees lifted Nakvin's spirits. The slight breeze under the canopy tousled his waist-length red hair as he stepped from the grass to the first moss-covered stones. His boots tapped a casual beat on the bare pavement till he stood before Nakvin with both arms behind his crisp green jacket.

Nakvin smiled. "I'm surprised you're not helping my grandson tinker with the ship."

"I have more important things to do." Jaren's emerald eyes briefly darted to Elena.

"Why don't you pull up a seat and we'll chat a while?" Nakvin gestured to one of three comfortable wooden chairs. "We've hardly seen each other in the past six months."

Jaren didn't move. "I had important work to do then, also. Thankfully, it's almost done."

Unease darkened Nakvin's gladness. She hadn't given it a name when Elena stood, knocking over her chair, and cried, "Mother!"

A tremendous force pushed Nakvin out of her chair and onto the lawn beside the patio. But Elena's concerns proved misguided when Jaren's right hand emerged from behind his back holding the lavender rod he'd taken from Xander. He pointed the smooth crystal cylinder at Elena.

The ground didn't quake. There was no peal of thunder or flash of light. The goddess of the White Well simply folded to the ground.

Nakvin couldn't remember rising to her feet or rushing to her fallen daughter's side, but that's where she found herself. Elena wasn't breathing, although that wasn't necessarily abnormal.

"What did you do to her!?" Nakvin shouted at Jaren.

"I fixed her," he said matter-of-factly. "I partitioned your influence—and Astlin's—away from Thera's soul. She should be herself in a moment."

The full weight of Vaun's will bore down on Nakvin. She fought to keep him out, but her strength soon failed. In the instant before Shaiel crushed her resistance and Avalon's last defense, Nakvin asked the monster with Jaren's face, "Who are you?"

A black wave cascaded down Jaren's red hair like nightfall on an autumn wood. His fine features softened further to become undeniably feminine. The emerald irises paled to resemble silver coins laid on the eyes of the dead. A slender hand emerged from the once empty right sleeve. As if to leave no doubt, wings clad in feathers black as ink burst through the back of the coat. Their tips touched pillars four rows apart.

"Don't you know your own father?" Zebel mocked.

Sharp nails dug into Nakvin's arm as she was roughly hauled to her feet. She clung feebly to Elena's dress, but the white satin slipped from her grasp.

"Come away, daughter," Zebel said, pulling Nakvin toward a tower that suddenly stood where the lake beyond the patio had been, "You don't want to be here when she wakes up.

36

Teg had been lying on the burned-out building's rough concrete floor long enough for the front half of his body to go from agonized to numb and back when a diversion finally came.

Unfortunately, it wasn't the diversion he'd hoped for.

Teg knew the situation had changed when a shrill cry echoed between the concrete canyon walls, followed by the ominous sound of several thousand men marching. Using just his thumb and forefinger he widened the cut he'd made in the plastic that covered the missing wall and looked down the street.

This is bad, he thought.

The column of troops was advancing toward the gate that stood across the road. No, it was worse than that. The soldiers, greycloaks, and feral Night Gen weren't marching *toward* the gate. They were marching *through* it.

Fallon is barging through your door, and he's bringing thousands of his best friends with him, Teg thought, hoping the warning would reach Elena through the prana thread she'd woven between his soul and her nexus.

There was no answer. Vaun's army continued pouring

through the gate. Teg faced the grim possibility that something had gone horribly wrong; that Avalon was lost, and his friends with it.

So what if they are? Teg steeled himself with a reminder that reality was what it was, and a ha'penny plus all the wishing in the world would buy half a cent's worth of salt. If he was the only one left, then seeing his mission through to the end wasn't vital; it was mandatory.

Teg watched the column march into Avalon. He would wait until the street was empty; then leave his perch, get to the square unseen, and find a way into the House of Law.

His plan hit a snag when the giant image of green hills under grey skies faded. The gate was closed, but two companies remained in the street. And several more were returning to the square, just to make Teg's job harder.

Harder, but not impossible. Much of the city had burned down in the Cataclysm, a lot of what survived had been demolished, and most of both had been replaced with new construction. But the street layout seemed largely unchanged.

If Teg's mental map was correct, the House of Law now occupied the block where City Hall, two of Serapium's top hotels, and the settlers' museum had stood. Smugglers' lore held that a private underground rail line had once connected the Mill to City Hall, supposedly so the Transessists could meet with city officials in secret.

The tunnel was said to have been sealed after an unknown incident, but some—including Jaren—had claimed there were still ways in. Some accounts even mentioned a lift that had gone up to City Hall or one of the hotels.

Searching for a tunnel that he'd never seen himself, that might've been just a rumor, and that probably didn't exist anymore if it ever had, was certainly a long shot. But Serapium's underground had gotten him this far. With a little luck it would take him the rest of the way.

And considering how today had gone so far, Teg thought his luck was due to change.

Stepping right from her quarters to the *Sinamarg's* backup bridge disoriented Celwen; not only due to the sudden transition from darkness to bright light, but because she and Gien had traveled more than a mile in an instant.

At least he did not fuse us with a bulkhead, Celwen thought as her vision cleared.

The auxiliary control station was a tall cylinder with walls of dark ridged crystal-metal and a white ceramic floor spanning thirty feet in diameter. A control dais rose from the center of the deck.

A thrill raced up Celwen's spine when she saw that, besides the green-robed Magist, she was alone. Gien's velocitation and the chaos engulfing the ship had gotten her to the control room first, but the real command crew wouldn't be far behind.

Celwen dashed to the top of the dais and initiated the sympathetic bond. She didn't realize how much she'd missed the incomparable feeling of oneness with the ship until her senses merged with the *Sinamarg's*.

"Someone's coming," said Gien.

Celwen's ears heard Gien's voice and the clatter of approaching footsteps. The *Sinamarg* saw four black-uniformed command crew led by Admiral Raig rushing down the hall toward the control station's door. Celwen sealed the entrance with a thought. In her excitement she almost forgot to shield the room against translation.

"Area secure," Celwen said.

The sensation of something squirming around an ice chip in her stomach nearly made Celwen vomit. She took a deep breath and discerned that the feeling was actually coming from the *Sinamarg*. Liquid Sign had burrowed into the agricultural caverns and was feeding on the abundant biomass, but Lykaon pressed his furious attack on the still-growing Anomian.

They are only three decks below us. A bead of cold sweat ran down Celwen's face.

Pounding and angry demands sounded through the door. With no time to waste, Celwen activated the telepathic comm and broadcast her thoughts to the fleet.

This is Lieutenant Celwen. Shaiel has betrayed us. His Left Hand Lykaon and the Anomian scourge he brought aboard have severely damaged the ship and slaughtered scores of our brothers. I have taken temporary command of the Sinamarg...

Thousands of angry minds flooded the comm, hurling accusations and invective at Celwen. The nexic shield repelled a translation attempt; then another. Soon translators all across the ship were bombarding Celwen's defenses, each frantically trying to breach the room. Her pulse raced. A concerted effort could easily batter down the shield.

Please! Celwen shouted over her outraged crewmates. *You must listen! Our alliance with Shaiel was a mistake. We can regain our rightful place in the Middle Stratum without him.*

Hellish cold filled Celwen stomach as if she'd swallowed liquid nitrogen. She doubled over on the dais, gasping for breath. Bombarded by ever more breach attempts as ships throughout the fleet joined in, Celwen needed a moment to pin down the source of the cold. When she did, she barely stifled a scream.

Temperatures in the *Sinamarg's* bowels had suddenly plunged close to absolute zero. The Anomian infection had died off—not just in the caverns, but throughout the whole ship. Nothing in the affected areas had survived.

Except for Lykaon.

Celwen looked upon the caverns, frozen with fear, as horrible golden light faded to reveal an enormous wolf standing alone upon frozen rocks. Its ravenous yellow eyes seemed to stare into hers through the sympathetic link. With a growl of cold rage, Lykaon sprang up to the cavern's roof and started digging through the ceiling. The black stone yielded to his claws as easily as rotted wood.

A hand rested lightly on Celwen's shoulder. She came back to herself and saw Gien smiling down at her through the lattice of his veil.

"You can hide for a long time," he said. "I know. You can run for years and years across the stars, but your sins always catch up. Because evil is of the Void, and doing wrong makes it a part of you."

A strange calm fell upon Celwen, and with it new resolve. Ignoring the translators hammering on the shield, the fists pounding at the door, and the beast climbing up from below, she stood and bared her soul to the fleet.

I am Lieutenant Celwen of the Sinamarg, *and this is my*

confession. I conspired with our enemies against my father. I betrayed him to follow my childhood ambition of becoming a pilot. He strongly objected to me joining the fleet. Having fought against the foe that drove us into the darkness, perhaps he foresaw the grave peril that awaited our return—the temptation of the oppressed to become oppressors.

The legion of angry thoughts fell silent, as did the hallway outside the door. The translators' siege relented. An entire fleet waited on Celwen's next word.

The Guild earned destruction. The Cataclysm gave it to them but robbed us of our vengeance. We punished the peoples of Mithgar and Temil in the Guild's stead; perhaps justly. Now Shaiel commands us to slaughter our kin.

Celwen had lived in fear of having her crimes exposed. And while her confession did bring shame, it brought even greater serenity.

Yes, the Light Tribe fled to the protection of demons. Should we boast that we fled to the outer dark? What of the demons in Shaiel's service who have butchered our people? I accept your condemnation for my crime. But I implore you to hold Shaiel to the same standard. Reject him and regain your freedom!

Breathing a sigh of relief, Celwen lowered the nexic shield and unlocked the room.

The door slid open. Raig stood at the threshold, heading a train of three other senior officers. Celwen met his blue-green eyes unflinching and saw none of the hatred that had festered behind them for days.

"Admiral," Celwen said, "I wish to surrender myself into your custody, sir."

Raig bowed his silver-haired head. When he raised it, his face held the neutral expression of one colleague facing another.

"Understood," the admiral said. "Before I officially place you under arrest, do you wish to make a statement off the record?"

Celwen snapped to attention. "Sir, an associate who aided me on Temil is currently staging an operation in defense of our Light Gen kin. I request that the *Sinamarg* set course for Cadrys to render support."

"Request acknowledged, Lieutenant," said Raig. "But granting it will require further discussion with the senior staff. Assaulting the seat of Shaiel's power is not a decision to be taken lightly."

The floor behind Raig erupted in a shower of metal and sparking crystal. The forepaws, head, and shoulders of a giant wolf emerged from below. The commander closest to the breach had no time to scream before massive jaws bit him in half. The other two officers' cries were cut short as the beast's thrashing horns gored them to death.

Raig dove into the control room. Celwen sent an urgent mental command for the door to shut, and its lower edge descended to the floor just ahead of the wolf's blood-flecked nose.

"Okay, you were right," Gien said as he backed into the far curve of the room opposite the entrance. "We're definitely too close."

Celwen almost told Gien to evacuate her and Raig from the room, but that would leave a ravening demon loose on the ship and leave Teg at the mercy of Shaiel's servants on Cadrys.

Attention all translator stations! Celwen broadcast through the comm. *Lykaon is attempting forced entry to auxiliary control. Three senior officers down! Requesting immediate ejection.*

The door buckled, swinging up and inward with a loud bang. Raig barely managed to roll out of the metal slab's path. A horned head covered with blood-matted fur plunged through the entrance, its fanged maw snapping; murder blazing in its yellow eyes.

Celwen took command of the control room's emergency translator and targeted Lykaon. She set the range at maximum, somewhere in the space over Temil, and activated the device.

Humming green-white light surrounded the wolf's head. Lykaon snarled and thrashed as the translator strained to convert his bulk into prana and fire it into space. The target seemed unnaturally resistant, because the translator's light began to fade.

The doorframe bowed with a piercing squeal of twisted metal, and Lykaon thrust his left foreleg into the room. Black bloody claws raked the air dangerously close to Celwen's face. Her fear was tempered by a rush of triumph when the light green glow returned, growing in radiance as translators all around the *Sinamarg* focused on the demon wolf.

But again the light began to fade, along with Celwen's hope. Not even the combined power of the flagship's translators could remove Shaiel's Left Hand from the *Sinamarg*.

This is Admiral Raig.

Celwen glanced away from the wolf's seeking claws and saw the admiral standing at the controls of a wall-mounted comm.

Raig continued. *All transport stations on the* Sinamarg *and all vessels in the fleet, translate this rabid cur off my ship!*

Celwen gladly complied, fixing the emergency translator

on Lykaon once more. Blinding light engulfed him. Under her telepathy-assisted direction, every translator in the fleet pulled Lykaon's molecules apart and scattered them across the system.

The silence that prevailed in the enemy's absence was almost deafening. Raig leaned against the ridged wall and heaved a weary sigh.

"Permission to set course for Cadrys?" Celwen asked.

Raig straightened and stepped to the foot of the dais. "Granted, Lieutenant, but Cadrys is three days away at our best speed. We may only be able to avenge your friend."

"I know a shortcut!" Gien shuffled over to stand at Celwen's other side. He looked up at her on the dais. "I'm from Cadrys. Let me take over, and we'll be there before you know it."

"What is he on about?" asked Raig.

A glorious realization dawned on Celwen. "Gien is a skilled nexist sir, with a particular gift for velocitation. Through the sympathetic bond, he should be able to move the ship as easily as he moves himself."

Raig frowned. "That is a grave risk. Can we trust him with our lives?"

"Shaiel knows that we severed our alliance, sir," Celwen said. "Our lives are in danger regardless of Gien's actions. Striking at the heart of Shaiel's regime before he can launch a reprisal is our best option."

"Besides," said Gien, pointing at Celwen, "you're gonna arrest her, anyway."

Raig smiled. To Celwen's surprise, he actually issued a deep, hearty laugh. "I must concur," he said. "You are relieved,

Lieutenant, but you are not yet dismissed. I have a final task for you if we survive the voyage to Cadrys. Magist Gien, you have the wheel."

37

Astlin telepathically searched a town on Seele's lower slopes for survivors while Xander ferried the wounded to Faerda's temple aboard the *Kerioth*. She was helping a group of Gen soldiers rescue a family from the tar-covered ruins of their house when a huge square of space on the field below was suddenly cut away.

It was like a window looking out on a large city under a black sky. Thousands of men dressed in grey or blue were marching down the street that now led onto the field. But Astlin hardly noticed the advancing army for the nightmarish creature that half lumbered; half slithered at its head.

Astlin dropped a pumpkin-sized chunk of masonry, almost hitting her foot, when she saw in the rotted flesh what she'd only seen before in shadow.

Shaiel's Will! But how? He fell from the Serapis *and burned up in a prana field.*

Xander had once mentioned a being called a kost that could cheat death by taking other people's bodies. Later Zan, while claiming to be possessed by a kost, had praised Tefler for ridding him of another. Could he have meant Shaiel's Will? It would explain how the creature had first appeared as Astlin's sister, and how it had survived getting fried in prana.

Ranks of Lawbringers with curved grey swords and blue-uniformed soldiers carrying rifles were rushing around the kost and through the gate. They were only a few minutes' march from the foot of the hill.

No one had expected Shaiel to get past Elena and Nakvin—at least, not so soon after the first attack. Anris had sent a quarter of his army to search for wounded and divided the rest into four groups; each stationed below one face of the hill. From Astlin's position on the west slope, it looked like the division on the field below her was outnumbered five to one.

A string of pops like firecrackers—but much louder—rose up from the plain as the Gen division opened fire. Greycloaks and Cadrisian soldiers staggered or doubled over, but none fell as they continued their advance.

They have aura projectors, Astlin thought. *Strong ones.*

The Light Gen had less protection. Their armor was Worked with protective auras, but when the Cadrisians returned fire, almost every shot that found its target took down a Gen.

Astlin cast about in desperation. She noticed a crowd of Light Gen soldiers gathered under a spiraling wooden pavilion supported by a ring of timeworn stones. She skimmed a few men's minds and learned that Anris had ordered them take the field while the north and south divisions moved to reinforce the west.

Astlin was starting to regain confidence when several dozen grey-brown shapes sped through the gate and galloped toward the Gen ranks. They looked like large wolves, but even from the hill she could see red slashes across their right eyes.

"They brought *Isnashi*," Astlin cursed under her breath.

Xander, she called out telepathically, *Shaiel's army is attacking from the west. Can the* Kerioth *give Anris air support?*

I see the enemy coming through the gate, Xander replied. She could sense his frustration. *The Gen are too close for me to risk using the ship's weapons.*

Astlin looked down on the field. Shaiel's troops had cleared the gate, which closed behind them. Gen fell to Cadrys guns, *Isnashi* jaws, and Lawbringer swords.

Shaiel's Will surged forward. The colossal beast didn't share Xander's qualms about friendly fire, because the torrent of yellow-green vapor he breathed enveloped a handful of his own men as it cut a swath through the Gen ranks.

Astlin heard the men's screams and smelled the sharp stench of chemical burns. She shook with rage when she saw that only corroded armor remained of the Gen who'd taken the brunt of the monster's breath.

I'm going down there, she told Xander. Instantly she stood on the field before the titanic beast.

The residue of the monster's breath stung Astlin's eyes, but she saw that its body resembled an elephant's, except far larger and covered with bruise-colored scales. Black meat and partially fossilized bones showed through its armored hide, and ragged skin stretched over its bat-like wings. Its four feet ended in hooked talons larger than swords. A massive tail curved across the grass behind it.

A memory from Astlin's life beyond the world came back to her. *And the dragon stood before the woman...*

But Astlin knew that neither she nor her enemy quite fit the words.

Shots rang out. Men screamed. Wolves howled. And the giant serpent's neck bent down, bringing Astlin face to face with a long horned skull partially clad in dead flesh and scales. Utterly black pits like postholes stared at her.

Cold laughter drove a gust of acrid air through cracked teeth the size of pike heads. "What prodigy is this, that we now are met in that realm which once was perdition and shall anon be worse?"

"You didn't have the sense to stay dead," said Astlin. "I'll teach you better this time."

"Oh!?" The monster's head snaked around to speak in her left ear. "You also escaped the grave, my lambkin. Though 'tis doubtful you'd endure another death as well as I."

"Let's find out who dies better," said Astlin.

A Gen spear jutted from the ground nearby. Astlin pulled it free and channeled the momentum into a powerful swing. The metal point slammed into the beast's head with a hollow crunch. A shock ran up the shaft, but thanks to Anris' training Astlin kept control of the weapon.

Shaiel's Will roared. He raised one foreleg, but Astlin spun out of the way before the talons came thudding down, sending up tufts of grass and soil.

A pair of greycloaks rushed her. Astlin released her light, halting their charge and making them drop their swords. She narrowly dodged the monster's next blow, which crushed the entranced Lawbringers underfoot.

Astlin turned her light upon Shaiel's Will, who recoiled with a shriek from the sapphire glow. She stabbed its neck again and again, piercing the thick scales. But on the final thrust, the spear got stuck between stony plates. Astlin was so focused on pulling her weapon free that she missed the tail lashing from her right. The blow hit her like a truck, and she landed on her back in the middle of a fierce melee between Avalon's soldiers and Shaiel's priests.

Astlin telepathically stunned the greycloaks standing over her. The Gen ran them through, allowing her to stand. She concentrated, mending her torn muscles and crushed bones.

A surprising distance away, Shaiel's Will was trampling Gen soldiers who'd rashly followed her example and charged him.

I need a new weapon, she thought.

"Serieigna!" Xander stood to Astlin's left holding his black, diamond-bladed spear. Without hesitation he tossed it to her.

Astlin caught the weapon by its ebony shaft. It felt light and perfectly balanced. But she looked at the deathless beast whose rampage she'd barely slowed. A spear—even one so fine—was no match for Shaiel's Will.

Xander's term of endearment echoed in Astlin's mind. The word meant *Beautiful Flame* in Nesshin, though she still couldn't pronounce it. Astlin's thoughts turned to Sulaiman's fiery sword. Her attempts to form a weapon from all four elements had been spectacular failures. What if she tried using just one?

Astlin drew the elemental fire out of Xander's spear. Heat radiated from the shaft, which began to glow, but Astlin commanded it not to burn her. The red hot weapon trembled as the others had before they'd exploded. Astlin shed her light to bolster her will, and with the rushing sound of fuel added to a blaze, the other elements burned away, leaving a spear made of red flame clutched tightly in her hands.

"You are truly capable of wonders, my love," Xander said. "Now use them to crush this cursed beast!"

Pride warmed Astlin's heart, but her enmity toward Shaiel's Will burned hotter. "Let's both crush him."

Astlin angled her nearly weightless spear downward and in front of her with a red flourish. She and Xander walked side by side toward Shaiel's Will, their silver and sapphire lights blending into the color of a clear sky. The chaos of battle calmed before them as Shaiel's troops lowered their weapons to stare in awe.

A Cadrisian just beyond the light's reach took aim at Astlin, but without pausing she cast her spear at the rifleman. The solid flame burned through his chest and he fell, firing his weapon into the air. Astlin willed the spear back to her, and the blazing red shaft vanished from the corpse's chest as it appeared in her hand.

Besides two more soldiers whom Xander nexically compacted into milk crate-sized cubes, no one else challenged him and Astlin as they came to stand before Shaiel's Will. The great beast and the two Zadokim formed a peaceful island in a sea of war.

"Two by two they come now to the slaughter!" Shaiel's Will boasted.

Xander didn't waste words. He stretched his open hand toward the monster, and a thunderclap sent its massive head whipping sideways on its long curved neck. The beast recovered, and its maw darted toward Xander, who funneled his power through both hands in an effort to keep the snapping jaws back. But this time the nexic waves broke around the giant head, not even slowing its descent.

Astlin threw her spear. Its fiery tip sank into the roof of the monster's mouth, and Shaiel's Will pulled back, bellowing in pain.

Xander nodded to Astlin. "Thank you," he said before nexically hurling a company's worth of swords and pikes into the beast's exposed underbelly.

Shaiel's Will screamed. It broke the weapons sticking out of its belly with one foreleg and shook the ground as it came down on all fours. The tail slap had made Astlin wary enough to notice the ragged wing bearing down on her. She willed herself to a position beside the beast's left hind leg and watched the lance-like wingtips tear the ground where she'd stood a second ago.

A jolt of dread passed through Astlin's mind when she saw the other wing covering the spot where Xander had been standing. But his silver radiance shone from the other side of the monster as if the full moon had fallen to earth. Shaiel's Will flinched.

Astlin unveiled her own light and dashed around her titanic enemy, slashing at its legs. Scales and flesh parted with the stench of seared rotted meat while Xander pelted the beast with a hail of nexically launched missiles. Whenever fangs, claws, wings, or tail struck down at her, Astlin would vanish and reappear out of reach.

"Petty gods flaunting your borrowed crowns," the monster cried. "Behold the glory of Shaiel, which is death!"

The golden light that burst out from Shaiel's Will caught Astlin before she could will herself away. She braced herself against the freezing sallow blaze as her flaming spear guttered and died. Icy cold invaded the bare skin of her hands and face and seeped through the Worked fabric of her dress.

Pure white light drove back the tainted gold. Warmth rushed back into Astlin's body as the white glow's source approached. Astlin saw that it was a Gen dressed in furs with stone beads braided into his long hair and bright markings on his coppery face.

"Jarsaal?" she said.

"You call my name rightly, souldancer," Jarsaal said. His hazel eyes looked her up and down. "Though perhaps I misname you."

Astlin's words tripped over themselves. "What are you...? How did...? Why?"

Jarsaal raised his hand. The white light that surrounded him and Astlin faded. The awful gold light was also gone, and she saw that a circle of Dawn Gen shamans surrounded Shaiel's Will. To her relief, Xander stood a short distance away looking unhurt.

"We are Faerda's priests," said Jarsaal. "Our goddess called, and we answered. She opened the way, and we came."

The Dawn Gen worship the White Well. Elena must have brought them here.

A pack of sleek brown and red wolves raced across the field and fell upon a group of *Isnashi*. Both packs of skin changers collided in a snarling mass of flying fur and gnashing fangs.

Jarsaal surveyed the torn, tar-covered field with disdain. "The Dawn Tribe shuns the Land of the Unclean, but we are glad to oppose the Defilers who pervert our Mother's gifts wherever we find them."

"Soft-brained savages," sneered Shaiel's Will. "The trollop who masqueraded as your goddess is no more. With her last breath she called you here to die!"

Cold fear stabbed Astlin's heart. *Elena can't be dead!*

But if Elena was still guarding the gate, how had Shaiel's army gotten in?

Astlin heard the seductive voice of despair. Even Jarsaal's stern face fell. The circle of priests muttered darkly to each other.

The beating of powerful wings drew Astlin's eyes to the sky, where saw a winged giant diving to the ground. He landed on one knee, and his purple-skinned, leather-armored body rose to its full towering height.

"Still your serpent's tongue, Forranach," Anris rebuked Shaiel's Will. He drew his large hooked sword and strode toward the beast like a gardener approaching a shrub he meant to prune. "False prophecies of our deaths will not forestall your own."

Astlin and Xander fell in with Anris, and Jarsaal joined them. Looking at the foes advancing on him and the ring of priests surrounding him, Shaiel's Will laughed.

"Death forsook me long erenow," the monster said. "Yet those whom Shaiel favors gain a reprieve from death, though their silver threads be severed."

Astlin wondered what the snake meant. She thought he was stalling for time until she saw movement among the bodies strewn across the battlefield. To her horror, dead greycloaks and Cadrisian soldiers rose and took up their weapons again.

"Such is the folly of rebellion against the Lord of Death!" crowed Shaiel's Will.

"Not every lost cause is folly," said Anris. "Almeth's Resistance failed, yet the children of Gen who fought with him survived. They stand against you now, as do I. Defend yourself!"

The malakh spread his wings and shot toward Shaiel's Will

like lightning. His hooked sword flashed, and a horn the size of an oak branch fell from the beast's head. The Will of Shaiel loosed an earsplitting shriek and took to the air with Anris in pursuit. Their battle gave Astlin the impression of a dove fighting a vulture.

"Faerda's messenger shall cast the serpent from the sky," Jarsaal declared. "My brothers and I must cleanse this land of the restless dead."

"What about Elena?" Astlin asked.

Xander laid his hand on her shoulder. "The kost is a liar. And even if his lies hold a kernel of truth, we cannot challenge a power capable of slaying Thera—not alone. The enemy is inside the gate, and the Gen are outmatched. Let's even the odds."

By Astlin's will, a jet of flame sprang from either end of her closed fist, forming a burning red spear.

"For Elena, Nakvin, and Seele," Astlin said.

Light blazed from Astlin and Xander's foreheads as they charged the blue-grey tide of Shaiel's army. With a ground-shaking cry, the survivors of the west division followed. Jarsaal ran before them in wolf shape to join the priests who fought the undead with flashes of holy light.

38

Teg saw lights and heard nervous chatter from the intersecting tunnel up ahead. He crept along slowly, hoping to get close enough to find out what was happening while staying hidden.

A violent tremor rocked the tunnel. The rails under Teg's feet clattered. The lights up ahead flickered, and grit rained down from the ceiling. The nervous babble turned to cries of panic and rhythmless pounding of a human stampede.

Teg reached the abandoned tunnel's intersection with the working track and crouched down in the shadows. Peering around the corner he saw a crowd—mostly bureaucrats judging by their costly but unimaginative clothes—trying to force their way aboard a train. A squad of blue-uniformed soldiers waged a doomed battle to impose order.

Of special interest to Teg was the lighted sign above the wide stairway leading up to the surface that read "Settlers Common Station". The Common was the plaza where the House of Law stood. The fact that this was the station serving it meant Teg was on the right track.

Actually, he wasn't. The track he needed was the defunct line that had run between the Mill and City Hall. Unless all the old smugglers' tales were total bullshit—unlikely in Teg's experience—the way into the abandoned tunnel was somewhere nearby.

Teg had started back down the line when another quake nearly threw him facedown on the track. He steadied himself against the wall and heard an authoritative male voice blaring over the now frenzied crowd.

"Attention! This is a public safety announcement. The Voice of Shaiel has declared a state of emergency for all of our lord's subjects within the Serapium urban core. Proceed without delay to the nearest orbital strike shelter in a calm, orderly fashion. Repeat; this is a…"

Screams drowned out the public address system, but Teg had heard enough to make him smile.

Looks like Celwen's here.

Teg hurried toward a service corridor, turned the corner, and almost shot the person who surprised him before he realized who it was.

Celwen is here!

The Night Gen officer stood frozen, her green eyes staring at the mirrored white gun he'd drawn on her. She'd traded her sharkskin outfit for a snug black and silver jumpsuit. Her long black hair was tied at her neck.

Teg holstered the gun. "I'm not sorry for that."

Celwen pressed a hand to her chest and took a deep breath. "You have no idea what I went through to get here. If you will give me no apology, how about a word of thanks?"

"Thanks," said Teg.

Celwen sighed. "My ship is in orbit taking heavy fire from Shaiel's fleet."

"One ship? Didn't you bring any support craft?"

"No." Celwen shook her head. "The *Sinamarg* used a special means of travel unavailable to other ships. It carries four squadrons of small *Yeleq*-class vessels of the kind you brought to Temil, but nexus-runners are vulnerable to weapons based on Workings."

"True," said Teg, "but ether-runner shields can't block nexism."

"The surface batteries are the real danger," Celwen said. "The sphere's defenses are being coordinated from the House of Law. Admiral Raig sent me to help you infiltrate the Cadrys Navy's command center and cripple their resistance."

Teg nodded. "Sounds like fun."

"We have a short operational window," Celwen warned him. "Raig will destroy the House of Law, whether or not we are in it, rather than risk losing the *Sinamarg*."

"That's a problem," said Teg. "There's an instant win ticket that will hand the war to one lucky player somewhere in that building. Our best shot at victory is blown if Raig brings down the house."

Celwen crossed her arms. "We had best get going, then."

"You know a way in?" asked Teg.

"I scouted the area nexically before translating down," she said, smiling. "There is a closed tunnel below leading to a lift that will take us straight to the House of Law's basement."

Teg smacked his fist into his palm. "I knew it! Lead the way."

Celwen led him down ten flights of grimy concrete stairs to

an even grimier service tunnel filled with cold humid air. The narrow corridor gave on another disused rail line where a rushing sound echoed up the tracks.

At first Teg feared an approaching train, since the noise got louder the farther down the tunnel they went. But there were no oncoming lights and no tremors shaking the ground.

About a hundred feet down the track, Teg's flashlight beam fell on the source of the noise. Water poured down the right wall through a large crack in the ceiling and into a pool that spanned from Teg and Celwen's feet to the bricked up wall where the tunnel ended.

"Looks like your people busted a water pipe," said Teg. "We're on a mission with zero margin for error and a countdown to certain death. Can they avoid throwing *more* obstacles in our way?"

"There are anti-orbital cannons nearby," Celwen said. "Our gunners are doing their best to make surgical strikes that specifically avoid our entry route, but they cannot stand idly by and let the enemy bombard them."

Celwen's statement was punctuated by the biggest impact that Teg had felt yet. This time he did topple forward, plunging into the cold filthy water and losing his flashlight. He surfaced in total darkness as loud creaking gave way to a deafening crash and dusty air rushing from the tunnel's far end.

"Are you okay?" Teg shouted over the gushing water and the sounds of rocks settling.

"Yes," Celwen said uncertainly. "But the cave-in blocked the way back, and the ceiling looks unstable."

"Is there a way forward?"

Celwen fell silent for a moment. At length she said, "There is a steel door between this tunnel and the one that leads to the lift, but it is underwater."

"Time for you to go diving again," said Teg. "Hop in. The water's cold as hell and tastes like junkyard mud."

A gentle splash and small waves rippling through the pool signaled that Celwen had taken Teg's invitation.

"How do you know what junkyard mud tastes like?" she asked.

"You clearly didn't grow up in the bad part of a big city," said Teg.

The roof shifted again with a loud crack. Gravel-sized debris pelted Teg's head.

Teg blindly reached for Celwen. "Guide me down to the door."

"The water is too muddy for me to see through," Celwen said, "and my nexic sight is not always reliable."

"You got us this far," said Teg, "and there's no going back."

Another series of cracks and groans sounded from above. Teg felt Celwen's small smooth hand take his big rough one.

"Ready?" he asked.

"Yes," she said. "And if we are to die here, there are few men I would rather share a grave with."

Is she coming on to me? Teg wondered. Instead of asking, he took a deep breath, waited for Celwen to do the same, and dove into the black depths.

Celwen soon took the lead. She was a more skilled swimmer than Teg, and soon she'd led him to a spot against the wall about a story down.

The water muffled the rumbling of the roof giving out. A jagged slab of rock jutted down into the pool. If not for the water and his protective aura softening the impact, Teg might have lost his right arm instead of just having a chunk torn out of his biceps.

Celwen thrashed, but Teg fought through the pain and held her to ease her panic. Calming her down cost him time. His chest was already feeling tight, and the regeneration that was already healing his arm didn't reduce his need for oxygen. In fact, he probably needed it more than most people.

Removing herself from Teg's embrace, Celwen pressed his hand to a hard, pitted surface. Teg knocked on it and heard a hollow thud made tinny by the water. That had to be the door. He felt around until he found a seam; then ran his hand down it. A surge of relief almost distracted him from the burning in his lungs when his fingers touched a rusted handle.

Teg pulled on the handle. The door didn't budge.

Locked!

There wasn't much time left. Teg's blood rushed in his ears. If he could've seen at all, he was pretty sure that the edges of his vision would be going dark.

Teg patted down the front of the door, trying to find the lock. His search became frantic despite a lifetime of experience warning him that haste didn't help at times like this. It occurred to him that Celwen could find the lock, but he had no way to ask her where it was.

Or did he? Teg pulled on Celwen's wrist, bringing her forearm closer, and traced the word *LOCK* on her sleeve.

Nothing happened.

Teg tried one more time, forcing himself to go slower despite his urgent need for air. There was a pause. Celwen's arm tensed. She grabbed Teg's wrist in both of hers and pressed it against a raised circular bump below the other handle of what turned out to be a set of double doors.

There was no more time. Teg drew one of his guns. Worked pneumatic pistols fired just as well in space as in an atmosphere, so he was pretty sure his would work here. He held the muzzle about an inch from where he remembered the lock being and pressed the trigger.

There was a small pop. A shockwave coursed through the water. Teg pushed on the doors, but they didn't budge.

Finally succumbing to panic, Teg pounded on the door with his bare left fist and the butt of his gun to no effect.

Celwen took hold of his wrist and forced his hand down onto the handle. She grasped the rusted metal and tugged.

Of course it would pull *open,* Teg grumbled silently to himself.

Pulling against the surrounding water pressure made Teg's wounded arm ache and his tortured lungs burn, but between the two of them, he and Celwen managed to plant themselves against the wall and force the heavy door open.

A torrent of water streamed through the door into the unseen space beyond. Too exhausted to struggle, Teg let the flow carry him along. He washed up on a bed of gravel where he lay coughing and gasping for air.

It was a couple of minutes before Teg regained enough lung function to call out Celwen's name.

"I am here," she called from somewhere nearby. "*We* are here. Look!"

Teg realized he'd had his eyes closed since diving under the surface of the pool. He opened them and saw pale orange light spilling over multiple sets of tracks coated in decades of dust now turning to mud. He stood and looked in the direction of Celwen's voice.

Just beyond her lithe, dripping form stood a large brick shaft. The top was lost in the darkness high above, but the door set into its base was wide enough to drive a drifter through.

"That lift leads up to the House of Law," Celwen said. "It is almost certainly watched. They may already know we are here."

Teg stepped up beside Celwen, drew his other gun, and offered it to her. "Time to stop being subtle, then."

Celwen took the gun. Teg started toward the lift, his boots sloshing with every step, and she walked right beside him.

We should have planned this better, Astlin thought to Xander as they waded through the middle of Shaiel's army. The enemy fell back from the Zadokim's light, and bullets fell away from Xander's nexic barrier. But amid the chaos they'd been cut off from the Light Gen army and the Dawn Gen priests.

Sulaiman said that bold swift action is preferable to meticulous planning, Xander replied. *Besides, we have our pick of targets.*

Astlin wished she could be as optimistic as Xander. A hostile sea of humanity raged across the ground, while Anris dueled Shaiel's Will in the sky above. The malakh's hooked sword hacked at the giant kost, but Shaiel's Will fought on unfazed while Anris grew ever more battered, bloody, and tired.

If only I could help him, Astlin thought. But the outnumbered Light Gen needed her even more.

Held aloft on its rotted wings, Shaiel's Will clawed at Anris with its right foreleg. The malakh swooped aside—right into the descending left paw. Nails like scimitars shredded the back of Anris' leather armor and the skin beneath. He had no time to recover before the massive tail connected with his midsection, batting him up toward the beast's gaping maw.

At the last second Anris rolled in midair and thrust his left arm toward the monster's decayed face. Avalon had no sun, but the ball of light that formed in the malakh's hand blazed like a summer noon.

Shaiel's Will turned its head away from the dazzling light. Anris used his upward momentum and spin, gripping his sword in both hands and bringing its heavy blade down on the monster's long thin neck. The curved edge clove stony scales and rotten muscle.

The beast's snakelike neck lolled down against its chest, dangling by a thread. Silence fell over the battlefield as all eyes looked skyward. Shaiel's Will thrashed blindly. Its tail whipped empty air.

Anris struggled to right himself while trying to strike past the flailing talons. He must have seen an opening, because he held his sword like a batter expecting a perfect pitch. Before he could strike, the monster's hind leg snagged Anris' wing.

The malakh spun sideways, and Astlin held her breath, sure that Anris would fall. But he hooked his sword's blade on one of the beast's exposed ribs and hung from the hilt, clinging to his foe as its massive forelegs bludgeoned him.

Anris' right hand released his sword's hilt and grabbed the monster's rib. He continued to hold on, supported by one arm, while wielding his blade left-handed. He chopped mercilessly at the wounded neck, and with a guttural cry his final blow sent the beast's head tumbling like a grisly kite with no wind.

Astlin and Xander joined in the cheer that went up from the army of Avalon at their captain's victory. But Anris fell away from the giant decayed body and pinwheeled toward the ground alongside it.

Xander stretched out his arms as if hoping to catch the falling malakh. And he did, thanks to his nexic gift and foes too distracted by their leader's earthshaking fall to open fire. He laid Anris gently on the trampled grass, and only then did Astlin see the terrible wounds that Avalon's captain had suffered.

The lavender skin of Anris' face was swollen with bruises and streaked with blood. His left wing was a shredded ruin; the white feathers stained red. His arms and legs were crisscrossed with deep gashes and frostbitten from contact with Void. His right arm and shoulder bore puckered chemical burns.

Shaiel's army came out of their trance and leveled a hundred weapons at their three worst foes. Unhindered by words, Xander asked Astlin to join her will to his, and she immediately consented. The wave of nexic force that burst outward from the Zadokim instantly cleared every foe from an arena-sized circle around them.

Over the groaning piles of her fallen enemies, Astlin saw green and gold banners approaching from the north and south. The standards of Avalon stood tall, rippling in the wind.

Astlin knelt beside Anris. "Help is coming," she said softly.

Anris didn't stir. His chest hardly rose and fell.

"It comes sooner than we thought," said Xander.

Astlin looked up to see a brown wolf leap over the tangled

mass of Shaiel's soldiers. It landed in the circle on two legs that brought Jarsaal Malisar, Chosen of Faerda, to the malakh's side. Jarsaal worked in silence as he knelt down and bathed Anris in the healing light of the Well.

"How long until he—" Astlin started to ask.

Anris sat up like a man waking from a bad dream. His chest heaved as his light brown eyes darted back and forth. Only old blood and several fresh scars remained of his once mortal wounds.

"Relax," said Astlin. Both of her hands failed to cover one of the malakh's. "You won. Shaiel's Will is dead."

Anris looked at her. His face was relieved but weary. "Forranach is a wily and ancient worm. False hope hides what you already know. A kost cannot die until his soul's true house is destroyed."

39

Even though they knew he was coming, Teg had never had an easier time breaking into a secure facility. Help from a nexist who could scout out enemy positions through walls more than made up for losing the element of surprise.

Not that there was much of an opposition to surprise. Besides the security teams sweeping the halls—always several steps behind their quarry, thanks to Celwen—Teg only saw scattered bureaucrats sprinting down bronze-paneled halls, their expensive shoes clicking on slate floors as stray papers fell from the bundles in their arms.

The House of Law brought up memory's from Teg's mercenary career. A Temilian dictator's mansion on the eve of a coup, the offices of a Stranosi financial firm after a bank run, the campaign office of an indicted Salorien mayoral candidate—all had wallowed in the same manic despair.

After climbing several flights of stairs, sneaking through a dozen dark offices, and crawling through at least one bathroom window, Teg and Celwen reached a balcony surrounding the level under the iron spire. The wide ledge gave a commanding view of the city, and Teg watched scattered drifters flee between stern-faced towers from shafts of green-white light that slanted down into the city.

Though buildings shook and clouds of smoke rose into the air, the impact sites were free of the spectacular explosions that Teg would have expected. He voiced his puzzlement to Celwen.

"The *Sinamarg* is bombarding the city with translator-based weapons," she explained. "They do not inflict damage with concussive force or heat, but by reverting targets to prana. Disintegrating a structure's foundations can destabilize the ground, as we discovered down in the tunnels, but collateral damage is rather light."

"Efficient," Teg said as he looked to the black sky overhead. "And more precise than anything we've got."

Sunlight glinted off the vast planes and edges of the Night Gen flagship, which continued its orbital strike while shooting at the smaller ships that swarmed it. The blocky Cadrys Navy corvettes chipped away at the huge dark gem with blue and red rays and torpedoes that Teg only discerned when they detonated on impact.

Teg fixed his eyes on Celwen's ashen face. "Can you call in an orbital strike?"

Celwen gave a start. "I thought you did not want the House of Law destroyed."

"I like to have backup plans," said Teg. "Can you call in a strike or not?"

"I can contact the admiral over a dedicated telepathic link," she admitted. "I could suggest a target, but the final decision would be his."

"Just curious," Teg said as he slid his knife between the panes of an office window and raised the sash. Foregoing the Formula irked him, but the sword hanging overhead called for speed over caution.

Still, a deadline wasn't a license to rush in blind.

"Anything fun waiting for us in there?" he asked Celwen.

Celwen's green eyes looked inward. At length she frowned and said, "This floor seems to have been evacuated, but one area of the northwest corner is blocked from my sight."

Teg swung his leg over the windowsill. "They must be hiding something important there. Show me the way."

Celwen led Teg through an abandoned, paper-strewn office to an empty hallway clad in yellow glazed brick. A tremor ran through the floor, and emergency sirens disturbed prevalent solemnity that Teg likened to a temple or a tomb.

"Which way?" Teg whispered.

Celwen pointed left to an ordinary-looking oak door at the end of the hall. As they stalked toward it, Teg felt a fascination with, and a fear of, the forbidden that only the door to his father's workshop had ever inspired.

Teg made damn sure to apply the Formula this time. As he ran his hands over the door's every panel and line, what had always been practical work slowly began to feel like a preparatory ritual for entering a sacred place.

"Hurry." Celwen's voice was barely audible. "The *Sinamarg* is taking heavy fire. They cannot delay a strike on the building much longer."

Though the warning fanned the urgency that smoldered in the back of Teg's mind, he wouldn't be rushed. When the

Formula was complete he stepped back from the door having found nothing. No alarms, no traps that he could see, and no sound on the other side.

Teg drew his ether metal pistol. Celwen held hers at the ready in both hands. With every precaution taken, Teg turned the bronze handle and pushed the door open.

The room beyond was a large, iron and bronze-paneled square with smaller square alcoves off the corners. The stench of blood and viscera hit Teg's nose before his eyes caught the pale nude body splayed atop the black marble slab at the room's center. Blood ran down a groove in the marble and through a brass grill set into a depression in the slate floor. The regular tap of its dripping was almost hypnotic.

Something long and wormlike swung down from above and whipped Teg's right hand. His gun flew from his grip and skidded across the floor.

Shock snapped Teg out of his trance. He glanced upward and saw a twisted hybrid of man and rat wearing filthy grey robes crouched on a narrow ledge above the entrance—much as its image had adorned Bifron's door.

"I know you," said Teg, recalling their prior meeting at the top of a tower in hell.

The freak perched above the door hissed through chisel teeth. It and two other plague-bearers had ambushed Teg once before, infecting him with a pox that only a deal with the devil had cured.

But this time it was alone.

Teg went for the knife at his ankle, but the big rat pounced, knocking both of them to the floor. Teg's head barely missed landing in the blood pooling around the drain.

Celwen's scream was louder than the shots she fired. The first two rounds missed, spraying Teg's face with flint chips blasted from the floor. He felt the rat's hairy misshapen body jerk as one bullet hit home. Another passed through the rat and, thanks to Teg's aura, merely burned into his right thigh instead of blowing a hole through it.

Teg cried out in pain, and Celwen held her fire. He'd have preferred her to keep shooting, but the huge rat's weight pressing down on his chest kept him from putting the thought into words.

Crooked yellow claws gripped an ancient knife whose bloody blade descended toward Teg's face. He gripped the rat-thing's hairy wrists and struggled to push it back, but his foe's twisted form concealed unexpected strength.

While Teg had his hands full keeping the rat from carving out his eyes, its dripping fetid mouth lunged forward. Teeth like a pair of leather shears pierced Teg's aura and his shoulder. He cried out again; not just from the wrenching pain, but because he felt infectious heat spreading from the wound.

Celwen rushed toward the grisly wrestling match. She dodged the creature's bald lashing tail and pressed the gun to its ribs.

Before Celwen could pull the trigger the rat's hind leg struck out, driving a clawed foot into her midsection. She fell to the stone floor, doubled over in pain.

Teg felt his shoulder itch as the gnawed flesh knitted itself back together. The heat of the infection cooled.

This is not *how I go out.*

Kicking Celwen had thrown the rat off-balance. Teg heaved with all his strength, driving his enemy back as he rose to his feet. The slavering jaws snapped at Teg's face, but he inclined his head to one side, suffering only a nipped ear.

"Keep your germs to yourself," said Teg. "They don't like me anymore."

Teg pistoned his knee up into the rat's lower jaw and heard its teeth crack. He pivoted, slamming his foe against the marble altar, which crashed to the floor along with the disemboweled victim lying upon it. The rat-thing collapsed onto the ruins in a foul heap.

Celwen was staggering to her feet, a pained grimace on her ashen face. Still holding the gun in one hand, she clutched her stomach with the other.

"You still fit for service?" Teg asked her.

Celwen nodded but failed to be entirely convincing.

"I doubt they were just hiding a big rat in here," he said. "See if you've got a clearer view from the inside."

Teg crossed the room and retrieved his gun. He was checking it for damage when Celwen spoke.

"The wall behind you!" she cried hoarsely, pointing at the left wall with a bloody hand. "There is a chamber beyond, clad in thick steel, with no way in. It is dark and empty, except for something…*wrong*."

The description piqued Teg's interest. "Can you describe what's in there?"

Celwen closed her eyes and fought to slow her heavy breathing. "A golden stone," she said at last. "Too large to hold in your palm."

"A giant gold nugget?" Teg said in disbelief. "That seems a little tacky for Vaun."

"Not gold," said Celwen. "Amber. There are ancient things entombed inside; dead things—a spider the size of my hand feeding on a dragonfly."

She stared at him, her eyes wide with horror. "Something came into the stone! It is alive and dead at the same time; hideous."

What most people would have called mad rambling reminded Teg of stories Yato had told the Nesshin kids to make them behave. His mind wandered from there to the bowels of the *Exodus*, where Nakvin had called Fallon a name from those morbid tales.

"A kost," Teg thought aloud. "It keeps its life in a *vas*, just like Thera's. Fallon's soul is hidden in here, and the rat was guarding it!"

Icy fingers dug into Teg's soul. He tried to fight them, but all his strength couldn't wrest his soul from their intangible clutches. Alien thoughts flooded his mind; memories terrifying in their inhumanity.

"Woe to the thief when the master returns to find him plundering his house," a cold voice whispered to Teg. He realized it was his own and screamed.

"Teg!" Celwen cried from an impossible distance. Her form blurred as Teg's vision faded to shades of grey and gold.

"I am deprived of flesh, owing to the vagrant malakh," said the pitiless voice in Teg's head. "Yours shall serve as recompense."

The devouring cold leeched away Teg's reason, but visceral

revulsion moved his arm to press the white gun' warm barrel to his head. An instant before he pressed the trigger, the invading presence left him.

"Call down a strike on the room!" Teg shouted to Celwen.

The rat leapt to its feet. It leered at Teg with empty black pits in place of eyes. He recognized the cold malice in its voice.

"You shall not slay yourself," Fallon said through the rat demon he'd possessed. "That pleasure is my just due."

Reflex moved Teg's hand again; pointing the muzzle not at him, but at the rat-kost. He pumped the trigger, producing a series of subdued pops with such little recoil that all seven shots punctured the grey robe's chest in a tight pattern. The monster that wore it lurched backward.

"Call in the strike!" Teg shouted again.

This time, Celwen bolted from the room. Teg turned to follow her, but before he'd taken three strides, the soles of his boots stuck to the floor like industrial magnets on an iron sheet.

"We both have outstayed our time," the kost-rat said from behind him. "What matters our passing to the turnings of the world? Your soul and mine shall descend to the Void."

Teg looked down and saw the floor under his feet glowing gold. He pulled a fresh magazine from his jacket and reloaded.

"You first," said Teg. He twisted around and aimed at the half-rat, half-human face. Worked bullets flew from the white gun in such rapid succession that the muted crack of each shot overlapped the echo of the last. The monster's head disintegrated, and its twitching body fell for the last time.

The glow at Teg's feet faded, leaving him free to run.

But he couldn't run, as much as his sense of self-preservation begged him. Because with the rat dead, the only one who knew the location of Thera's *vas* was brooding inside a chunk of amber in the next room.

Teg cast about the chamber. Besides the door he'd entered through, and the drain in the floor, the only other exit was a balcony off the upper right alcove with a fifty story drop beyond. He holstered his empty gun and walked toward the door, though every nerve in his body urged him to run.

Teg's lifespan had been miniscule compared to Fallon's, but Teg had been around long enough to know the kost's type when he saw it. Anyone who willingly stuck his soul in a piece of rock clearly had trouble letting things go.

As expected, the ice-cold hands were pawing at Teg's soul again before he reached the doorway. Teg didn't waste time fighting. Instead he turned on his heel and ran all out for the balcony.

Fallon possessed Teg's body just before they reached the balcony's edge. But that was okay, because the momentum that Teg had built up carried them over the low stone railing.

Teg was vaguely aware of his body flipping end over end through the air as the plaza rushed up to meet it. Fallon's mind had swallowed his, and was taunting him on the way down. But as before the mental connection was two-way.

Hey, the corner of Fallon's soul that had been Teg said to rest of the kost. *Don't think about where Thera's vas is.*

Fallon wasn't remotely human, but even his reptilian psychology wasn't immune to the old cognitive trick. In their shared mind's eye, Teg saw a deep chamber where Smith's clockwork form labored over a red gem and a rod of clear crystal.

Their real eyes—or the black pits that Teg supposed had taken the job—saw a pillar of green-white light streak down from the sky.

Fallon's spirit shrieked in helpless rage as the orbital strike enveloped the building's northwest corner, where his soul's true house resided, mere inches from his host's feet. The black mist that had frozen Teg's soul burned away, leaving him blessedly alone in his head. He rejoiced at his newfound freedom and his most satisfying kill to date.

But only in the second before he hit the pavement.

40

Nakvin stared across green hills to the war raging below Seele's western slopes. Even at this distance, the drydock built into the hill where the *Exodus* had crashed afforded a panoramic view of the battle for her kingdom.

This used to be my kingdom, she corrected herself. And the admission was like a shard of ice piercing her heart. The numbing cold was a relief compared to her anguish over Elena.

A winged shadow fell from the sky over Seele. Standing behind Nakvin, Zebel clicked her tongue.

"Shaiel's Will met his match," Zebel said. "I warned Fallon about his pride. Of course, that's the trouble with prideful people. They don't listen."

Nakvin noted her father's hypocrisy with a rueful laugh but said nothing. Zebel had fooled and betrayed her, striking down Elena and giving Shaiel free entry into Avalon. Far more humiliating than the political coup she'd achieved were the deep emotional wounds she'd inflicted.

Now the two of them stood atop an observation tower atop the drydock. The round building's roof was sheltered under a domed canopy supported by four fluted pillars. Nakvin was sure that Zebel had chosen this spot because it allowed her to watch Seele's destruction in safety.

And she'd brought Nakvin to make her watch, too.

Nakvin rounded on her father. Zebel still looked like a mirror image of her, but with folded black wings. The former baalah had discarded Jaren's uniform jacket and Worked the rest of his clothes into a diaphanous light green shift that left disturbingly little to the imagination.

"Since you're in a gloating mood," Nakvin said, "tell me what you did with Jaren."

Zebel smiled, exposing a pair of small fangs. Her silver eyes glinted. "There was nothing to be done. Our dear Captain Peregrine blew himself to atoms at Tzimtzum." Her expression soured. "I'm the one who suffered! Every second on that rusted tub with those unwashed Nesshin was worse than an eternity in hell."

"So Elena and Astlin couldn't read you telepathically because you have no soul," Nakvin mocked.

Zebel tossed her loose black hair and sniffed. "Your socially stunted daughter and her dimwitted friend simply failed to comprehend what is beyond their experience. Those Anomian locusts lack souls, and none of them could have used the partitioning rod. Few besides me can wield it well enough to cleave the soul of a goddess!"

"Then what are you?" Nakvin asked.

"Your own stake in the matter no doubt drives your curiosity," said Zebel.

Nakvin crossed her arms. "And your vanity drives you to

answer. You couldn't resist bragging now if you wanted to."

"Trying to regain a semblance of control?" Zebel smirked. "You can do nothing but play your assigned role in the paroxysms to come, just as I can only follow my nature. My body and soul are one, a composite formed by the *Nahash* himself to advance his inevitable triumph."

"Aren't you supposed to be Shaiel's Right Hand?" asked Nakvin. "Vaun won't be happy about your divided loyalties."

Zebel laughed. "Shaiel fancies himself the Lord of the Void. He's just an upstart who will presently be shown his place."

The tower shook. Nakvin braced herself against a pillar to keep from toppling over the edge. The clouds above Seele parted, forming a blue circle in the grey sky. Dread unlike any Nakvin had known clutched her heart.

"Behold!" Zebel exulted. "I succeed where all failed before me. Thera has awakened!"

Elena, was Nakvin's only thought as her last spark of hope died.

"Come, daughter," said Zebel. "We will aid Thera in slaying Shaiel and casting down Zadok. Fulfill the end for which you were made, alongside your issue and your sire!"

Nakvin's heartbreak fed her rage as she spun to face Zebel and began the motions of the Steersman's Compass.

Zebel shook her head. "You would vent your anger on me? It will profit you not at all. I am nothing. You are less than nothing, and your feckless grandson is nothing's pale shadow! I know you, daughter. All your long life, you have lusted for acceptance; for family. You cannot raise your hand to your father."

Nakvin's hands fell to her sides; not just because Zebel's

words rang true, but because while Nakvin was fashioning Tefler had strode up the tower steps to stand behind his great-grandfather.

"Grandma's got a soft spot for you," Tefler said.

Zebel rounded on her great-grandson just before he ran her through with a shadow sword.

Tefler's left hand twisted the blade. "I don't have her inhibitions."

Zebel looked down at the grey scimitar piercing her stomach and chuckled. "I am no shard of a stumbled angel cloaked in tarnished light! That blade bears the breath of my father. It cannot slay me."

Tefler's face was emotionless as he raised his right hand. A nimbus of prana covered his fist, which was closed around the hilt of a mirrored white scimitar.

"This can," he said.

Zebel fought to pull free of the grey sword that had impaled her, but its white twin severed the head from her shoulders, cutting short her final scream. Her decapitated corpse slumped to the floor. A second later, so did Nakvin.

There was only the hard stone beneath her and the hard vacuum where her heart had been. Then someone helped her sit up. He was wearing armor and had light brown hair and strange eyes. Nakvin knew him. He was one of the last family members she had left.

"Tefler?"

"Yeah," he said. She smelled machine oil and blood as he leaned closer.

"What are you doing here?" asked Nakvin.

431

"I was down at the dock helping them make repairs to the *Serapis*." Tefler raised the mirrored white blade. "Found this in the hangar. Xander wanted Cook to have it, but he's dead, so I figured—"

Nakvin's reeling mind didn't register the rest of what he said. "How did you know about Zebel?" she asked.

"I didn't," Tefler admitted. "I wanted to get Jaren's opinion on recalibrating the drum turrets, but I couldn't raise him via sending. So I followed the Void thread tied to his rodcaster."

Nakvin stared at the jacket that lay beside the stairs. The butt of a large gun peeked out from under the dark green fabric.

"Void thread?" she repeated.

Tefler helped her up. "A little trick I learned while poking around the local ruins," he said. "A rodcaster can shoot down a small ship. I'm not handing out firepower like that without keeping tabs on it."

"Oh," said Nakvin.

"Where is Jaren, anyway?" Tefler asked.

Nakvin faltered under a sudden weight. Tefler kept her from falling.

"Zebel…" she began to say. But fear and revulsion twisted her words, which emerged as a near-whisper. "Zebel killed him."

Tefler squeezed her shoulder. "Sorry."

"So am I," she breathed.

The light of a hundred suns shone from behind Nakvin, which was unusual because Avalon didn't even have one. She turned and felt a hot breeze on her face as a loud rumbling emanated from a dome of blinding white light on Seele's west face.

"That much prana could run a city for a year," Tefler said. "Or kill one instantly."

"I think Elena just did," said Nakvin.

Astlin fought at the head of Avalon's army beside Xander, Anris, and Jarsaal. Though reinforced by the north and south divisions, the Gen were still outnumbered since the enemy had been reinforced by their own dead.

Both sides' formations had broken down, leaving two wide chaotic lines shooting at, charging, and retreating from each other. Gen and Cadrisian soldiers traded gunfire. Greycloak swords cast living shadows that froze their victims where they stood. Faerda's Chosen fought *Isnashi* tooth and claw.

Alongside Xander, Astlin cowed the enemy with her light while Anris cut men down with his scythelike sword. At the same time, Astlin's spear flashed across the field and returned to her hand, sending a soul to the Void with each throw. The enemy answered with a hail of bullets, but the wall of nexic force that Xander projected before the vanguard turned every shot.

Jarsaal thrust at the enemy with his own wooden spear, and the prana he channeled was a godsend against undead soldiers who proved harder to kill a second time. The White Well's light burned them to the bone on contact, and bursts of white radiance scattered across the battlefield marked the presence of Dawn Gen priests.

Astlin's spirits rose when she saw that the enemy line was about to break. Only a force of undead soldiers—identified by their grisly wounds—stood in the way.

Looking for Jarsaal, Astlin caught a white flash off to her right.

Too far off, she realized. Jarsaal had broken off to aid a fellow shaman who'd been overwhelmed by greycloaks. The shades bound to their grey scimitars swarmed over the surrounded priest, preventing him from summoning the Well's light.

Jarsaal fought his way to the fallen shaman's side and erased the shadows with a prana burst. He was checking the motionless priest when a loud crack rang out and Jarsaal fell to one knee.

"Xander!" shouted Astlin. "Jarsaal's hit. Can you shield him?"

"Not without exposing us," Xander said grimly.

Astlin scoured the enemy line and saw a Cadrisian in the distance aiming at the Dawn Gen. She threw so hard that her arm throbbed and went numb, but her burning spear struck the ground in front of the gunman.

The spear faded from the ground up and reformed in Astlin's hand. The Cadrisian was beyond the reach of her weapon, but not of her mind. Luckily, almost getting skewered by fiery missile had distracted him, giving Astlin just enough time to invade his thoughts. His next shot blew off the top of his own head.

Forcing a man to kill himself twisted Astlin's stomach in knots. She took little comfort from knowing that he'd get back up in a minute or two.

Jarsaal was limping away from the shaman he'd sadly failed to save. The greycloaks were closing in, and Jarsaal's body compacted itself into the form of a lean but still wounded wolf. Surrounded, he ran straight toward a shocked Lawbringer and leapt.

A dark grey shape sprang from the melee to Jarsaal's right, taking him in midair and driving him to the ground. Jarsaal wrestled with the *Isnashi*, but the larger, unwounded wolf pinned him down as the Lawbringers closed in.

Astlin struggled to cast her will over the *Isnashi* and the circle of greycloaks, but she was still shaken from her last telepathic attack. Two greycloaks escaped her mental net and ran their curved blades through the injured wolf. Its corpse reverted to a Gen clad in hides with brightly painted beads in his hair.

A deafening roar and searing radiance interrupted Astlin's grief-stricken cry. Shaiel's army stared in helpless awe at the terrible light on the hill.

Astlin turned with all of her comrades to see that an entire town had vanished in a sudden whiteout. The light soon faded, leaving the hamlet apparently untouched.

Astlin had no trouble picturing her destination on the slopes above. The town that had been deluged with prana was the same one she'd searched for survivors.

Appearing in a narrow lane beside Xander, Astlin saw that the buildings and streets were undamaged, though the cobblestones were hot beneath her feet. But something immediately struck her as wrong, and a moment later she realized what it was.

Gen architecture was airy and lively, designed to stand in harmony with its surroundings. Astlin noticed with a start that the oaks and willows that the buildings had complimented were gone. Shrubs and even grass had left bare soil in their place. Looking at the town now was like hearing a lone instrument play a song written for a full orchestra.

"Everything living is gone," said Xander.

His words revealed the true horror that Astlin had hidden from herself. She sent her will out over the village as she had before, listening for the thoughts of living minds.

Her blood ran cold when she realized there was nothing to hear.

"There were hundreds of people here less than an hour ago," she said. "Now there's no one left."

A tremor passed through the street. Chimes hung from houses' eaves jangled, and clay pots that had survived the death of their flowers crashed to the pavement.

"Perhaps we are not entirely alone," Xander said.

The quake had come from the public square. Astlin's mind found the small common with its pavilion of wood and old stones just as empty as the rest of town.

No, that wasn't quite true. There was a deeper emptiness in the hamlet's heart; a lack so profound that it took on a being of its own.

Astlin shared her mental image of the square with Xander, and they were there. For a second time, though, the reality differed from Astlin's memory.

The delicate seashell-like roof had been blown from the pavilion and scattered across the square. Now the age-old stones stood free, like rotted teeth biting through the ground.

A solitary figure waited just outside the ring. Light brown hair fell in waves to the small of her back, and white skirts descended from there to the ground. Her white-sleeved arms were stretched out in front of her as if to embrace the ancient circle.

"Elena!" Astlin called out.

Elena's head turned, and Astlin's breath caught in her throat. Bright gold eyes gleamed with cold contempt in place of the goddess' strange but mindful rose-colored irises. Without a word, she faced the ring of standing stones once more.

"What is wrong with her?" Xander asked.

Astlin tried a second time to reach Elena's mind. Once again, she found only a glaring absence.

"I don't know," Astlin said. "Elena's always been strong enough to shut me out, but whenever I tried to make telepathic contact with her, I always had a weird sense of thinking to myself. That's gone now."

The sharp crack of splitting stone rang out from the center of the circle like a call to silence. The pavement encircled by the ring crumbled and sank as the ground shook.

A shadow passing overhead drew Astlin's attention to a winged form descending toward the square like a falling star.

"It's Anris," she said.

Xander looked up. "If he has left the battle, whatever's happened to Elena is far worse than we thought."

Anris landed on his feet between Elena and the Zadokim. The malakh still wore his torn leather armor, and he sported fresh wounds from the continuing battle on the field below.

"I have dire news from Tefler," he said. "Zebel used the rod of partition on Elena. Her soul has truly become Thera's!"

Shock stole Astlin's words.

"So that is how Shaiel opened the gate," said Xander. "Thera betrayed us to her brother."

"If only that was the worst of it." Anris took a step toward Elena. "Lady Thera, cease this destruction, I beg you!"

Elena lowered her arms but didn't turn around. "Who invokes my name?" she asked in a soft, distant voice. "Are you my father, that you dare bid me cease the work for which I was made?"

Anris' jaw clenched, and his purple face paled.

"Knowing what befell her father, I would tread lightly," Xander said

"If you know what she's doing," Astlin said to Anris, "tell us. We'll do whatever we can to help."

Astlin had never seen fear in Anris' eyes—not during her training, not when he led his men in battle, and not when he'd fought Shaiel's Will. She saw it now, as he stared at the collapsing ground within the ring of stones.

"You know that Zadok devised this cosmos as a contest between good and evil?" the malakh said.

"We discussed the subject with him at some length," said Xander.

Anris went on. "The Righteous One pooled his own life force into the White Well, yet he lacked a comparable source of evil to fill the Void."

"Doesn't prana turn into Void after it's used up in the Strata?" asked Astlin.

"Yes," Anris said, "but a force was needed to draw down the light, like a black hole's gravity. Without such a force, all prana would remain locked in the Well. The Strata would not have formed, and there would be no life."

Xander asked the question that now chilled Astlin. "Where did Zadok find such a power?"

The ground shook again, and the hole deepened beyond sight.

"Your crowns reflect perfect light from the world beyond," said Anris. "There, evil is not a substance; merely a shadow cast in the light's absence. Zadok envisioned a world where evil would have its own being, and so he thought, could be destroyed. Thus he built his ideal order where the shadow lay deepest."

A tremor from far below the hill signaled a gust of bitter cold air that flowed out between the standing stones.

Astlin shivered. "Where is the deepest shadow?"

"The prison of the *Nahash*," Anris said somberly. "The Serpent who deceived the world beyond lies bound beneath our own. These standing stones, which are scattered throughout hell, were raised by its Builders. They are supports touching hell's foundation in the Ninth Circle—the roof of the Serpent's cell. And Thera is delving into it."

How can we stop a god?

Astlin racked her brain for an answer. Something that Shaiel's Will and Anris had said came back to her. They'd called the light that she and Xander reflected crowns, and it was true that they granted certain authority in Zadok's world.

Astlin made a leap of faith. "Try willing the hole closed," she told Xander. "We might be able to reweave Avalon like Nakvin can."

She unveiled her sapphire light, which was soon joined by Xander's silver. The six stars' pure rays shone between the standing stones, and Astlin focused all of her will on closing the pit. She could actually sense Xander's authority striking the fabric of Avalon like an iron staff.

Moving by inches, the pit began to close.

"The Zadokim have issued their edict!" Anris rejoiced. "The Serpent's chains shall not be broken."

Thera wheeled on her opposition. Her face remained impassive, but her eyes blazed with golden malice. A force that made Xander's iron will seem like straw pressed back against the Zadokim with calculating brutality.

Resisting Thera's will was like trying to stop a slow train by standing on the track and pushing. Astlin tore off the veil she'd only lifted. Her light outshone Xander's, setting the whole square afire with glory and making Anris fall to his knees.

The full brilliance of Astlin's crown delayed, but didn't check, Thera's invincible will. The pit sank deeper toward the Ninth Circle and the utter corruption waiting below.

A sudden impulse stirred in Astlin's soul. She'd felt it while breaking the Nexus' hold on Teg and vying against Shaiel for Xander. The small placid voice told her to abandon her own will; to stop reflecting the light like a mirror and let it shine through her like a window.

Astlin almost gave in, but she hesitated out of fear—the deep-rooted fear of losing herself like Zadok's shards lost themselves to the Nexus.

Xander, whose own light was fully revealed as a dazzling silver diadem, shook his head. "She is too strong!"

Anris leapt to his feet with a cry and charged Thera, swinging his great hooked sword. The goddess held up her hand, palm outward, and Anris froze in mid-stride. To Astlin's amazement, even dust motes hung motionless in the air around him.

Thera spread her fingers, and dozens of white orbs like pearls made of light flashed into being, floating over every inch of Anris' giant frame.

Astlin tore her will away from the pit and mentally beat against the frozen block of time that bound Anris. But Thera closed her hand into a fist, and the prana pearls converged on Anris. They sank into his purple skin, turning it to blazing light that spread throughout his body like wildfire.

Despite Astlin's cries of protest, Anris flared into a white inferno that washed over the square and sent tongues of flame reaching higher than the rooftops before fading as if it had never been. The ashes of the malakh's armor drifted to the ground, and his blade shattered on the pavement with the bright chimes of broken stained glass.

Wrath consumed the last of Astlin's restraint. She raised a trembling fist to Thera. "I'll drag the damned snake out of that hole and shove it up yours, you murdering bitch!"

"I am surprised at you, Serieigna," said Xander. "And also impressed."

Thera stretched out her hand toward Astlin, who managed to will herself across the square an instant before a blinding white stream of prana tore through the space she'd occupied. The ray engulfed entire houses in its arrow-straight path through town and across the hill's flank. A high-pitched ringing followed in its wake, which left buildings whole but kindled a long swath of trees into towers of white flame that burned down to nothing.

"Astlin!" Xander cried, staring in horror at the smoking ground where she'd stood.

"Over here!" she called back to him from the plaza's other end.

Xander heaved a sigh of relief. "Do not scare me like that."

Still standing by the ring of stones, Thera looked at her hand and said, "This power is wrong. Had not Shaiel usurped the Void, I could have carried out my work unaided. More's the pity for this world. The *Nahash* will make you beg for death at my hand, but your prayer must go unanswered."

"I will never pray to you, Mother of Demons!" Xander vowed. He thrust his hands upward, and a surge of force rushed toward Thera, ripping a hail of flagstones from the ground and carrying them along like driftwood on the crest of a tidal wave.

The invisible tide forked at the center of the square, passing around the ring of stones while leaving them and Thera untouched. Flagstones hurtled by on either side of Astlin to scour the faces of buildings with the sound of a cannon barrage.

Xander rose from the ground. His body gave off sounds like stepping on green twigs. He didn't scream but only made agonized grunts.

"You first had this gift from me," said Thera, holding her outstretched hand toward Xander. "I will slay you with it, in memory of our former bond."

The burning spear was streaking toward Thera before Astlin was aware of throwing it. Thera's other hand lashed out, releasing a massive yet tightly controlled force that not only stopped the spear but shot it back toward Astlin, who found she couldn't move. The shaft didn't burn her, but it drove the air from her lungs as it rammed into her stomach and burst into a thousand fading embers.

The same force that bound Astlin lifted her into the air and squeezed her like a giant's fist. She could sense Xander pouring forth his power in a desperate attempt to loosen Thera's hold on both of them, but it seemed that the best he could do was prolong their agony. Astlin fought through the pain, focusing her will on healing splintered bone and crushed organs.

"You only delay this flawed order's rightful end," Thera said. "Surrender and return to the light that is denied me."

A shadow fell over Astlin's thoughts. A larger shadow fell across the town. She looked upward, and there she saw the tapered oval keel of the *Serapis*.

Two figures descended from the great ship on solid columns of air. One wore flowing white robes. The other's breastplate glinted under his red cloak.

Nakvin. Tefler.

Tefler hit the ground running near the square's west edge. He stopped just beyond Thera's reach.

"I know what you're doing, Mom," he said. "You've got to stop."

Nakvin rushed to her grandson's side. Astlin felt heartbreak from the queen that dwarfed her own physical pain.

"Elena," Nakvin said gently. "We love you, sweetheart. Please don't hurt anyone else."

Thera's gold eyes seemed to look through her mother. "Existence hurts everyone. I will make it stop."

Prana surrounded Tefler's hand. He drew the white scimitar and pointed it at Thera.

"Don't make me do this," he said.

Seeing the ether metal sword finally cracked Thera's icy expression. She scowled and thrust both hands toward Tefler.

Nakvin pulled a lavender rod from her robe and aimed it at Thera. The goddess' attention was suddenly fixed on her as the rod unleashed a tremendous nexic power that Astlin found chillingly familiar.

It's the partition rod. Nakvin's trying to restore Elena!

Through the rod, Nakvin wielded strength many times greater than her natural power. Sadly, she was still no match for a goddess.

Thera sent forth the will of an entire nexus against the assault on her soul. The rod in Nakvin's hand cracked, and she wisely let go before it exploded in a shower of amethyst fragments that the upraised sleeve of her robe deflected from her face.

"You lack Zebel's will," Thera told Nakvin. "The rod was harmless to me in your hands."

Nakvin didn't shrink from the rebuke. "I thought it might be, but I was pretty sure that dealing with it would take your mind off them."

Astlin had immediately visualized herself beside Thera when, as Nakvin rightly guessed, the goddess' crushing will had released her. Before Nakvin finished speaking, Astlin's spear was arcing toward Thera's head. A shock ran up the solid fire shaft as it struck what felt closer to diamond than flesh and bone.

The fist that Thera drove into Astlin's side struck faster than she could follow and harder than she'd thought Elena capable of hitting. The blow ground ribs to powder, punctured Astlin's right lung, and left her gasping at Thera's feet.

"Stop it!" Tefler cried as a stream of sallow light rushed from his left hand toward Thera. She answered with a flood of prana, but Xander's will pulled Thera's son to safety beside him.

"Laudable spirit," Xander said, "but poor planning."

Astlin's mind restored her body. She felt Avalon's fabric warping and saw Nakvin and Thera engaged in what looked like a staring contest but was really a battle for the realm itself.

"Xander," Astlin called out, "help Nakvin!"

She added her authority to Nakvin's, shining sapphire light on Thera that was soon mingled with Xander's silver radiance. With one accord they commanded Avalon to bind the goddess.

We've got her! Astlin thought. She and her allies' combined strength forced Thera to her knees within an area of space that was now heavier than the huge ship overhead.

A ship toward which Tefler was quickly ascending via airlift.

Astlin remembered the end of her first battle with Fallon. *He's not thinking...*

She hadn't known that there was a sending worked into her dress until Tefler spoke to her through it.

"Hold Thera for a couple more minutes," he said. "I'll rig up an anti-Malefaction field and blast her out of my mom."

Nakvin must have gotten the message too. "Tefler, no!" she shouted. "It won't work."

The brief distraction was all Thera needed. She burst her bonds with a sound like the sky tearing. A wave of force pushed her three opponents back the plaza's edge.

The goddess raised her hands toward the ship above. There was no time to warn anyone aboard before unseen hands took hold of the massive hull like a child clutching a model plane and pushed down with a force that overwhelmed its engines. The shadow of the *Serapis* stretched over the town and the whine of the ship's overtaxed drifters grew louder as it fell.

Astlin turned all of her light on the crashing ship. Even with the engines' help, fighting to keep the *Serapis* aloft against Thera's will was like an ant straining against the boot about to crush it. But if Astlin failed in her impossible task, it would cost the hundreds of souls on board their lives.

The shrill whine stopped. Black smoke poured from the *Serapis'* stern as its drifters burned out. Astlin would have buckled under the terrible burden of the ship's weight and Thera's will, but Xander and Nakvin once again joined their strength to hers.

Astlin's brief swell of triumph fled as the *Serapis* continued its descent. Together she, Xander, and Nakvin had almost been strong enough to hold Thera. But even all three of them couldn't hold back her destructive will and a multimillion ton ship.

The great ship's bow tilted downward, and Astlin thought she could see the bridge crew's horrified faces through the quickly approaching canopy. The impact would kill everyone in the square—except, she thought darkly, for Thera—but Astlin dismissed the urge to run.

If we don't stop Thera here, thought Astlin, *there's no stopping her. I owe it to the people of this world to die trying.*

Thera stood before the ring of standing stones, her arms stretched over her head as the gale raised by the ship's approach made her hair writhe like serpents. There was no pity behind her gold eyes.

Yet the sight no longer held any fear for Astlin. *I've died before,* she thought. *It's the worst experience I ever had, but I know what's waiting on the other side. I came here to save as many souls as I could. If it was just one; that's enough.*

The small voice returned, asking for Astlin's surrender.

I was proud and willful, she thought. *I don't deserve this.*

As the *Serapis* sped toward her, Astlin reached up to the stars hovering just above her forehead. She wasn't surprised when her fingers touched a circlet of polished stone. She lifted the crown from her head in both hands, held it up to the clear sky, and let go with all her might. Her crown faded into the blue.

Inexhaustible light emptied itself into Astlin's soul and lifted her up. Her black dress and the red hair blown in her face by the wind turned a gleaming white brighter than the Well.

These are only shadows, she realized, looking at the hill, the town, and the ship above them. *And I'm just a servant, but I've been raised above the one Thera serves.*

With less effort than it took to move a piece on a chessboard, the will that Astlin shared with the light plucked the *Serapis* from Thera's grasp and gently lowered it toward the ground.

Thera gestured toward the stone ring. A sound like the cracking of a black egg rose from deep below, and nothing flowed out of the pit. That was the only name Astlin could give to the non-color that made blackness look like a rainbow. It poured from between the standing stones, slithering around Thera and rushing toward Astlin.

The incomprehensible fear of waking from a nightmare to find one of its horrors invading reality shook Astlin's soul. In her fear, she closed her eyes and willed the light to force the nothingness back.

Astlin opened her eyes. A circle of bare soil lay where the ring of stones had once stood around the pit. The blacker darkness was gone.

But so was the light.

The *Serapis* fell once more, and Astlin could only watch helplessly as it dropped toward the square.

Silver rays of light bathed the great ship, and Astlin felt Xander's nexic power pressing against its keel. Nakvin extended her arms toward the *Serapis*, and together the two of them pushed the falling ship so that it came down a few blocks from the square. The sound of buildings being crushed was like a rockslide, and a strong wind carried choking dust. But the ship was mostly intact.

Astlin ran to Xander as he stood panting and caked in dust. She embraced him with arms clad in dusty black sleeves.

"That was incredible!" she exclaimed.

Xander tousled her dirty red hair. "High praise from someone who supported the ship by herself. How did you do that?"

Astlin stared at the grit-coated flagstones in shame. "The light did it through me," she said. "But I got scared by what came out of the pit. I tried to control the light, and it left me."

Xander cupped her chin and gently lifted her face to look at his. "You are too hard on yourself," he said. "The light leaves no one unless we forsake it."

As if to confirm Xander's words, three points of sapphire light briefly glowed above Astlin's brow.

Astlin kissed his cheek and took the bitter grit that stuck to her lips as a penance.

Nakvin screamed from the middle of the square. Astlin reflexively looked toward her just as the circle of earth where the pit had been erupted. Thera rose from the crater she'd made, covered head to toe in black dust. Her eyes burned like eclipsed suns.

"You think this a victory?" Thera said, her voice all the more terrible for holding none of the fury of her eyes. "The Builders left other rings. I will seek one after you have all died for your insolence."

41

Teg woke up on cracked pavement near the edge of a big square hole that had been the House of Law's northwest corner. Smoke billowed from the pit and vanished against a black afternoon sky pulsing with green, red, and blue flashes.

The only sounds were distant screams and the wail of air raid sirens. Nothing moved within the square. Teg took advantage of the eerie solitude to heal from the fall that he and Fallon had taken but only he'd survived.

Despite the stabbing pain of moving his shattered arm, Teg patted the still active aura projector on his belt. Thanks to the cigarette pack-sized device, the fall hadn't killed him. Truthfully it hadn't killed the kost either. Teg owed that to the orbital strike on Fallon's *vas*.

Which reminded Teg of what he'd seen in Fallon's last memory and what he'd come here to do.

A burst of green-white light beside him made Teg close his eyes and brace himself for disintegration. But he felt only a warm breeze and heard a familiar voice.

"Sleeping on duty is gross negligence," Celwen rebuked him.

Teg's newly healed bones ached as he sat up. He opened his eyes and saw the Night Gen pilot standing over him. A smile brightened her ashen face.

"I sleep in on Wellday," he said, extending an arm. She took his hand and helped him up. He surveyed the deserted plaza and the building's exposed cross-section.

"You have earned the rest," said Celwen. "The death of Shaiel's Will has thrown the enemy into disarray. Cadrys will be ours before the rest of the fleet arrives from Temil."

"I aim to please," said Teg. "But don't sell yourself short. You called in the strike. It's good to see you got out before the hammer fell. And you didn't bleed to death internally."

Celwen looked to the battle raging above. "I translated back to the *Sinamarg*, and Gien treated me."

"Isn't he the guy Astlin told me about?" Teg frowned. "Chews his own fingers, she said. You sure you can trust him?"

"If not for him," said Celwen, "the *Sinamarg* would not have come in time, and you would have faced this mission alone."

Teg raised his hands in a placating gesture. "Hey, you're a big girl, and I don't tell folks their business. But I can tell you where Thera's *vas* is and how we can pinch it like a fat kid's pocketknife."

Celwen's grey brow furrowed. "I do not know that expression. Is it peculiar to Keth?"

"Yes," said Teg, recalling one glorious fall day in the park. "Yes it is."

"Stop teasing and tell me where the *vas* is," said Celwen.

Teg moved to the edge of the pit. "I pried some intel out of the kost while we shared a brain. Mirai Smith's down in the tunnels working on the *vas* in a secret lab. It's nexically shielded and guarded by a greycloak-led platoon. Best of all, Shaiel's Blade is inside keeping an eye on Smith."

Celwen stepped up beside him. Her voice echoed the worry on her face. "I will ask the admiral to send a special operations team."

"Let's table that for now," said Teg. "I think we can extract the *vas*, and possibly Smith, with zero losses on our side."

"How?" Celwen asked.

Teg checked his gun. Its ether-metal frame wasn't even scratched. The action still worked smoothly, so he reloaded.

"First," he said, "we need a Lawbringer's cloak. The best place to find one is back inside the House of Law. We should have a much easier time getting in now that the wall's gone."

Entering the House of Law did prove much easier the second time. Hunting down a greycloak and relieving him of his trademark garment was only slightly harder thanks to Celwen's help.

They regrouped in a neglected corner of the sub-basement near the tunnel lift doors. Teg pointed out that taking the elevator down when they'd exited the tunnels would have placed them right outside Smith's lab.

"I was under threat of imminent death," Celwen said. "Besides, I am clairsentient; not omniscient."

"No offense meant," said Teg. "Even if you'd found the lab, you'd have missed the nexically shielded guards—not to mention Izlaril. Doing things at the right time is a big part of doing them right."

"Go on and do it then," said Celwen.

Teg wiped some of the former owner's blood from the grey cloak before donning it. The cloth was rough-woven, and wearing it actually made him feel colder.

Since Teg made it a rule to know his enemy, he'd learned all about Lawbringers from Tefler during his six months in Avalon. Their cloaks were Worked with sending, plus a Malefaction that did the same thing only better. He hoped it would add credibility to the con he was about to run.

"Izlaril Nizari," Teg said while calling up Fallon's last sight of Izlaril, kneeling in a bulky Guild Enforcer's uniform amid strange machines.

"Yes, Teg Cross?" the answer came immediately in Izlaril's soft, husky voice.

The response didn't rattle Teg. "You speak in haste," he said with cold menace. "Shaiel's Will calls upon you. The mercenary attempted to invade my sanctum and is now my host."

Izlaril's voice sounded confused, which was good. "Your *vas* survived the Night Gen attack?"

"You doubt me?" asked Teg, letting irritation creep into his voice. He called up another of Fallon's stolen memories. "You did not question my prior host when he freed you from the bowels of the Mill."

"Your pardon, lord," Izlaril said like a cadet caught with scuffed boots. "If it does not try your patience, why does Shaiel's Left Hand no longer rest upon me?"

Teg looked to Celwen. "Was the rat-thing Shaiel's Left Hand?"

She shook her head. "Tzaraat was Shaiel's Voice. The Left Hand was Lykaon. He died on the *Sinamarg*."

"Thanks," Teg told her. "I get Vaun's parts mixed up." To Izlaril he said, "Lykaon has fallen to the Night Gen's treachery. You may take his place, if you will perform a final task as Shaiel's Blade."

"Shaiel's Will now holds his Blade," said Izlaril. Teg could almost hear him groveling. "Wield it as best pleases you."

It took all of Teg's discipline to keep from grinning. "The souldancer Smith conspires with Shaiel's foes. Kill him."

Izlaril's silence was all the confirmation Teg needed. He threw off the gory cloak, took Celwen's arm, and dashed from behind the palettes of plastic drums where they'd hidden.

"Come on," Teg urged her. "We need to get down there before it's too late."

"What about the guards?" protested Celwen.

Teg shot her a deadpan look. "The guards are aspects of Vaun. Smith is who Vaun expects to serve him the universe on a golden plate. Izlaril thinks Vaun ordered him to kill Smith."

Celwen didn't look like she understood. She would when she saw the lab. Teg ran with her to the oversized lift doors and called the car.

Screams and the rattle of automatic gunfire echoed up the shaft as Teg and Celwen rode down. He let go of her arm, but she grabbed his and held on tighter.

"Still got the pistol I lent you?" he asked.

Celwen opened a pouch in her jumpsuit's right thigh and drew out the mate of Teg's ether metal gun.

"Good," he said. "Keep it handy."

The lift arrived one floor below the forgotten rail station. Even though the car had stopped, Teg still felt like he was sinking. The large doors opened on an even larger hallway with white brick walls and a red metal grate running along the right side of the concrete floor. The hum of nearby machinery was the only sound filling the damp air.

"Where is everyone?" Celwen asked as she looked around, holding her gun at the ready.

Teg didn't waste words telling her. He disabled the lift controls with his knife and hurried down the empty corridor. The hallway took a right turn up ahead. He rounded the corner and found the first bodies choking a double set of steel doors.

Celwen stifled a gasp. Teg stepped over the blue-uniformed corpses—each bearing exactly one mortal wound—and entered the room beyond. Celwen groaned as she followed.

Teg found the lab as Fallon had remembered it for him. The dim, uneven light came only from glowing white screens and tall tubes filled with rose-colored mist. A scent like lightning hung over the banks of strange machines connected by bundled cables running along the walls.

The only difference from Fallon's memory was the mass of dead bodies lying about the room. Most wore blue jackets. Some wore grey cloaks. All had been well-armed, but that hadn't stopped them from being efficiently and brutally slaughtered.

The machines' hum was even louder here, but Teg heard halting breaths coming from his right. He picked his way across corpse-strewn floor plates to stand before a figure sitting against what looked like the mutant child of an operating table and a drill press.

The rasping figure wore a padded grey jumpsuit drenched with blood. Some of it, Teg saw from the bullet holes in the tough fabric, belonged to the uniform's wearer. Despite the gore that matted the man's lank black hair and streaked his ugly face, there was no mistaking him for anyone but Izlaril Nizari.

"You. Lied." Izlaril spoke between shallow breaths. His eyes remained focused on the hazy twilight ahead of him.

Teg aimed with steady precision. Three pops put two rounds in Izlaril's chest and one in his forehead. The labored breathing stopped.

"Fighting isn't the best way to win," said Teg. He knew Izlaril couldn't hear him, but the lesson would've been wasted anyway.

"It's safe to come out, Smith," Teg shouted. "Let's go home."

There was no reply.

Teg turned to Celwen, who was staring at the dead Son of Haath. "We need to find the *vas* before backup gets here," he said. "Let's split up and—"

A funnel of small gears twisted down from the ceiling, sounding like a box of screws in a tumble dryer. The oily cogs assembled themselves into an insect-like body with a jaundiced skeletal face.

"Wait," said Mirai Smith. "Let me help you."

"Like you helped the Magists and Vaun?" said Teg. "Why should we trust you?"

Smith scowled. "Don't blame me for doing what I must to survive—which now means showing you this."

A metal arm emerged from the shifting mass of gears. Its three-fingered claw held what looked like a large ruby, but Teg thought he saw anguished faces reflected in its blood red surface. He could almost hear their screams.

An irresistible urge compelled Teg to reach for the gem.

Smith tried to pull it away, but Teg was faster. His hand closed around the ruby and pried it from the souldancer's metal grasp.

Now Teg definitely heard a voice—a familiar one—calling to him from the stone. This wasn't the first time a rock had talked to him, and because past incidents hadn't been remotely pleasant, he almost resisted looking into its facets.

Teg! the ruby said in an airy feminine voice. *Come into the gem.*

"Elena?" he wondered aloud.

"Yes, Master Cross," someone said from the doorway. "My obstinate sister inhabits the *vas*, as in part do I."

It was hard not to look at the gem, but Teg finally tore his eyes away from the glittering abyss as a gaunt man with drab brown hair swathed in a grey shroud enter the room. The corpses heaped near the door rotted to black dust in his path, and he trod upon their ashes.

Celwen pressed her back against the wall, squeezing her eyes shut like a child scared of monsters in her closet. Smith collapsed into a riot of gears that skittered into the darkness.

Teg found it hard to muster much fear, possibly because the gem was keeping him in a state of dreamlike detachment.

"Hey, Vaun," he said. "It's been a while. Not long enough, really."

Teg expected Vaun to lecture him; to make threats or even launch into a rant. Instead the god of the Void did something far worse.

He smiled.

"With every living breath you give offense," Vaun said, "but I take none. Invading my sphere, breaking into my house; even slaying my servants, I shall overlook all for the great service you have rendered me."

Let the ruby take you, Teg! Elena pleaded from the heart of the gem. Did it growl with hunger?

"You *wanted* all your lackeys dead?" asked Teg. "Wish you'd called me sooner."

Vaun now stood within arm's reach. The cold he gave off should have turned everyone to freeze-dried statues but didn't somehow.

"My Will, Hands, Voice, and Blade were a dear but fair price for victory in the game between my sister and me. The stakes are quite beyond your understanding, but the battles at Temil, in Avalon, and in the skies above us are mere echoes of a contest waged in eternity."

Teg interrupted with an upraised hand. "I know this speech. I'm an insignificant puppet, and you're the grand strategist pulling my strings. There. Saved you some time."

"Zadok split himself into mortal shards to gain new perspectives," said Vaun. "Mortals occasionally provide useful insights. My Will was of particular use in that regard. Striking my sister's death blow through Thera's *vas* did not immediately occur to me. But she told you of the possibility, and when my Will learned it from you, so did I."

The sinking feeling that had nagged Teg became an express elevator to the Ninth Circle.

"Oh shit," he said.

Vaun's left hand drew a wicked-looking sword from his shroud. Its straight single-edged blade had a hilt that looked to have been sculpted from coral made iron.

"I will not demean us both by asking for the *vas*," said Vaun. "I will grant you untold honor as the only man to die twice by my hand."

Vaun pointed his sword's tip at Teg's gun. "You may attempt to defend yourself. Slaying you in a duel and executing you are the same to me. I shall collect the *vas* afterward."

Shots rang out, but not from the gun in Teg's hand. After a whole magazine's worth of muted pops, Shaiel turned to Celwen, who stood aiming Teg's other gun at him. Her face had the passive, vaguely confused look of a passenger on a crashing ship numbed by the enormity of her fate.

"Cross has been a galling foe, but an honest one," Vaun chastised Celwen. "His swift noble end is not for traitors such as you."

Vaun leveled his sword at Celwen. The shadows around her came alive, stretching into twisted hands that clawed at her, leaving white frostbitten trails on her grey skin. She cried out in fear and pain.

Sparks flashed from the corner of the room behind Teg. Smith stood on five mechanical legs while the sixth pointed a crystal rod at a smoldering machine.

"Hurry!" shouted the souldancer. "Escape while the nexic shield is down!"

"You have crafted a new partitioning rod," Shaiel said approvingly. "Using it to disable the shield testifies to your genius, but it will be made to serve me."

Teg raised his gun and fired; not at Vaun, but at the swarm of shadows holding Celwen in their icy claws. Shadowy arms exploded on contact with the Worked bullets, and Celwen struggled free. She closed her eyes in concentration, and green-white light filled the room. Teg felt himself rising.

Vaun's cry of rage made Teg feel like his skull had been replaced with ice and cracked with a hammer. The translator's light died, leaving Teg, Celwen, and Smith trapped with Shaiel.

He'll kill you, Teg, Elena said. *You asked me not to let you die. I can't grant your prayer now. I'm sorry. Thera is loose in Avalon. She'll kill my mother, Astlin, and everyone there unless you join me in here.*

Teg was reeling from Elena's sudden revelation when a strange little man in green robes with a net over his face ran in through the wall on Teg's right.

Now I'm hallucinating, Teg thought as the newcomer, who was probably some kind of projection judging by their similar beards, grabbed Celwen's arm and ran with her through the left wall.

Vaun seemed to see it too, because he said, "Let the Magist and the traitor run. They will face my judgment soon enough."

With a motion imperceptible even to Teg, Vaun half-turned and thrust his grey blade through Teg's chest. The mercenary's heart froze instantly, and it shattered when Vaun's right hand struck the sword's spine.

Teg might have slid from the blade and fallen among the other dead men. He would never know since his awareness had contracted to black, silent numbness.

No. Something else was there with him—the last echo of a beloved voice.

Let the vas *take you! It's your last chance.*

Teg let the *vas* take him.

Light, color, and sound returned in one cacophonous flash. Teg floated in a rosy mist. The ruby was gone from his hand. Instead he held a black diamond. Actually, it must have been the other way around since the diamond was way too big to fit in the palm of his hand—or inside most star systems.

Elena floated between him and the vast diamond, and Teg understood the problem. His mind was trying to process information that went beyond his experience. There was no *here* or *there*; *big* or *small*. He didn't really even have a hand.

"I'm glad you came," Elena said with a smile. Her long wavy hair and white dress looked brighter than normal. Her eyes weren't the same rose hue as the ether around them, but were almost the same light brown color as her hair.

"Me too, honey," said Teg. And it was true. He was. "Where are we?"

"This is Thera's nexus," she said. "The *vas* is a silver cord encompassing her entire soul woven into the form of a gem. You let it pull you in when Vaun killed you. That's how I could bring you here."

"I guess that makes sense," said Teg. A troubling thought came to him. "But why are you here?"

Elena's smile faded. Her head bowed, and the sorrow Teg saw when she looked at him again would've broken his heart if Vaun hadn't done it first.

"Because I'm dead, too," Elena said.

Shock eclipsed Teg's grief. "You're a goddess. How is that possible?"

Elena pressed a hand to her chest. "I was the shadow Thera cast on the world. Cut off the light, and the shadow dies. Vaun severed me from Thera, but the silver cord I attached before you left Avalon drew you toward her nexus instead of Zadok's."

"So Vaun killed Thera?"

"No," Elena corrected him. "Just me, Thera's shadow. And it's a good thing, too. I was about to kill everyone in Avalon and release something that would have killed everyone else."

Teg racked his brain and hit upon a solution. "Okay. Your soul's in the *vas*, right? And your body's in Avalon. We get Smith to put them back together, and everything's fine."

Elena shook her head. "Shaiel emptied the *vas* of everything but the soul fragment that's still joined to him."

"Sounds risky," said Teg. "Why would Vaun leave part of himself in there?"

"To be the seed for a new composite soul enslaved to him. He's taken Smith to the Void, and it will flood Zadok's creation once new souldancers are made."

A sigh passed Teg's ghostly lips. "I had to try. What comes next?"

Elena's smile returned. "You think the world is better off in the hands of the Zadokim. How would you like to be one of them?"

The question hit Teg right between the eyes. "Like Astlin and Xander? Didn't they have to die first?"

Elena just stared at him.

"Right," said Teg. "To be honest, this is weird. I was always indifferent toward the gods. I'm not sure that becoming one is the best idea."

"Only the Zadokim have a hope of defeating Shaiel," Elena said. "Zadok won't interfere. Astlin and Xander can't win on their own, but Astlin showed me how I can send others back to help. And no one knows Vaun better than you."

"Alright," said Teg. "How do we do this?"

Elena stretched her arm toward Thera's nexus. Teg thought he saw a faint light glimmering through it, a million miles away.

"Astlin gave you a vision," Elena said. "Follow it through my nexus to the light of the world beyond. If you make it there, finding the way back will be up to you."

"Isn't that supposed to be as hard as going back to a dream you had years ago at the exact moment you left?" asked Teg.

"You need something that anchors you to this world," said Elena, "an attachment strong enough to make you choose the dream over reality."

Teg searched his heart. "I don't think I ever had anything like that," he said at length.

Elena's face fell. She tried to project confidence, but Teg could see the fear in the brown eyes that he found prettier than her rose ones.

Teg stroked Elena's hair. "I'll do my best," he promised.

Tears rimmed the girl's eyes. "Thera's nexus will take me when you leave. Even if you come back, this is the last time we'll see each other."

A rare feeling kindled in Teg's heart, and realized that he felt it for her. He hugged Elena. "I love you, kid," he said. "Take care."

She buried her face against his shoulder and wept softly. A wave burst out from the black diamond, and visions flooded Teg's mind. He saw a young girl lying in the sun on green grass watching clouds, climbing into her parents' bed during a storm, celebrating a birthday surrounded by laughing friends, and surrendering her heart to a young man with dark hair and olive skin.

It was the life that Elena would have lived if she hadn't been tortured and warped by her fathers; that she might have salvaged with the help of her family and friends.

Until Vaun Mordechai's sick little game had killed her.

A final image came into Teg's mind from Elena's. She was in her mid-teens, sitting at her father's workbench in his special room. They were cleaning his guns.

Her and Teg.

Elena lifted her tear-streaked face, and Teg finally recognized her eyes as his own.

"If I could have chosen my father," she said in a halting voice, "it would have been you."

The spark in Teg's heart burst into all-consuming flame. And what it yearned to consume most was Vaun.

"That's the right dream," said Teg. He wiped away Elena's tears and kissed her on the forehead. The faint lightning scent that usually hung around her had been replaced with the aroma of violets.

He gave her one last squeeze, let go, and let Thera's nexus pull him in.

As he passed through the impossibly vast diamond's black surface, Teg heard Elena call out to him.

"Tell my son what I never could."

Teg looked back into the ether.

Elena was gone.

With resolve hardened by joy, sorrow, and hate, Teg blazed

through a labyrinth of shimmering planes toward inescapable darkness and the promise of light on the other side.

I'll come back for you, Vaun, he swore. *And I'll take every minute you stole from Elena out of your pale frozen hide.*

42

Astlin wished that Nakvin would cry. Or scream. Or even break into mad laughter. Instead she sat beside the crater that had been a ring of stones, cradling her daughter's body amid the distant clash of battle.

If I looked into her mind, I might be able to help, Astlin thought. But she couldn't bring herself to spy on a grieving mother. She stood and watched as Nakvin held Elena and caressed her dust-coated face.

Astlin had no words to express her thanks when Xander drew close and wrapped his arm around her.

Is it wrong to feel more relieved than sad? She asked him mind-to-mind.

Xander pulled her closer. She rested her head on his chest. His robe smelled not unpleasantly of the dust, blood, and sweat of battle.

We were tested against a god and prevailed, Xander replied. *That is no cause for shame.*

Astlin shivered to think how close they'd come to failing. They'd fought with everything they had, and Thera had taken it.

Then she'd pronounced a death sentence that had somehow claimed her first.

She just collapsed like a rag doll.

Looking at Nakvin tending Thera's body on the hard ground where she'd fallen, Astlin heard Elena's voice echoing from her memory.

"What little room my heart has for others comes from you two. It's only right that you both have a place in it."

Astlin turned her eyes away, and Xander held her as her tears mixed with the dust on his robe.

With great effort, Astlin reined in the grief, anger, and gratitude warring in her heart. She turned to face Elena's body again.

Nakvin's eyes met hers. Astlin saw sorrow on the queen's face, but also a weary half-smile.

"I'm sorry," Astlin said softly.

"Don't be," said Nakvin.

"But I used to hate her," said Astlin. "I tried to kill her."

Nakvin sighed heavily. "You didn't kill her, Astlin. Zebel did. And I was too blind to see it coming."

"That's half right." Teg's voice preceded him as he strode into the ruined square. He looked just as he had when he'd left, but something about him had changed.

Astlin stared. Xander whispered a prayer. Nakvin released Elena and stood.

Teg joined the small vigil. A scowl twisted his face as he said, "Vaun killed Elena."

Nakvin's face hardened. Her silver eyes burned.

The ringing of armor drew Astlin's eyes northeast to the

mouth of a broad street. Tefler stormed into the square, his red cloak flowing like flame. A crowd from the wreck of the *Serapis* trailed behind him.

Tefler marched up to Teg. "Shaiel killed my mother?"

"Yeah," said Teg. "Right after he killed me."

Tefler blinked his multicolored eyes. "Wait. What?"

"Your mom had trouble showing how she felt," said Teg, placing both hands on Tefler's shoulders. "But she always loved you. She wanted to say sorry for not telling you while she could."

Tefler usually wore a look of lively mischief. Now his expression was as blank as Vaun's mask. He looked at the ground.

Nakvin's voice revealed the rage building inside her. "What happened, Teg?"

"Things were running smooth," said Teg. "I had Smith and the gem. My contact was about to get us out when the corpsicle himself showed up. He did for me and hit Elena through the *vas*. Now he's got it and Smith."

Xander struck his palm with his fist. "Then we go to Cadrys and take them back."

"Vaun lost Cadrys to the Night Gen," said Teg. "He's back in the Void, getting ready to pour it out on us. That's where we'll find Smith and the *vas*.

"Elena sent you to warn us," Nakvin said, her voice filling with pride. "That's twice now she's brought you back."

"She sent me," said Teg, "but she didn't bring me back. Not like before when she jumpstarted my corpse with prana and pulled my soul out of the Snare before the Void took it."

Astlin's heart lifted as she realized what was different about

Teg. "You escaped the Nexus!" she said. "You made it to the light and came back."

Teg shrugged. "I remember seeing a big light. But Elena's last words stuck with me, so I came right back."

"You didn't live in the world beyond?"

"It was tempting," said Teg, "but murdering Vaun seemed more important."

"Yes," Nakvin said. "It is. But even the four of us might not be a match for Vaun."

"Shaiel dies today." Tefler was shaking as he looked over the faces of Nakvin and the Zadokim. "Even if I have to storm the Void alone."

"Luckily," said Teg, "you won't have to. Elena sent reinforcements."

Astlin felt the light shining down on her before she saw a winged form descending from the sky. Anris landed beside Nakvin, three stars shining at his brow like amethysts. Even kneeling, he loomed over her.

"Your Majesty," he greeted Nakvin, bowing his purple-skinned, white-haired head. "It is my honor to serve you again."

Both of Nakvin's hands couldn't contain Anris'. "Please," she said, "get up. I don't outrank you anymore."

Anris rose to his full, towering height and smiled. "Very well. Perhaps you will agree to ally yourself with a fellow monarch."

The malakh's smile was reflected on Nakvin's face like moonlight on a dark pool. "It's just good to have you back," she said.

"Thank Lady Astlin." Anris bowed his head to the female Zadokim. "She showed me the way."

"Now we may have a chance!" said Xander.

"All shall be as the great light wills," said Jarsaal. Everyone turned to see him walking into the square from the west. Three points of emerald light hung above his painted forehead. Behind him, the battle still raged at the hill's foot.

Astlin didn't realize how heavily Anris and Jarsaal's deaths had burdened her until the sight of them lifted the weight from her shoulders.

Thank you, Elena.

Xander welcomed the Dawn Gen shaman into their company. "We are glad to have you back, but you spoke of the great light. Didn't you mean Faerda?"

"I have seen the pure light of which Faerda is only a sign," said Jarsaal. "I am grateful to her for guiding my steps, and will honor her request to slay the lord of the Void."

Astlin's soul burned with zeal, yet her eagerness was soon tempered. "Vaun needs to be stopped, but we've still got his army to deal with."

"Then let us deal with them," said Anris. In ten strides he crossed to the square's west edge, where the lack of trees gave a clear view of the battle below.

Astlin and Xander joined Anris. Teg moved to stand at Astlin's right and Jarsaal stationed himself at Anris' left. Lined up on the hill overlooking the battle, the Zadokim all unveiled their crowns.

Except for one.

Teg looked at the constellation of sapphire, silver, amethyst, and emerald stars.

"How are you guys doing that?"

Astlin turned to him and pointed at her glowing crown. "This?"

"Yeah," said Teg, "that."

The question puzzled Astlin. "It's easier than not doing it. The light already wants to shine through you. Just let it."

Teg paused for a moment, rocking on his heels as he looked upward. "I don't think it wants to shine through me."

"Never mind," said Xander. "Just focus on the task at hand." Suddenly he was holding his diamond-tipped ebony spear.

Astlin followed Xander's lead. Gouts of flame shot from both ends of her closed fist and formed into a spear of solid red fire.

Jarsaal raised his arm. His fingers were curled, as if around an invisible spear shaft. A dazzling white ray slanted down from the sky, streaked through the space between his thumb and fingers, and lanced into the enemy ranks below like a thunderbolt.

Teg lightly slapped Astlin's shoulder with the back of his hand, nodded to Xander, and pointed at Jarsaal.

"You guys should be packing *that*," said Teg.

"Do not waste time attacking them piecemeal," Anris said. "Shaiel's Will led them here. Let us combine ours to cast them out!"

Nakvin interposed herself between Anris and Jarsaal. "You're not exiling anyone from my kingdom without me."

Astlin doused her spear and connected her fellow sovereigns' minds, sharing Anris' plan between them. As one, they put forth their authority.

Greycloaks, Cadrisians, and *Isnashi*; living and dead, were lifted up from the battlefield. The enemy's confused cries merged into a frightened babble as they hung in the air like a low dark cloud of men and beasts.

A second movement of the monarchs' will tore open the sky, revealing a monstrous black cube suspended in rosy mist. The Zadokim's final decree sent Shaiel's army flying back to him through the gate.

Astlin covered her light and looked to the sky. There was only a widening circle of blue fringed with silver clouds. The gate to Shaiel's nexus was gone, along with his servants.

"That was fun," said Teg. "Think we'll see them again?"

Astlin's glowing sense of triumph darkened. "Shaiel doesn't let souls escape from his nexus."

The buzz of mingled voices behind her interrupted Astlin's brooding. She turned to see uniformed Gen and Mithgarders filling the square. Rosemy beamed at her from among the Nesshin who stood at the front of the crowd.

The people and the Zadokim faced each other for a long moment. Then, in an act that stunned Astlin, every Gen and man in the square dropped to one knee, sounding like a company of drummers striking a single note.

Only Tefler, standing beside Elena's body, remained unbowed.

Such a profound show of respect should have embarrassed Astlin, but somehow it felt right. All five Zadokim quietly accepted the people's homage.

"What now?" asked Xander.

"Now," said Teg, "we take the war to the Void and rain hell down on Vaun's head."

"Can we really kill a god?" asked Astlin.

"We don't have to," said Teg. "Thera's *vas* still holds a piece of Vaun's soul. We get the ruby, we sever Vaun from Shaiel's nexus, and he's stuck as a big black cube floating in the ether."

Nakvin frowned. "Won't Shaiel just take a new form?"

"It took Thera and Zadok eons to pull the same trick," said Teg. "I doubt Shaiel has that long."

43

Teg and his allies traversed a cracked, coal-black plain under a starless vault. Only the horizon's sickly golden line divided land and sky. Each footstep on the frozen ground hissed like dry ice. Teg thought of the cold as a living thing. Perhaps it was.

Nakvin and Tefler walked with them, and not just because they had the biggest score to settle with Vaun. It had taken all five Zadokim plus Nakvin to overpower Vaun and open a gate from Avalon to the Void. And now that they were in this frigid sub-hell, only the prana channeled by Tefler and Jarsaal kept them alive.

"Does anyone know where we're going?" asked Teg, looking out across the endless black waste. "I'm just following Astlin."

Astlin put her hand to her heart, closed her eyes, and frowned. "I'm following the pain. Shaiel's trying to block me, but even he can't keep the Strata from screaming."

"Is he creating a new souldancer?" Xander asked. It was hard to say whether he sounded more concerned for the universe or his bride.

"I think so," Astlin said with a shiver that probably had

nothing to do with the cold. "The victim has some nexic talent. Besides that, all I can tell is where he's being tortured."

"Shaiel will flood a whole Stratum with Void if the souldancer is completed," said Anris. "For that poor soul's sake, and all the souls of an entire world, we must stop this travesty."

"We should've brought a ship," said Teg. But he was just complaining for complaining's sake. They'd been lucky to force open a gate big enough for two of them to pass through at once.

After a few more minutes of walking, Jarsaal pointed toward the horizon. "There."

Teg strained his eyes, but a moment passed before he saw grey metal glinting in the gold-tinged distance.

"It's a big ball," he thought aloud.

"Big enough to hold a city," Astlin said.

"If we can see where we're going," said Teg, "why not will ourselves there?"

"We cannot bring Nakvin and Tefler with us," said Xander.

"Let's make the distance shorter," Nakvin suggested. "The Void is artificial. It should respond to us like Avalon does."

"Can we get past Vaun?" asked Astlin.

Nakvin jabbed her finger across the wasteland. "If we could punch through from another realm, we should be able to bend space a little."

The other four Zadokim joined their light to Nakvin's will. Teg even helped a little, although he and the light weren't on the friendliest terms. The metal orb grew to dominate the black landscape until Teg realized he was standing before it.

The perfect sphere floated as high as Seele's summit. The other Zadokim's bright crowns, and the prana envelope surrounding them, reflected dimly from the dark metal. The only sound was the cracking of frozen stone.

"Should we knock?" asked Teg.

Tefler drew the bulky rodcaster from his red cloak. "I'll ring the bell." He took aim and pulled the trigger. A humming cone of distortion blasted from the barrel and struck the orb like a gong. The single deep note shook Teg's bones.

The vast sphere's metal skin peeled back from a point directly overhead, forming a black square aperture. Warmth issued out like the breath of a star-eating beast.

"You'll have more use for this than me," said Tefler, passing the rodcaster to Teg along with two large golden shells.

He was right. Though Teg had taken a quick jaunt to Cadrys to retrieve one of his ether metal guns—Celwen still had its mate—even the superbly Worked pistol paled before the other Zadokim's weapons.

"Thanks," Teg said as he accepted the heavy single-shot gun. He popped it open, removed the spent shell, and loaded one of the two remaining rounds.

"Remember," Tefler warned him. "Those rounds only disrupt Malefactions."

"I got it." Teg kept the rodcaster in his right hand while drawing his Worked pistol with his left. He felt ready for anything.

Especially killing Vaun Mordechai.

"The door's open," Astlin said, "but I can't see in."

Anris moved to the head of the group. "Wait here. I will fly into the orb and back. You can share what I see with the others that we may weave the Void to carry us in."

"I don't think we'll need a lift," said Teg.

The inverted pit seemed to grow larger as he stared. He'd thought of the dark square as a monster's maw; now it was descending to swallow them.

Astlin pressed close to Xander. Jarsaal droned a Gen chant. A hooked blade like a storm of sand and embers formed in Anris' hand. Nakvin and Tefler faced the approaching portal with stern determination.

To his surprise, Teg's thoughts turned to the light beyond. *You're probably miffed that I walked out on you, but I'll be up front. Whatever reasons you had for letting me come back, I'm here for revenge. If you don't think Vaun has it coming, we're done. Otherwise, I could really use some help.*

There was no reply to Teg's inner dialogue. More than likely it was a monologue, but he'd find out soon either way.

The orb's jaws closed around them. Teg saw only darkness beyond the small bubble of prana, but the unendurable cold was gone. The air held a dry musk like an empty insect shell.

Something like a winter moon suddenly shimmered at the center of the orb, casting harsh light over the interior. Teg saw that the surface rose in jagged crests as if the inner layers had melted, fallen toward the center point, and cooled. Dark openings dotted the serrated towers' faces like casting errors caused by air bubbles.

"Astlin's more right than she knew," said Teg. "This thing isn't just big enough to hold a city, it *is* a city."

"Most astute, Master Cross," Vaun's voice boomed from every direction. "I am impressed that you required only one other Kethan to make that conclusion. The old jokes exaggerate your people's doltishness at least twofold."

Teg exchanged a sour look with Astlin.

Tefler charged to the front of the group. "We won your sick game, Vaun." Prana engulfed his hand as he drew the white sword. "Time to learn what happens when you take your best shot and miss. Will you come out and fight, or do we level this empty city around whatever rat hole you're hiding in?"

Vaun's laughter was like the last breaths forced from a giant's lungs. "The light beyond is not the only escape from Zadok. Souls wholly given over to Teth find refuge in the Void. I am the lord thereof, and those become one with it are my servants. I raised this city as their abode."

Shadows stretched from every crevice of the jagged towers and streamed down the narrow streets toward the invaders. A broken chorus of whispers, wails, and mad cackling preceded the writhing torrent.

"Shades of the impure," Jarsaal cried. "Shun their touch, and cleanse them with light!"

The other Zadokim stood back to back, crowns blazing. The shadows shrank back from the mingled lights' majesty, only to be burned away by Astlin and Xander's spears, cut down by Anris' sword, and annihilated by Jarsaal's prana bursts. Bullets from Teg's Worked gun killed the things, but he did his best to conserve ammo.

Tefler broke ranks and waded into the shadowy mass. The shades recoiled from his white sword as if he wore a Zadokim's crown. The curved mirror of its blade sliced the two-dimensional creatures like they were made of black paper.

While the shades fell before Tefler, a wall of shadow closed in behind him, cutting him off from his friends.

"Tefler!" Nakvin cried. She dispensed with the Compass and simply thrust her hand toward the shades converging on her grandson. Clear globes filled with rosy liquid floated among the shadows. Nakvin pulled her arm back as she clenched her fist, and blue bolts arced between the globes, making them burst into clouds of flame that howled like a whirlwind and smelled of lightning.

Teg didn't see how the inferno could have missed Tefler. But the flames cleared, leaving him untouched and the road behind him clear as he fought his way forward.

"Follow him!" Teg called to the others. He didn't know where Tefler was headed, but going there together was better than letting the enemy divide them.

"Smith is that way, too," said Astlin. "The pain keeps growing the farther we go."

"I'll take that as a good sign," Teg said as a shot from his pistol erased a lunging shade .

The Zadokim advanced. Teg and Astlin kept the path ahead clear while Xander and Anris cut down the shades that harassed them from behind. Jarsaal's raised hand sent white bolts burning into the shadows encroaching on Tefler. Nakvin supported him with incendiary Workings as novel as they were potent.

They caught up with Tefler at an intersection of six roads surfaced with a web of overlapping iron strands as thick as Teg's arm. A building that looked to have been formed by pouring molten lead into a giant ant colony reared its craggy towers up ahead.

"Smith's making the new souldancer in there," Astlin said. "I think he's almost done!"

"Then that's where we need to be," said Teg. "Are you guys good for one more push?"

Pitch blackness fell again, lifted just as suddenly, and was followed by an even more fleeting darkness. Teg looked up and saw two winged shadows—a huge pool of night with a serpentine neck and tail, and a much smaller but still unnaturally large black bat.

"That can't be who I think it is," grumbled Teg.

"Do you know who *they* are?" Tefler asked, pointing to the building with his sword.

A huge lupine shape came plowing through the lesser shadows between it and the Zadokim. Like the winged terror above, the wolf was joined by a smaller though still freakishly large companion—a giant rat.

Teg remembered standing before a dark signal beacon atop a tower in hell. "Yeah. I've met the whole lovable gang."

The harsh white moonlight turned sickly gold. A chill descended, and shades surged in from the sides, ignoring the Zadokim's crowns. Xander, Jarsaal, and Tefler fought to hold them back as Nakvin took over the rearguard.

The wolf and the rat charged closer. Pieces of their shadowy flesh boiled away under Teg's bullets and Astlin's spear, but the giant shades didn't slow. The absence of heaving breath through snaggled teeth and the lack of tremors from the beasts' galloping footfalls gave Teg a disturbing sense of unreality.

"Teg!"

Anris' cry woke Teg from his daydream. The larger flying shadow was diving at him on silent wings. A flurry of motion above warned him of the likewise inbound bat-shade.

Teg rolled left, brought up the rodcaster, and aimed the barrel upward. His angle lined up both winged shades. The bat's dark talons were about to tear Teg's face when he pressed the heavy trigger. A buzzing haze spread from the rodcaster's muzzle, scattering both giant shades like sunlight on morning fog.

Teg rose from his knees and saw the rat decapitated by a flaming red arc as it neared Astlin. He only remembered the wolf when Anris' cry became a scream.

The malakh was big, but the shade-wolf had swallowed him whole. Three amethyst lights could be seen dancing in the black like erratic shooting stars as gold light flashed around them.

Worked bullets posed as much of a danger to Anris as they did to the wolf, so Teg hurried to remove the spent rodcaster shell and reload. The used round chimed against the metal web underfoot and fell into the abyss between strands. Teg was slotting his last shell into place when twin prana bursts turned the world into a whiteout.

When Teg's vision returned, the golden light and the black wolf were gone. Shades still darkened the streets, but they stayed far back from Tefler and Jarsaal, who'd unleashed the Well's light.

Astlin rushed to where Anris lay on the cold metal web. His once lavender skin was blackened beyond recognition. The feathers of his wings crumbled to powder at Astlin's touch. She knelt beside him, her eyes closed, for several moments before burying her face in her hands.

Bare feet padded on iron, reminding Teg of a risen corpse treading on the floor of a morgue. Vaun approached from the direction of the metal ant colony, shrouded in grey and holding the same long single-edged sword that had killed Teg.

Tefler advanced to meet the lord of the Void, brandishing Elohim's white mirrored blade. His armor rang in martial rhythm with each step. His strange eyes held no fear.

"You wish to join your mother?" Vaun asked Tefler. "Your hope is vain. For betraying your holy orders, I shall keep your soul here with me, frozen and blind."

"Hold him for me," said Tefler.

Sapphire, silver, and emerald light washed over Vaun like a triple sunrise, but his dead expression never changed as he slowly pressed forward.

"Three of you could not hold my twin," said Vaun. "You will not detain me. The Harpy has no authority in the city I made, and Cross is a botched nonentity."

"One you can't keep dead," Teg stated as he fired the rodcaster. The Void-disrupting cone slammed into Vaun, who shielded his face and bellowed as buzzing distortion battered against him.

Tefler charged into the disruption cone, wincing slightly as he swung. The white sword cut into Vaun's stomach and forearms, leaving cauterized wounds in his pale divine flesh.

The last golden shell gave up the ghost, and the buzzing cone vanished.

Now it was up to the Zadokim. They couldn't stop Vaun, but their combined light slowed his next blow from the speed of thought to inhumanly fast. Teg, Astlin, Xander, and Jarsaal were inhumanly fast, too. They pummeled Vaun with a hail of spears and bullets before his grey sword could cleave Tefler in half.

Of course, there was a chance that Tefler might've been hit.

But he was in full view and a much smaller target than Anris, so Teg felt comfortable firing at Vaun from the side while Tefler attacked head on.

Vaun was stuck on defense. The Zadokim's weapons left no lasting damage, but the charred wounds inflicted by the white scimitar refused to heal. Everything was going fine until Vaun disappeared.

Teg had died twice before, and he found the silence left in Vaun's wake eerily similar.

"Where is he, guys?" Teg called out, casting about the iron city for any sign of Vaun.

"No idea," Astlin said between heavy breaths. Her blue eyes were wide with terror beyond what Vaun could inspire. "But something's happening inside." She pointed toward the building. "I think something's gone wrong."

"Wrong for Vaun? Or wrong for us?" asked Teg. "And how can anything go more wrong for us than the Void taking a Stratum?"

Astlin's scream came an instant too late for Teg to react. He didn't blame her. Outside the Zadokim's light, Vaun was faster than any of them. The familiar icy pain of Vaun's sword impaling him—this time from behind—immediately numbed his limbs. Teg slouched like a rag doll, held up by the blade and the superhuman strength of Vaun's arm.

"I dislike loose ends," Vaun spoke into Teg's ear. "And much like the late Captain Peregrine, it galls me to leave a job unfinished. You will die beyond my sister's help and return to the light you forsook, as you forsake all who trust in you."

A branching chain of iron blocks crackling with electricity

rushed toward Vaun through their air. Teg could still turn his head, and he followed what could only be described as electrified metal vines back to Nakvin's hands.

That one's really weird, he observed through his agony.

Weird or not, the metal branches turned to red dust on contact with Vaun.

"Your Workings will not avail you, harpy," Vaun chided Nakvin. "For all your considerable skill, you are not divine."

Teg knew that Vaun would kill Nakvin when he finally shut up, and that had sounded like a full stop.

He's right, Teg confessed to the light beyond. *There's never been a cause I went all in on. I'm a mercenary to the core. But when the client says "Go there and do this," I go do it. So tell you what— my fee is saving my friends' lives. Pay it, and I'm yours.*

Warmth spread through Teg's body, filling him with courage that shone from his brow like three garnets. He pictured the space behind Vaun and was there, firing his last five rounds with such speed that the subdued reports came right on top of each other. Three went into Vaun's back, and the last two entered his face as he turned.

"That was for Keth," said Teg. His throat tightened when he realized that he was defenseless, but Astlin, Xander, and Jarsaal surrounded Vaun.

With a scream to crack planets, Vaun released a sea of sickly golden light. Teg willed himself out of the blast radius. He arrived behind a bladelike building near the sealed entrance. The fractional second of exposure had left his skin blackened and numb.

Astlin appeared next to him. "Focus on making your body look like your soul," she said.

Teg was familiar with the concept. A moment later, he was whole.

"Looks like you came to terms with the light," Astlin said, poking one of the deep red stars of his crown.

Teg looked around the corner and down the street. Sallow light emanated from Vaun in waves. Raw Void had already flowed from the intersection into the surrounding blocks. A comparatively small bubble of prana guttered amid the golden flood, sustained by Jarsaal and Tefler with Nakvin inside.

"We reached an agreement," said Teg, "but the client's gonna have a hard time holding up his end."

"The Void is mine!" Vaun raged, his voice carrying across the iron city. "It will rise and drown you all. Abandon hope while Teth and I are one!"

Xander suddenly arrived. "He is right. None of us can leave the city by our own power. All four of us must join forces."

"But Jarsaal's pinned down with Nakvin and Tefler," said Astlin. "If he breaks away to help us, they'll die."

"We may all die if he does not," Xander said, gesturing to a squirming darkness that surged inward from the city's edge.

The shadows were rallying to Vaun.

Teg pointed to the termite mound towers. "We can't run now. Not when Vaun's about to get himself a new pet souldancer."

Lightning flashed from the metal ant colony's towers, shattering their roofs. Peals of thunder shook the city's foundations, but Vaun's scream was louder.

That must be what "Something going wrong" looks like, thought Teg.

Vaun must have thought so too, because the Void's light died.

Teg, Astlin, and Xander traversed the distance to their friends in an instant. Thankfully, Jarsaal and Tefler's prana dome had kept them and Nakvin from harm.

"Are you three alright?" asked Astlin.

"Don't worry about us. Look at him!" Nakvin said, stabbing a finger toward Vaun.

The lord of the Void staggered back from his foes. His dead face was etched with a pleasingly bewildered look.

"What happened to him?' asked Xander.

Teg pushed against the fabric of the Void. Nothing pushed back.

"Looks like our boy ain't divine anymore," he told the others. "That's what he gets for playing god with souldancers."

In the ensuing silence, Tefler approached Vaun. "Give up yet?"

Vaun's perplexed look hardened into a scowl. "I did not cross the stars, pass through hell, and ascend the throne of the Void to end kneeling at your feet!"

Vaun feinted, Tefler fell for it, and the grey sword ran deep into his right arm.

Nakvin gasped. Teg understood why. Vaun might have lost his godhood, but he was still a better swordsman than Tefler. Their blades crossed only once before Vaun's grey sword sliced open his opponent's leg.

"Come, kings and queens of Zadok's folly!" said Vaun, turning to his small audience. "I who courted godhood am reduced again to nothing. Slay me and show yourselves just!"

Teg looked over his friends' faces and saw the same scornful pity that he felt.

"You have your humanity back, Vaun," Astlin said. "Let me send you to the light."

Vaun advanced on Tefler, who stood on one leg clutching his right arm. Blood stained his white shirt and pants the same color as his cloak.

"Slay me before I slaughter this oath breaker as I did my whorish sister," ordered Vaun.

Teg was reaching for his knife when Tefler released a flash of prana that healed him and halted Vaun.

Tefler stood firm. "She was my mother," he said. "Meet her great-granddad."

The white sword burst into black flames as Tefler swung it down. Vaun raised his own weapon to block, but the flaming scimitar cut through Vaun's blade and buried itself in his forehead. Black fire shot from his eyes.

Tefler pushed downward, parting Vaun's skull and cutting down to his throat. Vaun Mordechai's mortal remains folded to the ground. Sulfurous smoke rose from the corpse.

"Every Kethan's in your debt, kid," Teg said to Tefler. "Me and Astlin, I mean."

Astlin joined hands with Teg, held on tight for a moment, and let go.

Nakvin stared at her grandson in horror. "What did you do?"

"I used a little of what Mom released," Tefler said, examining the blackened stump of a blade joined to a mirrored hilt that had been the sword called Elohim. His hand no longer glowed with prana, but the white metal didn't burn him.

"These are ill portents," said Jarsaal.

Teg started toward the only building he'd ever seen struck by lightning from the inside.

"I'm sure there'll be horrific consequences for us all," he said. "Right now, I'm more interested in whatever the hell happened in there."

44

Nakvin had gone back to Avalon with Tefler in tow; taking Anris' body with them. Jarsaal, who had little interest in clay tribe perversions like souldancers, had likewise returned to his people on Mithgar.

It fell to Teg, Astlin, and Xander to comb through the wreckage of Smith's iron city lab. Luckily, its layout matched the one under the House of Law, except the walls were interwoven metal lattices instead of brick. Smith was here, too—at least parts of him.

Xander led the search, following a trail of tiny gears between banks of singed equipment that still smelled of smoke and lightning. The path ended at a pile of gears on the threshold of a rectangular door in the room's far corner.

Several things about the door struck Teg as odd, like its lack of a frame and the huge clockwork towers he glimpsed on the other side.

"That is Kairos," Xander said somberly, "which means Smith is dead."

"But what could've killed him?" Astlin wondered with audible unease.

"It was the father of thunder," said a fussy little man in green robes and a black cap who came bustling toward them. "He's like you, but he's two people like me."

Teg instantly recognized him, despite the absence of a net and the presence of copious blood on his face.

"We need to stop meeting in secret evil labs," said Teg.

Astlin's brow furrowed. "Gien? What are you doing here?"

Gien laced his bloody hands. "Shaiel found us after we left the lab under his house. He made threats and offered us things."

"Us?" Teg repeated as a knot formed in his stomach. "Is Celwen here?"

"Yes," Gien said with a vapid grin and gleaming eyes. "Right here."

"Take me to her," said Teg.

Gien frowned, but his smile soon returned. "You don't understand. It's hard to explain, so I'll show you." He hurried back into the maze of machines.

Xander muttered something in Nesshin. Teg turned to see him and Astlin staring at the Kairos gate. A thin man dressed in black with dark woolly hair and pale skin stood in the doorway and beckoned to them.

"Who the hell is that?" asked Teg.

"I will speak with him," Xander said. "Go and keep an eye on Gien."

Xander stepped toward the gate. Astlin shot concerned looks between him and Teg but finally followed Xander.

Teg went looking for Gien and heard him shouting excitedly from a room off the right side of a short corridor. Teg followed Gien's voice, and what he saw when he set foot inside the doorway riveted him to the spot.

The destruction was worse in here, as if a thunderstorm had broken out inside the relatively small room. Scorch marks on the iron walls showed where lightning had struck, and fierce winds had strewn arcane instruments across the floor. Teg recognized parts of two items—the broken halves of a clear crystal rod and the shards of what had been a large ruby.

All of that was troubling enough, but what really raised Teg's hackles was the hulking steel frame to his left near the end of the room. He'd seen pictures of similar racks in histories of the Purges—specifically those dealing with Guild interrogations of captured Gen.

The torture rack was facing away from Teg. He could see that someone was shackled to it, but not who.

Gien stood beaming amid the shambles at the center of the room.

"What happened here?" Teg asked him.

"Shaiel wanted Smith to make a souldancer. They decided to use Celwen since her father made a good one. I helped, but when we cut out the soul fragment, something pushed back from the Stratum on the other side, like there was already a soul merged with it."

"Another soul?" Teg asked numbly.

Gien nodded. "Then the father of thunder was here. His eyes are like pearls on black velvet. He took the *vas* and cut Shaiel's shadow from the Void. He said I could become Celwen. I asked him before he went after Smith."

Izlaril's words came back to Teg: *"She opened Bifron's door— the black one—and entered."*

Teg's stomach turned. *Celwen called down Bifron's curse, but*

490

I led her to his door; just like I led her into Vaun's hands.

With heavy steps, Teg moved to stand before the torture machine. He expected to find the body bruised and burned. What nearly made him vomit were the clear signs of *gnawing* on the surprisingly little of it that remained.

"You ate her," Teg said more to himself than Gien. "She helped save us all, and you butchered her."

"No!" said Gien. "She's part of me, now. I *became* her!"

Teg left the two bodies in the room where Celwen had died and met up with Astlin and Xander in the main lab. Their faces looked as haunted as Teg supposed his did. The door to Kairos was gone.

Teg wiped his splinterknife on a swatch of green silk that he let fall to the cluttered floor.

"I'm done here," he said.

The months flew by, as time did when Teg kept busy. He and the other Zadokim had plenty of work to do healing the scars of the Cataclysm on Keth—not to mention destroying all of the verdilaks. But many hands made for light work, as Teg's mother had often said, and a day came when he stood with Astlin near the fountain in the small Northridge park where they'd been children.

"It's too quiet around here," said Teg.

A half-smile raised the corner of Astlin's mouth. "There were less than a thousand survivors on the whole sphere. We've practically got the place to ourselves."

"Don't get me wrong," said Teg. "Quiet is better than a horde of dead folks giving me false weather reports."

He looked to the sky overhead. Fittingly, it was a clear sapphire blue.

"So," Teg asked, facing Astlin again, "What's next for you?"

"Xander wants to rebuild his tribe," she said. "The *Theophilus* survivors already declared us their king and queen."

Teg raised his eyebrows. "The ruler of eight whole people. Don't tell Nakvin. She might get jealous."

Astlin laughed, and Teg realized it was one of his favorite sounds. *I bet nobody in the next world laughs like that.*

"I don't plan on ruling anybody," said Astlin, "just teaching them how to reach the light. Hopefully they'll teach others."

"The Nesshin can spread the word faster than you could by yourself," said Teg. "Smart. Have you chosen a spot for all this nation-building?"

"The population we've already got is from Tharis," Astlin said, "so we'll start there."

Teg sucked air through his teeth. "The universe hands you an almost unlimited selection of real estate, and you pick a noxious ball of asphalt that was a desert *before* the Cataclysm?"

Astlin's expression became somber as she looked at the empty buildings surrounding the park. A breeze carried the scent of violets.

"Tharis is Thera's sphere," she said. "There should be at least one good thing with her name."

"Yeah," said Teg. "I miss that."

Astlin looked at the green grass under their feet. At length she said, "We could use another set of hands—a mercenary who knows Tharis and can reshape matter and space at will."

"I'll pass the offer along if I run into someone who fits the bill," said Teg. "Me, I was just passing through on the way to my next job and thought I'd look in on the old neighborhood. Running into my childhood friend is enough to change my mind about Providence."

Astlin's face was grave when she looked up. "You're going back, aren't you?"

Teg shrugged. "I was in a hurry on my last visit to the light. Figure I'll take my time; see this other world everyone's gushing about."

Astlin stepped forward and wrapped her arms around him. The black silk of her dress was smooth against the cotton shirt under his open jacket. Her hair smelled like roses.

Teg gave Astlin a squeeze in return and patted her once on the back. They let go at the same time, and he started down the concrete walk toward the park gates. But curiosity got the better of him when he was halfway to the exit, and he stopped.

For a moment, Teg was afraid that he'd look back to find Astlin gone, but there she stood on the grass by the brick fountain, as regal as any great lady from an opera. She gave him a forced smile, and he hoped that her story wasn't a tragedy.

Teg asked the question that had haunted him for months. "That guy in black from the door to Kairos—who was he? What did he say that left you and Xander so spooked?"

Astlin looked like Teg was standing on her grave. "He said he was Almeth Elocine. He said we'd undone everything he'd set in motion to fix his mistakes, that Zadok's universe is in our hands now, and that he can't help us anymore."

Teg mulled over Astlin's words. He considered turning back,

joining Astlin and Xander on Tharis, and helping the other Zadokim run the world.

Then he thought of Tefler's last words to Vaun, and Gien's last words in that cursed room in the Void.

There's not much time left for this place, he concluded. *And besides, there'll be more coming after I'm gone.*

Teg walked through the park gates and into the boundless light.

Glossary

Anomians: Beings without definite qualities descended from an order of transessists who sought to free themselves from the limitations of human nature. Constantly modifying their own essences cost the Anomians their souls, and they became a plague scouring the cosmos for new living and nonliving properties to exchange with their own.

The old gods banished the Anomians into the outer darkness, where the Night Gen later encountered them and spent centuries driving them even further from the light of the stars.

Atavists: A sect of Zadok worshippers denounced as heretical by the Nesshin. Atavists believe that all creatures are fragments of the one divine Nexus. Individual existence, which Atavist doctrine calls an illusion, is responsible for all suffering, sin, and conflict. Thus, the chief spiritual aim of every Atavist is to return to a state of oneness in the Nexus.

Avalon: The Light Gen's home in exile. Originally confined to the Sixth Circle of hell ruled by Mephistophilis and Zebel,

Avalon was freed from the baals' soul tithe by Zebel's daughter Nakvin. The Light Gen's domain has since expanded to include all of the former Nine Circles except for the Ninth.

Bhakta: The lowest rank of Shaiel's priesthood. The literal translation is "retainer".

Cardinal Spheres, the: Numbering four, these worlds were the wealthiest and most powerful planets before the Cataclysm. In descending order of prestige the Cardinal Spheres are: Mithgar, Keth, Temil, and Cadrys.

Cataclysm, the: A universal conflagration that swept through the ether, burning the cosmos from the inside out. Its cause remains unknown, though the point of origin seems to have been in the ether over Mithgar. The only survivors were those occupying prana-infused, elemental fire-resistant, or ether-partitioned locations.

Dawn Tribe, the: A collective term for Gen who remained on Middle Stratum spheres during the Purges. Surviving in isolated pockets, the Dawn Gen emerged from hiding after the Cataclysm destroyed the Guild. Their culture has regressed to a pre-industrial lifestyle led by shamans.

Ether, the: A universal medium through which light travels. "Ether" is used when referring to a quantity of this substance, while "the ether" refers to the region it occupies.

The ether boasts a number of extraordinary qualities. It has practically no mass or viscosity and allows objects traveling through it to exceed the speed of light. Ether is also highly volatile and combustible.

Ether-Runner: A ship built to travel quickly through space by traversing the ether. Almost all ether-runners are piloted using a sympathetic interface called the Wheel.

Factor: The user of a Working; named for the act of fashioning prana.

Faerda: A primordial animistic deity worshiped by Gen in ancient times and, by the Dawn Tribe after the Cataclysm. Outsiders misinterpret Faerda as the divinization of the White Well, but her followers claim that their goddess is present in all life, everywhere, and at all times.

Gen: An immortal race of the Middle Stratum holding a place in the hierarchy of being one step above humans. "Gen" is the word for "people" in that race's tongue, and is both singular and plural. The word's pronunciation varies between Mithgarders, who render it "Ghen", and Kethans, who prefer "Jen".

Greycloaks: Properly, Lawbringers; members of Shaiel's priesthood identified by their eponymous uniform. They wield shadow swords and the power to manifest the Void.

Guild, the: Properly, the Sublime Brotherhood of Steersmen. Though it was a private professional fraternity, the Guild acted as a self-appointed regulatory agency. Its primary functions were advancing the science of ether-running and regulating the construction of ether-runners and Wheels. The Guild's authority was thought to rival the combined power of all current and former political bodies.

Human: The race holding the middle position in the whole hierarchy of being. Called the clay tribe by the Gen, humans possess intelligence but have limited life spans.

Isnashi: A sect comprised of Night Gen who perverted Faerda's gift of skin changing to serve Shaiel.

Kost: A kost (pronounced "kosht") is an evil undead being that survives death by transferring its soul into a Malefacted object called a *vas*. A kost can possess the body of a living or once living being in the vicinity of this vessel. Even if the host body is slain, the kost's soul will return to its *vas*, making the kost incredibly difficult to permanently kill.

Light Tribe, the: Members of a Gen enclave that survived the Purges by taking shelter in hell's Sixth Circle. Descended from the nobility of the more refined tribes, the Light Gen took their name from their self-imposed mission to keep the flame of civilization alight.

Malefaction: An effect produced by fashioning Void according to the user's thought patterns. The practitioners of such techniques, called "Malefactors", have attained infamy belying their historically small numbers.

Midras: A god whose cult gained dominance in antiquity. The ancient dualistic faith associated Midras with the sun, life, fire, compassion, and virtue. The god of light's priests were famous for traveling the countryside dispensing justice in lawless lands.

Mystery: One of the ancient liturgical rites of the Gen, whose shamans practiced the first known systematic tradition of fashioning prana.

Necromancer: A common derogatory term for a disciple of Teth, though in practice the term has been applied to social pariahs of varying backgrounds. The study, manipulation, and attempted reversal of death is but one branch on the Way of Teth.

Nexism: A cosmic mechanism for manipulating space, time, matter, and thought by will alone. Properly the domain of higher beings, nexism is rare among the Gen and all but unknown to humans.

Nexus-Runner: A spacefaring vessel resembling an ether-runner in general function but powered and operated by nexism.

Night Tribe, the: Descendants of refugees from the Guild's Purges (mostly Gen, but encompassing many races) who fled into the emptiness beyond the Middle Stratum's last stars. Living in darkness for millennia has strengthened the Night Gen's will to survive and hardened their hearts against the peoples who cast them out.

Nine Circles, the: Hell; variously described as either a place or state of torment reserved for the wicked after death. Ancient peoples' concepts of hell differed between religions and even among sects of the same faith. Few cults lacked such a notion entirely.

Prana: This primeval force is the basic building block of matter and the animating principle of all living things. Also called the light of the White Well.

Princes of Hell: Three surpassingly potent and evil beings who ruled the Nine Circles following the departure of hell's creators. Once human, their unrivaled wickedness earned them infernal honors outranking the baals; and dread curses whose corrupting effects birthed nightmarish plagues among mortals. The three princes, in ascending order of rank, are Tzaraat, Hazeroth, and Lykaon.

Shadow Caste, The: A secret order of powerful human Factors who stole the gifts of immortality and nexism from Gen prisoners of war. After clandestinely seizing control of the Guild, the Shadow Caste grew restless in their search for purpose. They finally decided to end the universe, setting in motion the creation of the souldancers, the Arcana Divines' expedition to hell, and the Cataclysm itself.

Following this failure, the Shadow Caste set themselves up as the ruling Magisterium of Temil and resumed their apocalyptic schemes. The order's current members are Magists Kelgrun, Vilneus, Zoanthus, Belar, Rathimus, and Gien.

Snare, the: Pejorative term for those realms created by the old gods to capture their followers' souls, thus preventing them from rejoining the Nexus after death, e.g. heaven and the Nine Circles.

Sons of Haath: An elite enforcer company employed by the Guild during the Purges and patterned after the legendary spy and mercenary Haath. Although the Guild's Transessists failed to duplicate Haath's nexism, they imbued his namesakes with other, equally formidable abilities.

Sphere: An inhabited world of the Middle Stratum, synonymous with "planet".

Steersman: The pilot of an ether-runner (the term is gender neutral) who can control a ship through the Wheel. When describing an individual with Guild training, the term became a capitalized proper noun. Most Guild-trained Steersmen were powerful Factors.

Stratum: A discrete region of the cosmos. Except for the Middle Stratum, all Strata are defined by their uniform composition.

The Strata are arranged in descending order of potency, beginning with the Fire Stratum located just below the White Well, proceeding downward to the Air, Middle, and Water Strata, and ending at the Stone Stratum located just above the Void.

The Middle Stratum is the balancing point of these forces and is synonymous with mundane space. The ether is not a Stratum, but surrounds and permeates all Strata. The realms of the Snare are sometimes called Strata, but this usage is not technically correct.

Telepathy: The power to nexically perceive, alter, and even control others' thoughts. Telepaths are as feared and distrusted among nexists as necromancers are among Factors.

Teth: An esoteric concept describing the flow of prana from the White Well into the Void. The principle defies easy definition, since its followers claim that Teth encompasses all areas of cosmology, philosophy, morality, and natural science. One of the major tenets of Teth is the dominance that entropy exerts upon all things.

Thera: A primeval entity alternately worshiped and despised in a number of ancient faiths. Theological opinions on Thera's nature vary, though most cults thought her a goddess. Necromancers consider her a personification of Teth. The Nesshin styled her the daughter of Zadok and queen of demons who brought evil into the world through her patricide.

Transessence: The process of exchanging the properties of substances through Workings.

Void, the: The lowest region of the cosmos, where prana flowing from the White Well settles once it has lost all of its potency. The Void is a nearly infinite abode of darkness and absolute cold where life cannot exist.

Wheel, the: A sympathetic control interface allowing a steersman to merge his awareness with an ether-runner.

White Well, the: A vast concentration of pure prana located in the ether above all of the Strata. The Well provides the raw material for all energy, matter, and life; as well as Workings and Mysteries. Some religious traditions equate the Well with Zadok's divine power, which was separated from the creator upon his death.

Working: An effect produced by fashioning prana according to the user's thought patterns, particularly via any method among a number of systems developed by the Guild.

Zadok: Nesshin creator deity worshiped by other faiths under different names. Killed at the beginning of time by Thera, his daughter and first creation, Zadok is prophesied to rise at the eschaton and judge every creature.

Zadokim: Souls who have escaped the Nexus and returned from the light beyond the cosmos by Zadok's leave. Unlike the shards of Zadok, Thera, and Shaiel, Zadokim exist of and for themselves, independent of any nexus.

The following is a preview of:

THE OPHIAN RISING
Soul Cycle Book IV

Brian Niemeier

Ceyhan and Iyana

Only fools liken Tharis to hell, Ceyhan reflected. Indeed, the Ninth Circle's frozen crags made him long for Tharis' burning dunes. Sleet like icy chips of glass stung his face as he trudged through dirty snow that the howling wind had gathered into knee-deep drifts.

A pang of guilt roused Ceyhan from his musings. *Wretch!* he chastised himself. *What matters your comfort compared to Iyana's life?*

Best to focus on the task at hand than to compound his guilt. The Ninth Circle was forbidden by ancient decree of Queen Nakvin. Ceyhan's upbringing at his parents' court on Tharis had instilled a deep aversion to defying royal commands. If only Iyana had been better disposed to obedience by her similar childhood in Seele.

Similar, but with crucial differences, Ceyhan thought as he slogged up a treacherous slope. Rocks like the horns of frozen devils stabbing up through the snow tore his cotton breeches as he passed. Luckily, the cold numbed the pain.

Ceyhan and Iyana had both been raised as the children of

monarchs. But whereas he was the adopted heir to Xander and Astlin of the Nesshin, Iyana was Nakvin's second natural child. Avalon's queen often spoke of Iyana's older sister, even though Elena had died before the younger princess' birth—twenty years ago for her and two hundred in the Strata.

Which was the second difference between them and the reason he was breaking royal law to track his beloved through hell. Though mortal, Ceyhan was prophesied to return as a Zadokim like his parents. Unlike her parents, Iyana was born mortal—the sad state of all Gen descendants more than two generations removed from a pure-blooded ancestor. For her daughter's sake, Nakvin had stretched time so that only one year passed in Avalon for every ten years without.

Cresting the ridge of ice-coated grey rock, Ceyhan racked his brain for new ways to console his beloved. He had already defended her honor against more than one churl who'd used Iyana's mortality to question her parentage, even though her fiery red hair and emerald green eyes were clearly the patrimony of Captain Jaren Peregrine.

Though giving slanderers a taste of his sword was highly satisfying to Ceyhan, his dueling victories brought Iyana small comfort. Her certainty that she would be lost forever after her death resisted all arguments of priests, theologians, and mystics.

Perhaps if I promise Iyana that Mother will guide her to the light beyond...

A bitter wind bearing the taste of decay buffeted Ceyhan as he struggled along the knife-edged ridge. He pulled the saddle blanket he'd taken from his mount tightly around him, drawing courage from the warm scent of horse infused into the dark, patterned wool.

The sleet thinned, and he saw her. Iyana stood near the edge of precipice against the leaden sky. The winds whipped her light blue gown and tossed her long hair like a scarlet banner.

"Iyana!" Ceyhan cried. His voice carried over the wind like a trumpet blast.

The princess turned toward him but kept her eyes lowered to the frozen ground. "Ceyhan," she said, "you came." She issued a curt laugh. "He was right about everything."

Passion urged Ceyhan to run to her, but a dark warning from his soul made him tread lightly toward the cliff's icy edge.

"Who was right?" he asked.

Iyana gazed into the stormy sky as if the roiling clouds were projections of her mind. "I never knew his name. His hair is iron grey and white like these peaks. His eyes are pearls immersed in dark pools."

Ceyhan cautiously stepped onto the precipice. His dark brown braid flailed in a sudden gust of wind from the pit below, and he secured it inside his makeshift cloak. "What did he say?"

"What no one else had the courage to tell me," Iyana spat. "He taught me things—many things that Mother forbade me to learn."

"Your absence grieves her terribly," Ceyhan said. A few more steps, and Iyana would be in reach. "Come away from the ledge, and I will take you back to her."

Iyana shrank back like a cornered beast, coming perilously close to the abyss. "Mother would have come herself, if she'd known where to find me. Only you knew, my love."

"You spoke to me in secret of your fascination with this place," Ceyhan said. "If you had confided in your mother—"

Iyana's laughter soured. "She cares only for soothing lies. My teacher tells me the truth!"

A shadow passed over Ceyhan's heart. "What truth?"

Iyana finally met his eyes. Her expression, like that of a jackal sighting a fresh kill, chilled him more deeply than the wind.

"That you would die today," she said.

Fear quickened Ceyhan's steps. He crossed the slick rocks to Iyana's side and grasped her right forearm. The new vantage point gave him a dizzying view of untold depths churning with black mists below. The unbidden memory came to him of a bull carcass writhing with maggots.

"This place is poisonous," he said. "We are leaving!"

Ceyhan readied himself for Iyana to struggle. To his surprise she stood firm, drew a silver bracelet on a slender chain from her sleeve, and clapped the thin metal circle around his wrist. Ceyhan pulled his arm back, but the silver chain bound his right wrist to a matching bracelet on Iyana's left. The chill air failed to leech away the metal's warmth.

"What are you playing at?" he demanded.

A triumphant smile brightened, but did not warm, Iyana's pale, lovely face. "I've outgrown games. My teacher showed me how to make this chain as serious and final as death. Our fates are now bound!"

Some false prophet or Ophian agitator has filled my love's mind with error, Ceyhan thought. Drawing his sword, he looked forward to slaying Iyana's deceiver on its double-edged diamond blade. But first, he would cut the trifling chain that hindered him.

"This isn't a mere silver chain," Iyana warned, "but a silver cord. Your great blade is no more threat to it than a letter opener."

The barb pricked Ceyhan's pride. He took his sword in his left hand, pulled the chain taut, and struck the fine silver links. A flash of sallow light repelled the diamond blade and a surge of numbing cold tore the sword from his grip. The peerless weapon—a gift from his father—vanished into the abyss.

Ceyhan's cry of dismay was cut short as Iyana lost her footing on the icy rocks. She fell screaming over the edge, and terror twisted Ceyhan's stomach as the chain that tied him to Iyana wrenched him off of the precipice to join her in the black depths of the pit.

What Ceyhan feared would be an eternal fall ended abruptly when the chain snagged on a jagged outcropping. Sharp pain shot through Ceyhan's arm as the bracelet arrested his descent with a jolt, digging into his wrist and crushing bone. A wet thud like an ostrich egg cracking diverted his attention to his right, where Iyana hung, swaying limply in the wind. The back of her blue gown and the grey rock wall behind her head were both painted crimson.

Ceyhan called to his beloved. Her name echoed from the surrounding cliffs, but she did not stir. Reaching across to her with his left hand drove white hot nails through his right wrist, but he set his jaw against the pain and touched the side of her fair, blood-spattered neck. Finding that her heart no longer beat broke his own.

Lightning flashed in the black mists far below, accompanied with thunder like peals of laughter. Panic replaced Ceyhan's sorrow. No one knew where he and Iyana had gone. His sword, which had been Worked to send messages, was lost, and he lacked sufficient skill as a Factor to fashion a sending with one arm.

Ceyhan raised his eyes to the cliff's edge high above. The rock face was too sheer to climb, even unencumbered by a broken wrist and Iyana's body. Her teacher had been wrong about the date of Ceyhan's demise, but death from the cold was certain unless he could escape.

Mother! Though he lacked her telepathic gifts, Ceyhan hoped that his desperation would make his thoughts heard across the cosmic gulf between the Ninth Circle and Tharis. The abyss answered with mocking thunder, and he stared hopelessly into its heart.

Sickly golden light shone down from above, and cold that made the endless winter seem like a warm spring day ravaged Ceyhan's battered wrist. The sallow gleam was emanating from the chain that bound him to Iyana. As Ceyhan watched in dread fascination, a golden aura surrounded her corpse. Iyana's eyelids fluttered as if she were waking from troubled dreams, but instead of eyes, they opened on black voids like mirrors of the pit.

"Ceyhan," she rasped.

Iyana's hellish awakening did not make Ceyhan scream. Feeling tendrils of dead golden light burrowing toward his soul like ravenous worms ripped a scream from his chest that joined the awful thunder in a chorus of terror and wicked glee.

Ceyhan's left hand drew his belt knife by reflex. The mundane weapon, no longer than his hand, was useless against the shackles binding him to the horror that had been his love, but his frenzied fear had a different object. Ceyhan hacked at the delicate wrist below Iyana's bracelet, bringing his knife down again and again until the last shreds of muscle and skin could no longer support her weight. She fell without a word.

There was a sound like a metal snake slithering over frozen rock. The pain in Ceyhan's wrist was eased as the silver chain slid from the outcropping, plunging him into the abyss. By then, he was too mad with fear and grief to care.

Acknowledgements

Thanks to Larry Correia, Vox Day, Jeff Duntemann, Declan Finn, L. Jagi Lamplighter, Russell Newquist, Jason Rennie, and John C. Wright.

Special thanks to the beta readers who helped make *The Secret Kings* the best book it can be:

Ben

David

D.J.

Glenn

John

Paul

Wes

About Brian Niemeier

Brian Niemeier is a John W. Campbell Award for Best New Writer finalist. His second book, *Souldancer*, won the first ever Dragon Award for Best Horror Novel. He chose to pursue a writing career despite formal training in history and theology. His journey toward publication began at the behest of his long-suffering gaming group, who tactfully pointed out that he seemed to enjoy telling stories more than planning and adjudicating games.

Besides writing novels, he has contributed short stories to Sci Phi Journal.

Visit Brian at http://www.brianniemeier.com/

Follow @BrianNiemeier on Twitter.

Honest reviews are vital to helping others make informed reading decisions. Please consider leaving a review of this book on Amazon.

54796751R00293

Made in the USA
San Bernardino, CA
24 October 2017